Marcus Herniman was born (or at least found in a cradle) in North London, and has led something of a changeling existence ever since. He studied Medieval Literature and Art at the University of Exeter, and now lives and works in the Island of Jersey. *The Fall of Lautun* is his third novel.

Also by Marcus Herniman from Earthlight

The Siege of Arrandin
The Treason of Dortrean

THE FALL OF LAUTUN

MARCUS HERNIMAN

EARTHLIGHT

LONDON • SYDNEY • NEW YORK • TOKYO • SINGAPORE • TORONTO

www.earthlight.co.uk

First published in Great Britain by Earthlight, 2003
An imprint of Simon & Schuster UK Ltd
A Viacom Company

1 3 5 7 9 8 6 4 2

Simon & Schuster UK Ltd
Africa House
64–78 Kingsway
London WC2B 6AH

www.simonsays.co.uk

Simon & Schuster Australia
Sydney

A CIP catalogue record for this book is available
from the British Library

ISBN 0-7434-1512-4

Typeset by Palimpsest Book Production Limited,
Polmont, Stirlingshire
Printed and bound in Great Britain by
Cox & Wyman Ltd, Reading, Berkshire

for
Linda K. Pletz
one of Michigan's finest daughters

and for
Stuart Quigley
who knows well the wisdom of laughter.

– nor seek to shape our dreams
nor simply to survive them
but to learn to be ourselves within them.

MAPS

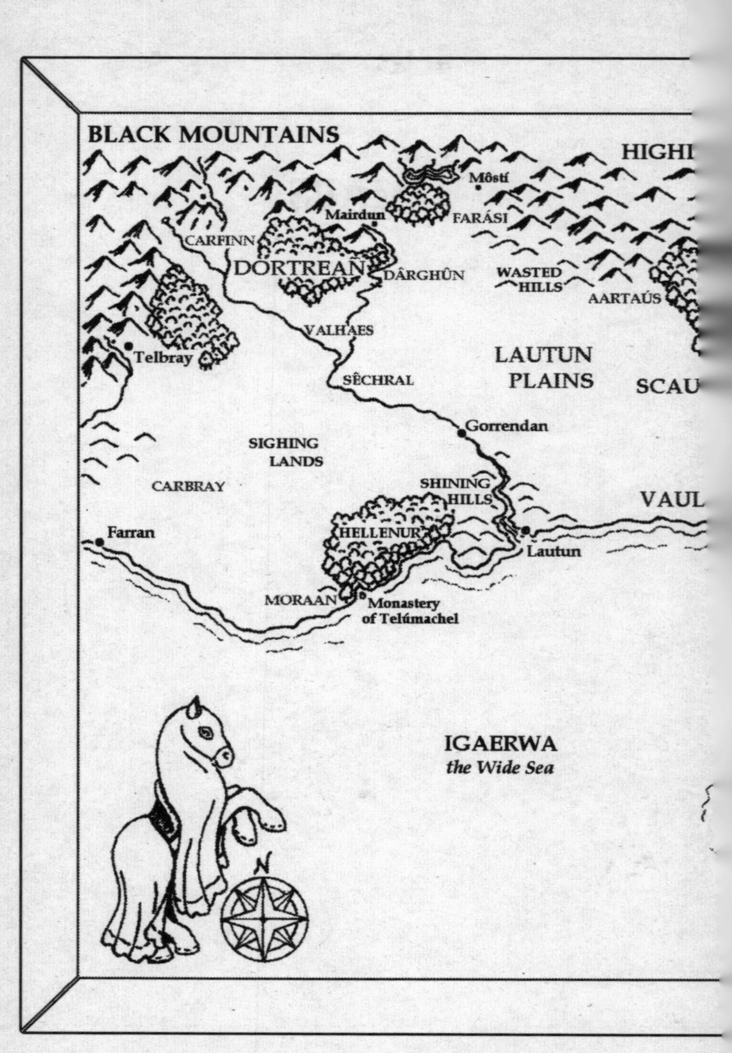
BLACK MOUNTAINS
HIGHI
Môstí
Mairdun
FARÁSI
CARFINN
DORTREAÑ
DÂRGHÛN
WASTED
HILLS
AARTAÚS
VALHAES
Telbray
LAUTUN
PLAINS
SÊCHRAL
SCAU
Gorrendan
SIGHING
LANDS
CARBRAY
SHINING
HILLS
VAUL
Farran
HELLENUR
Lautun
MORAAN
Monastery
of Telúmachel
IGAERWA
the Wide Sea
N

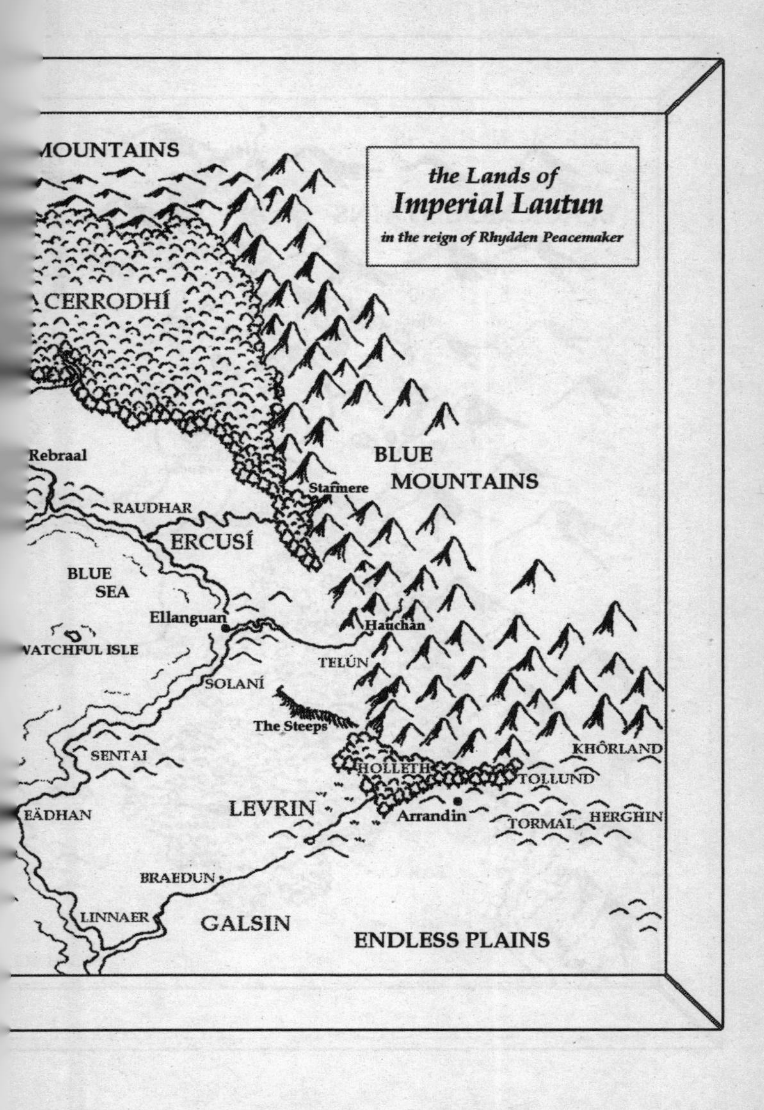
the Lands of
Imperial Lautun
in the reign of Rhydden Peacemaker
CERRODHÍ
Rebraal
BLUE
MOUNTAINS
Starmere
RAUDHAR
ERCUSÍ
BLUE
SEA
Ellanguan
Hauchan
TELÚN
SOLANÍ
The Steeps
SENTAI
HOLLETH
KHÔRLAND
TOLLUND
EÄDHAN
LEVRIN
Arrandin
TORMAL
HERGHIN
BRAEDUN
LINNAER
GALSIN
ENDLESS PLAINS

BLACK MOUNTAINS
White
Manor
Sîrnae
Twin
Watchers
TARÁGIN
Tungit
Isle
CARFINN
Flaming
Woods
DHÛLANN
Black
River
TELBRAY
WOODS
old
causeway
Telbray
Alvinaah
Kray
TARAAS
SIGHING

Dortrean
and the lands around
in the reign of Rhydden Peacemaker
0 1 2 3
Leagues
NORTHERN
WOODS
Mairdun
FÂGHSUL
DORTREAN FOREST
Rolling
River
DÂRGHÛN
ford
DORTREAN
ford
CARDHÁSI
Grey
River
VALHAES
Whitespear
Head
SÊCHRAL
LANDS
N

Prologue

We have heard of Halgan, High Priest of the Sun, First King of Khêltan; how he came up from the south, and fought by our forefathers in the Bright Alliance, where the great demon was cast down; and how afterwards he marched north, driving the darkness from the hills and forests of our homelands, and founded the Fourth Kingdom at the feet of the Black Mountains.

We have heard also how that kingdom fell; how Halgan – so beloved by the gods and his fellow men, friend of both noghru *and Fay – grew cold and cruel as the mountain snows, so that men named him anew, 'the Chill'; and how the beauty and wisdom of fair Khêltan was cast down, and destroyed by avenging fire, so that for two hundred years the land lay waste until the Lords of Dortrean came. And then it was told among men that Halgan himself did not die, but that he waited beneath the Black Mountains; and that he would return with vengeance from the cold darkness, should evil folk call upon him.*

But now, in these latest days, we have heard a new tale. Khêltan was betrayed not through her own lord's pride, but through the envy of other kingdoms; and though Halgan fled indeed, it was down a path of deep wisdom – to sleep as one lost through the long ages, until the enemy captain should return; and then wake, for the defence of all free peoples in their hour of great need.

From Corollin's address to the Reformed Council

Erkal Dortrean stood back from the desk, preparing for the second time that evening to take his leave. Rinnekh Ellanguan dragged himself from his chair and stood up. Courtesy obliged Erkal to wait for him.

'I am still not happy about T'Loi's guards remaining here,' Rinnekh said again.

Erkal sighed, in no mood for Rinnekh's games.

Five of the Souther warships had now left the Ellanguan harbours, bound – at the Emperor's command, and escorted by two of the Emperor's own ships – for the Braedun *commanderie* farther south along the coast, where they would be garrisoned against the threat of another assault from the Eastern Domains. The remaining two warships were to sail with the early morning tide, and Erkal was to go with them. The Souther Ambassador T'Loi was to stay behind as an honoured guest in Ellanguan. To have denied T'Loi the use of his personal bodyguard would have been taken as a deep insult, undermining the still fragile treaty of peace between Lautun and the South, and proclaiming him the hostage he truly was. Given the continuing unrest within the city, there was also a certain practicality in letting T'Loi's own men protect him, rather than taking members of Rinnekh's household guard away from their other duties.

All this Rinnekh knew, because Erkal had already told him. And besides, as Lord Steward of Ellanguan, it had been Rinnekh himself who had first secured this treaty with T'Loi. The two of them too obviously had a close personal understanding.

So it was a game of delay, keeping Erkal here at this late night meeting when he had an early start the next day. And he scented other games afoot. T'Loi was not here, though he had been at just about every other meeting that Erkal had had with Rinnekh over the removal of the Souther ships since the Emperor's departure. That might have suggested that Rinnekh's concerns about T'Loi were genuine, were it not for the presence of his pet Truthsayer, Baelar. To have a Truthsayer monitor a meeting between the Lords of two Houses Ancient was tantamount to insult. But then Dortrean's position within imperial politics was still far from secure, sailing too close to the winds of treason over the whole question of the departure of the Easterner armies and the continued presence of the Southers within the Six Kingdoms. Erkal was not minded to risk that position further by rising to Rinnekh's foolish bait and challenging Baelar's attendance. And in fairness, he conceded to himself, he did not trust Rinnekh either.

'None of us is entirely happy about any of this,' he said, 'least of all the Emperor. T'Loi is your problem, my Lord – though I dare say that he will behave himself, for a while. Now if you will excuse me?'

Rinnekh nodded reluctantly.

Erkal gave him a formal bow, his right hand clenched against his chest. Not that he thought the upstart Steward deserved such homage, even in his own palace; but it brought to the fore the black silk band about his scarlet sleeve – a mourning token for his elder son Solban, murdered less than a week before here in Rinnekh's own city, over this same bloody business with the Southers. Such small challenge Erkal allowed himself. Let Rinnekh be mindful of that.

He gave a more cursory nod to the Truthsayer, and to the unnamed mage lurking by the window, and strode toward the door.

The mage was one of at least three whom Erkal had seen roaming the Steward's palace of late, all of them clad in robes of the blue-green of Ellanguan, their faces hidden behind the deep brim of their hoods. By rumour they were magi of Sollonaal's following, from the College of Magi in Ellanguan. What this one was doing here, Erkal could only begin to guess. The window drapes were of the same colour as his robes, and throughout the meeting the man had stood silent as though trying to blend into them unnoticed – except that his repeated sniffling had betrayed his efforts.

Erkal paused at the door, and glanced back at his host. 'I expect you'll be glad to see the back of me,' he said lightly.

He ignored Rinnekh's protests, turned, and went out past the guards and down the broad stair to the East Hall.

The palace was all but deserted at this hour of the night, with just a few of the household sweeping the floor and setting the hall to rights in the dwindling light of the small summer hearth-fires. Erkal climbed the far stair and followed the upper landings toward his bed in moody silence.

There were no guards at his door, but the main living chamber of the Dortrean apartment was filled with welcoming lamplight. To his right as he came in, a long-legged young man sprawled sleeping in a high backed chair, his dark hair across his face, with one hand cradling a pile of folded linen in his lap.

Erkal stopped short. In that first moment he thought that he beheld his dead son Solban returned again. But it was only Kierran, the youngest son of his old friend The Arrand. Kierran, who had come with him from Arrandin – and partly against Erkal's better judgement, since The Arrand himself was failing fast – as an extra pair of eyes to watch his back.

The Earl ran a weary hand through his dark blond hair, and smiled sadly to himself as he latched the door shut. In truth, Kierran was very little like the sober minded Solban. For one thing, Solban would never have fallen asleep halfway through packing his belongings for the morning.

From what he knew of The Arrand's sons, neither would Kierran.

The thought sent a chill warning to his stomach, tugging him alert for other signs of danger. The apartment was quiet. The door in the far wall was open, and dimmer lamplight and firelight lit the bedchamber beyond. Though untidy with the business of making ready to depart, there were no obvious signs of struggle.

Erkal crossed swiftly to crouch down at Kierran's side. The young Lord was sleeping peacefully, his breathing slow and deep. With a silent prayer of thanks to the *Aeshtar*, he moved on to the open door.

There was no one in the room beyond, nor telltale sign that anyone had been there recently save Kierran and himself. But

Erkal was still wary. He picked up two knives from amongst the gear on the bed and slid them beneath his belt, then went back out to waken Kierran.

It took a good deal of shaking to rouse him, and then a hand over his mouth to hush him as he came suddenly awake and sat up.

'Has anyone been here?' Erkal asked him quietly.

Kierran shook his head. 'I was just packing,' he said. 'And then I felt tired, and sat down for a moment. But—' His voice trailed off. His deep grey eyes were wide and blinking as they returned the Earl's gaze.

Erkal did not like the feel of it. Ellanguan was no safe place to be, even in the Steward's palace. He would not have put it beyond Rinnekh to have planned some mischief here, while he himself was called away to their meeting. And there were doubtless many others who would have had the skill to make Kierran sleep – whether through drugs or some magical art – to gain entry here for their own purpose.

He drew the knives from his belt and handed one to Kierran. 'We may have company,' he said.

He led the way to the end door of the living chamber, and through into the narrow side hall beyond. A single lamp of green and gold glass shone softly from the top of the tall press, but otherwise the hall was empty.

'Your Grace,' came Kierran's voice behind him.

Erkal turned. Kierran was crouched down in the doorway, studying the floor. There were dark patches on the pale grey stone before him, and more scattered up the wall.

'Blood,' said Kierran. 'Still wet.'

Erkal frowned, casting his gaze around the hall in the dim light. The air seemed to grow thicker, pressing in upon him.

'But not much,' he said quietly, signalling for Kierran to join him; 'and only there.'

Together they checked the rooms that opened off the hall, and then they went back to search the bedchamber and bathroom beyond. But there was no more blood, nor any other sign that anyone had been there. So far as they could tell, nothing had been moved or taken.

Erkal locked the outer door of the apartment, satisfied that they were now truly alone. Kierran had picked up his bundle of linen again, and was standing restlessly in the middle of the living chamber.

'Should we tell the household guards?' Kierran ventured.

'I had rather not,' Erkal replied. 'They would only raise the alarm, and the Souther Ambassador would be most upset. I do not want to have to deal with T'Loi at this hour. Also, whoever was here seems to have taken pains to keep their presence secret. I do not wish them to know that we are aware of them. Not yet.'

Kierran looked puzzled for a moment, then his eyes widened in understanding. 'You think whoever it was might come back?'

Erkal nodded. 'Or perhaps others, who knew why they were here.'

'How do you know there was more than one?'

'The blood. From the way in which it fell, I should think that one person was standing by the door, and that a second person took him unawares and cut or stabbed him.'

'One man alone could have cut himself, by accident,' said Kierran doubtfully. 'And it is said that the Easterner wizards shed their own blood to cast their spells.'

'Not quite so messily, I think,' Erkal reassured him. 'But then why go away – especially if you were asleep? No, I think that two were here; and that the second either killed or overpowered the first, and then took him away, not wanting to be discovered.'

'He must have used magic to do it.'

Erkal shrugged. The memory of the hooded mage in Rinnekh's chambers flickered uneasily in his mind. Though there were now a handful of magi whom he liked well enough, his inherent distrust of the Council of Magi as a whole remained. High Councillor Sollonaal and the Ellanguan Magi fawned too much on the Steward Rinnekh for his liking; and then the Emperor's most trusted adviser, the Archmage Merrech, had for long been Dortrean's adversary at Court. This mysterious visit had something of the feel of one of Merrech's riddling gambits. And then again, the Southers and Easterners both practised magics of their own – the kind of magic that had brought about Solban's death.

'A strong man could have carried him,' he said aloud.

'But at least it seems he was friendly,' said Kierran. 'I mean, he got rid of the enemy at the door, and no harm came to us. So perhaps we have someone friendly watching over us.'

He carried his bundle over to the long settle, which had a pair of large leather saddlebags hung over the back.

'Perhaps,' Erkal allowed. 'Or he could still be an enemy, wanting to remain unknown. If he thinks we are unaware of him, we may be better able to catch him if he returns – if we can stay awake.' He managed a weary grin. 'Well, I guess Rinnekh had left us little enough chance of sleep tonight anyway. There will be time to catch up on our rest on the voyage south.'

He went through into the bedchamber to sort out his own gear, though Kierran had already done most of the cleaning and packing for him. With the suddenness of the war against the East, and all the business that had come after, he had been travelling light for quite some time now. Even the scarlet tunic he had on had been made hurriedly for him here in Ellanguan, and did not yet feel properly his own.

Kierran came and stood by the curtained corner post at the foot of the bed, watching him.

'We could ask the Braedun priests in the morning,' he suggested presently. 'I mean, if no one else comes tonight. The priests might be able to tell us more about what happened here, with their arts.'

'They might,' Erkal allowed. 'But this is not your father's palace. Rinnekh will not take kindly to having *heathen priests* – as he calls them – snooping about the place; nor do I wish to draw his attention to this matter by inviting them up here.

Someone from Braedun will no doubt come to meet us down in the lobby, but I would ask that you do not speak to them about it until we are well out to sea. Not unless other things should happen tonight that make it necessary.' He looked straight at Kierran as he said this, until the young Lord nodded obediently. 'Even so, we have a long voyage ahead; and you can expect the danger to increase as we go further south.'

Kierran leaned against the bedpost, his dark eyes glancing from the Earl to the doorway and back again.

'Is it wise for you to sail with the Southers?' he asked. 'Kelmaar have offered to take us straight to the *commanderie*, by magic.'

'So have Braedun,' Erkal returned. 'Prime Councillor Sollonaal has even offered to send us with one of his magi. But no. I can not so distance myself from the Souther commanders at a time when trust desperately needs to be built – especially when T'Loi is being held here in Ellanguan. Call it a gambit, if you will. I have sent instructions ahead to the *commanderie*, but I must sail in the Braedun ship as escort to the remaining Southers.'

There was also the fact, Erkal had to admit to himself, that he had no desire to arrive early, to watch the noble Braedun knights having to move out of their ancient and beloved *commanderie*. The grief and anger over that removal would not make his dealings with the Southers any the easier.

'The Braedun ship is no match for Souther warships,' said Kierran, raising a dispute they had had before.

'These two warships are battered and sparsely repaired,' Erkal reminded him, 'and scarcely at full strength. And the Lords of Braedun have great mastery over wind and weather.'

'And will one of the Magi be coming with us – one we can trust? Morvaan, or Rhysana perhaps?'

Erkal gave him a warning frown. 'You forget Dortrean's distrust of the Magi. Just because we worked well with them in Arrandin does not mean I wish to have them around me all the time. I am more than content with the faithful strength of

Braedun. Besides, Rhysana is with child, and your father wants Morvaan with him.'

Kierran looked away. There was sadness in his young face at the mention of his dying father, but also something else, more akin to disappointment. Erkal thought that he could guess the reason for it.

'I don't suppose,' he said more gently, 'that the Magi would have any more news of Kellarn than we do, if that is what you were hoping.'

Erkal had no certain knowledge of where his younger son Kellarn now was. But Kellarn would prefer it that way, he thought. The boy had fought well in and around Arrandin, drawing the unwanted attention of the Emperor Rhydden; and given Dortrean's dangerous political position, and Rhydden's equally dangerous shifts of mood with those he chose to play with, Erkal could not blame Kellarn for wanting to make himself scarce. And then Kellarn was off on a secret errand of his own, helping to guard against the return of the ancient demon captain who had ruled these lands fifteen hundred years before – that same demon whom the Easterner armies had worshipped, and whose servants had, perhaps, brought about Solban's death. So it was safest for all of them if his whereabouts remained unknown.

Though Kellarn and Kierran were firm friends, Erkal did not think that his son had ever spoken to Kierran about his errand. Kierran himself had never mentioned it. And the subject of Kellarn was not something that Erkal wished to discuss, here within the unfriendly walls of Rinnekh's palace.

Kierran sighed, and tilted his head up in determination. 'We shall have to go by sea then.'

Erkal smiled. All the Arrands were poor sailors, as a rule. With the many troubles of the last week, it had not occurred to him until that moment that young Kierran might prove no exception.

'You don't have to come, you know,' he said. 'I doubt that

you would want to remain here, but the priests could take you back to Arrandin, or wherever you wish to go.'

'Where you go, I go,' said Kierran stubbornly. 'You need me more than ever now.' It was just the look that Kellarn would have given him. Erkal could make no answer.

I FIRE IN THE WATER

Chapter One

The *noghr* steward Markhûl thrust open the library doors, and bowed with fierce dignity for the two ladies to pass through. Rhysana smiled as she nodded to him, mindful of his discomfort.

The long hall of the Dortrean manor library stretched away before her in muted shadow, opening out at the far end to the right, whence the gentler northern light of the summer morning chiefly came. On either side, from floor to ceiling, the white stone walls were lined with deeply recessed shelves, stacked with tomes and codices and scrolls of every size and hue, and carved caskets and other treasures standing quietly in between. Rumours of enchantment whispered to her in the dim light, and she caught the sweet, refreshing tang of peppermint on the air.

By rights, they should not be here at all. It was unthinkable that two magi should be left alone in the Dortrean library for any length of time, even though both were counted as family friends. Dortrean's traditional distrust of the neutral Council of Magi had kept these doors barred to any attempt at research for many generations. But the Lady Ellaïn – daughter of the present Earl, and running the manor in his absence – had so commanded it. Ellaïn had work of her own to do, for which she required Markhûl's assistance; and she had felt that Rhysana would be more comfortable in the quietness of the library than among the bustle of the household. The steward, though displaying an uneasiness bordering on outrage, had been obliged to defer to his lady's wishes.

Accompanying Rhysana was the journeyman mage Corollin,

of whom she knew little enough, save that she was the adopted daughter of the Archmage Morvaan and a close friend of Kellarn of Dortrean. They had not yet seen Kellarn that morning. At Markhûl's suggestion, Ellaïn's two sons had now gone galloping off to chase him out of his rooms and down to the library.

Corollin went at once to the long central table, her booted feet sending whispered echoes of their own along the shelves as she strode across the floor. To please Ellaïn – or perhaps Rhysana herself – she had put on hooded robes of soft strawberry gold, rather than the warrior's tunic and breeches in which she had arrived the night before; and her dark hair was wound into a plaited crown about her head, much like the silver fair crown that adorned Rhysana's own. But though this manner of dress lent her a gentler appearance, it brought more strongly to mind her training as a scholar and mage – which could only serve to increase Markhûl's agitation.

'Is there anything else?' the *noghr* asked from behind them. Rhysana turned back, raising one hand slightly to signal that there was not.

'I expect Kellarn will be here soon, thank you,' said Corollin.

The steward glared warning to each of them in turn, as though he suspected any mage – no matter how friendly – capable of plunder the moment his back was turned. Then he bowed deeply once more.

'Try not to touch anything,' he growled. He went away, pulling the great doors shut quietly behind him.

Rhysana sighed.

'He's probably gone to find Kellarn himself,' said Corollin. 'Would you like to sit down, my Lady?'

'In a moment.'

Rhysana moved on further into the room, glad of the gentle exercise to ease her legs and back, and drawn by the lure of the forbidden shelves. Though Ellaïn had been anxious for her health, she did not feel particularly unwell that morning. Her faint sickness at breakfast, she told herself, had had little enough to do with her state of expectant motherhood, and was simply her apprehension at the task set before her. She needed to speak to Kellarn and Corollin alone.

She had been startled the night before by Kellarn's outburst against the Emperor, following the news of his brother's death; and she was now certain that Kellarn and Corollin had discovered more about the impending return of the ancient demon Lo-Khuma, which might be vital knowledge for Rhysana and her colleagues to learn. It seemed that the gods had brought them together at this moment, here at the Dortrean Manor; and the gods alone knew when – if ever – another such chance might present itself. She must question them while she could. And then she was also worried about Kellarn himself, and what his oath against the Emperor might drive him to do.

It had already occurred to Rhysana that Corollin might be the easier of the two to question, while they were alone. Corollin was herself a mage, and so more likely to be amenable to the Council than a son of Dortrean; and as a journeyman she was far below a high councillor such as Rhysana in standing and power, though barely a couple of years of age lay between them. Indeed, there were some high councillors who would have demanded answers from Corollin on such an urgent matter. But Rhysana felt that she could not do so while they were both guests under Dortrean's roof. And besides, she would have been loth to do so in any event, because she believed in the right of other people to personal privacy, and doubted the wisdom of wresting knowledge by force or fear where it was not freely given.

And then there was the wonder of the library in which they now stood, so long denied to the Council. Even the ancient Warden of the libraries in the College of Magi in Lautun – who seemed to know by heart the contents of almost every other book collection in the Six Kingdoms, without having to refer to an index – could scarcely begin to guess at the unknown treasures stored here. It was as though the books were calling to her, pleading to be taken down and opened, to reveal their hoarded words. Their secrets, they whispered, were far more valuable than anything Corollin might have to say. Rhysana let her legs carry her to the nearest shelf.

'I suppose that there is no harm in just looking?' she ventured aloud, glancing back over her shoulder at Corollin.

The journeyman returned the look with an even gaze from deep blue eyes, neither smiling nor frowning. Rhysana reminded herself that this was no college student, to be so easily drawn. For a moment, she wondered who was testing whom.

'Better not,' she answered herself. Then she smiled, and went to sit in one of the formal chairs beside the table.

A tray had already been set there, with tall jug and tea bowls, no doubt at the instruction of Ellaïn. Corollin poured for them both. Rhysana took the bowl from her and sniffed delicately at the fragrant steam. This was the source of the peppermint she had noticed earlier, though there was a hint of other herbs blended with it. Corollin sat down, facing her across the table.

'I am worried about Kellarn,' Rhysana began. 'But you know him better than do I. After his outburst last night, do you think he is about to do something rash – like riding off to confront the Emperor at the Summer Court?'

'Not today, I think,' said Corollin, with a brief smile. 'Nor for many days yet, if I can dissuade him. But he has sworn vengeance, and that oath will bind him.'

Rhysana nodded. 'He blamed the Emperor for Solban's death. But does he have proof of that?'

'He appears to believe so,' Corollin allowed.

'And what do you believe?'

Corollin considered the question. 'Kellarn usually does what he says.'

Rhysana smiled, conceding the block. She toyed absently with the silver handles of her crystal tea bowl.

'In his oath, last night,' she said, 'Kellarn spoke of demons serving the Emperor and his counsellor, the Archmage Merrech. You both played your part in the war against the Easterners, so you know that the power of the demon captain Lo-Khuma was behind that assault. And from what both your father and Kellarn have told me, I believe that you have had other encounters with the servants of that demon.'

Corollin dropped her gaze, and then nodded.

'The priests of the *Aeshta* Orders have foreseen that Lo-Khuma now seeks to return,' Rhysana went on, 'but not the manner of his coming, nor how he may be prevented. And as a journeyman mage yourself, you will appreciate that our own Order has made little study of demon lore, since our Council precepts proscribe it.'

'I seldom think of myself as a journeyman these days,' said Corollin. 'Or at least, the lore of Zedron which I am studying seems to make so many demands, in so many different ways, that sometimes I feel as raw and unlearned as any College novice.'

'We all feel like that at times,' Rhysana laughed. 'The more we know, the more we realise how much we have left to learn.'

'But don't get me started on my studies,' said Corollin. 'We could be here for hours.'

'Another time, perhaps,' said Rhysana. 'But in short, if you or Kellarn have learned more about the demon's return, or how he may be prevented, then I would urge you to share this knowledge – either with the Council, or with the priests of the *Aeshta* Orders if you prefer.'

Corollin stared down at her tea, as if debating within her own mind. Rhysana sipped from her own bowl, and waited.

'You already know,' Corollin said at last, 'that the Enemy draws close, seeking a way to return, and that his power is at work within the waking world. Whether there are specific events foretold that herald his coming, I have not learnt. But in truth, he needs but one person, or creature, with the correct knowledge and power, to open a way and summon him into the waking world from the Realms beyond. He nearly achieved this last year, close by here in the Black Mountains, but the Sun priests and the Fay drove him back. He still has many servants hidden in the world. One might be calling him even now, as we speak; or perhaps a few days hence, when the moon is at the dark.'

'But this is terrible!' Rhysana cried. She set her bowl down too swiftly, spilling a little of the tea on to the polished wood. 'Do his servants now have this knowledge?'

The memory of the final night of the siege of Arrandin came unbidden to her mind. One of the greater priests among the Easterner hosts had summoned the ancient lieutenants of Lo-Khuma against them – huge demons, thrice the height of a man, with heads like horses' skulls and manes of fire. But for that summons, the priest had had to draw strength from a number of his own minions gathered around him. So even with the correct knowledge, how much greater power might be needed for the demon captain himself to be called, Rhysana could scarce begin to imagine. There was some small comfort in that.

'Perhaps,' Corollin shrugged, taking a napkin from the tray to mop up the tea. 'But now that the Easterners are marching home, and the Southers have agreed to peace, the Enemy may choose to bide his time and plan anew. I was simply telling you what we learned from the elvenfolk of the Fay.'

'The Fay?' Rhysana echoed.

At that moment the library doors burst open, and Kellarn of Dortrean came quickly in. His white linen shirt, though clean, hung untucked outside his breeches, and his sandy fair hair was wet and brushed straight back. He appeared to be clutching half a sourbread roll in one hand. Though his face was flushed from his precipitous arrival, to Rhysana's mind there was still a paleness about him, a shadow around the eyes, as though he had slept badly. From Kellarn's unguarded expression as he saw her, she guessed that she herself must look worse than she felt.

The two women rose as one to greet him with due courtesy, both because he was their host and because he was far above them in precedence by right of Blood Noble.

'Ellaïn said for us to wait here,' Rhysana explained. 'I fear that Markhûl was a little put out by it.'

'Are you going to throw us out?' asked Corollin cheerfully.

He waved his bread roll at them to sit down, and shut the doors behind him. Rhysana took the napkin from Corollin, and finished cleaning up.

'You are welcome, Rhysana,' said Kellarn, 'but I'm surprised to find you still here. Won't they miss you back at the College?'

'The students have gone down for the summer now,' she said. 'Besides, I think we need to talk – if you feel able.'

Kellarn nodded. 'You might even surprise a straight answer out of me,' he grinned. He came over to the table and helped himself to some tea.

'Tell me again about the Southers,' he said. 'I wasn't really listening last night.'

Rhysana nodded, smoothing the folds of her dark blue gown into place. 'They are mostly gone from Ellanguan now, though Ambassador T'Loi remains. The Emperor has given them the Braedun *commanderie* as a garrison, in case the Easterners return. Your father was to sail down there with them.'

Kellarn cursed beneath his breath. His misgivings clearly ran as deep as Rhysana's own.

'Kierran of Arrand is with him,' she added.

'Kierran?' His face shone with sudden hope, as swiftly shadowed by a cloud of dismay. 'What is Rhydden playing at? Is he going to kill my father too?'

The directness of the question startled her. 'The Emperor has left Ellanguan, sailing for Lautun. He should be there any day now.'

'Erkal will have the priests of Braedun to protect him,' put in Corollin; 'and Kierran too.'

'For what comfort it is worth,' said Rhysana, 'the priests of Kelmaar believe that whoever – or whatever – caused your brother's death has also left Ellangaun, some days ago, before the Souther ships set sail. Or so Hrugaar said.'

'Probably with the Emperor,' Kellarn muttered.

'How is Hrugaar?' asked Corollin.

'He is well,' Rhysana smiled. 'He is to be our new Council Secretary, now that Iorlaas is Prime Councillor, so I hope to see him more often.'

'Hrugaar as Secretary?' Corollin gasped. 'Why would the Council choose him? I thought he caused far too much trouble in assemblies.'

'Iorlaas chose him,' Rhysana corrected her. 'For that very reason, I think. But we shall have need of his sense of humour in the coming days.'

She turned her attention back to Kellarn. He was staring down at his tea bowl, chewing over the last of the sourbread roll.

'You said last night,' she began, 'that you believed Rhydden was responsible for your brother's death. How are you so certain?'

'Isn't it obvious?' he threw back. 'You said his last words were, *Kellarn was right.* The only major thing Solban and I ever disagreed upon was his loyalty to the Empire. Surely that means it was his beloved Emperor who destroyed him.'

'It is said that he had a disagreement with the Emperor, over sending the Souther ships to harbour in Renza,' Rhysana allowed. 'Yet he was obeying that very order at the time of his death. While Rhydden may share the blame, in part, for giving the command, that does not make him wholly responsible.'

Kellarn sighed heavily, and glanced sideways at Corollin. After a moment, the journeyman gave a slight nod in return.

'Rhysana, you have been a good friend to my family,' he began. 'And if your Council of Magi is neutral – well, perhaps someone neutral is what I really need right now. And Mellin said last night that we ought to start talking to each other.'

Rhysana felt her heartbeat quicken. She schooled herself to calm. 'You do not have to tell me, if you would rather not,' she said.

Kellarn shook his head. 'We were followed and attacked on

our way here,' he told her; 'five days ago now. One of the two who attacked us was a shadowfay changeling.'

She nodded, but said nothing. The shadowfay were the evil corruption of the immortal elvenfolk of the Fay, beautiful and terrible. In ages past they had worshipped Lo-Khuma; and in recent years they had again turned their malice against the Six Kingdoms, striking at the Lords and Magi of the Court Noble.

'The other was one of the Emperor's Black Destriers. He had a pendant with their badge upon it, a black horseshoe on gold. The changeling summoned a demon against us, a thing of madness and confusion. Corollin and I managed to destroy it.'

'It was one of the *Ulhennar*,' said Corollin. 'A creature of terror from the ancient strife of the gods.'

Rhysana did not recall the name, but she shelved it away in her mind for later. 'Five days,' she said, counting back hurriedly. 'That would have been the day following Solban's death. Surely you are not suggesting that it was the same creature?'

Kellarn's face turned paler still, and his eyes widened.

'No,' said Corollin in her deep, thoughtful voice. 'It was the second day after we passed through Rebraal. They could not have picked up our trail so quickly, unless they had the means to find us and get there by magic. I don't think either of them would have had the power.'

'The Emperor's Archmage would,' said Kellarn.

Rhysana nodded slowly. The Archmage Merrech would indeed have the power to do so. 'But why would Rhydden or Merrech want you dead?' she demanded.

'Why not?' Kellarn countered.

Rhysana picked up her tea bowl. 'To be blunt,' she said calmly, 'it would serve no useful purpose, that I can see. Nor is it Rhydden's way – nor Merrech's. His Eminence plays games with people, driving them to bring about their own downfall; and the Emperor learned from him. They might spy on you, or take you hostage to bring pressure on others. But your father is already trapped in the web with the Souther armies; and your Lady mother now returns to the imperial palace with the Empress, easily within Rhydden's reach.'

'What?' cried Kellarn.

'We shall be keeping an eye on her at Court, of course,' she assured him. 'Which is why we need to know as much as possible about what happened to Solban, and why you think Rhydden is responsible; so that we can be prepared to protect her – and others – if necessary. The more so, if you are planning vengeance against him.'

Kellarn and Corollin looked away. Neither of them spoke. Rhysana sipped her tea deliberately.

'The attacks on Solban and yourselves might not have come at Rhydden's own bidding,' she reasoned. 'You know already that the priests of Mairdun believe that there is a danger from within the imperial household, which might put even the Emperor at risk. We had thought that it might be an agent of the Easterners or Southers. Yet you tell me that this shadowfay changeling rode with the Black Destrier, and that it was the changeling who summoned the demon against you.'

'The Destrier was an ally of the shadowfay,' said Kellarn. 'He had one of their knives, which they give to their sworn friends. And the other side of his pendant had the same symbol as the one I gave you in Arrandin, which came from the Easterner warrior: the lozenge in the square, the ancient sign of the enemy captain himself. Do you really think that one of the Emperor's most trusted circle of spies could have kept *that* secret from Rhydden and his foul Archmage?'

Rhysana felt suddenly stifled, even in the cool tranquillity of the library. Her unborn child stirred fretfully inside her. She had the urge to cry out in denial, to shout that it could not possibly be so; that even Rhydden and Merrech would never sink to such betrayal. And yet she could not do so. The spark of truth had kindled within her, spreading through her thoughts like wildfire. Rhydden knew, and Merrech knew. They had known all along. She forced herself to breathe deeply, and took another sip of tea with trembling fingers.

'What became of the pendant?' she asked.

'It is in the keeping of the elvenfolk of the Fay,' said Corollin. 'They will keep it safely hidden from the shadowfay, and from the Emperor's servants.'

Rhysana nodded. The pendant was the proof of Kellarn's story – proof which would speak for itself to the Magi and the *Aeshta* priests, with their arts. If Rhydden or Merrech knew of it, as surely they must, then they would be searching for it now; and anyone who carried it would be in deadly danger.

'Look here,' said Kellarn, leaning forward nervously. 'I'm not sure how much of this you should tell the Council. If the *Aeshta* Orders get wind of it – or even some of the *Vashta* priests – they might do something stupid and make everything much worse.'

Rhysana returned his gaze steadily. 'The Council already knows that there is a danger within the imperial household,' she said; 'and we have it in mind that the shadowfay are stirring again, and that they have served Lo-Khuma before. I shall enquire whether the madness of the *Ulhennar* might explain the death of your brother, and others, in Ellanguan; for that may help us to prevent further deaths. But otherwise you have made your oath before the gods, and I shall leave the gods to speak of it, if they will.'

Kellarn grinned at her in relief.

'For the moment,' she added. 'I want you to promise me, however, that if you do go seeking vengeance against Rhydden, you will not do so alone. If he can call upon the shadowfay and demons for allies, even you might be hard pressed to handle them all.'

Kellarn ducked his head, but then looked backed at her. 'I promise,' he said.

'How did you overcome the *Ulhennar*, by the way?' she asked.

'With my sword. But Corollin helped.'

Rhysana glanced at the journeyman in silent question.

'I controlled the one who had summoned it,' Corollin explained. 'But it destroyed him. Against the creature itself, my strength was too weak – though the Fay call it but a lesser terror.'

Rhysana nodded. 'And this is our great fear with the demon captain himself. We can strive against his servants; and thus far, by the grace of the gods, we have survived. But who among our priests and magi has the strength to stand against him? And we are weaker yet, after the war. Even the matrix of power we found in Arrandin might not be enough to hold him back.

'Our friend Hrugaar has been hunting through the oldest records, in the hope of finding other foretellings of the demon's return, and how he may be defeated. That search has so far proved vain. But have you learned aught that you can tell us of this, from the Fay? Or from the dragon?' she asked Kellarn.

He sat back at the mention of the Father of All Dragons, but did not relax.

Corollin picked up the covered jug and poured more tea for them all. 'Long ago, a way was opened for Lo-Khuma to enter the waking world,' she answered after several moments. 'He brought an army of demons behind him. And as you know, it was the forefathers of the First Kings who drove him back – both through strength of arms, and through great strength of will, using the gifts of power they had.'

'Gifts unlike those of our own Magi,' Rhysana sighed. 'Though not so different, perhaps, from the powers of the *Aeshta* priests.'

'But the First Kings also took thought for the time when the Enemy might return,' said Corollin, 'and how they might lend help to those who had to fight him.'

'In what way?' demanded Rhysana.

'No!' Kellarn said quickly.

Corollin frowned at him. The two of them stared at one another, while Rhysana looked on. It was Kellarn who finally shrugged and turned away.

'It was a secret kept hidden even from the Fay,' Corollin explained. 'But together the Kings made an artefact, and hid the parts of it separately, in many different places.'

'What manner of artefact?' Rhysana asked.

'That is still unclear. We are not even sure how many pieces there were, though it seems likely there may have been one for each of the Six Kingdoms.'

'And have any been found?'

Corollin nodded slowly. 'Four – those made by the Kings of Hauchan, Ellanguan, Khêltan and Cerrodhí.'

'And where are they?'

'Safe,' said the journeyman. 'Only the two of us know anything about them, and a handful of the Fay – and now you, of course.'

Rhysana nodded. There were still some details that they were not willing to tell her.

'I take it that this is another matter which I should keep to myself?' she said. She did not expect them to answer. 'So why are you telling me?'

Kellarn looked up, as if seconding the question.

'The horselords of Lautun must have made one part of the artefact,' Corollin answered. 'You are better placed than we are to find it.'

'Am I?' said Rhysana. 'Why?'

'You have access to the College libraries in Lautun – and to the imperial palace during the Summer Court. And it was you who found the great defence matrix in Arrandin, and learned how to use it.'

Rhysana wanted to protest that her success in Arrandin owed much to the work of her colleagues; and that she was hardly at liberty to search the imperial citadel, whatever freedom she might have in her own College. But Corollin's reasoning was sound enough under the circumstances.

'What am I to look for?' she asked.

'We don't know, exactly,' Corollin admitted. 'Each King knew only of his own part, and was sworn not to speak of it nor to reveal where it was hidden. But if Hrugaar has been hunting through ancient records, as you say, perhaps he will have found some clue to help you, without realising it.'

'Perhaps,' said Rhysana doubtfully.

'Four pieces have come together again, after fifteen hundred years of waiting,' said Corollin. 'If you are meant to find another, you will.'

'Other people are hunting for the artefact,' Kellarn put in, 'and they aren't friendly. We found out about them some time ago, in Ellanguan. It's possible they may have found the Lautun bar already. The search could prove very dangerous.'

To Rhysana's mind, anything connected with Lo-Khuma was bound to be perilous. She waved the warning aside. 'Bar?' she asked.

Kellarn shifted uncomfortably. 'The other pieces are metal bars, with jewels in. The Lautun part may be something else, of course.'

'I see,' she said. 'That leaves the Sixth Kingdom of Farodh. Is that where you shall be heading next?'

'That is the part we are looking for,' Corollin allowed. 'But it may not be hidden in the marshes of Farodh at all. The first bar we found was hidden far beyond the borders of Six Kingdoms.'

Rhysana nodded again. By implication, the object they had asked her to find might also be hidden almost anywhere within the world, and with no clue as to its whereabouts. She did not share their confidence in her own ability to find it.

Kellarn was staring moodily into his empty bowl. With Solban's death, she wondered whether his fear for his parents' safety might seem more pressing to him now than this improbable search, even though the fate of the Six Kingdoms turned upon it.

'Well,' she said aloud, 'I had not really expected to see you at the Summer Court. Yet for what small comfort it is worth, it seems to me that you have a habit of turning up where you are most needed, Kellarn – whether you realise it or not.'

She smiled at him, and he managed a wry smile in return. Rhysana sensed that it was time for her to go.

'Thank you for letting me see your library again,' she said, standing up. Kellarn and Corollin were on their feet a moment later. 'It must be the dream of any scholar in the Six Kingdoms – so many unknown or forgotten treasures, just waiting to be read.'

'They're not forgotten,' said Kellarn. 'Nor unread.'

'Have you read any of them?' she countered.

'A few,' he answered crossly.

Rhysana coloured in embarrassment. 'Forgive me my Lord, I did not mean to offend.'

'No.' Kellarn sighed, and ran one hand back through his hair. 'No, my Lady, it is I who should apologise. Dortrean is honoured by your praise of her treasures.' He bowed to her across the table, and Rhysana gave a gentler bow in return.

'A true son of Dortrean,' she smiled. 'Just like your father. Such kind courtesy will stand you in good stead, when you are Earl in your turn.'

Kellarn's bearing briefly faltered. 'I never wanted to be Earl,' he said.

'Or Emperor, perhaps?' she ventured.

'No!' said Kellarn, startled. 'Never that!'

'Then give time to thought,' she said. It was not the moment Rhysana would have chosen; but it needed to be said, and she might not have another chance. 'If you take vengeance on Rhydden, and he dies, then his dynasty comes to an end. His nearest heirs are but distant cousins, in Vaulun. Other Houses Noble will stake their claim for power; and Dortrean is foremost by precedence, if not by blood ties with the imperial line.'

'Why have another Emperor?' Kellarn challenged. 'Why not a council of Earls, presiding over the Court Noble?'

'Others may not share your views on that,' she answered.

'And what if the new Empress is now with child?' put in Corollin.

'Then at best we would have another Interregnum,' said

Rhysana, 'until the child came of age. Either way, the Court Noble would be tearing at one another's throats for power, until a strong hand controls them again. And with the Southers on our shores, and the Easterners still minded to war, that might prove the end of the Six Kingdoms as we know them.'

'So are you saying I should leave Rhydden alone?' Kellarn demanded.

'No,' Rhysana answered. 'I am just reminding you that it does help to think about the consequences of removing an Emperor, before you do it.'

After Rhysana had gone away, Kellarn fetched his sword from his room and went to the family shrine to Hýriel. The shrine filled the whole of the northwest tower, and unlike the rest of the White Manor it was lined entirely in the smooth, polished black stone of the surrounding mountains. High overhead, a clerestory row of window arches was open to the summer morning outside. The only other light came from the huge bronze bowl of fire that stood in the centre of the square floor.

There were a few tall chairs set at intervals around the walls, but no one else was here at this hour of the day. Kellarn pulled off his boots and socks and padded barefoot across the floor, circling to the left of the flames. Then he sat down cross-legged on the cool flagstones – facing South toward the fire, as near as he could guess it – with his great sword balanced across his knees.

Kellarn breathed deeply in the welcome shadows, letting his gaze rest on the sword as he surrendered to the calm stillness of the shrine. The patterned hawks and serpents and hounds seemed to shift and dance along the blade in the firelight.

It had not occurred to him before, until Rhysana had mentioned it, that the demon of the *Ulhennar* which this sword had destroyed might be the same creature responsible for his brother's death. Corollin had thought it unlikely; but it fuelled the thought in Kellarn's own mind that had he gone to Ellanguan, instead of chasing after the Fay, he could have saved his brother's life. Did that leave Solban's blood upon his own hands?

And yet, had they not gone to Starmere, they might not have met the moon fay Losithlîn; and it had been Losithlîn who had given them the fourth bar. It seemed as though Solban's life had been the price to pay for achieving that part of their quest.

Kellarn hoped and prayed that the lives of his father and mother – and Kierran of Arrand – would not be demanded of him as well. Yet if he turned aside from this quest, to try to save them, then there might be no chance of defeating Lo-Khuma, and the whole world as he knew it would be lost. So for now he had to trust to the gods, and to the strength of Braedun and Rhysana's magi, to keep his family safe from harm. But such trust did not come easily to Kellarn.

He turned his thoughts to the next journey ahead, the search for the Farodhí part of the artefact. Losithlîn had advised them to seek help from the Guardian of Telbray Woods, south of Dortrean, which was in itself a difficult and dangerous challenge. The Guardians were the ancient keepers of *Aeshta* lore, who had dwelt deep in the forests since the earliest days of the Six Kingdoms – until, that is, the Emperors of Lautun had hunted them all down and killed them in the previous century. To deal with the Guardians or their secrets was still punishable by death under imperial law, though officially none were now left alive to worry about.

The moon fay Losithlîn – serving in place of a Guardian for the great forest of Cerrodhí – had told them that one true Guardian still lived within the Telbray Woods; and that that Guardian could tell them if any of the ancient Kings and Queens of Farodh were now reborn among the living. How they were meant to retrieve the memories of the old Kings, whether dead or reborn in other lives, Kellarn did not know, though he supposed that some of the *Aeshta* priests might have the power to do so. And whether those memories would be of any help in their quest was quite another problem. But Losithlîn had advised it, and it did seem less long-winded than searching hundreds of square miles of marshland in the abandoned wastes of Farodh.

Their other choice, with perils enough of its own, would have been to journey beyond Telbray Woods to the imperial cities of Telbray and Farran, to hunt through whatever records they could find. Kellarn doubted that there would be anything of use here in the Dortrean library, though Corollin might have thought it worth looking.

'Collie?' said a woman's voice.

Kellarn opened his eyes and looked up. Corollin was standing on the other side of the flames, her strawberry gold robes glowing bright against the shadows.

'When had you thought to leave?' she asked, circling round toward him. 'And are there any maps here that we might look at?'

'We don't need a map,' he said. 'We just follow the river south between Carfinn and Dhûlann, and cross at the old causeway. Telbray Woods are on the other side. I've done it any number of times.'

'And once inside the woods?' she pursued.

Kellarn gave her a rueful grin. 'No maps to be had – or not that I know of. But there is a path. We shall have to hope that the Guardian finds us.'

Corollin nodded. 'What about the Sun Temple?'

Kellarn frowned. The priests of Torollen, *Aeshta* Lord of the Sun, were powerful allies against the demons of Lo-Khuma, and they had no great love for the Emperor; but they could sometimes be over eager in their fiery zeal. The stone fay Sarnîl, who had helped rebuild the temple, had warned against telling the priests too much of their tale until the time was right.

'I should like to see it,' said Corollin.

'I should, too,' he said with an effort. 'And it is on our way. If we leave tomorrow morning, Mellin could ride there with us.

If she talks to them about horses, perhaps they'll ask us fewer questions.'

'And today?'

'Today you can teach me how to stand up from a tumbling roll,' he grinned. 'And later I should like to spend some time with my nephews – once Mellin has finished drilling them in the stable yard.'

Chapter Two

Rhysana did not return home to the Lautun College until late that afternoon. She had gone first in her magical *leap* to the Dârghûn manor house, in search of her husband Torkhaal and their son; and had been persuaded by the Lady Rogheïn Aartaús of Dârghûn to stay for a noon meal, and for some hours thereafter. Torkhaal himself was partly to blame. Through his close friendship with the late Prime Councillor the Lord Herusen Dârghûn, he had come to be treated as an adopted member of the family; and now that Herusen's many grandchildren had mostly passed into their teens, the household welcomed the chance to make a fuss of Torkhaal and Rhysana's own little boy, Taillan.

They had gone there the day before, bringing the last of Herusen's belongings from the College, and to test his grandson Aidhan for magical talent. Aidhan, now fully thirteen and on the threshold of his manhood, had proved more promising than anyone had really expected. He was also possessed of exceptional mental gifts similar to those of his grandfather, which were only just beginning to show. Torkhaal was thus eager to take the boy to see his kinsmen among the Môshári Order, to discuss his future training. He had left the manor almost as soon as Rhysana arrived, taking the embarrassed Aidhan with him in his magical *leap*. Rhysana and Taillan had stayed behind to wait for them, and to speak with Aidhan's mother Serinta – herself a former votary of the *Aeshta* Order of Aranara, and no stranger to psychic gifts and the demands of magical discipline. So by the time that they had returned to the relative peace of their own College apartment, the day had flown by and it was time to get Taillan bathed and ready for bed.

Still, Rhysana's day had not been entirely wasted after she had left the Dortrean manor. She had managed to tell Torkhaal of her conversation with Corollin, and of what the elvenfolk of the Fay had said about Lo-Khuma's return. She had also told him of the demon of the *Ulhennar*, and raised the question of whether such a creature might have been responsible for some of the deaths in Ellanguan. Torkhaal in turn had passed this information to the Môshári, who had promised to spread the word to the other Orders. She had not told him about the rest of her conversation with Kellarn; and though he sensed that she was unsettled after her visit to Dortrean, he knew better than to press the point.

Mage Councillor Hrugaar came in just after she had settled Taillan to sleep. He was on his way to Iorlaas' study, so his visit had to be brief. Iorlaas was a stern taskmaster, and with his first imperial Court as Prime Councillor only a few days away he was making great demands on Hrugaar's time to help prepare for the ordeal. Since Hrugaar himself was but newly made Council Secretary – and since the previous Secretary, Oghraan, had left much in disarray and was less than forthcoming in offering to help him out – the whole business was proving far more of a headache than he had anticipated. The formal protocol which Iorlaas required was not Hrugaar's strongest subject; and the other magi who might have helped him – Rhysana and Torkhaal among them – had been noticeably absent over the past two days.

Nevertheless, Hrugaar was more inclined to laugh about his problems than to complain about them, so his visit was a welcome diversion. In between his cheerful banter, Rhysana discovered that the Emperor's ship had arrived the previous evening, sailing on up the White River estuary straight to the imperial citadel on the far shore. Hrugaar and Iorlaas had watched – from a safe vantage within the imperial palace itself, and aided by magical means – while Rhydden and his household disembarked. He was thus able to reassure her that the Lady Karlena of Dortrean had appeared in good health, and in charge of those around her rather than constrained by them. The Empress Grinnaer had looked far less well, and Karlena had ordered a litter for her to be carried up into the citadel from the wharf.

'Rhydden should never have made her make the voyage,' said Rhysana. 'There was no need. His Eminence could have brought her here in a single *leap*.'

Hrugaar shrugged. 'Perhaps he doesn't trust her. The rumour is in Ellanguan that she was sleeping with her brother.'

'You should not listen to gossip, Ru,' she tutted. 'But I am surprised at Iorlaas. I had not thought that he would go spying on the Emperor's doings like that.'

'He seemed to like the idea, when I suggested it.'

'You are leading our new Prime Councillor astray,' Rhysana frowned. But she was only teasing, and Hrugaar grinned in answer.

'He has a good sense of fun, deep down,' he said. 'He just needs the chance to show it more often.'

He went away soon afterward, with the promise to return later if he might. Rhysana did not wait up for him. She left Torkhaal to speak with him alone, if he would, and took herself early to bed. The night air from the city was still hot and stuffy, with the threat of a storm, and she was tired and needed to think.

She worked a simple spell to cool the air of her bedchamber a little, and undressed and climbed into bed. Taillan was snoring softly. Rhysana left the covers thrown back, and breathed deeply to calm her thoughts. Before the fourth breath, she was asleep.

She awoke as the first light of dawn crept in through the window shutters. Torkhaal must have closed them when he came to bed. Rhysana lay there for a few moments, listening to the carolling of the College martlets outside and her husband's quiet breathing. Then she stirred herself to get up.

She was heavier now, and her movements a little slower, and the effort of rising awoke him. Torkhaal growled and reached one arm around her. She looked back, and saw that his dark eyes were open and he was smiling.

Rhysana smiled and gave in, rolling back into bed and into his arms to kiss him. She had work to do, but it could wait. With the dangers they had faced in the past few months, and those that still lay ahead, she wanted to treasure these moments while she could. And she did love him so very much.

She giggled at her own foolishness. He chuckled in answer, and kissed her again.

She could feel his *presence* surrounding her, with the touch of feathered wings, and the warmth of his passion rising. His fingertips brushed down her spine, and then round to stroke her swollen belly, and then slowly circled up around her breast.

He gave another playful growl as she pushed him away, rolling him on to his back. She kissed his mouth once more; and then worked her way down his body, while he settled into deep purrs of contentment.

The sun was fully up by the time that Rhysana was washed and dressed, but the cloister garden still lay deep in shadow beneath the towers of the library building. It must have rained overnight, she thought, for everywhere was clean and damp and fresh, and the air was sweet with the scent of honeysuckle. The finches and titmice and martlets all chirruped at her as she made her way along the pillared walkway, and larger seabirds wheeled and shrieked in the brightness overhead. But with the College term ended and the students returned home, there seemed to be no other magi about at this early hour.

Though sleep had overtaken her the night before, she felt that her thoughts must have sorted themselves out while she slept. Or perhaps it was just her nature to see things more clearly in the morning light.

She was still deeply worried about Kellarn's oath against the Emperor – which, so far as Rhysana could see, could only lead to calamity and strife, whichever way he played it. Then again there was the news that one of Rhydden's Black Destriers was both a servant of Lo-Khuma and an ally of the shadowfay. She found it impossible to believe that neither the Emperor nor the Archmage Merrech had been aware of the fact; and the betrayal of the Six Kingdoms that that implied, by those very rulers supposed to protect them, appalled her. That in itself gave good cause for Kellarn's oath of treason to be fulfilled, if only to prevent a far more dreadful calamity. And then there was the quest for the unknown artefact, into which she had now been drawn.

Rhysana mentally upbraided herself for not having questioned Hrugaar about his research in Ellanguan, and whether he had found mention of the First Kings making provision against Lo-Khuma's return. She must remember to ask him.

Not that Rhysana intended speaking of the quest, or of Kellarn's oath, to anyone. Not until Kellarn or Corollin were ready for her to do so. For one thing, those were matters revealed to her in trust and friendship. For another, she had seen at once the great need to keep such things secret. And she realised now, somewhat to her surprise, that she felt confident enough to trust their judgement in this.

The question of the Black Destrier – and where Rhydden and Merrech themselves might stand in relation to Lo-Khuma and the shadowfay – was something that she wished to consider further before she spoke of it. In truth, Rhysana did not know to whom she might speak of it at all.

Torkhaal was her husband, her comforter, her rock; but he was also younger than her, and her junior on the Council, and too often inclined to let his heart persuade his head. Though she knew that she could count on his support, she did not feel that he could give her the advice that she needed. To ask Hrugaar without first speaking to Torkhaal did not seem fair. Besides, his fay blood gave him a rather different view of the life of the world. Rhysana was not sure that she was yet ready to hear what he might have to say.

Had Herusen still been alive, she would of course have gone to him. Only now did she begin to realise how much she had come to rely on his quiet wisdom over the past few years, since she had joined the ranks of the Council. She might have asked the Archmage Morvaan, though she knew him less well; but Morvaan was still in Arrandin, and preoccupied with the state of that city and the failing health of The Arrand. Or else there was the Archmage Ellen – except that Rhysana had no idea where she was, and Ellen guarded her privacy fiercely.

Being thus left alone to consider the problem, Rhysana had decided to do what she supposed any born scholar in her place would have done. She was going to the library.

Or to be more precise, she was going to see the Warden.

She let herself in through the patterned bronze doors, and made her way slowly up the sweeping stair of the library hall. He was waiting for her at the top, a shadow among shadows in his hooded robes of grey.

'Mistress,' the dull, familiar voice greeted her as she reached the landing.

'Good morning, Warden,' she said, bowing.

They studied one another for a moment in silence. Then Rhysana glanced around her, wondering if there were any ears nearby to overhear them.

'You have seen the library of the White Manor of Dortrean,' he said. It was more a statement of fact than a question.

'I have, Warden,' she nodded. 'But no catalogue was shown to me, and I doubt that the present Earl may be persuaded to provide one for us. The next Earl – perhaps.'

'Your name shall be honoured among generations of magi, Mistress,' he told her. 'This is a great achievement.'

'I have achieved nothing yet,' she demurred. 'But there is a possibility.'

'As I have said.'

He turned and led the way up the second stair, waiting

patiently for her on the small landing at the top. The morning sunlight came through the coloured glass of the window behind him, surrounding him in a misty aureole of many hues, though his robes remained the same featureless grey. Rhysana came up beside him. The low door to the reserve collection of the *aumery* library was just to her right; but he made no movement toward it, and she was reluctant to go in without his invitation.

'You have a purpose, Mistress?'

'I do.' Rhysana drew a deep breath. 'The First Council cleared the fortress of Whitespear Head and sealed it, after Illana was overthrown. I need to know what they found there.'

'You have more than once perused the Council Records.'

'I have,' she nodded. 'Enough to know that they are far from complete. There must have been other records made at the time, which were perhaps considered unsuitable for any but the High Council to see. I need to know what was taken from Whitespear Head – and what might have been left behind.'

It had come to her that this was the obvious choice. The Archmage Merrech was all but obsessed with the evil Illana, and with the unsolved riddle of her most notorious work, the *Argument of Command*. Rhysana herself had perceived that there was some connection between the text of the *Argument* and the lore of the Easterner wizards concerning the return of Lo-Khuma – whether through influence from one to the other, or both drawing upon a common source. So while she had long suspected that Illana was the key to understanding Merrech himself, it now occurred to her that this might also explain the connection between Lo-Khuma and the Emperor and his Black Destriers.

There was also the fact that Illana had lived some thousand years before, much closer in time to the defeat of Lo-Khuma and the founding of the Six Kingdoms. It was therefore possible that her fortress held records of the earliest days of the Kingdoms which had not survived in Ellanguan or

Lautun. And it was also a fact that Illana was held responsible for the ruin of the Wasted Hills, the erstwhile seat of the High Kings of Lautun; and there was no knowing what ancient and royal treasures might thereafter have found their way into her hands.

Beyond all this there was the news that Illana herself – long absent, and preserved by some unknown power – had but recently entered the Realms of the Dead. The priestess Ilumarin of Aranara had brought the tidings to Torkhaal here in the College library, having thought it important for Rhysana to know. She had not said why; but it had occurred to Rhysana that perhaps some of the magic at Whitespear Head might now fade or change with Illana's final passing.

'The treasures that were brought back were given to the library,' said the Warden. 'Some were sent to Ellanguan. The *chaedar* will show you what is here. The great among the First Council had knowledge of what was left behind. They made no catalogue. There were no written accounts, other than those which you have seen.'

'So that knowledge died with them?' she pursued.

The Warden seemed to shift beneath his robes, almost as if he were fidgeting.

'Their memory is with us,' he recited.

For the Warden himself, it was no less than the simple truth. As a high councillor, Rhysana knew that he had indeed been here in the library ever since the days of the First Council, and spoken even with the First Founder Caraan in person; and it was whispered among the High Council that he thus had close personal knowledge of the work and studies of former magi. Rhysana had never had occasion before now to question him upon that point; and he was besides a firm believer in the right of all magi, past and present, to personal privacy, so that she would have hesitated to do so.

Yet though he had recited the words in his accustomed dull, mechanical voice, there was something in his manner which somehow begged the question. Rhysana drew a cautious breath.

'Warden,' she ventured, 'was part of that knowledge entrusted to you, for a time when another High Council might have need to hear it?'

For answer he turned and brought his arms up before his chest. Rhysana could not see what he did next – both because he now had his back to her, and because his hands were forever hidden beneath the long sleeves of his robes – but a moment later a doorway appeared in the far corner of the landing, where there had been none before. There was no door, just an opening on to the top of a narrow stair leading down into darkness. The Warden glided straight toward it.

'Mistress?' he invited, without pausing. Rhysana hurried after him.

The staircase was so narrow and so steep, that had she been a month greater with child Rhysana doubted that she could have managed it on her feet. She kindled a ball of her own silver-blue magelight, and sent it bobbing down ahead of her to light her way. The Warden himself seemed to have no need of it.

They had descended perhaps half the height of the library building when the stairway took a final turn, and she saw daylight coming up to greet them. They came out into the corner of a small vaulted chamber, barely four paces square, with what Rhysana took at first to be large round windows upon three sides. But at second glance she realised that they were more like mirrors, or magic portals, fully a fathom wide and bordered with heavy frames of gold.

The middle mirror – upon her far right as she came in – showed a broad river under morning sunlight; and it was from this that the bright daylight within the chamber chiefly came. On the far shore of the river stood a line of low, rugged cliffs, with a tumble of wooded hills beyond. Rhysana knew it at once for the promontory of Whitespear Head, at the meeting of the Rolling River and the Grey.

The mirror to the left showed only empty darkness – except perhaps for the beginnings of a narrow bridge, close down beside the lowest part of the frame. The third, which was just to her right as she entered, looked on to a world of pale scintillating mist, like the heart of a sunlit cloud.

The fourth wall had no mirror at all, but the biscuit coloured stone of the College buildings had been worked to frame a circular opening of similar size, filled with a honeycomb of many recessed shelves; and in the corner beyond stood a slope-fronted desk and a tall four-legged stool. There also seemed to be a circular pattern to the smooth flagstones of the floor, though Rhysana had no time to study it just then.

The Warden went straight to the middle mirror, and laid his covered hand upon the gilded frame. The view within dipped and swooped forward across the river waters, until they seemed to be standing close in beneath the looming cliff. Rhysana felt a sudden chill of apprehension.

From this distance – looking through the mirror, as it were – she could see that part of the cliff was not altogether real. It was a veil of power, a *glamouring* to conceal what lay behind. The true rockface reached back into a shallow cleft, with a short flight of smooth-hewn steps leading up to a pair of sizeable stone doors. The doors were shut fast, and sealed at the midpoint with a medallion of power that pulsed and swirled with ever changing hues; and from that seal were spun countless strands of power that ran out to weave the web of *glamour* to conceal it. Even seen thus, through the scrying mirror, the sense of bonded power was staggering. And when she looked away, Rhysana found that sparks of colour still trailed across her sight.

'The doors of the fortress of she who was named Illana,' said the Warden, 'sealed with the combined strength of the High Council in the five hundred and fortieth year of the Six Kingdoms reckoning. Once in every generation its strength shall be renewed. Only with the white steel rod of the Prime Councillor of All Magi may this seal be safely opened.'

The Prime Councillor. Rhysana's heart sank, and she felt that she could have wept in frustration. Had Herusen been alive, she was sure that she could have persuaded him to help her; and that he would have gone with her to Whitespear Head, taking as many magi with him as he saw fit, to see her safely inside. But now he was gone, leaving an altogether different successor behind him. Iorlaas knew her hardly at all, and even less about her work on Illana. He had not the links with the *Aeshta* Orders to understand the true threat of Lo-Khuma's return; nor would he likely countenance the opening of Whitespear Head – for whatever reason – without prolonged debate in the High Council. And if the High Council learned of her intent, then so would the Archmage Merrech.

'Were there no other ways inside?' she demanded.

'Of those that were known to the Council, this one alone remains.'

'There must be another way,' she said.

The Warden made no answer. Instead he lifted back his hood, revealing a mane of snowy white hair and a full beard, and bright eyes that sparkled in welcome. Rhysana gave a little cry.

'Herusen?' she gasped.

'Um, not exactly, my dear,' he said, in a voice that was very much Herusen's own. 'I suppose you might say that I am Herusen as the Warden remembers him. Remember what you learned when you first came to us on the High Council. The Warden is part of our work, and becomes part of us; and so we become part of him. In a sense. But he seldom chooses to reveal it in this way.'

'So it is not really you at all?' She felt more confused than disappointed.

'Yes and no. It is no matter. Look!' He turned his face toward the mirror. With an effort, Rhysana tugged her gaze away from his face to obey.

'You need the rod to open the seal,' he told her. 'You do *not* need the Prime Councillor himself. Any mage of sufficient power could handle the energies involved. The Archmage Morvaan could do it – or Ellen, perhaps.'

'But what if Iorlaas objects?' she countered. 'Or are you suggesting that I borrow the rod without asking his permission?'

'I made no suggestion,' he answered easily. 'I am merely telling you how you may get inside. If, when and why you should wish to do so, I leave to your inestimable wisdom.'

'But that is what I lack,' she said. 'Oh Herusen, why did you have to leave us so soon?'

'I did what I had to do,' he said. 'The rest I leave to you, and what's-his-name.'

'Torkhaal?' she supplied. 'Hrugaar?'

He gave her a last smile, pulled his hood forward over his head, and became the Warden again.

'Herusen Dârghûn, Flower of the Staff,' he said, 'Prime Councillor of All Magi. His memory is with us.'

Almost, Rhysana fancied, there was a note of sadness in the ritual words.

'Yes, Warden,' she said. 'His memory is with us.'

He raised his sleeve to the golden frame, and the view of the cliffs spun away into the distance once more. Then he led the way to the recessed shelves on the other side of the chamber. Rhysana fished out a handkerchief from the pockets of her indigo robes, and wiped her eyes before she followed him.

The Warden lifted down a small codex bound in dark grey leather and offered it to her. Rhysana tucked her handkerchief inside her sleeve, and pulled out and put on a clean pair of gloves before taking it from him. The codex did not look look particularly old, and there were no markings on the cover that she could see. Rhysana opened it carefully.

The first few pages were laid out as an index, penned in one of the magical alphabets used by the Magi that would require but a simple *screening* spell to read with ease; and then there were two or three pages left blank after that, as though the index were not yet complete. Rhysana turned past them swiftly – and then her heart skipped a beat. For there in the codex before her was a detailed drawing of the doorway and hewn stair that she had seen in the mirror, with the seal of the High Council and the strands of the *glamouring* spell laid out in a tracery of silver ink.

'I thought that you said that there were no other written records, Warden,' she said aloud.

'There were not,' he replied.

Rhysana looked at him, and then back at the codex in her hands. And suddenly she understood.

'You have put this together yourself,' she said, 'from what was told to you at the time.'

The Warden gave the slightest nod beneath his hood. 'I have tried, Mistress. The information is far from complete. High Councillor Saelwan, in particular, was a poor observer with no sense of scale or direction, and it was a great labour to make head or tail of what he had seen – though his knowledge of the making and use of incense for magical purposes has seldom been equalled, and it was said that he could tell one horse from another by scent alone. The work is thus of limited value, and should not wholly be relied upon as a guide.'

Rhysana skimmed ahead through the pages. There was a good deal more of the magical writing, all penned in the same beautifully even hand. There were also more drawings and plans, marked with words and symbols in different coloured inks. The workmanship was exquisite, and the value of the knowledge that it might contain made her hands tremble a little in excitement as she held it.

A soft whisper of chimes sounded from somewhere outside, and the air around her stirred as if with a gentle breeze. The *chaedar* – the unseen attendants of the College library – had arrived. The Warden moved toward the centre of the floor.

'You may borrow the codex for as long as you wish,' he told her. 'But keep it hidden, and return it only into my keeping when you are done.' He motioned for her to join him.

'Thank you, Warden,' she said, closing the book in her hands. She was at a loss what else to say.

He leaned toward her a little, and would have lowered his

voice if he could. 'Beware of His Eminence, Mistress. He knows—'

Another chime sounded, and the musical voices of the *chaedar* whispered all around them.

'Knows what?' Rhysana prompted.

'Too much,' he answered. 'Too little. Iorlaas, Prime Councillor of All Magi, has need of me. Mistress?'

He touched her lightly on the arm, and they were back on the upper landing again. There was no sign of the hidden doorway in the corner.

The Warden stepped back and motioned for her to go in through the *aumery* door. Then he turned and glided calmly down the stair toward the Lower Library, as though nothing out of the ordinary had passed between them.

The Emperor Rhydden was still dressing when his Counsellor came to find him.

'Are we not to be permitted one morning of peace to ourself before our Summer Court begins?' he said irritably.

He turned back to study himself in the long mirror while the two household men brought his shirt. Though now into his late thirties, Rhydden prided himself that he could still pass for ten years younger. His shoulder length hair was still thick and raven dark, with no trace of grey. His chest and upper arms seemed a little broader, more powerful than they had been. Yet the light in the chamber lent his skin an oddly drawn, pallid look, as though he had spent too long out of the sun.

'There is always tomorrow,' the Archmage Merrech said smoothly. 'His Highness has a meeting with his guard commanders in little more than an hour.'

'We are well aware of the fact,' Rhydden scowled. 'We intend to ride before then.'

The men lifted the white shirt over his head, and shook it down around him.

'Of course, Sire.' Merrech signalled with one pale hand, and the household attendants went out swiftly, closing the doors behind them. The Emperor sighed, and turned round to face him.

'And what will our guard commanders have to tell us?' he asked.

'Little of note.' The Archmage began the work of lacing Rhydden's shirt himself. 'They should not keep His Highness long.'

'Yes,' said Rhydden, 'there are times when I do not miss Solban's thoroughness. But I was sorry to lose him.'

'Of course, Sire.'

'So what have you discovered, Counsellor? Is there news of Tighaún?'

'None,' Merrech answered. 'I have been unable to find him.'

Rhydden frowned. Tighaún of Vaulun was one of his better Black Destriers. He did not like the fact that there had been no word from him in the last six days – not since he had picked up Kellarn of Dortrean's trail, west of the Great Forest.

'Could his changeling friend have betrayed him?' he demanded.

'Perhaps,' Merrech allowed. 'Or he might be keeping them both hidden, beyond even my arts to discover. The shadowfay have no word of him either.'

'They are hardly to be trusted,' said Rhydden. 'Could Kellarn have killed both Tighaún and the changeling, and kept that hidden from us?'

'It is possible Sire, though unlikely. The girl with him is a journeyman mage; and they may have had help from the forest creatures, as they did when they escaped Mataún.'

'Tighaún is not such a fool,' Rhydden countered.

The Archmage shrugged. 'There has been no report of Kellarn returning the horses to Mairdun; nor has he been seen in the village of Môstí, nor abroad on His Highness' own lands. Nor have I been able to find him. I believe that he has either gone to ground in the forest of Cerrodhí, or returned home to the White Manor of Dortrean.'

'But you do not believe him to be dead?'

'Not yet, Sire. Were that the case, the Lady Karlena would have heard.'

Rhydden nodded. Though Kellarn's mother was kept with the Empress' household, here in the citadel, she still had her own accomplished methods of gathering news from the world outside. Had the heathen priests of the *Aeshta* Orders learned of Kellarn's death, they would no doubt have sent word to her at once – and then his own spies would have learned of it, even had Karlena not told him herself.

Merrech went over to fetch his black tunic. Rhydden turned back to the mirror.

'One wonders what Kellarn might be doing in Dortrean,' he said. 'Erkal's troops should return there from Farran any day now; and then of course there is the new Sun Temple. Is that Taràgin mage still in Ellanguan?'

'Mage Councillor Hendraal, Sire? So I understand.'

Rhydden slid his arms into the proffered tunic, and then turned to let the Archmage fasten it.

'Have Rinnekh lean on him,' he said thoughtfully; 'either through our ambitious friend Sollonaal, or one of the *Vashta* priests as appropriate. Taràgin has lands within spitting distance of the Sun Temple. Perhaps Hendraal should pay his noble kinsmen there a visit, to see what is happening in Dortrean.'

'Taràgin himself is like to be coming to Court, Sire,' Merrech observed.

'So much the better,' said Rhydden.

He tugged the high collar to sit more comfortably about his throat, checked it in the mirror, and then crossed the room to the small side table where his personal jewel casket had been set.

Dortrean's age-old alliance with the *Aeshta* Orders still troubled him. He comforted himself that he had gone some small way to undermine that by sending Erkal to the Braedun *commanderie*. No matter their long friendship with Dortrean, when the Lords of the Braedun Order beheld Erkal overseeing their removal from their own headquarters to make way for the Southers, at the Emperor's request, their trust in the Earl himself would be weakened. The other Orders would also begin to have their doubts. And if the Braedun business went off smoothly, then it would pave the way for other moves to divest the *Aeshta* priests of some of their influence and power.

Erkal's growing friendship with the Magi – or at least with those magi who had been with him during the siege of Arrandin – was a more complex question.

Rhydden sought and found the jewel that he wanted, a white gold ring set with a single pale blue stone, and slid it on to the third finger of his left hand. He smiled at the familiar tickle of power that ran up his arm to nestle at the back of his head. Then he stroked the gathered green stones of the Easterner necklace which the casket also held.

He smiled again, briefly, amused at the irony of the tribute that Herghin had sent him – and that a mage born of the Môshári should have brought it to him. Rhydden doubted that any of them, perhaps not even the Easterner woman who had worn it, had understood its true value. Though long treasured as bridal gifts among the Easterner clans, such jewels had a darker, more ancient history, remembered only by the shadowfay. Enchanted with the proper power and rituals, they had once forged the bond between a chieftain and the patron demon of his clan; and though the Archmage Merrech had assured him that no such spell was now laid upon this necklace, he had allowed that the arrangement of the stones might be close enough to the ancient patterns to be suited to the purpose.

Had any of the Easterners had the wit to know, they could have used it to summon their great demon and bind him to their purpose. Instead they had come as grovelling servants, awaiting their master's return.

Of course, Erkal had been foolish enough to return a similar jewel to The Vengru. The priests of Kelmaar had avowed that there was no enchantment set upon it; and as sworn enemies of the demon captain, Rhydden doubted that they would either have lied or parted with it had they believed otherwise. But it might be only a matter of time before the servants of Lo-Khuma in the Eastern Domains discovered what could be done with the Vengru necklace, and summoned him into the waking world. It brought another sense of urgency to Rhydden's own position in the war. He could not let the demon's power pass beyond his control.

He closed the casket lid firmly, and turned back to his Counsellor.

'What do you make of your new Prime Councillor?' he asked.

'Iorlaas, Sire? He is a lesser fool than Sollonaal. He is a faithful servant of Holy Serbramel, and hopes to keep the peace between the Council and the Court Noble – though he would not set aside ten centuries of Council wisdom and tradition to achieve it.'

'Could the *Vashta* priests gain sway over him, do you think?' Rhydden wondered.

'Not in Council matters, certainly,' Merrech returned. 'Nor has he ties of blood or close friendship with the Houses Noble. Iorlaas' neutral stand should prove interesting – and perhaps useful.'

Rhydden nodded, and led the way through into the murrey chamber where he was wont to break his fast. Three of the younger attendants in the golden livery of Lautun scrambled to attention as he entered. He waved them away, picked a fresh-baked roll from the tray, and went over to the open window.

'And what of the lovely High Councillor Rhysana?' he asked. 'Has she yet learned to bend Iorlaas' ear as she once did Herusen's?'

'Not yet, Highness – although her troublesome friend Hrugaar now acts as Iorlaas' secretary. Rhysana herself appears to be continuing Herusen's work, watching with the *Aeshta* Orders for signs of their Enemy's return. She has been in

Dârghûn, and her husband Torkhaal was yesterday with the Môshári.'

'We hardly suppose,' said Rhydden, 'that she has released her notes on the Arrandin defences to the High Council?'

The hooded Archmage snorted in answer.

The Emperor sighed, and gazed out through the window. Beyond the grey slated roofs of the guard quarters and the squared court on top of the north tower of the river wing, the great White River estuary glittered in the early morning light. On the farther shore, some miles downriver, the sprawling city of Lautun was still half hidden beneath the blue shadows of the folded hills behind. But already the first of the imperial ferry ships was making its way down with the receding tide, its terracotta sail furled and its golden horsehead prow trotting untroubled through the foaming swirls. Over the next two days, the ferries and other ships would make that journey several times, up and down across the river, bringing the Lords of the Court Noble and their households for the Summer Court. Several had already arrived here in the imperial citadel over the past few days.

'We trust that our paths shall cross again during this coming Court,' he observed. 'She makes such a charming adversary.'

'Like Karlena, Sire?'

'The Countess of Dortrean has a gift for finding answers that work, Rhysana for raising questions.' Rhydden frowned. 'Was there something else, Counsellor? Our stallion awaits us.'

Merech had come round to his right, into the deeper shadows beyond the panelled window revere.

'The question of the Southers in Ellanguan, Highness,' he hissed. 'Ambassador T'Loi retains a sizeable household and guard. With the Earl of Dortrean now gone, the number left behind is causing concern in the city.'

'Erkal should have objected to that,' said Rhydden.

'So did he, Sire – or so I understand. He bargained for the least number that courtesy would allow, without declaring T'Loi hostage once more.'

'And you do not trust Rinnekh to deal with them?'

'I do not trust T'Loi,' the Archmage countered. 'Your Rinnekh may underestimate him.'

The Emperor took a bite from his roll. He needed the Souther armies, given the threat of a renewed attack from the East. But should the God-King prove less amenable than T'Loi had hoped, Rhydden did not want Southers in Ellanguan helping to defend the city against their own countrymen. This present peace was too fragile to test their friendship thus.

'You were best to go there yourself, Counsellor,' he said. 'Whisper in our Lord Steward's ear – and have a word with our Destrier, Baelar. Perhaps T'Loi can be persuaded to send some men away, for the sake of our Empire's peace.'

'And if he refuses?'

'We persuade him some more,' said Rhydden lightly. 'Tomorrow is the dark of the moon. The *Aeshta* Orders will be watching for something to happen. Let Rinnekh give them something to think about.'

'You do not require his service tomorrow night?' the Archmage questioned.

'We do not,' said Rhydden. 'Rinnekh and T'Loi may better serve us by drawing unwanted eyes elsewhere.'

Chapter Three

A larger company than Kellarn had expected set out from the White Manor that morning. His sister Ellaïn had announced that she wished to bring her two boys along for a day's outing to the Sun Temple, with two guards of the household to see them safe home again afterward.

They crossed the Ringstream south of the manor, and then followed the sun east and south around the sheer blackstone cliffs of the double-peaked mountain known as the Twin Watchers which guarded the entrance of the Dortrean valley, keeping to the west of the Grey River. The way was shorter than upon the eastern side of the river, though arguably the going was slower, and it meant that they had to pass through the Tarágin manor lands. Tarágin, though retainers of Dortrean, had a long tradition of giving birth to powerful magi which made their relationship with their overlords somewhat strained. But the Tungit Isle, where the Sun Temple stood, could only be reached from this side. Had they taken the eastern route, they would have had to cross the deeper fords of the Grey River south of the Tungit Isle to come back to it; and Ellaïn was not willing to risk her young sons in the deeper waters.

Kellarn rode at the head of their small band, with his younger nephew Korren at his side. Both of Ellaïn's boys had their mother's golden hair, and were dressed in tunics of Dortrean red that morning as befitted the occasion; and Korren, newly turned nine, already showed promise of being as wayward and adventurous as his uncle. Terrel, the elder by two years, had more the quiet seriousness of his father Jared – or of Solban, at that age. He was riding at the rear with the two guardsmen, asking them questions and trying to share in their low laughter. Ellaïn and Corollin rode in the midst, talking constantly – or at least, his sister was talking in her sweet, easy manner, with Corollin putting in a deeper note here and there. Ellaïn had kept to the grey of mourning, for Solban's sake; but her grey gown was embroidered with many coloured flowers, and her hair was caught in a net of gold scattered with tiny red garnets, and her mood was more summery and festive than it had been the previous day.

Mellin Carfinn was away to Kellarn's right, her chestnut gelding both joyful and impatient on the familiar ground. With her dark green riding habit, and her long yellow gold hair held back in a simple black netted snood, her appearance was more sombre and formal than the rest. But her energy seemed boundless as ever, and she flashed him a smile whenever she caught his eye. Knowing Mellin as he did, Kellarn began to think that she might be planning something.

Their way lay through gentle hill country with stands of white-barked birch, and elms and oaks and willows and alders all in their rich summer finery. The day was fine and hot, the blue summer sky fading into a shimmering haze east beyond the river. To their right the great cliff walls of the Twin Watchers glittered like coal in the sunlight, shoring up huge heather-covered slopes, with glimpses of snowy peaks impossibly high above, peeping down through their veils of trailing cloud. They passed the dark towered manor house of Tarágin upon their left, quiet but watchful in the mid-morning heat; and then ahead in the distance they caught their first glimpse of the golden domes of the Sun Temple, bright as a flame fallen into the lap of the land.

In all Kellarn's young life the old temple on the Tungit Isle had been little more than a faded memory, a cluster of paved terraces and mostly fallen stones, resting on a long, tapered island in the midst of the Grey River. It had been held a holy place and a haunted one, not to be visited lightly or after dark – though Kellarn himself, like many reckless teenagers from previous generations, had done so.

But then Torriearn, Chosen Priest of Torollen, had come here with some of the elvenfolk of the Fay; and within the space of a few months they had rebuilt the Sun Temple anew in all its glory, to stand watch against the return of Lo-Khuma. The magic of that building was still the wonder of the *Aeshta* Orders – and the deep displeasure of the Emperor and the imperial priests of the *Vashtar*. Had the war with the East and South not turned their attention elsewhere, the Court Noble might have debated nothing but the implied threat from the new Sun Temple all summer long.

At length they turned their back on the mountains, and rode down to the river in the late morning sunlight. The Tungit Isle itself was perhaps three quarters of a mile long, with the six domes of the Sun Temple shining atop a low hill at its northern end. The narrower southern tip rose into a rocky promontory covered with pines and dark evergreens. Between these two heights the ground dipped down into a sheltered dell and bay on the near side, from which the boulders and shingle of the ford stretched out across the waters to the western shore.

On the lower slopes of the temple hill stood a timbered stable block and paddock, and a larger area of ground had been cleared and stones set there as though more building had been planned. Kellarn supposed that the sudden war in the east, and the loss of Torriearn himself in Arrandin, had put a stop to the work for a while.

'I don't see any dragons,' said Korren, as they came down to the river's edge.

'Dragons?' Kellarn echoed, startled. 'What makes you say that?'

'Cousin Mellin says they helped build the temple.'

'Does she now?' Kellarn relaxed a little, and chuckled. He had heard much the same, though he would not have expected it to be common knowledge, even in Dortrean. But Mellin was a close friend of the Sun Temple, and undoubtedly knew more than most.

'Well, if there are any around,' he said, 'they are probably staying hidden so they don't frighten the horses. Some dragons can disguise themselves as people, you know.'

'Oh don't encourage him, Col,' Mellin warned, drawing rein beside them. 'And you,' she said, fixing on Korren with her bright green eyes and wagging one gloved finger at him, 'are not to go staring at every priest and knight in the temple wondering if they are dragons in disguise, or you'll get us all into trouble.'

'Your fault for starting it,' Kellarn grinned.

Mellin tried to glare at him, but ended up grinning herself.

'But how can you tell?' asked Korren, undaunted.

'Tell what?' demanded Terrel, as the rest of the party arrived.

'Never mind,' said Kellarn. 'We'll explain when we get to the other side.'

Mellin led the way across the ford, guiding her horse with ease through the swirling waters. Kellarn rode behind, leading Korren, and then came Corollin with Terrel. Ellaïn and the two Dortrean guards brought up the rear. The ford seemed more shallow and level than Kellarn remembered it, so that he wondered whether the priests or the elvenfolk had done something to improve it. Not even the hem of Ellaïn's full skirted gown was wet when they reached the island shore.

Though Kellarn had seen no sentry posted, it was clear that they were expected. A handful of folk had come out of the stables to greet them and help them dismount, and three more had emerged through the temple doors and were already making their way down the winding path of the hillside with measured gait.

Kellarn sighed inwardly as he lifted his nephews down from the saddle. So much for an informal family visit. He busied himself with handing over the horses, allowing Mellin and Ellaïn to take the lead. Corollin hung back with him. The two boys raced on ahead up the hillside, but nobody seemed to mind.

The welcoming party met them at the foot of the path. There were two knights – a man and a woman – clad in formal white surcoats bordered with gold over good mail, and with burnished caps of leather and steel, and long swords at their sides. The third was a woman of about Ellaïn's age, round faced and dark haired, in simple white linen robes that suited her ample figure. She gave her name as Selîn, a lesser priestess of their Order, and greeted them with the blessings of all the *Aeshtar*.

As they made their way up the hill, Selîn explained that Holy Father Ûrsîn, the senior priest of Torollen upon the isle, was at present instructing the novices; but that they were welcome to stay and join the noon rite, and afterward to sit at table with him and eat. Ellaïn replied that they would be honoured to do so, if Ûrsîn could spare the time. Kellarn exchanged glances with Corollin, wondering if they could slip away early instead. But then they drew near to the temple doors, and he stopped thinking about anything else.

The outer walls of the temple building were of smooth black stone, sheer as a fortress, and seemed to spring up from the very rock of the isle itself. To the northwest, the wall swelled out into the great round tower of the chapter house, crowned with the largest dome of all. The temple dome – not golden like the rest, but of a rose coloured stone like a feldspar – soared up above the heart of the building, with the lesser towers and roofs and courts arrayed all around. The doors led in beneath the nearest dome, and were of the same black stone as the walls.

But as they mounted the outer steps and passed inside, the sombre black gave way to triumphant light and colour. They entered a squared chamber, with a ring of six pillars supporting the vaulted dome overhead. The dome was lined with gold, and the pillars and walls and four corners of the roof were all of white stone, more like chalcedony than marble. The floor beneath the dome was of polished black stone inlaid with silver stars, with a small fountain pool in the centre; but the four corners around were paved with jasper or marble, in colours proper to the *Aeshta* Lords for each quarter. Beneath the rim of the dome a circle of windows let in the sunlight through patterned glass of many colours, so that the air itself seemed filled with rainbow hues.

There were no statues here, nor carvings, nor raised altars upon the quarter floors; yet these were clearly lesser shrines to the gods, as one might expect to find in the outer courts of any great *Aeshta* temple. Kellarn's sense of wonder shifted a little toward self-consciousness, a twinge of guilt that he might have come here like any street urchin to gawp at a sideshow in a fair.

'The work is still far from complete, my Lord,' said Selîn, interrupting his thoughts.

'It needs nothing more,' he said. 'The gods are already here with us.'

The priestess looked taken aback, but she recovered herself to smile and bow. Kellarn nodded in return, though he was scarcely less surprised than she. What in the world had prompted him to say that? Everyone seemed to be looking at him.

'Have we time to see the temple?' Ellaïn asked, breaking the silence.

'Yes indeed, my Lady,' said Selîn gratefully. 'They will be making ready soon, but you are more than welcome.'

Terrel had taken Kellarn by the hand and was now dragging him across the hall, saying that he must come and see the stair. Korren bounced ahead of them eagerly.

They came to a flight of six apron steps, each of a different colour. The bottom-most and largest was again of polished black stone, but those above were of rarer kind – lapis and moonstone, azurite and red jasper, and rose gold sunstone at the top. As far as Kellarn could tell, each was made of a huge single slab without flaw or join. Their worth in gold alone was beyond price.

'Can you not feel the virtue in these stones?' whispered

Corollin, crouching down beside them. 'Each holds a great blessing, and they are balanced together in harmony.'

'I like the moonstone best,' said Terrel. 'It's like ice lit with blue fire – like the tales of the realm of the northern fay.'

'I think that the Fay had a hand in it,' Kellarn nodded.

'The senior priests of all the *Aeshta* Orders played their part in raising this stair,' said Selîn proudly, 'at Holy Father Torriearn's request. Here we see the union of the elemental lords – Earth, Water, Moon, Air, Fire and the Sun.'

'But where did they find precious stones of such a size?' asked Ellaïn.

Selîn shrugged. 'I was not here when the Temple was built,' she said. 'Holy Father Torriearn travelled far to find the stones he required. You would have to ask him.'

Kellarn opened his mouth, and then shut it again. They all knew that Torriearn was dead. Yet perhaps for the Sun priests – as for some of the other Orders – that was no great obstacle to conversation. He exchanged glances with Corollin. Should they need to speak with the dead Kings of Farodh in pursuit of their quest, that was a point worth remembering.

The two Sun knights went up the stair and opened the doors at the top. Selîn took off her sandals and followed them. Kellarn waited for Ellaïn and Mellin, and then climbed the stair slowly, holding his nephews' hands on either side. Corollin and the household men came behind.

Beyond the doors was a pillared cloister walk, opening on to sunlit courts to left and right; and straight ahead stood the Temple of Torollen itself, built all of the same rose coloured stone as its dome. Its tall doors were of golden oak, each carved with a rearing unicorn, and stood wide open in welcome.

Like the smaller chamber through which they had just passed, the main temple was square, and lined with the same white stone. But here the high golden vault of the dome was held up by twelve pillars of deep red jasper – some partly within the walls, and some standing clear – each on a plinth of rose coloured stone. The central altar was a weathered cube of the same rose stone, which had stood in the ruins of the ancient temple that had been here before.

The white floor was inlaid with a tracery of gold, and still wet from a recent scrubbing; and indeed the whole feel of the temple was of fresh air and soap, rather than stale incense and stuffiness. Yet if Kellarn had felt a fleeting touch of the hands of the gods in the outer shrines, it was as nothing compared to the sense of *presence* here. It was as though life and strength welled up from the altar stone, and flowed out along the patterned lines of the floor; and light and blessing flowed down from the dome over the high windows and walls and pillars in endless waves. It reminded him abruptly – and rather surprisingly – of the curtain of power guarding the Magi's chambers in the Arrand palace.

His nephews were tugging at his arms again. He suffered himself to be led forward, though steering them to the left as was the custom in holy places. They wanted to point out to him the many creatures pictured in the stained glass windows high above, and the tall braziers of wrought copper which stood cleaned and ready at the far side.

'There's your dragon, Korren,' said Mellin, pointing up to a window on the southern side.

They had to move round a bit further to see it properly, because of the bright sunlight behind. But then Kellarn could make out the long, snaking body, picked out in red and yellow and white against a deep blue sky.

'What does the writing say, beneath him?' asked Terrel.

'Firinaakr,' Mellin answered. 'That is his name.'

'How do you know?' asked Korren.

'Because it is, my young Lord,' said a man's voice.

Kellarn looked down again. A handful of other people had come through the doors and were walking toward them, led by Holy Father Ûrsîn himself. Ûrsîn was a homely man, somewhere into his thirties, and comfortably unremarkable with his light brown hair and diffident smile. He was simply clad in white tunic over brown breeches, though a sash worked with jewels and gold was draped over his left shoulder, denoting his priestly rank. Where Torriearn had been a man of action and challenge and fiery zeal, Ûrsîn's gifts were said to lie in quiet study and prayer, and in the successful day-to-day running of a monastery temple. Kellarn could believe that his quiet restraint might be invaluable in tempering the hot-headed knights of the Sun. Nevertheless, there were matters which he would rather not discuss with Ûrsîn at all, so that he had been hoping to avoid such a meeting.

'Firinaakr is a red-golden dragon,' Ûrsîn went on, addressing Terrel and Korren. 'When Torriearn gathered together the senior priests of all the *Aeshta* Orders and brought them here to discuss the building of this temple, Firinaakr came to bear witness. You might say he is a friend to us, in his own dragonish way. That is why we have his likeness in the window there.'

'Is he a sun dragon, Father?' asked Terrel.

'No,' said Ûrsîn. 'He is – well, something different. I am not a master of dragon lore, I'm afraid.' He turned to look at Kellarn.

'Are there any dragons here now?' Korren demanded.

'Children! Children!' exclaimed Ellaïn. 'You must not task Father Ûrsîn so.'

The priest held up his hand and smiled. 'Not in the temple, no,' he answered the boys. 'But the rocky hill with the pine trees, at the southern end of the island, we now call Dragonrest. If he is anywhere here, he is most likely to be there.'

'Can we go and look?' Korren asked Kellarn.

'Soon,' Kellarn promised, nodding.

'Forgive me my Lord,' said Ûrsîn, turning back to him. 'I see that you have brought the holy blade of Fire with you. Might we perhaps be permitted to see it?'

'In here?' said Kellarn doubtfully.

'It is a holy blade,' said Ûrsîn; 'and this is a temple of Fire and the Sun. But we can go outside, if you prefer.'

Kellarn shook his head. He drew the sword from its sheath and went down on one knee, presenting it hilt first toward the priest. The golden patterns glowed bright along the blade, and the sword seemed warmer and heavier in his hands than usual. Ûrsîn bent forward to look, and ran one tanned hand along the length of the blade, but a few inches above it, as though testing for a sense of heat or power. The other temple folk crowded around, and the two boys leaned forward over Kellarn's shoulders.

'You came by this in Sentai, I understand,' Ûrsîn said presently.

'It was in the treasury of my uncle of Sentai,' Kellarn replied. 'But it seems to have come from Dortrean, long ago.'

The priest nodded, and straightened up. 'And with this sword you slew the Easterner chieftain,' he said, 'and burned him with holy fire. It is a wondrous blade. One might be forgiven for wondering if it could have saved Torriearn himself, had the gods brought you there but a little sooner.'

Kellarn ducked his head. There were any number of deaths he might have prevented, had he been in the right place at the right time – his own brother's among them.

'I'm sorry,' he said.

'No,' said Ûrsîn, 'do not be. There is none here would hold you to blame. The gods in their wisdom have offered you other paths. And I may tell you now that Holy Father Torriearn has not yet entered the Realms of the Dead – though neither is he in the waking world, as far as we can discover. It would not be the first time that he has travelled through other Realms in the service of Torollen, beyond the reach of our knowledge; and perhaps that is where he has now gone. So here at the Sun Temple we still hope that he may return.'

'A month is a long time,' ventured Corollin.

'Perhaps,' said Ûrsîn; 'and perhaps not. But for now we can hope, and continue in our own service to the gods.' He signalled for his folk to move on.

'Of course,' said Kellarn, standing up and sheathing his sword again. 'The noon rite. Forgive me.'

'There is nothing to forgive,' Ûrsîn smiled. 'Wield the blade well, my Lord, with the blessing of Hýriel and Torollen, and all the *Aeshtar*.'

He brought his hands together in the familiar sign of blessing, with fingers spread like wings, and bowed and moved on.

Already there were many more people coming into the temple, making ready to take up their positions. Korren tugged at Kellarn's arm, and looked up at him imploringly with wide hazel eyes.

In spite of the wonder of the temple, or perhaps because of it, Kellarn did not feel that he wanted to stay for the rite. He was half afraid that Ûrsîn would want to call down some special blessing upon him, because of his sword; and given that he was not yet prepared to tell the Sun priests all that he knew concerning Lo-Khuma and the Emperor, he felt that he would somehow be playing Ûrsîn false before the gods by accepting it. Now was not the right moment. And his nephews were urging him to come away.

Kellarn took each of the boys by the hand, grinned an apology to Ellaïn, and beat a hasty retreat. Ellaïn waved him away with fond indulgence.

Mellin caught up with them on the slope outside, and together they left the path and followed the spur of the hill which ran down the eastern side of the isle, rather than going back to the stables and the bay. A single bell rang out from the temple buildings above, heralding the start of the noontide rite.

At the far end of the spur the remains of a small watchtower still stood guard atop a low mound. The weathered stones of the walls now scarcely reached above Kellarn's head, and were mostly overgrown with creepers and sweet golden honeysuckle, and the holm oaks that grew around provided a dappled shade. But the paved floor of the tower had been cleaned and swept, and a wooden bench was set against the north wall.

They tarried for a few minutes at the tower, looking eastward across the rolling farmland, and west toward the Carfinn hills of Mellin's home. But then the boys were eager to move on; and so they climbed down to the rockier ground at the southern end of the isle, and spent the better part of an hour scrambling among the pine trees in search of a dragon's lair.

If Firinaakr was there that day, not even Kellarn managed to find him. But his nephews did not seem too disappointed. There were many rocks to climb, and hollows to explore, and the cool shade of the pines was welcome in the heat of the summer day. None of them was in a hurry to return.

At length Kellarn sat down on a bank by the western shore, gazing up at the double peak of the Twin Watchers and the snowy ranks of the Black Mountains spreading out in the distance beyond. The hunt for Firinaakr had put him in mind of another dragon – *the* dragon, Ilunâtor – as bright and iridescent as the air above the mountain snows, and with that same sense of vastness; a wonder too wide and distant and *other*, beyond the reach of humankind. Like chasing the rainbow's tail.

In Arrandin, he had sensed that Ilunâtor had his own interest in the war against the Easterners, and in the role which Kellarn himself had to play. In the Nets of Starmere, the memory of the dragon had brought a confused dream of the Enemy and the Emperor, against both of whom Kellarn was now opposed. And now that he was seeking the help of the Guardian of Telbray Woods, the memory of the Father of All Dragons returned again. The moon fay Losithlîn had told them that the first Guardians had sat at the feet of Ilunâtor.

'You're not going back to the White Manor, are you?' said Mellin, sitting herself down beside him.

'No,' he said, turning to her. 'I thought that was obvious.'

Mellin grinned, undeterred. 'So where *are* you going?' she asked.

'South.' He picked up a pine cone and pitched it out into the water.

'South where?' she pursued. 'Telbray? Farran?'

'It's better if you don't know.'

He picked up another pine cone and toyed with it. Mellin snorted.

'Two nights ago you were swearing vengeance for your brother,' she said. 'You've barely arrived home and now you're leaving again, with scarcely a word. Ellaïn is very worried. So am I.'

'I told her we were going to Telbray.'

'And are you?'

Kellarn sighed. He looked around for his nephews. They were further up the slope, playing happily.

'Well we're not charging off to Lautun, to confront the Emperor,' he said in a low voice, 'if that's what you're worried about. We were only passing through Dortrean anyway, on another errand. And I really don't want to talk about it. Please, Mîsha?'

She smiled at her childhood name.

'Telbray City, or Telbray Woods?' she said quietly, without looking at him.

'Mîsha,' he growled.

'You would not lie to Ellaïn,' she went on, as if thinking aloud; 'but you might mislead her a little, for her own safety. She will assume the city, so you probably meant the woods – or perhaps the woods on the way to the city. Either way, I suppose I had better come with you.'

'What?'

'Since Markhûl was preparing food for you, I asked him to pack some for me, so you needn't worry on that score. I am well provided.'

'You are *not* coming with us,' he demurred. 'It is far too dangerous.'

'I have friends in the city. And friends in the woods,' she added in a whisper.

Kellarn looked at her.

'This is my home ground,' she smiled. 'You wouldn't expect me not to talk to my neighbours, would you?'

Kellarn twisted the pine cone round in his hands. If Mellin

did have friends in Telbray Woods – whether elvenfolk or other creatures, or even the Guardian – then her help could prove valuable. He had no doubt that he could trust her; and no doubt that she was stubborn enough to ride after them, whether they asked her or not. But he would rather not have involved her in this dangerous quest at all.

'We should get back to the temple,' he said. 'Let's see what Corollin has to say. And if she says no then it is no, do you understand?'

Mellin smiled. 'Thanks, Collie-dog. But I think she will see the sense in setting Ellaïn's mind at rest.'

They rounded up Kellarn's nephews and made their way back to the Sun Temple. Corollin and Ellaïn had already come out on to the hillside to look for them. Mellin at once broached the question of riding south with them to Telbray.

It seemed to Kellarn that Corollin was almost expecting the offer, though he was sure that neither of them had spoken of it before now. Since she had begun to study the lore of Zedron, Corollin had had other such moments of mystic foresight. She simply nodded and listened in her own quiet way, and then smiled in answer.

'Yes, of course,' she said. 'If Kellarn is content that you should come.'

Kellarn was not sure that he was content at all. Yet he could think of no other reason to dissuade her – not that he could speak of openly here before the doors of the Sun Temple – and simply to say no would seem churlish, and weigh little with the headstrong Mellin. Besides, Corollin knew as much as he did of the dangers of their quest. And his sister Ellaïn seemed much taken with the idea.

He managed a wry smile. 'I suppose so,' he said.

Within a short while they had said their farewells and collected their horses from the stable block. Ellaïn and the two boys went inside to eat with the Sun priest Ûrsîn, and they had the household men to see them safe back to the White Manor later in the day. Kellarn, Corollin and Mellin crossed over on to the western shore, and followed the bank downstream to the main ford across the Grey River beyond the southern end of the isle.

The waters of the ford were deeper and more treacherous here, still swollen from the thawing mountain snows. Kellarn's spirited bay Rúnfyr made heavy going of it, and sulked for a good while afterward; and had it not been for Mellin leading the way on her chestnut Wynborn, he might have balked at the crossing altogether. Corollin's gray Mistwise, though shorter than the other two and having almost to swim at some points, followed behind with her usual gentle temper and seemed not the least bit put out by Rúnfyr's thrashing and splashing.

Once safely up on to the far shore, they turned southeast and rode easily across rolling grassland slopes, glad of the warm afternoon sun to dry them and the wind of their speed upon their faces. Kellarn took the lead again, with the two women behind him on either side. Before long they could make out a broad stretch of woodland off to their right, no more than a couple of miles away beyond the river.

'Are those the Telbray Woods already,' asked Corollin, 'or part of Carfinn lands?'

'Neither,' Mellin replied. 'Those are the Flaming Woods, so called for the colours of their leaves in autumn. The Carfinn Hills lie beyond them, to the west, and Telbray Woods are still several leagues away, south of the Black River. But it is said that long ago the Telbray Woods ran all the way up past here to join the Dortrean Forest in the north, and that the Tungit Isle and the Flaming Woods were hidden in the heart of that one great forest. It was in the Flaming Woods, I think, that Torriearn first met Firinaakr.'

Kellarn glanced back at her at the mention of the dragon's name.

'Did you know Torriearn well?' asked Corollin.

'Quite well, I suppose,' Mellin shrugged. 'He has been a good friend to Carfinn over the last few years – he and his friends,

Tinûkenil and Gwydion, and the Moon mage Dakhmahl. Or *Dakhmaal* I should say, since he is a Mage Councillor now, is he not?

'So I am told,' Corollin agreed. 'We have not met.'

'It is because of them that I have friends in Telbray Woods,' Mellin went on. 'Where exactly are we going in the Woods, by the way?'

'We don't know yet,' Kellarn put in quickly.

They lapsed back into silence, listening to the drumming beat of the horses' hooves on the firm turf.

'We need to find the Guardian of Telbray Woods,' Corollin said at last. 'If there is still one there.'

Mellin said nothing. Kellarn turned to look back at her again.

'That was one of the reasons I didn't want you to come,' he said.

Mellin nodded.

'There are elvenfolk living deep in the wood,' she said; 'some of the wood fay who fled the great forest of Cerrodhí long ago. Perhaps you were best to ask them.'

They rode on, veering southward to follow the line of the river, passing along the borders of the Dhûlann manor lands. Dhûlann were lesser retainers of Dortrean, and the previous Lord, Valroc, had proved even more problematic to Kellarn's father than the magi of Tarágin. But when Valroc had died, a couple of years before, the succession had passed to his sister's son, Rinnakhal of Aartaús. Rinnakhal had since rebuilt the manor house – largely destroyed by fire at the time of Valroc's death – and married the lovely Lady Inghara, daughter of the Lord Rebraal; and Erkal Dortrean seemed well pleased with him. His father's kinsmen of Aartaús had also been respected horsebreeders for many generations, which made Rinnakhal a promising neighbour from Mellin Carfinn's point of view.

The land around them seemed more peaceful than it had under Valroc's rule, though the more tended parts and the manor house itself lay further to the east, hidden from view behind the hills. But as the afternoon wore on they caught sight of a large company of warriors in the distance, marching upriver toward them. Kellarn swore, and signalled a halt; then led the way off to one side, to the cover of some nearby trees.

'What's the matter?' Mellin asked him. 'They are probably your father's men returning from Farran. Ellaïn said that they were expected any day now.'

'I had rather not be seen by anyone,' said Kellarn. 'The fewer people who know where I am, the better.'

'The Sun priests know,' she pointed out.

'The Emperor is less likely to have spies in the Sun Temple,' he told her. 'Can't we just slip past them?'

'Some of them have horses,' said Corollin, 'though most are on foot. But if we have seen them, they have probably seen us. We were hardly taking pains to keep ourselves hidden. To stay out of sight now would only draw their attention the more.'

Kellarn swore again.

'I suppose it's a chance we'll have to take,' he sighed. 'If we ask them to guard their tongues about seeing us, it may not be so bad.'

'Unless the Emperor has men among your father's troops,' said Corollin.

Kellarn made a face. That was a possibility he would rather not have considered.

'Let me go first,' said Mellin. She nudged Wynborn around and led the way out from behind the trees, back on to the level ground nearer the water's edge.

They had ridden little more than a furlong when the marching host came clearly into view. Mellin's guess proved correct, for they were clad in the colours of Dortrean's retainers – the red and blue of Tarágin, and the scarlet and black of Dhûlann, and the golden orbed Sun crosses of the knights of Valhaes. There must have been well over six score of them, mounted and on foot, with wagons and gear trailing behind. Two outriders had already broken away from the main host, and were cantering toward them with hands upraised in greeting. They slowed their own pace as the horsemen drew near.

The first of the riders was Rinnakhal Dhûlann himself, clad in a scarlet tunic open at the throat and with a black sash tied about his waist. He was perhaps slightly older and taller than Kellarn, with long curling hair the colour of polished acorns; and he was unarmed, save for a long sword in a black sheath slung at his side. The second was a more seasoned warrior, clad in bright mail beneath his red and gold surcoat, but Kellarn could not put a name to him.

Rinnakhal knew Mellin at once, and bowed to her in the saddle as they drew rein. The second man he named as Lord Ierodh of Valhaes. When the two riders realised who Kellarn was, they bowed even more deeply and nodded to Corollin. They would have dismounted had not Kellarn forestalled them.

The news that the men had to offer was brief. The warriors under their charge had been sent down to Farran over a month before, at the time of the Emperor's muster; and once the Easterners had gone, and the Southers had given promises of peace, the Emperor had sent commands for the mustered forces to stand down again. Though the city of Farran was still uneasy, and many doubted that the Southers' promises would last, the Lord Steward of Farran had welcomed the chance to be relieved of the burden and expense of housing so many extra troops. The Dortrean warriors themselves were glad enough to be coming home.

Rumour had reached even Farran of Kellarn's own role in the war against the Easterners, and Rinnakhal praised him with due courtesy and a touch of cheerful envy. But he made no mention of Solban's death, and Kellarn guessed that he had not yet heard of it.

'Does Torreghal Valhaes ride with you?' he asked them. The marching troops were heading more to the northeast, away from the river – presumably toward the Dhûlann manor – and it was hard to make out their shadowed faces at this distance.

But Valhaes was the strong arm of Dortrean's defence, and Torreghal was his father's senior commander. He had half expected to see him riding there.

'Gone to Court, my Lord,' Ierodh replied.

Kellarn nodded. 'Rinnakhal,' he said, 'it were best if no one else knew that I have passed this way today.'

'I shall give the command, my Lord.'

'Also,' said Kellarn carefully, 'although our troops are standing down, it would be wise for all the Lords of Dortrean to stay on their guard in the days ahead. There have been spies abroad in Lautun, and some may already have come west across the Rolling River. This war has made my father more enemies, and some of them could prove very dangerous. Do you understand?'

'The shadowfay are stirring,' added Corollin in her deep, grave voice.

Rinnakhal's pleasant face hardened at the name. He drew himself up in stiff salute. 'We shall keep watch,' he promised.

'And Valhaes also,' said Ierodh.

Kellarn saluted in return, his right fist clenched across his breast. Then he nodded for them to go, and the two riders wheeled their horses and cantered away back toward the marching host.

'Were you going to tell me about the shadowfay?' asked Mellin, when they were out of earshot.

'Valhaes and Dhûlann lie closer to Lautun,' said Kellarn. 'Besides, you have the Sun Temple to protect you.'

'There are also shadowfay beneath the Black Mountains,' she reminded him; 'and some have strayed down into Carfinn lands in the past, and in to the Telbray Woods. I could wish you had told me before.'

'Would it have changed your mind about coming?' he countered.

'No,' Mellin allowed. 'But I should have liked to warn Ûrsîn, at least.'

'The Sun priests already know to keep watch for them.'

They let the subject drop. But Mellin's face was more set and determined as they rode on south.

Within an hour they came down to where the waters of the Black River flowed in to the Grey, and dismounted to stretch their legs and rest the horses. The Carfinn Hills now lay well behind to their right, and the land ahead on the farther shore was wilder open scrub. They had reached the borders of the Dortrean lands. The sun was climbing down in the west toward the distant mountains; and though still hidden by the lie of the land, Kellarn knew that the northern reaches of the Telbray Woods stretched beneath the shadow at the mountains' feet.

'Could we have crossed that river,' asked Corollin, 'if we had ridden over Carfinn lands?'

'No,' Mellin answered. 'At least, not without riding far out of the way to the west, to the lake of the Sîrnae, where the Black River has its birth. There is a weir crossing there. But the rocks are treacherous, and the horses would not have made it. And besides, the waters of the Black are poisonous to man and beast. Only here, where they join the Grey, do they become wholesome again.'

'The path into the woods lies farther south, anyway,' said Kellarn. 'It is still more than three leagues from here to the old causeway where we can cross the Grey River, and perhaps another four from there to the beginning of the path.' He looked at Mellin. 'Unless you know a better way in?'

Mellin grinned and shook her head. 'The path is probably the safest bet, for strangers.'

'And where does the path lead?' asked Corollin.

'Straight west through the middle of the woods,' said Kellarn, 'and then on to the city of Telbray on the other side. But it is not like the Holleth Road from Arrandin. Most folk take the longer way around the southern end of the woods, and avoid going in among the trees at all.'

'The woods do not welcome strangers,' Mellin agreed.

They mounted up again and carried on south. The land

on this side of the river now grew steadily less homely and tended, diminishing into broad grassland slopes with only a few lonely bushes and trees, and a cooler wind blew up from the southeast.

At length the river took a wide sweeping bend to run eastward across their path, and they drew rein as they came to the causeway. The sun had sunk low in the west, and would be gone within the hour, and long shadows lay over the land.

The old causeway itself was a line of huge stone slabs laid more or less straight across the river, banked around with smooth shingle; and in some tales it was said to be the ancient work of giants. The waters of the Grey River streamed over and between the stones in a constant roar, spraying white foam and rainbows in the evening sunlight. The ground on the near side was still churned and muddied where the Dortrean troops had come across earlier in the day.

They made their camp about a stone's throw back from the causeway on the near side, with a small thicket of holm oaks and holly for shelter. The horses had brought them far that day, and it seemed foolish to leave the relative safety of Dortrean soil so close to sunset. There were all manner of strange or unfriendly creatures which might stray down from the Sighing Lands or the Telbray Woods under cover of darkness; and here at least the river offered them some measure of protection.

The next morning dawned deep rose, with piled clouds gathering in the southeastern sky. Kellarn decided to put on his mailshirt again, now that they were leaving Dortrean behind.

'You'll be sweating kegs in that by mid-morning,' Mellin teased.

He handed her a dagger from his pack.

'I need to be able to defend you properly,' he said. 'This isn't some happy market day outing.'

'I know that,' she said. She looked down about her riding habit, then shrugged and thrust dagger and sheath into the top of one boot.

Corollin had also returned to her familiar garb of leather tunic over breeches of beechleaf brown, with her short sword at her side. Her white staff was strapped to Mistwise's saddle. She went to fill their waterskins in the river while the others finished loading up the horses.

It was still early when they set out. The causeway crossing gave them no problems, and Corollin paused on the far shore to study the ground before they mounted up. No one appeared to have passed this way since Rinnakhal and his warriors were here.

A louder swirl and a plop amid the steady rush of the waters drew Kellarn's attention back to the river. He sent Rúnfyr on ahead and walked back to the causeway rocks, his hands ready at his sword. There was no sign of anything, either within the water or beyond.

He was about to turn away when a flash of silver broke surface, and a fish soared into the air. It was fully as long as his arm, and mottled with green and hazel brown. Kellarn caught a fleeting glimpse of one large balled eye swivelled toward him; and then with a flick of its tail the fish plunged down again and was gone. The water sprang up in a circle behind it, forming a bowl of spray that sparkled like fine crystal, until the steady flow of the river swept it away. He laughed aloud in delight.

'What is it?' asked Corollin. But when he told them, it seemed that neither of the women had seen it.

They rode southwest across the open land, following more or less the route taken by the Dortrean warriors. The deeper green of the Telbray Woods was now clearly visible away to their right, rolling over hidden swells in the land all the way to the misty peaks of the Black Mountains some ten leagues distant. The warm air was already starting to turn sultry and sticky; and cloud shadows chased down across their path from the Sighing Lands, carrying the rumour of approaching storms.

After about an hour they turned more to the west, heading straight toward the edge of the trees. Here the open grassland thrust deeper into the woods, like a spearhead vale about a league in length. Kellarn knew that the path they sought began at the inner end of this vale. But when he had come here before – nearly three years ago now, following the death of the last Guardian, Gilraen – he had been travelling east from Telbray city with his father and the moon fay Tinûkenil. Finding a way out of the woods had not then been a problem. Finding the way in might prove less straightforward, although they had Mellin to help them.

As they rode in between the widespread arms of the woods, the forest noises grew louder in their ears – the endless murmur of the wind among the leaves, and the shrieks and calls of many birds. Crows jeered at one another from their treetop perches, and waddled and flapped across the ground as the three riders went past.

At length they reached the inward end of the spearhead and slowed their horses to a walk. The trees now hid the mountains from view, and the sun had disappeared behind the gathering clouds. Kellarn shifted the weight of his shield on his back, and peered in beneath the branches at the gloomy shadows ahead.

The Telbray Woods were not as dark as the shadowed forest of Cerrodhí, nor perhaps as ancient as the Holleth Woods north of Arrandin. But like the Dortrean Forest, these woods had strange enough tales of their own, and the merchants and travellers of the Six Kingdoms rarely ventured within. On Kellarn's previous visit here, both Tinûkenil and his father had insisted that they keep to the path at all times; and Mellin had told him that the path was their safest way.

On either side of the spearhead the eaves of the woods formed long curving lines, almost like a hedge. Here those clearer lines gave way to a more open spread of bushes and trees, and it was perhaps a hundred yards or more further in before the trees closed ranks again beneath their solid canopy.

They dismounted and led the horses in among the first trees, bearing more to the left as they went. Corollin went ahead, with Mellin to advise her, and Kellarn came behind keeping a watchful eye all around.

Before long they had found two pathways running off among the trees, about twenty yards apart; and a third, wider path, slightly farther off to the right. None of them liked the feel of the wider way, but it was hard to judge between the other two.

'Perhaps they join up further on?' Mellin ventured doubtfully.

'Some help you are,' Kellarn teased. 'I suppose we could split up and follow both for a little way, and see which one seems the better choice.'

'No,' said Corollin.

She lifted her staff from Mistwise's saddle, and handed the reins to Mellin. Then she went and stood midway between the two paths, holding the staff upright before her, and began to sing softly to herself. Mellin and Kellarn exchanged glances, and waited quietly.

After a few moments Rúnfyr grew bored and began to walk off. Kellarn pulled him up short. Rúnfyr tugged back on his own reins and took two more steps sideways. Not wanting to get into a fight with his horse at this stage, Kellarn gave in and walked a few paces with him.

Corollin turned back toward them. 'It is difficult to tell,' she said. 'I can get no sense of whether one path is better to choose than the other. Perhaps Mellin is right, and they join up further in.'

'Rúnfyr seems to have chosen for us, then,' said Mellin.

Kellarn looked, and saw that his horse had led him to the beginnings of the middle path. He grinned ruefully.

'I'm not sure I trust his judgement that much,' he said. 'Perhaps we should take the other one.'

Nevertheless, they decided that if Rúnfyr was happy, then they might as well go that way; and the other horses seemed content enough.

They set off deeper into the woods, with Corollin leading

again and Kellarn at the rear. They went in single file, for the way was overgrown and little wider than a bridle path for much of the time – though it was still clearly a path, and Corollin seemed in no great danger of losing her way. The song of birds grew muted as they moved further in, and the air was like wine, heady with the scent of leaf and bark and the moist richness of the woodland floor. They saw no sign that the other path joined on to this one, and after a while they left off looking for it.

Toward mid morning the ground began to rise, and the undergrowth thinned out, with more open stretches running away into the green shadows beneath the trees. The three of them had spread out a little along the line of the path and were walking quietly.

A flash of deep red among the trees caught Kellarn's eye, and was gone again. He slowed his pace on the path, pulling Rúnfyr to a halt beside him. After a moment the red winked in and out again, slightly farther ahead and to their left, and then reappeared in the small bowl of a dell. It looked to be a deer – a young stag, crowned with pale antlers. The beast turned and stood poised, watching him. Almost waiting for him, Kellarn thought.

Rúnfyr snorted and shifted on his feet. Corollin and Mellin had stopped to look back.

'What is it?' Mellin asked.

'A red stag,' he said softly. 'I think—'

The creature had gone again. Kellarn looked to either side among the trees, then blinked and shook his head as if trying to wake himself up.

'I think he wants us to follow him,' he finished.

'A stag?' asked Corollin doubtfully.

Kellarn shrugged. Now that the creature was gone, he felt a little foolish. But when it had looked at him, he had felt sure that it was waiting for him to follow.

'Where?' asked Corollin, leaving Mistwise and coming back along the path. Kellarn pointed toward the dell.

Corollin looked at him carefully, and then looked away through the trees to where he was pointing. She clasped her hands together and drew a deep breath. Kellarn guessed that she was searching through the trees with other, magical senses.

'There is something there,' she said presently, 'but I am not sure what. The life of the woods seems more alert, focused – almost wary. That way lies danger, more than welcome.'

'It could be a trick,' said Mellin. 'There are many mischievous creatures in these woods.'

'But could it be the Guardian?' Kellarn demanded.

Mellin shrugged. 'If we keep to the path, the woods will give us less trouble. Unless the Guardian comes to find us, we're probably better off looking for the elvenfolk of the Fay.'

'But will the path lead us to them?' asked Corollin.

'The path crosses the forest river,' said Mellin. 'The wood fay should be aware of us by the time we reach there, and with luck will come to speak to us. But that is still quite a long way ahead, I think.'

'Several miles,' Kellarn agreed.

'Perhaps the stag was being hunted by something else?' Mellin offered.

'It didn't look like it,' said Kellarn.

'Did you see which way he went?' asked Corollin.

Kellarn shook his head.

'Well if he wants us to follow, perhaps he'll come back,' she said sensibly. She went back to Mistwise, and they set off again along the path.

Kellarn followed reluctantly, his eyes still straying left to where he had last seen the stag. Though common sense – and the advice of both Mellin and Corollin – told against it, the urge to follow the beast was growing stronger. He was sure in his heart that it had been waiting for him.

As they drew level with the dell he called a halt again. The women looked back at him with measured patience.

'I need to go and find out,' he said. 'Just as far as the

dell there. Wait here for me on the path, where you can see me.'

Without waiting for them to argue, he handed Rúnfyr's reins to Mellin and set off at a quicker pace across the leafy carpet of the woodland floor. The air was quiet all around him, save for the trudge of his own feet and the shifting and blowing of the waiting horses.

He slowed as he came to the lower lip of the little dell, more or less where the stag had been standing. The ground ahead of him dipped slightly, and then swelled up toward a steeper bank on his right with open patches of earth and tree roots. Ahead and to the left, the outer edge of the hollow was flanked by ferns and hazel bushes. There were no obvious signs that the stag had passed this way at all.

Kellarn turned and waved to the other two. They seemed farther off than he had expected, but they waved back in an untroubled way. He moved on down into the dell, and across to the bushes on the far side. There was still open ground there, and the beginnings of what might have been a trail; and then again, in the distance ahead, he fancied he caught sight of a flash of deep red moving among the trees. He sprang forward a few paces down the slope, hoping for a clearer view.

The stag was nowhere to be seen, and the bushes now hid him from his friends upon the path. Kellarn sighed and resigned himself to going back.

Even as he began to turn a sense of sudden danger came upon him – a chill prickle running down his spine and tightening in his gut. His hand closed about the hilt of his sword.

A beast of sorts now stood between him and the dell. It had the likeness of a great cat, black as a winter midnight, and its bright green eyes were nearly on a level with Kellarn's own. Heavy forepaws flexed restlessly against the earth, and the great jaws were parted just enough to flash a warning of pale fangs.

Kellarn, like any follower of the *Aeshtar*, knew the beast at once for a panthress; and that the panthress was a guise of the Moon Maiden Haëstren herself, or one adopted by her messengers and servants. But what the Moon had to do with him, here or anywhere, was beyond him. He tightened his grip on hilt and sheath.

'Who art thou, that comes hither at the dark of the moon?'

The voice of the beast was deep, smooth velvet, and seemed to come from all around him; and its beauty was matched by its terror, which threatened to open his bladder at any moment.

'I am Kellarn of Dortrean,' he answered, bowing, without taking his eyes from that bright gaze. 'I come to seek the Guardian.'

'Foolish son of Fire. At the dark of the moon it is not you who seek the Dead, but the Dead who seek you. Turn back while yet you may.'

Kellarn felt himself jump at the mention of the Dead. And yet it seemed as though the panthress knew all his thoughts already, and all about his quest – as though they were but continuing a conversation begun some time ago, somewhere else.

'I may not turn back,' he said.

'You are free to choose.'

'I will not,' he said. 'The demon captain will soon return. I must brave the Dead to find the way to stop him.'

'May, will, must,' the panthress growled. 'So you will set yourself against Lo-Khuma, and turn the fates of the world, and save all. Yet when the Guardian Gilraen was killed, you were there. Did you raise hand or voice to save him? When the Lords of Carfinn were lost, you were there. Did you save them? When your brother died, you were elsewhere. Could you not have saved him?'

'I could not,' Kellarn whispered. 'I did not.'

'You did not. How then shall you save all the rest?'

'I must try what I can,' said Kellarn. 'And not I alone, but Corollin, and others. I play but a part.' That was what the elvenfolk kept trying to tell him, to trust to the strength of others as well as his own. He was sure he had learned that by now.

The panthress seemed unimpressed.

'The moon is at the dark, when all life dies,' she said. 'Seek the Dead, and they will devour you. Seek to turn back, and I will devour you. All paths begin and end here.'

'I must go back to my friends,' said Kellarn, beginning to move.

'You will not find them,' the panthress growled. 'Go now.'

Kellarn stopped. 'What have you done with them?'

The great eyes stared at him, but she made no answer.

'Let me pass,' said Kellarn, drawing his sword.

The panthress growled more loudly. Kellarn's blade blossomed into red-golden fire and flew up from his grasp.

The shape of the great beast shifted, flowing up into the form of a tall figure robed all in black. Her face was hidden in empty shadow beneath a heavy hood.

'Go now,' she said, in a voice that was everywhere and nowhere. 'Chase after your red stag of dreams, Son of Dortrean. Go.'

There was no appeal to that hidden face, to the implacable poise of form. She made no gesture. Yet it seemed to Kellarn as he looked that somehow she dwarfed the woods around him, surrounded by a void before which the trees and bushes and the very ground itself were as fleeting and fragile as a fluttering veil; and he could not touch her. His own failure drove him away, with a rejection beyond measure.

With no will left to oppose, he stumbled back; fumbled and found his sword where it had fallen; and then turned and walked away, empty.

Chapter Four

'Make him run!' Taillan commanded.

Rhysana smiled. The wooden horse turned by the table leg and sped back swiftly across the open floor.

'His legs should move,' said Taillan. 'Make them move.'

'He does that for Dhûghaúr,' she said, 'but not for me.'

'Why?'

'Look!' said Rhysana. She focused on her spell, and the horse flew up to hover beside the casement window. Another flare of lightning lit the grey rain outside.

'He flies for me, because I am an Air mage,' she explained. 'Dhûghaúr is a mage of Earth.'

Taillan trotted over to stand beneath the toy. 'He should have wings.'

'He flies by magic,' she told him. She called the horse back into her hands. The boy ran after it, laughing.

There was movement in the outer hallway, and Torkhaal came through into the living chamber. His dark hair and robes were dry, so she guessed that he must have *leaped* straight to the College buildings from the imperial palace. He was far earlier than she had expected, and from the look on his face Rhysana guessed at once that something was wrong.

'What is it?' she asked.

A shadow had clouded her own heart all morning, though until now she had tried to pass it off as no more than the gloomy mood of the rain outside. There were several other possible causes that she had already considered. For one thing, today was the dark of the moon, when the servants of Lo-Khuma were thought to have greater strength to act. For another, the Archmage Merrech had been noticeably absent – whereas he usually put in an appearance the moment that Rhysana turned her attention back to the study of Illana. She was worried what he might be planning with the Emperor, or what else might be happening somewhere in the Six Kingdoms.

Taillan had scampered over to greet his father and been lifted up into his arms. Torkhaal kissed the boy's forehead, and stroked his silver fair hair as he carried him back toward her. Rhysana stood up from her chair.

'The Arrand has gone at last,' he told her. 'Morvaan brought word to the palace this morning, and Jared has returned with him now.'

Rhysana sighed, both saddened and relieved. At least it was nothing worse.

'Well, we knew it was only a matter of time,' she said sensibly. 'How has Jared taken it?'

Torkhaal shrugged. 'Difficult to tell. I asked about Ellaïn and the boys, but Morvaan said that the Sun priests would be fetching them. The Rite of Burning is this evening.'

'Yes,' said Rhysana.

Taillan wriggled impatiently, so Torkhaal set him down. The boy collected his horse and took it off for a canter around the room.

'Morvaan also offered to take Karlena down,' Torkhaal told her; 'but the Empress does not want her to leave the palace.'

'The Empress, or the Emperor?' Rhysana wondered.

'Grinnaer herself, I think. Rhydden could overrule her, of course, but Karlena did not seem to think it would be worth the fight.'

'Ellaïn will be in Arrandin,' she said. 'She can represent Dortrean well enough. If the Empress is likely to be with child, then perhaps the Countess of Dortrean feels that her duty is more toward the living than the dead.'

Especially, she thought to herself, if Karlena knew that her son was now thinking of overthrowing the present Emperor – in which case Grinnnaer's unborn child would be the next heir to Rhydden's throne. Yet she did not think that Karlena knew.

Torkhaal stroked her cheek. 'Shall you go to Arrandin for the Rite?' he asked.

Rhysana looked away. She was very fond of The Arrand and his family, and her first instinct was that she should go. But the Warden's codex called for her attention, and she had the worried feeling that she was running out of time. Yet it seemed churlish to begrudge the old man a few last hours of respect.

'I can stay with the boy,' Torkhaal offered. 'Or we can leave him with Lavan at the palace.'

'My brother is here for Court?' she demanded, surprised.

'For once,' he grinned. 'And Nereïs and the twins, and little Maïa.'

'Whatever possessed him to bring the children?'

'Ellen is with them, to look after them,' he reassured her.

'I love my Aunt Nereïs,' said Taillan, appearing at Rhysana's side. 'Can we go see her?'

'Go *to* see her,' she corrected him absently. 'In a while, perhaps – though I doubt that the Archmage Ellen will be too pleased to have another little boy running around her. You shall have to be very quiet and good.'

'I think that Ellen will want to go to Arrandin,' said Torkhaal.

'Yes,' she said. 'I need to speak with Ellen.'

Herusen – or the Warden's memory of him – had told her that the Archmage Ellen could open the seal on Illana's doors, if she had the Prime Councillor's rod. Ellen seemed a better choice than Iorlaas.

'Very very good,' Taillan sang.

Torkhaal was looking at her in question. Rhysana watched as their son skipped away again, and then laced her fingers between his and let his mental *presence* enfold her.

She had already told him of the Warden's codex, though not the details of where and how he had given it to her, and Torkhaal had known better than to press her upon that point. Of the role that Herusen himself had played, she had said simply that he had left a message with the Warden for when she was ready to hear it. The vision of the old man she considered to be a very private matter between herself and the Warden, which she might have hesitated to share with Torkhaal even had he been privy to the secrets of the High Council – which as yet he was not. And besides, she saw no point in renewing her husband's grief over Herusen's death.

From her study of the Warden's notes, Rhysana had swiftly gathered that the fortress of Whitespear Head had been planned around the patterns of a magical cube of nine – even as Illana herself had described those patterns in the *Mazes and Pyschic Constructs*. The fortress had been delved for her by the *noghru* of the Black Mountains, though their work had been left unfinished. The Council had not explored the full extent of it at the time of Illana's defeat. They had made mention of many magical defences and deceits, and aspects of the stronghold which baffled them, and hints of places which were better left unexplored; and all these the Warden had recorded faithfully in his account.

What the surviving magi had brought back from Whitespear Head had been mostly works by earlier authors, now housed in the College libraries, and some few jewels and magical treasures, and booty of war from Illana's broken armies. The bulk of her reported wealth seemed to have been paid away to the *noghru* for their work, and no one had dared ask for it to be returned. Illana's own work, save for a few scattered papers of little consequence, appeared either to have been destroyed or else hidden away beyond even the skill of the First Council to find it.

So much Rhysana had already told Torkhaal briefly the previous evening, though she let him sift through those details in her mind more fully now. Two of the works from Illana's hoard had referred to Easterner traditions, which she thought either he or Dhûghaúr might like to look up in the library;

though she also thought that the Warden would have mentioned them before now, had they any bearing on the matter of Lo-Khuma.

Having slept upon it, and then looked at the Warden's codex again earlier that morning, she felt that he had given her a better understanding of the overall layout of Whitespear Head than perhaps any one individual of the First Council had ever grasped; and thus she could make an informed guess – as much intuitive as reasoned – as to where Illana's most guarded treasures would have been hidden. There was an unmapped area in the upper part of the fortress, on the fourth and fifth levels above the riverside doors, not far from where Illana's private chambers had been found. Rhysana felt that she must go there as soon as possible, to see whether her guess proved right.

Why the rush? Torkhaal wondered.

Lo-Khuma. Merrech. There were fears and feelings she could not have put into words, even had Taillan not been there with them, which was why she had chosen to show him mind to mind. Apart from the inestimable scholarly value of discovering more of Illana's work, there was the chance that it held vital knowledge for their efforts to prevent the demon's return. And Merrech knew something. He might know what she sought, and try to prevent her – or let her find it for his own purpose. He might have spoken with the dead Illana. And with Illana dead, her magic at Whitespear Head might fade or change. Rhysana felt that she was running out of time.

Why Ellen? Torkhaal asked. *Why not the High Council?*

The Toad would know, she demurred.

Hrugaar's name for Merrech. Torkhaal chuckled mentally, in spite of himself.

Ellen can open the seal for me, if she has the rod, she went on. *But I need to ask her before I approach Iorlaas.*

Torkhaal read past the words.

You can not go in alone, he objected. *Whitespear Head is dangerous. The High Council should go with you – and us.*

Not you, she countered. *We can not both be risked, because of Taillan. And I have to go. I know more about the fortress, and as much as anyone about magical defences. I know more about Illana.*

But you need more than Ellen. And what if Iorlaas refuses?

Rhysana blushed, too slow to mask her rebellious thought. Torkhaal was far from happy.

I shall discuss it with Ellen, she reassured him; *and Morvaan too, if he can spare the time tonight.*

I don't want to lose you.

'Nor I you,' she said aloud, and kissed him.

Kellarn did not remember how long he had been walking. When he came to himself, he found that he was on a south facing slope. The trees grew less thickly here, and shafts of bright sunlight came down through the branches on to tall grass scattered with summer flowers and young saplings. A little stream chuckled its way down the hillside ahead of him, and the rattling calls of magpies sounded from the leafy canopy. The air was warmer here, and he felt sticky and tired beneath his mailshirt.

He unslung the star shield from his back and sat down, stretching his legs out before him. He took a mouthful of water from his own waterskin, rather than risk the unknown waters of the stream. All his food was back with the horses, and Corollin.

Kellarn thumped his clenched fist against his knee. It had been foolish to lose sight of the path, and of Corollin and Mellin. The panthress had said that he would not find them; but did that mean that they were in trouble, or simply that he himself was lost? Since Corollin and Mellin had stayed on the path, he could only hope that they would make their way safely to the elvenfolk of the Fay – or whatever other forest folk might be known to Mellin. For now, his own problem was to find a way back to the path, or to find the Guardian. The panthress had warned against either choice. But unless he were to sit here forever, there seemed to be nothing else that he could do.

He took another swig from his waterskin, and turned to reach for his shield; and froze.

One delicate hoof, bright as burnished copper, rested lightly on the midnight blue of the shield. Kellarn let his gaze run up the slender leg above, across powerful muscles bunched beneath the glossy chestnut hide, along the proud poised curve of the neck, and found himself staring straight into the face of the stag. Antlers of pale gold spread out above its head like a branching crown, and its great round eyes were of a lustrous deep hazel.

Welcome, Son of Dortrean, said a voice in his mind.

Kellarn gave a slight start of surprise. The stag stepped back, away from the shield. He tried to keep as still as possible, not wanting to frighten the beast away.

'You came to find me?' he asked softly.

I came to find you, the stag's voice replied. It was deep and sweet, with a smoothness of velvet hide, and reminded him somehow of the panthress. But where the voice of the panthress had been edged with danger, this voice thrilled with a sense of joy and promise, and delighted amusement.

The panthress is also the Guardian, the stag agreed.

Kellarn remembered the hooded figure in black. 'She sent me away. She thinks I have already failed.'

No. The denial was swift. *You come here at the dark of the moon. She showed you your darkest fears. But fear and hope are two sides of the same leaf.*

'But she sent me away.'

To me.

'The red stag of my dreams.' Kellarn nodded.

But it was no longer the stag before him. A young woman stood there, barefoot in the grass, clad in only a simple shift of white linen. Her arms were naked, and her red-gold hair flowed long and free down to her waist in burnished glory. Her eyes were soft hazel, like his own, but her skin had the honeyed smoothness of one of the golden fay. A flicker of red light played about her hand as she lifted his shield from the ground. Kellarn scrambled to his feet and bowed. She smiled in answer.

'Who are you?' he asked. 'Are you one of the Fay?'

She shrugged elegantly, and swept her hair behind one ear with delicate fingers.

'I serve as the Guardian of Telbray Woods,' she said. 'But you may call me Dyrnalv, if you like.'

Kellarn found himself gawping stupidly. She was fully a head shorter than he, and scarcely any older, slender and smooth as a temple novice, and as gentle and homely as any girl of his mother's household. She was altogether different from the dark figure who had been the panthress, and his mind was labouring to forge the link between the two.

'Fear and hope, life and death, all flow together in the dance,' she said, handing him his shield. 'Today is the dark of the moon, and it would not be wise for you to seek the Realms of the Dead. The Dead would hold too much sway over you. Tomorrow the moon will be reborn, and your hope the stronger. We will speak with them then. Come now.'

She offered him her hand, and he took it shyly in his own. There was no spark of power or magic at their touch, but the simple joy and excitement of holding another living thing.

'My friends, Corollin and Mellin,' he managed to speak at last. 'Are they safe?'

'I sent the forest folk to find them,' she said. 'They will bring them to us, safe enough.'

They walked together for some time without speaking. Kellarn was content to look around him at the trees and mosses, and the smaller flowers and plants peeping back at him from among the tangled undergrowth. There were many older trees here, oak and ash and chestnuts of huge and ancient girth; but also paler clearings in between and patches of sunlight, with younger trees and saplings barely his own height. As they moved on through the maze of hill slopes, his ears grew more in tune with the woodland noises; so that what had at first seemed like hushed stillness behind the calls of the magpies grew rich and alive with many interwoven sounds and rumours of all manner of living things, straying across his ears and heart in an endless harmony, at once vast beyond understanding and as familiar as breathing. Dyrnalv herself made no sound – or at least, none to compare with the trudge of his own feet and the whispered ring of his mailshirt – and yet she seemed wholly in tune with the woods, and content that he should take delight in it all.

At length they followed another stream down a steeper slope and came to the open shoreline of a long lake. The sun had already climbed well down in the western sky beyond its far end, and the waters shone dazzlingly bright with silver and gold. Away to the left, still a couple of miles distant, Kellarn could just make out a single grassy hill on the southern shore of the lake, ringed with the pale trunks of many birches. Dyrnalv followed his gaze, and spoke at last.

'Here is Alvinaah, the true heart of Telbray Woods,' she said, 'which few mortal men have seen in many a lifetime. You shall rest by the hill tonight, and then we shall see what the morrow may bring.'

'And Corollin and Mellin?' he asked.

'Take off your boots, Son of Dortrean,' she said. 'We must ford the stream barefoot; and the lake and the shore beyond are holy to the *Aeshtar*.'

Kellarn did as he was told, and wriggled his toes gratefully in the cool grass.

'Why did you bring me here alone?' he asked her.

'You told your friends to stay behind.'

Kellarn looked at her. She looked straight back at him, and smiled.

'It is you who must face the Dead,' she said. 'And you, more than they, who needed to see the life of the woods and understand it.'

'But why?'

'Have you not enjoyed our walk together?'

Without waiting for his reply she turned and led the way across the stream. Kellarn picked up his boots and splashed after her.

'You are the Son of Dortrean,' Dyrnalv said as they went on along the shore; 'and you bear the sword of Fire. The Dead will answer you, where to others they might not speak. But be warned, Kellarn: the answers of the Dead rebound upon the living. Ask wisely, or ask not at all. And remember that there is life in death, and death within life, and all are joined in the great dance.'

'Do you think I should not face the Dead at all, then?' Kellarn asked.

'You are free to choose,' she said simply.

Kellarn drew a deep breath, and then blew it out again resignedly. He would have asked her more, but knew not how to ask. She offered no more help.

As they carried on along the shore, he felt again the music of the forest; only now he sensed it more keenly, as though it thrilled upon the air above the waters and flowed up through the soles of his bare feet. The need for questions seemed to fade and be forgotten. It reminded him of his meeting with Ilunâtor.

Almost before he knew it, they had come to where a little stream flowed down from the bare hill to feed the waters of the lake. Tall tree-spirits walked out from among the pale birches – fair folk like the Fay, with flowing hair and slender limbs, clad in simple tunics like the Guardian herself. They brought bowls of water and sweet berries, and pale golden wine, and bade him rest and refresh himself with their sweeping gestures and soft laughter. Kellarn sat down upon the sweet turf, and gazed about him; and drifted into a dream of dancing leaves and sunlight.

When his dream passed into wakefulness again, the music and dancing were all around him. He was lying on his back. The sun had gone down behind the mountains, and the summer stars had leaped into the clear twilight sky overhead.

Kellarn sat up. A small fire had been kindled near the bank of the stream, and Corollin and Mellin were sitting on the grass beside it laughing merrily. The tree-spirits were dancing in the shadows beyond, their lithe figures glowing softly. The smaller, darker shapes of fauns were leaping and capering down along the shore, to the music of strings and pipe.

Fauns. Kellarn checked his gear hurriedly, but nothing seemed to have been taken.

'You've been asleep,' said Mellin.

'I grew tired of waiting for you,' he grinned. 'Where's the Guardian?'

'Somewhere about,' said Corollin. 'She said she'd be back tomorrow.'

'Ah,' said Kellarn. The two women seemed unconcerned, so he guessed that there was no point in talking about it further.

'I'm sorry about running off, earlier,' he added.

'So you should be,' said Mellin. 'But at least no harm came of it this time.'

Hrugaar let his gaze wander around the convocation chamber, only listening with one ear as High Councillor Sollonaal droned on. He felt strangely out of place – the more so because he was sitting in what would more properly have been Torkhaal's place, had he been here.

The circular chamber was in the central tower of the College of Magi in Ellanguan, and usually reserved for the meetings of the lecturing staff. It was thus the heart of Sollonaal's own domain – and presumably why he had chosen to receive Prime Councillor Iorlaas here, surrounded by most of his fellow lecturers, rather than in the privacy of his study. There were four doorways to the chamber, each flanked by carved and painted statues of the mystical beasts of the *Aeshtar*; and between the doorways a line of windows ran the length of the four arcs of the wall, with deep cushioned window seats for the magi to sit upon. The inner courtyards of the College were hidden in darkness outside, and the window panes reflected the scene within, lit by the golden glow of Sollonaal's power which formed a dome over the waist high cube of lapis in the centre of the floor.

Sollonaal sat in the south, arrayed in high councillor's robes of the blue-green of Ellanguan, with wide borders of cloth of gold to signify both that he was the Prime Councillor of the Ellanguan Magi and that he served the imperial god Aranel. There were two magi some distance apart to his right, and three upon the western side, all robed in the same blue-green but with stoles and hoods of different colours, red or white or sky blue. Other than the sandy haired Drengriis of Româdhrí, the Bursar of the College, all were magi of the imperial gods.

When Hrugaar had been a lecturer here under the Archmage Virlaas – the previous Prime Councillor of the Ellanguan Magi – he had sat by custom on the southwestern arc beside the coiling sea-serpent of Sherunar. But Prime Councillor Iorlaas, as a mage of the *Vashta* goddess Serbramel, had seated himself in the northeast; and since he required his Council Secretary close by him, Hrugaar had sat down upon his left beside the paws of the golden winged lion of Maachel. The lion reminded him keenly of Torkhaal in the difficult mood of the meeting.

Sollonaal came to the end of a very long cadence, and glared around the chamber in the heavy silence that followed. Since Drengriis had signalled some time ago that he wished to speak, Hrugaar gestured for him to proceed.

'I had not yet finished, Councillor Hrugaar,' Sollonaal said sharply.

'Wind it up then, for the love of Peace,' sighed Iorlaas. 'You have been going a good half hour.'

Hrugaar nodded to Sollonaal, then grinned an apology to Drengriis – who was himself sitting beneath the sea serpent's coils that evening. Drengriis shrugged in reply.

Prime Councillor Sollonaal sighed as heavily as Iorlaas.

'In summary then,' he said, 'the relationship between the Southers and the city is much improved. The merchants and tradesmen are used to dealing with them on a peaceful basis, as indeed they have done for the last several centuries. The Lord Steward Rinnekh has, to our surprise and his credit, forged a good understanding with their leaders under less than favourable circumstances. If there is any unrest remaining – which I grant is still apparently the case – it would seem to arise mainly from the heathen Orders and their followers, and among the most staunchly traditional and uncompromising elements of the city's inhabitants.'

'Those who still assert their independence from the Emperor,' Iorlaas supplied. 'But with regard to your Lord Steward, Sollonaal, I understand that there is a rumour in the city that he has made his own deal with the Southers, whichever way events may turn elsewhere. Have you any brief observations of your own upon that point?'

Hrugaar grinned. That was a rumour which he himself had passed on to Iorlaas, though he guessed that it must have been talked about in every tavern in Ellanguan by now. Sollonaal could hardly not have heard of it; and from the smooth smile and dismissive gesture that he returned at once, he obviously had.

'Rinnekh is the Emperor's favourite,' Sollonaal replied, 'and thus will have many enemies, particularly among those elements I have already mentioned. Having made great efforts myself to work peacefully with him, and to discover how his mind works – as far as it concerns the Magi, at least – I am persuaded that Rinnekh sets the concerns of the Emperor above his own, and will not betray those who are under his care.'

There is more to it than that, Hrugaar thought. But Sollonaal had clearly rehearsed his answer often enough to give the impression that he believed it, and he would be on his guard against any attempts by Hrugaar – or others – to read the thought behind the words.

'Thank you,' said Iorlaas. 'Councillor Drengriis, is there anything you wish to say now that can not wait until the New Moon assembly tomorrow?'

Drengriis considered, and then shook his head.

Iorlaas stood up. The other magi rose with due courtesy.

'I must say,' Iorlaas observed, 'that I am less confident than you over the whole question of the Souther forces in the Empire – though as you say, perhaps here in Ellanguan they are more suitably under control. I shall put the matter to the general assembly, before the Summer Court begins, so that I am aware of the feelings of all of our Order before I speak with the Emperor.'

'His Highness would take ill any meddling,' Sollonaal warned. 'He needs our support. Or, failing that, he needs our silence.'

'The Council remains neutral,' said Iorlaas. 'As onlookers we may make our observations on the game. It is up to the Emperor how he chooses to play.'

Sollonaal scowled. 'Rhydden is not as forbearing as you, Prime Councillor. If the Council oppose him, we become his next enemy.'

'Perhaps the Council will agree with you,' Iorlaas allowed, glancing around him at the other Ellanguan magi. 'We shall hear what they have to say tomorrow. Come, Councillor Hrugaar.'

He made his formal bow of farewell and led the way to the door between the winged lion and the gryphon. The subtle shimmer of Sollonaal's warding veil of power drew aside before him, allowing them to pass through.

Iorlaas went ahead along the narrow passage beyond, the pale green light from his hand reflecting dully from the darkened windows on either side and limning his dark grey hair and laurel green robes with a ghostly aureole. Hrugaar followed quietly, listening to the sounds of the Ellanguan magi as they broke up their meeting and began to move away through the other doors. Their mood seemed less than happy.

Iorlaas and Hrugaar turned left when they reached the far landing, making their way to the head of the northern stair. Two shorter magi, both robed in black, were waiting there for them. The first was Mage Councillor Dhûghaúr, smiling broadly as he caught Hrugaar's eye. The other, broad-nosed and palely nervous in Iorlaas' light, was the Earth mage Telghraan.

'The priests are ready, Prime Councillor,' said Dhûghaúr, 'though the hour is later than we had planned.'

'Blame Sollonaal,' Hrugaar grinned. Iorlaas waved for him to be quiet.

'Do you still wish to go?' Dhûghaúr asked.

'Of course,' said Iorlaas brightly. 'Having heard what the magi here have to say, it is only fair that Kelmaar and the other Orders should have the chance to speak. I need to know both sides of the story.'

It had been the Prime Councillor's own suggestion, though Hrugaar had at once supported it and had asked Dhûghaúr to make arrangements. Dhûghaúr had enlisted Telghraan's help, since he knew his way around the city better, and around this particular College.

Telghraan, meanwhile, was glancing anxiously from side to side, as if fearful of being overheard. Having been in much the same position himself with Sollonaal, Hrugaar could sympathise. Telghraan was the only other *Aeshta* mage, apart from Drengriis, now left on the College staff, and was obviously retained on sufferance by Sollonaal. Hrugaar doubted that he would have been invited to the meeting with Iorlaas, even had he not been busy elsewhere.

'The knights said to come to the postern gate,' Dhûghaúr told Hrugaar. 'They said that you would know where.'

'Can you *leap* straight there?' asked Telghraan. 'We are well past the sunset curfew.'

Hrugaar nodded, and the four magi moved to link hands. Iorlaas put out his light. Hrugaar breathed deeply to focus, gathering them mentally into his spell. A moment later they had swapped the stuffy landing of the College for the cooler air of the city night.

The northern wall of the Kelmaar School loomed before him, the blue-grey of the ancient stone slumbering deep in star-shadow. To his right, the long wing of the shrine of Maësta stretched out from the main body of the school, its high windows still glowing softly with candlelight, though the sunset rite would have come to an end some time ago. The streets around them were empty and silent, and the distant noises of the harbourfront carried clearly up into the city on the night wind.

Dhûghaúr had hardly let go of his hand before the small postern door opened and a wedge of light spread out across the cobblestones. The Lady Miranda of Kelmaar stepped into view. She was clad in the silver-grey surcoat of a holy knight of her Order, with the white teardrop of Kelmaar upon her breast, and her wild brown curls were tethered into a single tight braid at her back. The white steel mace at her hip flickered as she moved. She beckoned them inside, checked the street quickly to satisfy herself that they had not been observed, and then shut the door behind them and slammed the bar home. Telghraan smoothed his hair and tugged at his over-large robes, in an attempt to make himself more presentable.

Miranda led them through into a long teaching hall, bright with lamplight. To Hrugaar's senses the air was clean and fresh, with a slight edge of salt, and he could tell that the priests had prepared a warding spell about the hall to keep this meeting secret. Their hosts stood to greet them as they crossed the scrubbed flagstone floor.

To Hrugaar's surprise the reclusive High Councillor Maëghlar was there – frail as ever, and leaning heavily upon his grey staff. He stood before the great carved chair beside the hearth that had once been Master Trigharran's. To his right, provided with a simpler high backed chair, was the Abbot Shaünar from the monastery school of the Temple of Sherunar in Ellanguan. Shaünar was tall and hale, being somewhere in his early forties, with short dark hair and robes of deep sea green. His usually calm face seemed shadowed, as though stormclouds were gathering within.

On the nearer side of the empty hearth stood a younger woman in the grey and white robes of a priestess of Maësta, her brown curls braided prettily with many strands of silver thread; and she alone smiled as they approached. Hrugaar smiled back. This was the Lady Bromaer Kelmaar of Româdhrí, Miranda's older sister; and he knew that the two women had effectively been left in charge of the school since old Trigharran's death, while the Order regrouped in their *commanderie* manor to the east of the city. The blush of rose in Bromaer's cheeks and the sparkle in her eyes were as yet the only outward signs that she was carrying Drengriis' child.

Apart from these four, and the four magi themselves, there were just three other people in the hall. There was a guard at the door through which they had entered, and another guard at the door in the far corner – both clad like Miranda in grey surcoats over mail, and both known to Hrugaar from his many visits to the school.

The last person, standing before the centre of the long hearth, he had no knowledge of at all. She was clad in a curious hooded shirt and breeches of darkest charcoal grey, with supple boots and gloves of dull black leather. Her hood was thrown back to reveal a Souther face of rather severe beauty, scarcely softened by the silky raven hair that tumbled free across her shoulders.

'This is Mijal,' said Miranda, introducing them. 'She came to us just after the sunset rite. You need to hear what she has to say.'

'Indeed,' said Iorlaas evenly.

The Souther woman looked at them, her lip twitching toward the curl of a sneer. She seemed less than impressed with what she saw. Iorlaas gave her a formal bow, by way of apology.

Miranda completed the introductions, and they settled

Maëghlar into his chair. Another high backed chair was brought for Iorlaas, as Prime Councillor, and the three younger magi stood protectively around him.

'So what has the esteemed Lady Mijal to tell us?' asked Iorlaas courteously.

The Souther woman nodded for Miranda to speak.

'Mijal has been in the Steward's palace,' Miranda explained, 'though she is not one of Ambassador T'Loi's following. She serves another – another faction in the Court of the God-King, I think.' She looked at Mijal, who bowed her head in confirmation.

'They trust T'Loi even less than we do,' Miranda went on, 'and they don't like what he is doing here. They are worried that he and Rinnekh will make a bid for power in Ellanguan, and use their position to lend strength to a war against the God-King himself.'

'I have heard a similar tale,' said Iorlaas; 'though there it was said that Rinnekh and T'Loi would use their strength to help the God-King overthrow our own Emperor. Might it perhaps be, Lady Mijal, that your God-King fears that T'Loi will prove a stumbling block in his way to the taking of Lautun?'

'That's what I said myself,' Miranda agreed. 'But Mijal says that's not what the God-King wants.'

'Then why did he send his ships to attack us in the first place?' put in Telghraan.

The Souther woman laughed. 'He did not,' she said. 'The fleet of the God-King is a hundred times larger than the few poor ships that came this way. They were sent by lesser rulers of his Court, hoping to persuade him to join a war against you. Few of them now live to beg his forgiveness.'

'Either way,' said Shaünar, 'it would seem that neither we nor the God-King wish to have these Souther armies remaining on Six Kingdoms lands.'

'But the Emperor wants their help to defend against a second assault from the East,' Iorlaas reminded him. 'Would the God-King send other help, if those armies were withdrawn?'

They looked at Mijal.

'I may not speak for the God-King,' she said. 'He will send his own messengers to your Emperor, when he will. But this is another part of my story. There were princes who came from the East—'

'Chieftains,' Miranda supplied.

'Chieftains,' Mijal nodded. 'We believe it was these chieftains that urged the K'tarim – and others – to drive the God-King to an attack on your lands. They said that a new god was rising, a great demon, who would grant great power and riches to those who served him; and that the God-King would do well to find favour with him. And here in Ellanguan I have heard a similar tale – that the Eastern men who attacked you came to make ready a way for a great demon that is hateful to your kindly gods of the *Aeshtar*.'

'The ancient enemy,' said Maëghlar in his creaking voice. 'The God-King would do well to fear him.'

Dhûghaúr stirred uncomfortably at Hrugaar's side. 'So are you saying,' he demanded, 'that T'Loi's people would help the Easterners, rather than fight them?'

Mijal shrugged. 'T'Loi has commanded them to peace. But that was the reason the rulers of the K'tarim sent them here.'

'Can T'Loi keep control of them?' asked Iorlaas.

'He is highborn,' she nodded. 'They must serve him or die – unless one of their own lords, or the God-King himself, comes to command them otherwise.'

'And how likely is that?'

'We are keeping watch.' Mijal gave a thin smile.

'And who is *we*?' Hrugaar ventured.

'We who do not serve T'Loi,' she returned. 'Be thankful we do not. Three nights past, in the Steward's palace, one of his men was found hiding in the rooms of your Earl of Dortrean. He had a poisoned blade, but he was no great swordsman. We – removed him, secretly. No one knows of this. But strange to tell, T'Loi and Rinnekh blame you.'

Mijal gave her thin smile again. Hrugaar was uncertain whether she meant it to be a warning or a compliment.

'But Erkal Dortrean is safe?' he demanded.

'Safe for now,' she shrugged. 'One of my people watches him. We think he should be kept alive.'

'What are you to the God-King?' asked Shaünar.

'I am his father's daughter, the God-King Ascended,' Mijal said. She bowed briefly, raising her palms to her forehead in homage. 'Now I must go.'

Iorlaas and Shaünar stood up.

'Could you take command of the Souther troops?' Iorlaas asked her.

'No,' she said. 'And I do not trust the magi who come to the Steward's palace. Can *you* not take command of *them*?'

Iorlaas spread his hands in a noncommital gesture. Mijal smiled. She bowed once, deeply, to them all, and then strode lightly away across the hall. Hrugaar sensed a faint rippling along the air as the guard opened the door and took her out.

'Well, Mijal has confirmed our own guesses on a number of points,' observed Shaünar as he sat down again. 'Yet I find myself wondering about her purpose in coming here. Was it to warn us, or to discover how much we knew?'

'She spoke as honestly as she could,' said Bromaer. 'She lives a life of secrets, that much is plain. But in this, I think, she was trying to help us. I sensed no malice toward us within her.'

'Nor I,' Hrugaar agreed.

'To warn us,' said Maëghlar, sitting forward. 'There was more before you came, Iorlaas. The merchants may have made their peace with the Southers—'

'And their profit from them,' Miranda snorted.

Hrugaar laughed. Maëghlar frowned at the pair of them, and then went on. 'But the people of the city are afraid. They turn to the *Aeshtar* for comfort; and they turn to Kelmaar, because we have ever loved Ellanguan and been ready in her defence. And now Rinnekh hates us the more for that; and though we have not yet stood openly against him, his fear that we may do so gnaws deep into his coward's heart. We have proved a less willing tool in his hands than Sollonaal and the College Magi.'

'Mijal says there are always magi about the palace these days,' said Miranda.

'Though Drengriis seems to think that they are as concerned as we are about what might be going on,' put in Bromaer.

Hrugaar was about to say that he thought that Sollonaal had been selling out to Rinnekh all along. But at that moment there came a loud banging on the door at the inner end of the hall, and then a deeper tremor on the air as a young man burst in. Miranda whipped her head around to fix him with a gaze of steel.

'Lorghan!' she barked.

He skidded to a halt, fumbled a bow, then padded swiftly forward again to go down on one knee at Shaünar's side. Hrugaar recognised him as one of the younger guards in training, probably no older than sixteen. He wore only a loose blue shirt, unlaced and half tucked into his grey Kelmaar breeches. His hair was tousled, and his face and clothes looked smeared and grubby.

'My Lords,' he said. 'The school is burning.'

Miranda let slip a word that would cost her a week in holy penance. 'What? Where?' she added urgently.

'The west side,' Lorghan answered, scrambling to his feet again. 'The fire is on the stair and in the hallways, the mess hall is burning.'

Miranda was already moving, dragging him with her. 'Hrugaar, we need you!' she commanded.

'I shall come,' he answered, helping Iorlaas to his feet. 'Telghraan, can you find Drengriis please? He may still be at the College.'

'I am gone,' the Earth mage nodded. He closed his eyes, and vanished.

'We shall defend the shrine,' said Maëghlar, as Shaünar helped him up. 'Come along, Little Daughter.'

Bromaer did not appear to have heard him. She was looking up into the air before her, her eyes bright with reflected light. Hrugaar followed the line of her gaze, and to his lasting delight glimpsed a swirl of shimmering opalescent coils, hovering in the midst of the hall. Even to his fay-born sight they were little more than bright ghostly forms. There were two of them – mystic serpent messengers of the *Aeshta* Lords of Water – twining endlessly one about the other, speaking mind to mind with the priestess who had called them. For a moment, both turned their heads toward him; and then they were gone.

'I have sent word to our Order,' Bromaer said aloud, 'and to Father Shaünar's people also. They will send help soon.'

She turned her face to Hrugaar. 'Rinnir was in the Seaward Tower.' She waved her hand absently in the wrong direction. 'They may have forgotten him.'

Bromaer smiled and bowed to the magi, her hands sweeping together in the sign of *Aeshta* blessing; and then she was gone, hurrying to help Maëghlar and Shaünar to the northern door.

'Rinnir was brought here?' Dhûghaúr demanded.

'A few days ago,' Hrugaar replied. 'I thought that I had told you. The Môshári felt that he might fare better here, with the Masters from the Harperschool to visit him.'

'The fire will not be good for him,' said Dhûghaúr.

Hrugaar did not need the reminder. Rinnir had been a musician and storyteller, and a close friend of the dead Mage Councillor Salbaar. But his face and hands had been badly burned in the fires at Fersí village, east of Arrandin, when he had tried to rescue Salbaar – which was why the healers of Kelmaar came to have him in their care. The flames could only renew his memories of pain and loss.

'I am not much use at fire fighting,' said Iorlaas, 'but I feel that I should help. Should I summon the Council to the assembly chamber, and then bring those who wish to come back here?

'I regret,' he added, almost wistfully, 'that I have not

Herusen's skill to call individual magi here to me now. Not yet, at least.'

Hrugaar shook his head. 'Half of Kelmaar will be here the sooner,' he replied. 'You were better to go home and rest, to gather your strength for tomorrow. Kelmaar already think well of you, for coming here.'

'I am not so old that I need to be packed off home to bed,' Iorlaas returned testily. 'Now lead the way, Councillor Hrugaar. We shall all do what we can.'

There was no time for further argument. Hrugaar shrugged his acceptance, and set off swiftly down the hall. Dhûghaúr and Iorlaas hurried after him.

The door gave on to a long panelled gallery running to left and right, lit by the angry glare of firelight flooding in through the windows on the far side. There was no sign of Miranda and the knights. Hrugaar turned right, looking out through the windows as he went.

As Lorghan had reported, most of the long dining hall ahead to the west was already ablaze, its tall windows flickering like many coloured jewels as the flames danced and leaped toward the timbered roof. In the cloister garden below, perhaps a dozen of the younger novices and guards were gathered together, hugging one another and chattering in the night air, or staring up at the flames from beneath hastily donned cloaks and blankets. More people darted in and out of the kitchen door beyond, half hidden among billowing clouds of smoke and steam. The south side of the school, and the buildings behind to the east, seemed still to be safe beyond the fire's reach.

The long gallery came to an end at a door which led straight on to the minstrels' gallery of the dining hall itself. Hrugaar risked opening it an inch, then wrestled it shut against the rushing draught from the heat. Tawny flames scrabbled at the jamb.

'This one looks clear,' said Dhûghaúr, peering out through the shuttered grille of a stouter door to their right.

Hrugaar nodded. They pulled the door open and went out into the cloistered practice yard. The upper windows on the western side were bright with flame; and the ruddy light spilled down on to two men who had just come stumbling out from the shadowed walkway below.

The taller of the two was Sturannan – a senior knight within the school – though Hrugaar might hardly have recognised him. Nearly half his hair and beard had been scorched away, and his tunic hung in blackened tatters. The flesh beneath was scarlet and livid with many burns, and he was limping with painful dignity. The hand that clutched his sword was little more than a blackened claw.

The younger man supporting him was short and lithe of build, with dark shoulder length hair, and he wore the grey livery of Kelmaar with a short sword at his side. Though his fair face had, by custom, a look of sadness and injury, he seemed all but unhurt by the fire. Hrugaar knew him at once for the Lord Lïall of Solaní, a lesser cousin of the Lord Steward Rinnekh. But Lïall had long been estranged from his kinsman – and indeed from most of the Court Noble – and the knights of Kelmaar had taken him under their wing. Hrugaar was more kindly disposed toward Lïall than were most of the other magi, both because of his friendship with Kelmaar, and because they shared a common friend in the blind harper Saraï. The thought that Saraï might also be here filled him with sudden alarm.

'Hrugaar,' cried Lïall. 'Thank the gods you're here! Rinnir is still up in the tower.' He jerked his head back toward the northwest, rather than let go of the knight.

'I know,' said Hrugaar. 'But where is Saraï?'

'Renza,' said Lïall shortly. Saraï, like Hrugaar, was grandchild of the old Steward Gradhellan, and thus had a better claim – though unrecognised – to the Steward's throne than did the upstart Rinnekh. It had been thought wise to keep her safe outside of Ellanguan.

'I tried to get through,' Lïall went on, 'but the fire is too bad.'

'The fire is alive, Hrugaar,' Sturannan rasped. 'It takes human shapes. I have unmade two. Or one, twice. We must guard the shrine.'

'The Lady Bromaer is there,' put in Dhûghaúr, 'and High Councillor Maëghlar.'

'There are Southers in the school,' Lïall told them. 'I fought one down on the south stair, the other side, less than ten minutes ago.'

'Not all the blood is mine,' said Sturannan, nodding slightly toward Lïall's tunic. The movement turned to a grimace.

'The Southers started the fire?' Iorlaas demanded.

'Who else?' said Lïall bitterly. He turned and led Sturannan away across the yard.

'I can find the way to Rinnir,' Hrugaar told the two magi. 'You may wish to go to find the Southers.'

He drew a deep breath, and closed his eyes briefly to focus within himself. Then, with a whispered word of thanks to Sherunar, he brought forth a ball of liquid light within the palm of his right hand.

'But they said that the fire is *alive*,' Dhûghaúr protested.

'I heard,' said Hrugaar.

He raised his right hand, let the ball run freely down the length of his arm, across his shoulders and down the other arm, and then flipped it around with his left.

'Go back down the gallery, and turn right at the far end,' he told them. 'Go through that classroom, and then take the stair down from the landing beyond.'

He let the ball flow back again, feeling rather than watching as the light spread out across his sleeves. He dropped the ball to his right foot, and then flipped it up around his boots and breeches, and on up and around his collar and back down upon the other side, clothing himself in an outer skin of watery power.

'Councillor Hrugaar,' said Iorlaas sternly. 'This is hardly the time to be fooling around like any common juggler.'

Hrugaar kicked the ball of light high in the air, and let it come down upon the crown of his silver fair head. It burst like a bubble, scattering down around him like foam from a wave in the long bay of Ellanguan.

'What, are you still here?' he laughed. He reached out and brushed Dhûghaúr's forehead with his fingertips, leaving a shimmering mark like a crescent moon. Then he shooed them away impatiently and turned and ran away west, going in through the door from which Lïall and Sturannan must have come out.

Iorlaas has no feel for magic, he thought, as he moved in to the stifling darkness. *It must come from serving that dreary goddess of Justice. He misses out on the simple joy of the dances of the Lords of the* Aeshtar.

The room that he was in now was used as a sparring hall by the students on wet days, and also as a place to change and arm themselves. There were a number of benches around the walls, and racks for gear and practice weapons. The fire had not yet touched them, but the air was already thick with bitter smoke. To his far left was a door which led back to the main hallway and to the west stair, and it seemed to be from that way that the smoke chiefly came. He thought that he could also sense water there, an edge of dampness behind the smoke, as though the priests might have been using their power to fight the fire. But there was no sound of voices nearby, only the faint hiss and crackle of devouring flame.

Hrugaar did not tarry to find out. He turned instead to the right, and went through a low door into a narrow store passage lined with cupboards from floor to ceiling on either side. The door at the far end, to his left, would lead him straight into the lower chamber of the Seaward Tower.

The far door was already on fire.

Hrugaar took the challenge in his stride. He had wrapped his protective spell around him for just such a purpose. He knocked up the latch and pulled the door open.

The heat from beyond roared round him like a furnace. It was small wonder that Lïall had turned back. The hangings and settles and long oak table that had graced this lower chamber were all ablaze, and the painted ribs and bosses of the vault were turned to flaked and blackened stone. The heavy timbers of the main door across the hall – which led to the city streets outside – glowed bright as logs upon a winter hearth; and the worn stone stair, just to his right, served as a chimney toward the upper floors.

Though Hrugaar loved the Lords of the *Aeshtar*, and their unbounded joy in the dance, he found nothing to delight him here. This was Fire in its more dreadful aspect, running wild and devouring all in its path. It had neither the comfort of the hearthfire, nor the mystery of the forge, nor the terrible beauty of molten rock. It was just greedy, wanton and spiteful.

Yet though the glare of the fire half dazzled him, and the air seemed too thick and choked to breathe, the power of Hrugaar's spell held. He could endure the heat without hurt. He shielded his eyes with one hand, slammed the door shut, and sprang forward on to the stair.

The updraught seemed to carry him, spewing him out on to the smaller landing above. A second scene of burning filled his sight. But here the flames pressed closer in, and the grey oak of the panelled walls rippled with red and bright gold in baleful patterns. There were three doors, each leading to chambers used by the healers for those who were not part of the School or the Order. He guessed that Rinnir would have been settled somewhere here.

Hrugaar paused on the landing, reaching out with senses other than sight. He was now close to the southern end of the shrine of Maësta; and as he stood he could feel the power of the warding spell raised by Maëghlar and the priests, soaring up like a tall wave behind him, as though poised just before the fall. He brushed its strength and coolness with his mind.

Then a scream tore the air around him, and he knew that he had found Rinnir.

Hrugaar ran forward round the corner of the landing and burst through the open door. He was in one of the smaller rooms, with windows facing north and west, but only the nearer half of the room was yet ablaze.

Rinnir was sitting by the foot of the bed, in the middle of the floor, facing Hrugaar as he came in. He was clad in knee length breeches and a sleeveless vest, and his hands were raised as if in prayer. But crimson flame played up and down his bare legs and arms, and kindled his fair hair to a mane of fire.

Hrugaar gave a cry of dismay, searching the room with his eyes for blanket or drape with which to smother the flames. The curtains on the farther window were still whole. He made to move, and then stopped. Sturannan's warning whispered in his mind.

He looked again at Rinnir. The musician's eyes were still his own, filled now with a thousand tales of terror he could never tell. But his mouth was stretched wide in the mockery of a smile, with tongues of fire licking out between teeth and lips; and as Hrugaar watched, the fire swept up around Rinnir's frozen form, so that he seemed but a shadow within a body of living flame.

Hrugaar hesitated for a moment. He was loth to hurt Rinnir. But the fire would kill him, even if Hrugaar did not – even as it had devoured everything else in its path, save the knight Sturannan. The burning had to be stopped.

The fire creature leaped to its feet, dragging Rinnir like a puppet within. Hrugaar let loose a storm of ice and sleet around them, turning swiftly to pelting hail. Steam and smoke roiled through the chamber in sudden fury. Cut off from the fire around, the creature ate itself deeper into flesh and bone. Rinnir screamed.

Hrugaar seized hold of the man by the shoulders, building the strength of his spell. He must snuff the creature out, drive it from Rinnir's body before it killed him. Flame slithered along his arms, grappling in vain for purchase on the watery skin of power. The roar of steam and ice was drowned out by its hissing. And then it failed, and was gone.

Hrugaar let the storm fade, and cooled the steam away.

Rinnir slumped lifeless in his arms. He lowered him gently to the floor, and knelt down beside him on the bedded hailstones.

The last signs of life were fading. Hrugaar took a deep breath and plunged down into a healing trance, chasing after them. The spark that had been Rinnir himself was gone. The last memories were beginning to drift apart, scattering like leaves and petals on the surface of a flowing stream. Hrugaar could watch them, but it was not within his gift to draw them back. Besides, he thought, Rinnir would be happier now. And Salbaar would be waiting for him.

He let himself drift for a while, watching the bright petals of memory as he bade Rinnir farewell, and only slowly surfacing toward the waking world again. The room was now in darkness, save for the sullen glow from the flames beyond the doorway. The hailstones beneath him were melting to gritty sludge.

He became aware of noises from outside, of people gathering in the street below. At first he thought that it might be help arriving from the nearby monastery school; or perhaps the city guard, since the sunset curfew was still in force. But the voices were harsh and mocking. A man jeered loudly, hooting at Kelmaar's misfortune.

Hrugaar's fair face flushed with anger. He sprang to his feet, spoiling for another fight – or a shouting match, at least, through the bedroom window.

But as he stood up he was aware of another *presence* nearby; and with his fay senses he saw it, rather than with mortal sight. It stood at the nearest corner of the shrine of Maësta, rearing up through stone and timber to fully the height of the Seaward Tower. It had the body and shape of a man – though fashioned as if from water and light, with the lustre of pale moonstone – with the face of a panthress, and a mane like a lion's that glittered with remembered starlight. It was turned away from him, looking down toward the heart of the school, and a curved blade was in its hands. A second *presence*, like to the first, stood further to the east; and between them they drove back the fire from the shrine by the power that was within them.

Hrugaar understood. The priestess Bromaer – or those with her – had raised the guardians of the shrine. The people in the street, and even Hrugaar himself, were as nothing to the guardians. They had come to protect and defend, and the need of the school called them. His own purpose should be the same. He felt ashamed of his foolish anger.

He knelt to rest one hand on Rinnir's ruined body, in final farewell. Then he turned and ran out into the fire.

After Hrugaar had shooed them away, Iorlaas and Dhûghaúr hastened back across the yard and through into the long gallery. The door to the dining hall still held back the flames. Dhûghaúr glanced at the wooden panelling running the length of the walls, and guessed that it was only a matter of time before the fire came chasing after them.

'Councillor Hrugaar is growing quite out of hand,' said Iorlaas, striding ahead.

'He came close to death at Tollund,' Dhûghaúr reminded him. The thought had not been far from his own mind when Hrugaar had sent them back. He thought it tactful not to mention that his incorrigible friend might also be glad of a little excitement, after days of being tied to Iorlaas' sleeve while the new Prime Councillor prepared himself for the Summer Court.

'I am hardly surprised,' Iorlaas observed.

His pale green magelight sprang to life in his hand as they passed the last of the windows and entered the deeper shadow at the far end of the gallery. There was only one doorway to their right. They went through into another teaching hall, with rows of bench seats end-on to them as they entered, and three high windows looking west. The light from the burning glowered at them through coloured panes of purple and red. The two magi picked their way between the benches in silence, making for the door in the opposite wall.

The door opened just before they reached it, and a man and a woman came in. White light flooded around them, welling from a crystal hung about the man's throat. Both were dressed in the grey tunic and breeches of Kelmaar – and both reached at once for the swords at their sides.

'Peace!' said Iorlaas steadily, holding up his hand. 'We mean you no harm.'

'Hrugaar sent us,' added Dhûghaúr.

The two knights eyed them doubtfully, weapons drawn.

'Where is Hrugaar?' asked the woman.

'Back near the fire,' Dhûghaúr answered. He began to gesture with his hand, but thought the better of it as the knights shifted their swords. 'We left him in the yard. I am Mage Councillor Dhûghaúr, and this is Iorlaas, Prime Councillor of All Magi. We heard that there were Southers downstairs.'

The knights exchanged glances, as though not wholly surprised by his words. Then they made formal bows to Iorlaas, and saluted Dhûghaúr with their sword blades upright before them. The man's eyes kept straying to Dhûghaúr's forehead.

'We found none on our way up,' the woman returned. 'But we should be glad of your help down there. Left down the stair, and then take the door on your left at the bottom.'

She pointed the way with her sword; and then the two knights circled out and around them, and ran along the tops of the benches toward the gallery beyond. The door slammed shut behind them.

The two magi went through on to a small landing, lit only by the cool wash of Iorlaas' magelight. The low doorway ahead and to their left would take them on to the stair. Dhûghaúr pulled the teaching hall door closed, glad to get away from the fiery glare of the windows. But as he turned back to Iorlaas he saw that a much more present threat was upon them.

One of the other doorways on the landing had kindled to sudden flame; and stepping from it was a figure that seemed to take its shape from the very fire itself. In form it was like a ghostly warrior, with crested helm and rippling mail, and a tall spear in its hand. Dhûghaúr shrank back, scrabbling in his mind for some power that he could use against it.

Prime Councillor Iorlaas seemed quite undismayed.

'Stand, servant of War!' he commanded, flinging his magelight into a circle about the warrior's feet. Then he frowned, weaving rapid passes in the air with both hands while he kept the creature fixed within his gaze. Several dozen strands sprang up from the circle of light, deepening in hue to a rich summer green, weaving and knotting themselves with dizzying speed into a mesh that held the flaming figure from helm to heel. The warrior writhed and strained against the bonds, to no avail.

Iorlaas permitted himself the slightest sigh of satisfaction, and clasped his hands together at his waist.

'This,' he said without turning, 'would appear to be one of the lesser messengers of Fraërigr, *Vashta* Lord of War. Since Holy Serbramel, as you know, is the daughter of Mighty Fraërigr, her servants are granted some measure of authority over them.'

'But what is it doing here?' Dhûghaúr demanded. 'And what has it to do with the Southers?'

And how long will your spell last? he wanted to add.

'Interesting questions all,' Iorlaas agreed. 'I shall see what I can find out, before I dismiss him.'

He took two steps forward, until he was almost within arm's reach of his woven net of power. Dhûghaúr kept his eyes on the warrior, more than Iorlaas – both ready to hurl his own power at the thing, if it tried to attack, and trying to work out what manner of spell Iorlaas had contrived to contain the fire. He had also the uneasy feeling that the creature was something other than Iorlaas believed it to be.

How Iorlaas questioned it he could not fathom. He saw only that the web of magic shrank slowly in upon itself, green fire grappling against the red, until suddenly both melted together and vanished with a flash.

The door behind was still burning. The Prime Councillor seemed to be unharmed.

A moment later, two globes of magelight winked into life – Iorlaas' pale green, and Dhûghaúr's tawny gold.

'Well, that did not get us very far,' Iorlaas sighed. 'It refused to answer my questions, except with insults, and fought every inch of the way. But from what the knight of Kelmaar told us, there may be others about. We had better keep moving.'

Dhûghaúr looked at the burning door.

'Could you use a similar spell, to stop the fire from coming through?' he asked.

Iorlaas rubbed his chin as he thought about it, and then smiled.

'I do believe that I could,' he said. 'Thank you, Dhûghaúr. Perhaps I am of more use fighting fire than I had realised.'

He waved his magelight away behind him, spread his hands palms down in front of him, and breathed out. Instead of a woven web, a simple wall of green light spread up across the door and all around the frame. The flames were snuffed out, though the panelled wood of the door was still burning.

Then the teaching hall door burst open again, and a black robed figure stumbled through.

'Telghraan!' cried Dhûghaúr. 'Did you find Councillor Drengriis?'

'Gone home,' Telghraan shook his head quickly.

'Yet his errand was not entirely wasted,' came a voice from behind.

Telghraan pulled a face that only Dhûghaúr could see, and then ducked aside. High Councillor Sollonaal was approaching between the benches of the hall, the gold borders of his robes flickering ominously in the ruddy light from the windows. Another of the Ellanguan magi was with him, who by his height and thinness and shaven head could only have been Mage Councillor Eralaan – the Senior Lecturer of the Ellanguan College, and the most senior mage of Fraërigr now living in the Six Kingdoms.

Come to gloat, thought Dhûghaúr, irritably. But he clasped his hands together before his chest and bowed slightly, in the correct manner of formal greeting between magi of the Council.

'I am pleased to see you here, Sollonaal,' said Iorlaas. 'Although I must confess that I should not have expected it.'

'The sentiment is mutual, Prime Councillor,' the other replied. 'But whatever our problems with Kelmaar, I may not stand idly by while their school burns down about their ears. Were it our own College, I hope that they would also come to our aid.'

'Ah,' said Iorlaas. 'So you do hope to make political coin out of Kelmaar's misfortune, then?'

Sollonaal turned his vexation to a smile. 'The city is rife with discord,' he returned. 'If through simple help in time of need we can begin to build bridges of understanding with the heathen Orders, then that is all to the good.'

He glanced at the green wall of Iorlaas' power.

'The fire burns, Prime Councillor,' he said. 'It has reached the hallway behind us. As a mage of Aranel I am perhaps better placed to deal with it than you are, but all help will be welcome. Shall you come?'

'What about the Southers?' asked Dhûghaúr.

'What Southers?' Sollonaal demanded.

'The guards said that they had found none,' Iorlaas demurred. 'But do you go down, Councillor Dhûghaúr, and see what you may do to help. Take Mage Councillor Eralaan with you.'

Dhûghaúr could see some sense in it, in that Iorlaas would presume that Eralaan could handle any other flaming warriors of Fraërigr that they might meet. But he hesitated to leave Iorlaas in Sollonaal's care; and the gaunt Eralaan looked likely to prove a rather uncomfortable companion. He glanced at Telghraan, who wrinkled his broad nose in sympathy.

'Yes, Prime Councillor,' he said.

He waved Eralaan forward, and opened the low door to the spiral stair; and sent his tawny magelight bobbing down ahead of them into the darkness.

* * *

Telghraan sighed inwardly as Dhûghaúr went away. Sollonaal had been the very last person he had wanted to find when he went back to the College to hunt for Drengriis, and Eralaan would have come a close second. Had they known how blindly he had made the *leap* to bring them back here – Telghraan being unfamiliar with the school, and not knowing where the fire might have spread while he was away – they might have been less insistent on coming. But Sollonaal would brook no argument, and the young mage had not been minded to tell him. He had half hoped that he might indeed make an error in his return *leap*, carrying both of them with him to an untimely death.

It was not just the difference in faith, or age, that rankled between them. To Telghraan, Sollonaal epitomised the tortuous political side of the Council, which at best bored him senseless, and at worst made him contemplate murder. Iorlaas, whom he remembered from his student days in Farran, he found similarly dull and circumspect – though not spiteful like Sollonaal, nor so quick tempered.

Telghraan had gone to Arrandin during the war because he had wanted to take action where it was needed, with no thought of political gain. He had returned to the Kelmaar School for similar reasons. He admired High Councillor Rhysana and her friends because – to his mind, at least – they had the backbone and passion to act swiftly in time of need, and left it until later to worry upon what political toes they might have trodden. Rhysana's exceptional ability had made a great impression upon him; and Torkhaal was exactly the kind of Earth mage that Telghraan himself aspired to be – brave, passionate, loyal, and the father of a growing family. Dhûghaúr he found more timid, but good company when one got to know him. Hrugaar he did not know quite what to make of – a reaction not uncommon among Council members – though he liked him well enough.

Telghraan would have preferred to follow Dhûghaúr down the stair, had Iorlaas been minded to let him go; but the Prime

Councillor was already ushering him back into the teaching hall. He comforted himself that it was probably best to have at least one *Aeshta* mage with them in the school of an *Aeshta* Order. Following on from that thought, he supposed that it was a good idea for someone to keep an eye on Sollonaal.

He led the way back across the hall, and through into the long gallery beyond. The door at the far end was now ablaze, and flames spread out along the panelled walls to either side.

'I can quench the flames and slow the burning,' said Sollonaal as they hurried along; 'though it requires no little effort. Telghraan, run on and be ready to open the door at my word, so that I may have a clear view to work.'

Telghraan hitched up his long robes to avoid tripping over, and trotted on ahead. He did not much care to be ordered around by Sollonaal, but he was doing this for Kelmaar's sake, not his own. The light from the burning buildings outside shone brighter than ever through the windows, so that he had to shield his eyes with one hand from the glare as he ran. The fire had reached the roof, and the sky above the cloister garden was choked with smoke and smeared a ruddy brown.

He skidded to a halt as he approached the door, now sweating with the heat. Sollonaal had slowed his pace as he readied his power, and was still a dozen paces behind. Iorlaas was halfway between them.

Telghraan looked at the door latch with its iron ring, and wondered whether Sollonaal would put out the fire on this side before telling him to open it. He doubted that he would. Given time, he could have cooled the metal down – but he doubted that Sollonaal would wait for that, either. He would have to think of something else. He steadied his breathing, and drew strength from the stone floor beneath his feet.

'Now,' Sollonaal's voice echoed down the gallery.

Telghraan gathered himself, turned, and kicked with his right heel. The strength of Earth smashed the latch and flung the door wide open. Fire and smoke belched out around him, stinging his eyes and singeing his hair and robes. Telghraan swore loudly.

The next moment the fire died away, and the light around them grew dim. Telghraan rubbed his eyes and blinked.

Sollonaal's spell had cleared a path ahead. Beyond the open door was a wide minstrels' gallery, blackened and scarred, but now free from any flames. There was another door on the far side. To the left, the large hall which he had seen through the windows still burned, but the fire had been driven back from this end. In spite of himself, Telghraan had to allow that Solonaal might have done something useful.

He hurried out on to the blackened walkway, his eyes and face still smarting from the heat in the hall. Iorlaas followed close behind him. Down at the far end, beyond the flames, he could make out half a dozen or more people among clouds of steam, though their voices were drowned out by the roar of the fire.

He was almost halfway across when there was a deafening crack, and then a rumble like thunder; and the great roof beams overhead split apart and tumbled down.

Telghraan gave a soundless cry and turned back toward Iorlaas. But his legs were too slow and leaden, and his robes snarled around them.

Iorlaas staggered sideways. A long beam arced down and caught him full across the shoulders and head. The old man crumpled and fell. Timber and slate rained down around them, and choking dust and ash. Telghraan was battered to the floor.

As the noise died away, he slowly raised his head again. His legs were pinned by fallen timbers, and the stench of seared flesh seeped through the bitter ash. Iorlaas' body was all but hidden beneath the ruins.

He raised his head further, painfully, squinting through the reek. Sollonaal stood just beyond the open doorway, staring back at him with a look of utter hatred.

And then Sollonaal spoke one word and flame blossomed all around Telghraan, and overwhelmed him.

[illegible]

[illegible] the first time [illegible]

[illegible]

[illegible] and pressed [illegible]

[illegible] There was [illegible]

[illegible] which [illegible]

[illegible] the [illegible] had been [illegible]

[illegible] have done something [illegible]

[illegible] eyes, and [illegible]

[illegible] could make out half a dozen [illegible] more [illegible] of [illegible]

[illegible]

[illegible]

[illegible] the old man [illegible]

[illegible]

[illegible]

[illegible]

Chapter Five

Hrugaar was up on the west landing when he heard the noise. He had carved his way south from the Seaward Tower, bringing ice and sleet to kill the fire as he went. This upper floor held the sleeping quarters for the lesser priests and novices of the school, but by the grace of the gods he had found no sign that any had been left trapped here. The southern part of the landing and the great well of the west stair were still damp and clouded with steam, which upheld his earlier guess that one or other of the priests must have brought water here through their arts to clear a way out.

When Hrugaar heard the crash, he guessed at once that part of the building must have fallen. He iced the last of the flames nearby and set off at a run.

As he reached the top of the stair a high pitched scream echoed up to greet him – a death shriek, if ever he had heard one. He took the stair two steps at a time, sure footed even on the puddled treads, and leaping down half the second flight into the hallway below.

The passage was filled with flame, but the doorway at the far end was wide open, revealing the jumbled ruin of what had once been the minstrels' gallery of the dining hall. Amid the fallen beams and rubble, he thought that he could glimpse part of a black robed body burning. He thought at once of Dhûghaúr.

Hrugaar sped through the fire and out across the piled debris beyond, heedless of his own peril. Heavy rain leaped down to meet him from the open sky overhead, and the timbers hissed beneath his feet as the flames guttered and died.

He knew that he was too late. Fire had withered and seared the broken body, and the charred robes were turning to paste beneath the rain. The agony of death still shivered on the air. Yet as he crouched down among the wreckage, he felt a stirring of sudden doubt – or stubborn hope. Some instinct told him that this could not be Dhûghaúr.

'Hrugaar?'

He dragged his gaze away, and looked up. Lïall of Solaní was clambering toward him across the ruin, keeping close in to the northern wall. And then Hrugaar caught sight of a second figure standing in the doorway beyond, clad in robes of blue-green and flickering gold.

'Sollonaal!' he cried, not knowing whether he was surprised, or shocked, or simply furious. What in all the hells of the *Vashtar* was he doing here?

Sollonaal ignored him. He seemed to be staring past them, lowering his hands palms down in the closing gesture of a spell. The glare from the burning passage died away, and they were plunged into shadow. The dining hall was filled with smoke and steam, lit with a ruddy glow from below.

'Sollonaal!' Hrugaar cried again. 'Is this—'

He could not finish, could not say the name. Sollonaal looked back at him, as if noticing him for the first time.

'Iorlaas,' he answered hoarsely. 'The roof.' He gestured toward where Lïall was cursing in the darkness.

Hrugaar thought that he understood, and his heart sank within him. This body was too slight to have been Iorlaas. The Prime Councillor must have fallen nearby. But Iorlaas had been with Dhûghaúr.

He moved to help Lïall, flinging light like sea spray in the air around them. Iorlaas was half buried no more than three steps away. His dark green robes had escaped the worst of the fire, but Hrugaar needed no special gifts to tell him that they were too late. The Prime Councillor of All Magi was already dead.

'Did you find Rinnir?' Lïall asked him. He was clearing away the smaller lengths of timber with boots and gloved hands before trying to shift the huge beam across Iorlaas' back.

'Too late,' Hrugaar said aloud.

Lïall paused for a moment, then went on with his work.

'The other priests have started to arrive,' he said. 'They brought the rain.'

Hrugaar rested one hand on his shoulder, signalling him to stop. 'Too late,' he said again, gently.

He looked toward Sollonaal. The older mage was still standing in the doorway, his face pale and shocked in Hrugaar's light.

'Were you here?' he asked him.

Sollonaal nodded once. 'Telghraan brought us.'

Hrugaar finally understood. The ruined body behind him had been Telghraan, not Dhûghaúr. A wave of relief flooded through him, and then a sting of guilt and sorrow for Telghraan.

'Where is Dhûghaúr?' he demanded.

'Down below, somewhere,' said Sollonaal vaguely. 'Councillor Eralaan is with him. We came to do what we could.'

The High Council was shocked by Iorlaas' death, when they heard the news early the next morning; though less so, perhaps, than by the events surrounding it. They mourned also the frail High Councillor Maëghlar, who had fallen giving his last strength in the defence of the shrine of Maësta. The priestess Bromaer had said that he had died of a broken heart. The death of Mage Councillor Telghraan was noted with sorrow, though of those who attended perhaps only Rhysana and Hrugaar felt much sense of personal loss.

Hrugaar was there because Rhysana had asked him to be, as witness to what had happened. She felt rather sorry for him, sitting all alone beside the empty Prime Councillor's seat on the west side of the great assembly chamber, with seven members of the High Council – just over half of their remaining number – arranged in an arc around the eastern half. The Prime Councillor's chair was not singled out with a golden glow of power, as it had been after Herusen's death; but the early morning sunlight slanted down through the crystal dome overhead to bathe the white marble wall on that side of the chamber in summer glory, while the high councillors themselves sat in rainbow-flecked shadow.

The Archmage Ellen was enthroned in her accustomed High Council seat in the north, with Sollonaal facing her in the south. Rhysana herself was almost directly opposite Hrugaar, sitting just to the left of the ebon doors that faced the Prime Councillor's seat. The Archmage Morvaan and Asharka of Braedun were further round to her left, and High Councillors Lirinal of Dregharis and Ekraan of Eädhan to her right. The reclusive Ekraan, she knew, was only here because Morvaan had dragged him here. She guessed that Lirinal had come because Sollonaal had need of him – both because he was the only other Ellanguan mage on the High Council, and because he was the only other *Vashta* mage present apart from Sollonaal himself.

The main burden of the tidings had been known to all of them save Asharka before the meeting began. Hrugaar had come to find Rhysana in the College library soon after dawn, and then gone back to her apartment where they had been joined by Ellen and Morvaan for breakfast. Being thus forewarned, though hardly prepared, they had at least had time to draw breath before wrestling with the practicalities of the situation.

The events of the night before had not ended with Iorlaas' death. By the time that the priests of Kelmaar had brought the fire under control, there had been fighting and turmoil in the city streets outside the school. The city guard had been called out, and warriors of both *Aeshta* and *Vashta* Orders had tried to calm the fray; and then the palace guard had arrived, strengthened with Souther warriors from the household of Ambassador T'Loi. By dawn the Lord Steward Rinnekh had placed all of Ellanguan city under full curfew and martial law. High Councillor Lirinal had been up half the night dealing with frightened and angry merchants. Sollonaal himself looked bone weary.

'It does beg the question,' he said, turning to Hrugaar, 'what the late Prime Councillor was doing at the Kelmaar School in the first place. Can you enlighten us?'

'He had heard your report on how the tides in Ellanguan were flowing,' Hrugaar answered. 'He might be forgiven, I think, for wanting to hear what tale Kelmaar had to tell.'

'You are not here to think, Councillor,' Sollonaal told him. 'You are here to relate the facts as you know them.'

'And what did Kelmaar have to say?' asked High Councillor Lirinal.

'We had not much time, ere the fire was discovered,' Hrugaar answered truthfully. 'They said that they were worried at how often there were magi to be seen within the Steward's palace.'

He had told Rhysana over the breakfast table about the Souther woman Mijal, and together with Ellen and Morvaan they had agreed not to mention her at this meeting for fear of alerting Sollonaal to her presence in Ellanguan. The Archmage Ellen had objected that the High Council should still be told at some point; but Rhysana had sided with Hrugaar in keeping the matter secret a while longer. If Sollonaal was as much in thrall to Rinnekh as they now suspected, it would only serve to cause more trouble.

'Of course we are often in the palace,' Sollonaal replied with strained patience. 'This High Council needs no reminding of the delicate balance between rival powers in the city of Ellanguan, in particular with the continuing presence of the Southers in our midst; and there has been even greater wariness of our own Order of late, as rumours spread of our achievements during the siege of Arrandin. Since the Emperor himself distrusts us, we have had to work doubly hard to keep the favour of his beloved Rinnekh. And I may add that it is partly through our own labours that the Merchants' Guild and the *Vashta* Orders have now also reached some measure of understanding with our Souther visitors – enough, at least, to hold their peace. It is the stubbornness of the *Aeshta* Orders that continues to prove our greatest difficulty, as has been shown by the unfortunate events of this past night.'

'Perhaps it might have helped had you had more *Aeshta* magi on your staff,' said Ekraan pointedly; 'or taken better care of the ones you had.'

'And Councillors Dalzhaúr and Radhraan were only sent to the Ellanguan College to cover until the end of last term,' put in Asharka, waving her hand distractedly for Sollonaal to be quiet. 'They will no doubt wish to be returning to their own students in Arrandin. While I appreciate that the Prime Councillor was preparing for the coming Court – which sadly he will never see – the whole question of the staffing of the four Colleges is something that we must address as soon as possible. With the losses we have suffered over the past few months, it is vital that we take thought for the training of the next generation of magi.'

'I have two journeymen now awaiting their trials to join the Council,' Ekraan agreed.

'Councillor Radhraan, for one, has welcomed the opportunity to work with us in Ellanguan,' said Sollonaal. 'Given the shortage of magi willing to teach, perhaps we should consider keeping the Arrandin College closed for the time being.'

'One might argue that the Ellanguan College should close, given the turmoil in the city,' Ellen countered. 'There is far greater risk to the students there.'

'But the next term is still a good while away,' said Sollonaal, ignoring her. 'Ellanguan is being held at sword's point as we speak, and the Summer Court begins today. We must keep our sense of perspective.'

Hrugaar looked as if he was about to laugh. Rhysana stepped in hurriedly.

'What else do we know of how the fire started?' she asked.

Hrugaar cleared his throat. 'It seems to have begun down in the stores in the southwest part of the school,' he answered. 'One of the knights who found the fire says that he fought with a Souther nearby.'

'With respect,' Sollonaal sneered, 'that is just what he would say. But it was at night, and presumably he was one and alone. He might have fought anyone in the dark, and then assumed it must have been a Souther.

'It should be noted,' he added, sweeping his gaze around the assembly chamber to press the point, 'that no other intruders were found in the school, aside from this one brief incident.'

'I have no reason to doubt the one who told me,' said Hrugaar.

'You said that there were creatures of Fire that caused the burning,' said Asharka. 'Can you tell us more of those, Hrugaar, or whence they might have come?'

'They were like fire gone wild, shaping itself to human form,' he replied. 'I have not met the like before. Councillor Dhûghaúr said that the Prime Councillor thought that they were like the fiery warriors of Fraërigr – though Dhûghaúr himself did not wholly agree. The priests of Kelmaar believe that someone came in to the school and summoned them there; and then fled before they could be taken.'

'Which might suggest that Southers or Easterners were behind it,' Morvaan pointed out.

It had been the dark of the moon, the night when they had feared that the servants of Lo-Khuma might move again. What they might have hoped to gain from an attack on the Kelmaar School – apart from the chaos it had caused in Ellanguan – Rhysana had not yet managed to fathom.

'Or a *Vashta* priest of War,' Hrugaar added, 'if Iorlaas was right about the fiery warrior.'

Sollonaal thumped his fist down upon his knee, his face tight with anger. 'That is precisely the kind of thoughtless remark that precipitates bloodshed in the streets of Ellanguan,' he fumed.

'Though I trust,' said Ellen, 'that we of the High Council at least have the wisdom to consider the possibility in light of the facts available to us.'

Sollonaal visibly reined in his temper, and favoured her with a curt nod.

'Councillor Hrugaar,' he said, 'the late Prime Councillor – as some of those here present – may have been willing to indulge your wayward tongue. It might even be that it amused him. But I would remind you that the next Prime Councillor may be less favourably disposed to accept such lack of regard from his Council Secretary.'

Hrugaar stared back at him, his fair face serene and untroubled in the morning sunlight.

'And who is to be the next Prime Councillor?' asked Lirinal.

The Archmage Morvaan sighed. 'That is another matter which should be resolved quickly, with the Summer Court at hand,' he said. 'There is also the question of the admission of two more mage councillors to the High Council, which I have mentioned before.'

Rhysana smiled to herself. One of the two candidates was Hrugaar himself, which was why Morvaan did not name them now. The other was her husband Torkhaal. To Rhysana's mind, both would bring a welcome breath of fresh air to the stuffiness of the older Council. But both were *Aeshta* magi, which would push the *Vashta* magi on the High Council even further into the minority.

'To be fair,' said Ekraan, 'perhaps that should wait until after the election of the next Prime Councillor.'

'As Prime Councillor of the Ellanguan Magi,' said Sollonaal, 'I am willing to stand in again as deputy until that election is made. But in truth, I see no reason for any great delay. Given the briefness of Iorlaas' tenure, and the reasons put forward that determined his election, I would suggest that I am the obvious choice for his successor.'

'The nominations must still be made before the greater Council,' said Ellen.

'They debated the matter at length, less than a month since,' Sollonaal objected.

'But the situation has changed,' said Morvaan. 'Besides, a general assembly was set for this afternoon, before the Court opens, so we shall not have too long to wait. And by that time it is to be hoped that we may send word to other magi, urging them to attend. High Councillor Ferghaal, in particular, I should like to be here. His insight into the dealings between the Southers and the Braedun Order may prove important.'

'Ferghaal was coming anyway,' Asharka confirmed.

'In the meantime,' Morvaan added, 'I think that a few hours' rest might do our Ellanguan members no harm.'

The meeting came to an end and the magi stood up. Rhysana waited for Ellen and Hrugaar to join her, idly studying the twin carved eagles of her misericord seat to avoid having to speak to anyone else as they came across the patterned floor. She had half hoped that Morvaan would also join them; but he had already warned her at breakfast that he had much to do that morning, and he went away with Trialmaster Ekraan.

The shadowed lobby was deserted when the three of them went out through the ebon doors. Rhysana looked around, wondering whether they might still be overheard.

'Come back with me for a moment,' she offered, 'before you go to rest.'

Ellen gave her a knowing look.

'Who said that I was going to rest?' Hrugaar teased.

'I did,' she said, holding out her hands.

She took them in her *leap* to the small landing outside her apartment and led the way through into the living chamber. Torkhaal had taken Taillan out to play before the day grew too hot. Rhysana clapped her hands to summon the *chaedar* and ordered chilled cordial for them all.

'You are planning something,' said Hrugaar. 'I can tell.'

'Perhaps,' she allowed. 'I need to borrow the Prime Councillor's white steel rod of office. Can you find it for me?'

'What?' Hrugaar cried. For once, she had the rare pleasure of seeing him wholly surprised.

'Only for tonight,' she assured him. 'The Archmage Ellen knows all about it. You could bring it to me here later this afternoon, after the assembly.'

Hrugaar eyed the two women doubtfully, and then grinned.

'Perhaps,' he said. 'If I may play a part in whatever you plan to do.'

'I promised Torkhaal no less,' Rhysana told him. 'That is another reason why you need to get some rest.'

'And what is it that we are to do?'

Rhysana hesitated. If she told him of Whitespear Head now, Hrugaar would ply her with many questions and his inquisitive mind would never let him get to sleep; and he had the ordeal of the Council assembly ahead of him, with Sollonaal acting as Prime Councillor. For his sake, she might have considered waiting another day. But with the opening ball of the Court at the imperial palace that evening, it was her best chance of getting in to Illana's fortress while the attention of the Archmage Merrech was distracted elsewhere. The dreadful turn of events in Ellanguan had only served to increase her sense of urgency.

Ellen came to her rescue.

'Hopefully little enough,' she told Hrugaar, 'except to serve as moral support for Rhysana. Bring the rod here, safely and secretly, and then you shall find out.'

'Yes, Archmage,' he said humbly, giving her a bobbing bow. He turned slowly, as though reluctant to go.

'Shall you try to summon the dragon?' he asked over his shoulder.

'Dear gods, no,' Ellen exclaimed.

Hrugaar was still lingering. Rhysana smiled.

'Stay and have your drink,' she told him. 'You can sleep here, if you like – though Taillan may not give you much peace.'

'The guest chambers across the cloister would be quieter,' Ellen agreed.

Hrugaar went back to the long table, and took one of the tumblers that the *chaedar* had brought in. He handed another to Ellen.

'I would rather not return to Ellanguan just yet,' he admitted. 'I doubt that I could rest there now.'

The Emperor Rhydden was in one of his better moods as he climbed the broad stair to his own apartment. Given the number of problems that had already arisen that morning, his continuing good humour surprised even his imperial self.

He had just come from a minor battle of wits with Karlena of Dortrean. The Countess had intercepted him on his visit to the Empress' tower, informing him that Grinnaer was not well enough to see him, nor would she be attending the formal opening of the Court that evening. Karlena herself would oversee the final preparations for the feast on Grinnaer's behalf. Rhydden had returned a suitable volley of arguments, which she had dismissed with confident ease. These were matters in which the Emperor for once would not have his own way.

He should have married Karlena years ago. Though as Empress Consort she might have led half a dozen rebellions against him, she would have made a far worthier sparring partner than the feeble Grinnaer.

Then there was the latest turn of events in Ellanguan, of which even Karlena had not yet heard – or if she had, she had made no mention of it. The early reports from that city were not quite what Rhydden had expected. But he comforted himself that as the news began to spread it would draw attention well away from other happenings of the night before.

The memory surfaced briefly in his mind – the flare of golden power as Merrech had fastened the Easterner necklace about Rhydden's throat, and the hungry faces of Lord Drômagh and the War priest Môrghran of Fâghsul. He could still feel the echo of the inhuman strength that had surged in answer through his limbs, and still taste the boy's blood upon his lips.

Rinnekh had told him the rumours of what Môrghran did with the dead bodies of little boys, after the unholy rites were ended. The Emperor did not greatly care, as long as the man remained loyal.

His guard escort halted on the landing at the head of the stair, and Rhydden passed alone through the golden panelled doors. The Archmage Merrech was waiting for him in the squared white chamber beyond – a ghostly figure in robes of silver-grey, lurking in the pale shadows beneath the high western windows.

'Does our Lord Steward retain the upper hand in Ellanguan?' Rhydden asked, as the doors closed behind him.

'He does, Sire,' Merrech answered. 'Ambassador T'Loi has been obliged to place many of his own countrymen under guard, to help keep the peace within the city. Perhaps he might now be persuaded of the wisdom of sending some away.'

'Yet you believe otherwise.'

The Archmage spread his arms in a brief, open gesture. 'His Highness knows my thoughts on T'Loi.'

'It is not a situation we wish to last for long.' Rhydden mounted the low dais and draped himself casually in his gilded throne. 'Our Rinnekh will persuade him.'

'So it is to be hoped, Sire,' said Merrech, bowing his hooded head. 'We still do not know where the God-King himself stands on the question of war.'

The Emperor frowned. 'Yes,' he said. 'The K'tarim may perhaps serve us the better against the Easterners. Have our agents among them now reached the Braedun *commanderie*?'

'Those who count.' The Archmage traced one finger across the chequered round of the *sherunuresh* table beside him, and picked up one of the pieces. 'And His Highness now has the advantage.'

'Yes,' Rhydden said again. His hand strayed to the base of his throat. It felt strangely empty without the necklace there, as though part of himself were missing. 'The Master is now bound to our cause, and the Easterners must bow before us. It is a war they can not hope to win.'

'Yet still he is the Master,' Merrech warned. 'The power that binds will grow as the moon nears the full, and wane as she nears the dark; and he will seek by any means to break it. His Highness must weigh the limits of his own strength.'

'We have been through this before,' said Rhydden irritably. 'I must wait until the full moon before I make demand upon him.'

'And perhaps another moon, or more,' said Merrech. 'The Easterners are not yet here, and the strength of the *Aeshta* Orders is not yet broken.'

'The Orders are too weak,' Rhydden scoffed. 'They have not the strength to resist the great demon here in the waking world, not even with the Crown of Ferrughôr to help them.'

'If that was ever made, save in legend,' said the Archmage.

'It was made,' said Rhydden. 'The rulers of Lautun remember it, even after fifteen hundred years. With the necklace *and* the Crown, our command would be assured.'

'Yet no record of it has been found.'

The Emperor smiled dangerously. There had been that business with the librarian in Ellanguan a few years ago, though nothing had been found on him when he was taken. Rinnekh and his allies among the Magi were still searching in the Book Halls there.

'Your new Prime Councillor has gone,' he said aloud, changing direction. 'Will Sollonaal succeed him, do you think?'

'Perhaps,' Merrech allowed. 'There is to be an assembly this afternoon. We shall have to consider what he says in the debate.'

'And who will stand against him?'

The hooded Archmage returned the playing piece to the board. 'That, Sire,' he purred, 'is the more interesting question.'

* * *

The Archmage Ellen stayed long enough to finish her cordial, and then went away on business of her own. Rhysana packed Hrugaar off to bed, and he was soon deeply asleep. Then she settled down by the open casement window with the small codex the Warden had given to her, until her husband and son returned.

She spent the rest of the morning quietly with Taillan, while Torkhaal worked in the library; and then the three of them made the *leap* to the imperial citadel on the far shore of the river estuary, to visit her brother and his family in the Telún apartment there.

The long hallways of the river wing were already busy, with liveried attendants in the colours of many of the Houses Noble dashing hither and thither on various errands. A few of the nobles themselves drifted in the shadier parts of the enclosed garden of the old summer palace which lay beyond, bright as flowers in their finery; but most seemed to have withdrawn to the coolness of the loftier galleries or their own apartments to escape the heat of the day. If news of the latest troubles in Ellanguan had reached the citadel, it did not appear to have clouded the mood overmuch. Rhysana's brother Lavan had heard nothing.

They had their noon meal together on the balcony of the Telún apartment, looking out across the White River estuary, though it turned out to be more of an informal picnic. Rhysana sat with Nereïs and the two smaller children in the green shade of the hanging creepers, persuading Taillan not to pull Maïa's pretty golden curls, and Maïa not to punch him. Torkhaal was stretched full length on a rug with the twins Khyrfan and Mâghan – dark haired like their father, and growing taller by the day as they raced through their twelfth year – taking them both on in a game of *sherunuresh*. Lavan himself sat on the balcony parapet, surveying his family and the glorious summer day around him with obvious contentment as he sipped his pale wine. The worries of the world outside were not permitted to spoil the moment.

As the second hour of the afternoon approached, Torkhaal and Rhysana made the *leap* back to their College chambers, leaving Taillan in Nereïs' capable hands. Hrugaar was still sleeping peacefully as a baby. Rhysana left Torkhaal to wake him, and went through into the bathroom to wash and dress herself in her formal indigo robes, with the double sash of the High Council and a single black sash of mourning for their dead colleagues. Then she went out into the living chamber to let the menfolk ready themselves, while she turned her thoughts to focus on the coming assembly.

Before long they came out to join her. Hrugaar had changed his grey clothes for a set of black councillor's robes borrowed from Torkhaal; and with his silver fair hair and fine features, he looked far more handsome than he had any right to be. Her husband was in his familiar robes of darkest green, immaculate as ever. She made a show of pretending to remove a stray ebon hair from his shoulder.

'I suppose that will have to do,' she sighed; and then flashed them a mischievous half smile.

Hrugaar excused himself and went away, saying that he would meet them in the assembly chamber. Torkhaal took Rhysana by the hand and led her to one of the casement windows, where they could look down into the cloister garden.

'Ru tells me that you and Ellen asked him for the Prime Councillor's white steel rod,' he said quietly.

Rhysana felt her cheeks flushing with guilt. 'I do not want an argument,' she said.

'I am not arguing – yet,' he returned. 'I thought that you might have told me.'

'You were out with Taillan when we came back,' she explained, 'and you saw how much Ru needed to sleep. And I did not tell you this morning because I did not want to spoil your day.'

Torkhaal laughed uneasily. 'There are riots in Ellanguan, the new Prime Councillor is dead, Telghraan is dead, and now we shall have the whole assembly squabbling about it before we go on to the joys of Rhydden's Court. How in the world could you spoil my day?'

'You worry about my going.'

'Of course.' He held her closer to him – perhaps too close for comfort.

'We have been through this before,' she said, drawing away a little, but taking both his hands in her own so that he would not feel shut out. 'Ru and Ellen will be with me – and Morvaan too, if I may persuade him. They are Water, Earth and Fire, and I am Air. Together the gods will protect us. And Taillan needs you here – I need you to be here. I shall find it easier to focus if I know that you and he are safe together.'

'I know all of this,' Torkhaal growled. 'But I am still allowed to worry. When shall you go?'

Rhysana relaxed, and smiled. 'Later this afternoon, I think,' she told him; 'once the assembly is over and everyone has gone to the opening ball. If you are there, people will assume that I have stayed behind with the boy.'

'So you want me to lie for you?'

'No,' said Rhysana. 'You can just tell them that I am not there tonight, but hope to be at the palace either tomorrow or the day after. Not that anyone will care that much anyway, I expect.'

Torkhaal lifted one hand to stroke her cheek.

'Rubbish,' he grinned. 'Now is there anything that you need to warn me about before we go up to the assembly?'

'Not really,' she said. 'You know as much about the tidings from Ellanguan as do I. We shall have to think about candidates for the next Prime Councillor – though Sollonaal seems to think that he will be the likeliest choice.'

'Again.' Torkhaal pulled a face.

'Then there will be the naming of Council delegates who are to attend the Summer Court,' Rhysana went on.

'Why do I feel that we could write the assembly report without even being there?'

'Perhaps,' she allowed. 'But there may be more news from

Ellanguan. And besides, Ru needs our support. It is not easy to keep order in the assembly at the best of times, without having Sollonaal trying to lord it over him as our next Prime Councillor Elect.'

Erkal Dortrean shielded his eyes from the brightness of the afternoon, watching as the small rowboat slid alongside below. The Braedun sailors lowered a rope ladder for the Souther captain to come aboard.

They had left the open sea a few hours before, and were making their way up the long race of the Galloppi River estuary against the pull of the ebbing tide. The two great Souther warships with their tiered banks of oars had now drawn several lengths ahead, and the steady beat of their drums rolled back like a challenge across the water.

'Perhaps he is going to offer to tow us,' muttered Father Dharagh.

Erkal shook his head. 'He may want to know where to put ashore.'

His gaze strayed back to the nearer of the two warships, whence the Captain's rowboat had come. A man's body hung half naked there, swinging on a rope from the yard of the forward mast. Erkal had seen him being hauled up by the wrists, barely an hour since. From the looks of it, the man had already been dead or senseless by that time.

Kierran of Arrand stumbled across the deck to join them. 'Are we going ashore?' he asked hopefully.

Kierran, Erkal thought, had proved to be a better sailor than most of his family; which meant that he had ventured out from their shared cabin after only two days at sea – though he had yet to find his legs properly – and he had only been sick once that morning. The *noghr* priest Dharagh had also taken to the water far better than the Earl had hoped. There had been some teasing from the crew on the first day out from Ellanguan, when one of the younger priests on board had offered to cushion him on a cloud of air to allay the effects of the sea swell. The *noghr* had had his revenge the next morning, when he had kindled the holy fire of Hýriel upon the deck to observe the dawn rite. Of course, no harm had been done to the ship, and Erkal had managed to smooth over the incident; after which the dwarf seemed to have earned the friendship and respect of the crew, and instilled a healthy amount of terror into them to boot.

'Their ships are too large to go all the way upriver,' explained the priestess Hannaï of Braedun. 'They will make harbour at Neridh, at the head of the estuary, and the shipwrights there will help them to repair the last of their damage. All this has been explained to them. The warriors they carry will then make the march overland to reach the *commanderie*. Since the village of Neridh is on Linnaer lands, the Lord Linnaer has agreed to provide an escort to guide them.'

'And do we march with them?' asked Kierran.

'I had understood that you were to sail with us all the way to the *commanderie*,' Hannaï answered, before Erkal could speak. 'The journey on foot would delay your arrival by another day.'

Kierran looked at Erkal, but the Earl avoided his gaze. Though well past her three score years, Hannaï was Weathermaster for the Braedun ship and their official escort to the *commanderie*. She it was who had kept them abreast of the news from her Order – of the recent events in Ellanguan, and of the death of Kierran's father The Arrand, and of what was passing at the *commanderie* ahead of them – so far as the senior priests had informed her. Erkal did not wish to offend the Lords of Braedun by delaying his arrival any further, nor did he wish to impose upon Hannaï by obliging her to make the longer journey overland. But it had occurred to him that perhaps they ought to go ashore at Neridh, to keep a weather eye on the marching Souther warriors.

'Is the *commanderie* much farther?' Kierran asked.

'Less than a day away,' Hannaï assured him. 'The river journey will be easier on your stomach than the sea. And the tide will be turning soon, which will help.'

Whatever Kierran said next was lost with the commotion of the Southers coming aboard. The Captain arrived first, rolling over the side rail to land lightly on his feet. He was clad in a panelled ochre coat over black breeches and sea boots, and his thick grizzled hair had been brushed and tied back neatly for this meeting. Erkal knew him as A'lil, a lesser commander of the K'tarim fleet, whom he had met on two or three occasions in the company of the Souther Ambassador T'Loi. Behind him came two men, clad in similar garb and with long knives slung from their belts, who were clearly his personal guards.

The Southers bowed first to Erkal, and then to Kierran and Dharagh; and then A'lil alone gave a further bow to the priestess Hannaï. She nodded in return, but did not smile.

'Gracious Lord,' said A'lil, addressing Erkal in the language of the God-King's Court. 'We are soon to make harbour and send our armies overland, but there is danger of which you should know. May we speak freely here?'

'You may,' Erkal answered carefully, in the same tongue. 'Though my friends will understand little of your words, if you choose the beautiful language of the Su'lorim.'

Kierran looked as though he had understood nothing at all. The face of Hannaï was unreadable.

A'lil smiled broadly, and bowed in apology. 'Your pardon,' he said, changing to the everyday tongue of Lautun. 'The danger is this. We have found a spy on our ship, sent by our enemies in the Court of the God-King Among Us.' He raised one hand to his forehead briefly in homage.

'The one who now hangs from the mast?' asked Erkal, nodding toward A'lil's ship.

'Even so,' the Captain smiled. 'He was whipped until dead, while all watched, and now his body will feed the birds.'

'If he was already dead, why hang him?' asked Father Dharagh.

'It is our custom,' said A'lil. 'Among other things, it is – a lesson, for other men. This man was a spy, sent to kill. He thought to break the peace between our peoples, and to take the life of your Lord of Dortrean if he could.'

'You are sure of this?' demanded Hannaï.

'We do not doubt your word,' said Erkal swiftly, as the stormclouds gathered in A'lil's face. 'We give you thanks that this danger is now past.'

The Captain glared at Hannaï, but then forced a smile and bowed to the Earl in acceptance.

'One man is dead,' he said. 'We fear there may be others. On board my own ship I can keep command, and you are our ally. On land, others will command. New danger may arise. The Lord of Dortrean is wise and brave in heart, and much honoured among our people. But at this time I would advise him not to go ashore, but to sail on up the river – for his own safety, and for the good of both our peoples.'

A'lil bowed and smiled again. The Earl nodded in return. 'We were just speaking of this before you came,' he said.

It struck Erkal that the finding of the spy was more than timely; and that A'lil – or someone using him – might have other reasons for not wanting him to accompany the Souther warriors on their march.

He looked out across the water to the shadowed moorland cliffs of Galsin, and then north to the gentler orchard hills of the Linnaer shore. The village of Neridh was still some miles ahead, around a bend in the river, and whatever ships were there were hidden from view. The fishing boats and smaller craft that he could see were all huddled close in their own village harbours, and they had passed only one merchant ship in the open waters of the estuary. The Lord Linnaer, Erkal remembered, had sent few men to the siege of Arrandin, having been more concerned with the defence of this very coast against Souther attack. It thus seemed likely that he would provide strength enough to keep the Southers under control while they marched east toward the *commanderie*. Erkal's own presence might only serve to provoke conflict rather than to discourage it, if – as A'lil believed – there were those who sought to change this new found peace by killing him, or by taking him hostage.

'The wisdom of Captain A'lil and the wisdom of the priestess of Braedun are both in agreement,' he said aloud. 'We shall see your ships safely in to harbour, and then sail on ahead to the *commanderie*.'

The Souther Captain bowed deeply, and Hannaï favoured him with a small smile. Erkal glanced at Kierran in apology. The young Lord stared back, his grey eyes unusually wide in his pale face, as though trying to tell him something. The Earl nodded quickly, understanding. Kierran had remembered their unseen visitors in the Steward's palace, on the eve of their departure from Ellanguan. The dead man hanging from the yard arm might have been one of them.

As the Southers made ready to depart, Erkal wondered privately whether A'lil had just rid him of an enemy, or of a friend.

Rhysana counted thirty-two other magi in the great assembly chamber when the ebon doors were shut – being just over two thirds of the surviving members of the Council, and scarcely one fourth of the number of misericord seats available.

Apart from the seven high councillors who had been there earlier that morning, three more of the remaining five had now joined them. High Councillor Ferghaal of Braedun was just to the north of the doors, his white hair and beard cropped so short that Rhysana had to look twice to recognise him. She thought that the style made him look younger, if a little more severe. The elegant Trialmaster Foghlaar was on the nearer side of the doors to her, occupying the High Council seat with the twin carved eagles that she had used earlier on, so that Rhysana was obliged to take the next High Council seat around toward the south. The Imperial Counsellor the Archmage Merrech lurked in the shadowed recess of his usual seat on the northwest arc of the chamber, directly across from where Rhysana herself now was. But he had been there before she had arrived with Torkhaal, and had so far made no attempt to acknowledge her presence.

Sollonaal had contrived to look rested and refreshed in his gorgeous robes of turquoise and gold. Rhysana realised with a shock that he had sat down in the west, rather than the south, in the one High Council seat between the Prime Councillor's and the Archmage Merrech. Hrugaar, as Council Secretary, was standing barely half a dozen paces to Sollonaal's right.

The white steel rod lay cushioned on the Prime Councillor's seat between them.

But although Sollonaal had thrust himself so close to Herusen's former place – or Iorlaas' place, Rhysana reminded herself – it was the Archmage Morvaan who performed the warding spell to seal the chamber. He did it so subtly that his casual gesture might have been no more than a signal for Hrugaar to begin; but every mage in the chamber should have noticed the ripple of sunlit power which flowed around the white marble walls, unless they had fallen asleep while waiting.

It fell to Hrugaar to make the formal announcement of Iorlaas' passing, and of the deaths of Maëghlar and Telghraan. He did so simply, looking unusually solemn and sad in his stark black robes. The silence that followed in the assembly chamber was remarkable.

He then went on to give a shortened account of the burning of the Kelmaar School, and why Prime Councillor Iorlaas had been there; and what he knew of the events that had followed thereafter. As he spoke, the silence around him turned to whispers and murmurings, and then to the unmistakable rumble that heralded a coming storm.

Sollonaal spoke next, giving the news of the city from that morning. As he related it, it seemed that Ellanguan had stayed peaceful under curfew and that the misunderstandings of the previous night were being smoothed away. But then Mage Councillor Drengriis pointed out that the inhabitants of the Kelmaar School had been obliged to remove themselves to the monastery of Sherunar in the north of the city, and that the school itself was now held secure by Souther warriors and members of the Steward's household guard. There had been an outcry from among the *Vashta* priesthoods – and others – that the priests of Kelmaar had summoned guardians from another Realm to defend the shrine of Maësta; and the rumour now ran from the palace to the temple precincts that the *Aeshta* Orders would soon be required by the Steward to remove themselves from the city altogether, or at least to keep their presence there to a minimum.

There was a predictable uproar from the assembly. Sollonaal held up his hands for peace, bellowing – out of turn – that it was no more than a frightened rumour. Most of the magi ignored him. Hrugaar had to stand up and move out on to the floor to restore some sense of order.

'Time was,' said old Irzael of Farran, when Hrugaar signalled for him to speak, 'that Kelmaar were the right arm of the Lords Steward of Ellanguan to keep the peace in the city.'

'Times change,' said the deep voiced Ghîlsaan of Telbray, who was sitting just to Asharka's right. 'The new Steward follows the imperial gods of his master.'

'Not all the *Vashta* Orders find favour with Rinnekh,' put in Councillor Dalzhaúr, one of the Arrandin lecturers who had been moved briefly to the Ellanguan College the previous term. He was sitting facing Ghîlsaan in the northwest, as a mage of Eörendin. 'The priests of Arts are less welcome in the palace than before, and their school is still being used by the Southers as a garrison.'

'How fares the bursar, the Lady Eonnaï?' Hrugaar asked him. Dalzhaúr shrugged in answer.

'There you may have it,' said Councillor Liertiis, the Junior Lecturer of the Lautun College. 'Perhaps the Lord Steward Rinnekh is more your problem than the Southers. I have not heard that Farran are having such problems.'

Hrugaar gestured quickly for High Councillor Ferghaal to speak, before the arguments could begin.

'Fellow magi,' said Ferghaal, holding his hands palm out on either side of his closely cropped head in the prescribed manner for speech, 'Farran is not quite the forgotten city, west of West, that some of our Ellanguan brethren might have it be. There are many Souther traders who sail our way, and that caused us problems enough of our own in the recent war. While it is true that for now the Lord Steward of Farran holds peace – and perhaps the better since the armies of the Emperor's muster were sent home – it is but an uneasy peace; and what passes in the east of the Six Kingdoms can still tip the balance either way.'

He went on to speak about Braedun, and the progress of the priests and knights as they moved out of their *commanderie* and the Souther warships sailed up the Galloppi River; and how resentment of the Southers' presence was growing all the way along the coast down from Ellanguan, and also in the city of Arrandin.

'I must say,' ventured Kharfaal of Vaulun when Ferghaal paused, 'that this question of your *commanderie* strikes me as being somewhat sour grapes. The Braedun Order also has houses in Ellanguan and Lautun, Farran and Telbray, a temple in Arrandin and the monastery isle beyond the Shining Hills. Surely it can bear the small sacrifice of this one estate for the duration?'

'Would Vaulun suffer one of their palaces to be used by the Southers?' countered Hrugaar.

'For a year, and if the defence of the Empire required it, yes,' Kharfaal nodded.

'But you would negotiate with the Emperor to charge them for the lease,' put in High Councillor Lirinal.

Kharfaal smiled. 'Of course.'

A handful of the magi laughed. Rhysana found herself hating them.

'All this is beside the point,' scowled Ranzhaar of Stanva. 'The priests of Kelmaar believe that the Southers were responsible for the burning of their school, and indeed for summoning creatures of Fire to do so; and now Souther troops have a say in the control of Ellanguan city. Such summonings are proscribed by this Council, and it is our duty to call them to account.'

'One of our own Colleges could be next,' someone called out.

Rhysana was startled by the tide of feeling let loose by Ranzhaar's words, even though the warning signs had been there. Everyone seemed to be talking or shouting at once, and more than a dozen hands were signalling, vying for the right to speak. Hrugaar stood on the floor with his arms outstretched, calmly waiting for the storm to subside. As the magi quietened down, Sollonaal raised his hands to address the assembly. Hrugaar overruled him in favour of the Archmage Merrech.

The chamber was suddenly silent. Merrech raised his long pale hands on either side of his hooded head, as though savouring the moment.

'If Kelmaar believe,' he purred, 'that the Southers are responsible for the summoning – and this Council has no cause to doubt their word – then that is a serious charge. It behoves us to act. It is no longer a question of rival faith, or of the political needs of the Empire, but of a use of power which is against our precepts and which falls within our jurisdiction to reprehend.'

There were several murmurs around the chamber, but all were tense, subdued. Though many might have agreed with Merrech, their deep wariness of his loyalty to the Emperor gave them cause for doubt.

Watch the reactions, came Morvaan's voice in Rhysana's mind. He tucked a half eaten pastry away in the pocket of his grey robes, and leaned forward in his seat to speak.

'I need hardly remind this Council,' he said aloud, 'that the Souther empire is vast, with many lands and peoples. We are told that T'Loi was not among those rulers who allied themselves with the Easterners; and there have been other tragic events in Ellanguan, and elsewhere, in recent months, for which he and his people can not be held wholly to blame. Though one or more Southers may have been responsible for the attack on the Kelmaar School, their purpose may be at odds with that of their fellow countrymen who are here to help defend us.'

'But T'Loi must answer for them, as Ambassador,' said Irzael.

Morvaan nodded. 'Last night was the dark of the moon – a time when the servants of the ancient Enemy grow stronger. Only a month ago, as the moon neared the dark, the Easterners were on the brink of taking Arrandin in the demon captain's name. Those who were there saw the fiery demons that they summoned. We must consider the very real possibility that this attack on an *Aeshta* Order has far deeper resonance than one more petty stroke in the current politics of Ellanguan.'

Rhysana found it difficult to gauge the mood of the assembly as he spoke; or at least, to read anything there beyond the predictable. The *Aeshta* magi, in particular those who had been with them in Arrandin, were clearly on the alert, and most of them seemed to have considered the thought already. The *Vashta* magi, who counted for more than a third of those present, ranged from disdain or unease to apparent boredom. There was no great outcry, as there had been earlier. She wondered whether Merrech's intervention had put them all on their guard.

'It is good to see that the spirit of dear High Councillor Maëghlar lives on,' said Sollonaal, 'though I think that the Archmage overstates the case. Councillor Hrugaar, you would not say that the creature that you fought was a demon?'

'I should not have named it so,' Hrugaar allowed.

'Prime Councillor Iorlaas thought that it was a warrior of Fraërigr,' put in Dhûghaúr. 'But I think that he was mistaken.'

There were angry murmurs from both *Aeshta* and *Vashta* magi around the chamber.

'I myself saw no creatures while I was with him,' said

Sollonaal; 'and the flames that I quenched were but normal fire.'

'The priests of the *Vashtar* believe that the *Aeshtar* are demons,' said Ranzhaar of Stanva. 'Perhaps then they would perceive our enemies as friends?'

'Are you saying that the priests of War are responsible then?' challenged Eralaan, his bald pate reddening with fury.

'In Telbray it is rumoured that Iorlaas' death was part of an *Aeshta* plot,' said Councilor Stellaas.

Rumoured by the priestess Kaïra, no doubt, Foghlaar sent mind to mind for those in the High Council seats. The Reverend Mother Kaïra, High Priestess of Serbramel in the city of Telbray, was notoriously outspoken in her hatred of the *Aeshta* faith – though there had been little enough love lost between her and Iorlaas while he had been alive.

Rhysana half heard them, being more intent on watching Hrugaar. He had turned his back to her, facing Sollonaal, and stood very still.

'You were with him,' he said quietly to Sollonaal – though the acoustics of the chamber carried his words to Rhysana's listening ears.

'Of course,' Sollonaal replied.

'Iorlaas escaped the flames,' said Hrugaar. 'Why not Telghraan?'

'Why not Rinnir?' Sollonaal countered.

Leave it, Sollonaal! She flung the thought at him. From their reactions, the rest of the High Council must have heard her.

'Councillors, please,' commanded the Archmage Ellen. The magi fell quiet almost at once. Hrugaar turned and bowed to her in apology.

'As Mage Councillor Dhûghaúr of Moraan has reminded us,' Ellen went on, 'the late Prime Councillor took an interest in the welfare of the *Aeshta* Orders, though he himself followed another faith. Now the Summer Court is upon us, and Ellanguan is in as much of a mess as ever, and Iorlaas is gone. While I regret the unseemly haste, so close on the heels of his loss, we must give urgent consideration to the choice of our next Prime Councillor – one who will guide us and speak on our behalf in the difficult days ahead.'

The magi settled back into the cushioned recesses of their seats, as though relaxing with the return to more familar ground. At Ellen's prompting, Hrugaar invited Sollonaal to speak – since as Prime Councillor of the Ellanguan Magi he was by tradition the most likely candidate for Iorlaas' successor.

Sollonaal's election speech was as predictable in content as it was in length. Rhysana found herself fiddling with the sashes on her robes, and then struggling against a growing urge to pass water. She shifted position on her seat, and tried to occupy her mind by watching the reactions of the other magi as Sollonaal went on. Morvaan seemed more than half asleep, and many of the other councillors appeared as bored or irritated as she was. Hrugaar had sat down again, and was swinging his legs from side to side beneath his robes with a faint swishing sound like distant waves, which Sollonaal clearly found distracting. But there were a surprising number of magi who nodded their heads in agreement, rather than weariness, as he spoke.

Sollonaal sold himself as a keeper of peace, and urged that the Council should work closely with the Emperor's commanders, and with Rinnekh and the Southers, to ensure that the Empire remained peaceful and stable during this difficult time. The Council had, he maintained, enough influence to persuade the *Aeshta* and *Vashta* Orders to bury their differences for now and to work together in the face of the continuing threat of a renewed assault from the Eastern Domains. Provided that the Council confined itself to imperial directives, rather than favouring any one faction from within the Court Noble, he did not believe that their traditional neutrality in the internal politics of the Empire would be compromised.

Remembering her conversation with Kellarn of Dortrean, and the likely presence of Lo-Khuma's servants among the Emperor's most trusted agents, Rhysana thought Sollonaal's proposal far more dangerous than even the staunchest defender of Council neutrality might have realised. But she would have hesitated to risk explaining that in an open assembly, even had the Imperial Counsellor himself not been there.

High Councillor Ferghaal spoke next, proposed as a candidate by the Archmage Ellen. Given the Braedun Order's position, with the Southers in the process of occupying their *commanderie*, he said that he felt that he was not the best choice to speak on the Council's behalf before the Court Noble. Nevertheless he urged them to take action over the attack on the Kelmaar School, to help hunt down those responsible, and to challenge the presence of the Southers in the Six Kingdoms before their strength grew too great. Had the Archmage Merrech not spoken along similar lines earlier in the assembly, Rhysana felt that Ferghaal might have gained more support than he did.

Hrugaar then invited High Councillor Asharka to speak, since she had been a candidate in the previous election, though no one had proposed her as yet that afternoon. Rhysana knew before she began that Asharka would speak about the Colleges, and the urgent need for the Magi to rebuild their own strength and to ensure that their learning was passed on to future generations. Upon that issue most of the magi present – including Rhysana herself – were in ready agreement. Unlike Ferghaal and Sollonaal, however, Asharka held that the Souther presence was no business of the Council as a whole, whatever individual magi might choose to do about it. It was, she said, the responsibility of the Emperor and the Court Noble to deal with the Southers and to keep the peace; and that the *Aeshta* Orders were better placed to guard against the return of the demon captain or his servants. And if Ellanguan were considered too unsettled for the safety of their College students, then she suggested that the staff and students should be moved to the Colleges in Lautun and Farran for the next few terms to ensure the least disruption to their work.

'Does the High Councillor suggest,' asked Kharfaal of Vaulun, 'that after so many of our colleagues risked and lost their lives in the defence of Arrandin, we should now withdraw to lick our wounds and let the Empire fend for itself?'

'As a Council responsible for our Order and Colleges, yes,' Asharka replied. 'Now that the war is over, we must avoid being caught in the games of power played by the Emperor and the Court Noble. If we must withdraw to remain neutral, then so be it. Better that than to give our power into the wrong hands, or to lose it altogether. The late Prime Councillor Herusen himself has said as much in the past.'

From the muttering around the chamber, it seemed that few of the magi were inclined to agree with her.

'Given the present Emperor,' said Ranzhaar of Stanva, 'I do not suppose he would take kindly to our hiding away.'

'The afternoon is passing, Hrugaar,' said Sollonaal. 'Apart from Ferghaal and myself, are there any other candidates whom the assembly may wish the High Council to consider?'

Hrugaar turned his head slowly to look around the great chamber. Torkhaal and Dhûghaúr were whispering together in their seats at Ellen's left hand. Rhysana did not need to hear them to know what they were saying.

Shall you risk the wrath of the goddess, or shall I? Morvaan's voice asked in her mind. Rhysana smiled.

'Councillor Hrugaar,' she said aloud. 'I should like to propose the Archmage the Lady Ellen of Raudhar – if she will permit?'

It was worth it just for the look of surprise on Ellen's handsome face – surprise not at the proposal itself, but whence it had come. Rhysana understood better than most that Ellen had no desire to be Prime Councillor, and indeed considered any Archmage to be unsuitable for the role. But Ellen looked across to her, and nodded. They both knew that Ferghaal's close ties with the Braedun Order would tell against him in the vote, and that Asharka had not the strength of following among the greater Council; and that the only other choice was Sollonaal, whom neither of them wished to see in power.

High Councillor Ekraan took great pleasure in seconding the

proposal, and there were several murmurs of approval on either side. Sollonaal sat up straighter in his seat and smiled with calm confidence. Rhysana wondered how much of a challenge he truly felt Ellen to be.

The Archmage Ellen sat forward on her seat to speak, the summer sunlight shimmering on her silken robes of green and brown, and the glory of her hair glowing like fine burnished bronze. Since the use of magic by individual magi was greatly restricted in the assembly chamber, the splendour of her appearance was suitably impressive. But though no mortal *glamouring* had enhanced her beauty, Rhysana did wonder at that moment whether the sunlight carried some touch of favour from the gods.

Ellen spoke simply, without the need for lengthy arguments at this stage in the debate. She spoke with great respect of Herusen's achievements as Prime Councillor, and how he had fulfilled his duties to Council, College and Court Noble without denying one for the sake of another; and she held that any Prime Councillor should labour to do the same, to balance the needs of the Magi with the needs of the Empire in which they lived, and if necessary to offer his or her own life in the service of others – as Herusen had done, and Iorlaas.

With regard to the Southers, Ellen observed that the Houses Noble would no doubt debate the matter at length during the coming Court, and that they had the temporal power to deal with them. With regard to the use of power in contravention of Council law, she upheld that whoever was responsible should be suitably dealt with, working together with the religious Orders where appropriate.

Ellen's great strength, Rhysana thought to herself, was that she was effectively proposing to continue doing what the Council had done for centuries, and making it sound like common sense. That lure of stability rooted in tradition might win her much support – especially among the High Council, by whom the final choice would be made.

There were no other candidates proposed, so Hrugaar then

ran swiftly through the list of appointed delegates from the Colleges to the Summer Court. Torkhaal was now the only mage on the list for Lautun, but Hrugaar said that he would go with him since he had been planning to attend with Iorlaas. Morvaan would represent Arrandin. Drengriis of Româdhrí and High Councillor Lirinal were the two appointed from the Ellanguan College. Mage Councillors Ghîlsaan and Corrimaer were listed for Farran; but Corrimaer – looking younger and more forlorn than usual in her robes of laurel green and black – declared that she had no wish to go without Iorlaas there to guide her. Asharka, as Principal of the Farran College, said that she would try to find someone else.

'That concludes the business of this present assembly, I think,' said Morvaan. 'If the appointed delegates would be so kind as to remain behind briefly, I should like a quick word.'

'Are the High Council to make the choice of Prime Councillor this afternoon?' asked Ekraan.

'Tomorrow morning, perhaps,' Morvaan returned. 'I think that we may allow Iorlaas the dignity of one more night – and give ourselves the chance to sleep on it. Besides, there are two more of our number who should be here.'

The other high councillors gave their agreement. Most of them seemed to be as relieved as Rhysana herself that they were not expected to stay behind that afternoon.

'There is one more thing,' said Hrugaar, stepping out on to the patterned floor. 'The High Council are to elect our new Prime Councillor. Yet I think that perhaps it might help if the greater Council were to make a show of hands this afternoon, to aid the High Council in their choice.'

'The suggestion is highly irregular,' said Sollonaal at once.

'The election is held in closed assembly for good reason,' said Trialmaster Foghlaar. 'To require a mage to declare his support openly might be considered a breach of personal privacy; and what he shows openly with his hand, in the presence of others, may not reflect the true feelings of his heart.'

'I would not force anyone to vote, against their will,' Hrugaar returned. 'Yet I think that it might help. For one thing, the *Vashta* magi count for fully one third of the greater assembly, yet there are only two of them on the High Council.'

'I believe that the High Council does take that into account, Councillor Hrugaar,' said Ellen drily.

'Besides,' Hrugaar added, 'if I am to prepare the Council Records for this assembly, I should like to cast a true reflection of the feelings of those present.'

'I think that the High Council should abstain,' said Ferghaal; 'and any others who may wish to do so. But if the other candidates agree, I for one see no harm in an informal show of hands at this stage.'

Ellen pursed her lips thoughtfully, and then nodded to Hrugaar.

Sollonaal is caught, came Morvaan's voice in Rhysana's mind, echoing her own thought. It was Sollonaal's frequent claim in High Council meetings that he spoke for many on the greater Council – a claim which had been borne out on many occasions, and particularly in the run up to the last election, until Iorlaas had stolen most of his votes. Now Hrugaar was offering him the chance to prove that claim again. If Sollonaal won this informal vote, the High Council would have little choice but to elect him. If the vote went against him, or if he refused to let it take place, then his chances of becoming the next Prime Councillor of All Magi might be severely hampered.

Sollonaal folded his hands over the golden borders of his robes, and smiled. He had no choice but to accept Hrugaar's dare.

The Archmage Ellen beat him by eleven votes to nine. The High Council and two of the other magi abstained. High Councillor Ferghaal came nowhere near the running.

To Sollonaal's credit, he took the defeat with outward courtesy – if with no great good humour. Morvaan swiftly brought the assembly to a close. The magi rose and began to chatter together, splitting off into small groups to circle the chamber and go out through the ebon doors. Rhysana remained seated, waiting for Ellen to join her. Though her legs felt swollen and uncomfortable, the pressure on her bladder was now so great that she dared not risk standing for one moment longer than she had to.

Trialmaster Foghlaar and a couple of the other magi paused on their way out to comment on how well she was looking. Rhysana thanked them politely, more intent on what was happening on the far side of the chamber. Sollonaal and Hrugaar stood facing one another, not far from the Prime Councillor's seat.

'—little trick,' Sollonaal was saying quietly. 'You may have hoodwinked Iorlaas with your games, but I should advise you not to try playing the High Council.'

'Did I hoodwink Iorlaas?' laughed Hrugaar. 'I think not.'

'You dragged him along to the Kelmaar School, and precipitated this whole bloody mess.'

'Prime Councillor Iorlaas wanted to go,' said Dhûghaúr, appearing with Ellen at Hrugaar's side. 'I was there. As a mage of Justice he wanted to hear their side of the story.'

'He liked not the way you have cast your lot with Rinnekh,' said Hrugaar, 'dragging the rest of the College with you.'

'You acted most irresponsibly,' said Sollonaal sternly. 'I shall recommend to the High Council that they seriously reconsider your position as Secretary.'

'The High Council offered me the post,' returned Hrugaar. 'If they like not the way I fill it, they are free to ask someone else.'

Sollonaal drew himself up to his full height – taller than Dhûghaúr, but still shorter than either Ellen or Hrugaar. Then he gave a curt nod to Ellen, and circled past them to leave. Dalzhaúr and Eralaan hurried to join him.

Chapter Six

Most of the Council had now left the assembly chamber, the Archmage Merrech among them. Rhysana had not seen him go out. Though relieved to have avoided a confrontation with His Eminence on this occasion, she was still worried by his apparent lack of interest in her. The Warden had warned her *he knows*, but had offered no elaboration upon that point. Whenever she had turned to the study of Illana's lore in the past, Merrech had always seemed to be there ahead of her, waiting. Now that she was about to enter Illana's own fortress, the fact that he was ignoring her suggested to Rhysana that she might be mistaken.

Ellen came over to find her, with Hrugaar and Dhûghaúr in tow, and together they went straight to Rhysana's apartment. By the time that they had freshened themselves and made themselves comfortable, Torkhaal and Morvaan had returned and the unseen *chaedar* had brought crushed raspberry ice in crystal tumblers for them all. The Prime Councillor's rod of office lay wrapped in golden silk at one end of the long table.

'So what is this secret errand?' Hrugaar asked as they sat down.

'Put down your drinks first,' Rhysana instructed.

Hrugaar and Dhûghaúr obeyed.

'I am going to Whitespear Head,' she said simply.

For the second time that day she had the pleasure of seeing Hrugaar surprised beyond words.

Dhûghaúr sat bolt upright, like a startled rabbit. 'Not *the*

Whitespear Head?' he managed, when he found his voice at last.

'Illana's fortress, sealed by the High Council for a thousand years,' Rhysana nodded. 'You know the rest of the story. Herusen believed that the seal could be opened by an Archmage wielding the Prime Councillor's rod of office. Ellen and I plan to put his theory to the test.'

'But why?' asked Dhûghaúr.

'Why now?' asked Hrugaar.

Rhysana took a sip of her raspberry ice.

'We have known for some time that there may be followers of Lo-Khuma among the imperial household,' she said. 'I suspect that there may be a connection between the Easterner prophecies of Lo-Khuma – which one of their wizards referred to at the Khôrland parley – and the collection of songs known as the *Passing of Lordship* in Illana's *Argument of Command.* And His Eminence is obsessed with Illana. We have found no other reference to Lo-Khuma among the works recovered from Illana's hoard by the First Council; so it occurred to me that at Whitespear Head we might find the key to this riddle, to find out what Illana knew of Lo-Khuma, and thus what Merrech himself might know.'

'Do you think that the Toad might be one of the Enemy's servants?' cried Dhûghaúr.

'I think that he would know if any of Rhydden's household were,' she replied.

'Then so would Rhydden,' said Ellen grimly.

'That is part of what I am trying to find out,' Rhysana went on. 'It may also be possible that Whitespear Head holds lore of the Enemy's return that we have not found elsewhere, and perhaps even guidance as to how he may be turned back.

'I do not suppose,' she added, 'amongst all the texts that you have read during the past weeks, that any of you have come across mention of the First Kings making provision against the demon's return?'

She had tried to keep her tone light, almost wistful, not

wanting to reveal anything more of what Kellarn and Corollin had told her. But Torkhaal looked at her in question, and Hrugaar sat forward eagerly in his high backed chair.

'You have found something?' he demanded, his eyes flashing deep sea green.

'I have found nothing,' she demurred, truthfully enough. 'There may be nothing there to find.'

'There were magics at Whitespear Head which confounded even the First Council,' said Morvaan. 'I trust, Rhysana, that you have taken into account that you may find more than you are reckoning on? It is not a place to enter lightly.'

'I have studied the accounts of those who went there,' she assured him; 'what they remembered of the ways of the fortress, and of the magical defences.'

'Illana died a thousand years ago,' said Dhûghaúr, 'give or take twenty years. Surely most of her magic would have faded by now – or be deeply asleep, as was the power in the Arrandin matrix?'

Rhysana exchanged glances with Torkhaal, and he nodded.

'Illana is but newly dead, within the past few months,' he told Dhûghaúr. 'The priests believe that her life was somehow preserved *elsewhere*, not in the waking world, for all those years; and only this summer did she at last enter the First Realm of the Dead.'

Dhûghaúr wrinkled his nose at the thought.

'Does His Eminence know of this?' Ellen demanded.

'Quite possibly, by now,' said Rhysana. 'That is another reason why I need to go there as soon as may be.'

'Could the Easterners have played a part in her death?' Hrugaar asked Torkhaal. 'Or other servants of the Enemy?'

Torkhaal gave him a wry smile. 'That we do not know. My own worry is that it may make a journey through the fortress doubly dangerous.'

'But I know where many of the magical defences lie,' said Rhysana; 'and I know where I want to go – more or less – and have considered the safest route to get there. And Ellen will be with me, and Hrugaar.'

'And Torkhaal?' Hrugaar asked.

'I am not allowed,' said Torkhaal. 'One of us has to stay with Taillan, and face the joys of the Summer Court.'

'A task every bit as perilous,' Ellen observed.

'I shall go with you as far as the gates, I think,' said Morvaan, 'to see you safely inside. But my old bones are not suited to clambering about underground.'

Rhysana smiled at him in thanks, and Torkhaal looked slightly happier.

'I am not sure that I am the best person to go with you,' said Hrugaar. 'I have not had much luck of late. Three lives slipped through my fingers yesternight, when I was close at hand to save them.'

'But Dhûghaúr came back alive,' said Rhysana.

'And Sollonaal,' said Morvaan.

'It might help if you tried to like Sollonaal a little more, Hrugaar,' Ellen told him.

'What, in the hope that he may also lose his life?' Hrugaar grinned.

Ellen drew breath to make answer, but then favoured him with an inscrutable smile.

'I shall go with Rhysana,' said Dhûghaúr. 'You may have need of an Earth mage.'

'And what am I?' asked Ellen.

'Too precious to risk,' he replied stoutly. Ellen smiled again.

'Thank you Dhûghaúr,' sighed Rhysana. 'That is just what my husband needed to hear.'

The little mage looked confused for a moment, then hung his head in apology. Torkhaal thumped him gently on the shoulder.

'So when do we leave?' Hrugaar asked.

'In a little while,' said Rhysana easily. 'You have time to change and to gather your thoughts. And I need to pay a visit to the library.'

* * *

It was nearly an hour later before the magi were ready to set out. Rhysana said goodbye to Torkhaal privately, though with no great sense of foreboding or finality. She knew that she would be coming back; and her own hope seemed to take root and blossom within him. Their matching wedding rings of pale wood clicked against one another as their hands parted.

She had gone to the library to see the Warden and to take another look in the great mirror at the cliffs of Whitespear Head, since she would have to be the one who took the other magi there in her magical leap. The Warden had seemed calm and unruffled as ever, reminding her with his usual practicality to take due care of any manuscripts that she might happen to find. But as she had taken her leave of him on the library stair, he had called after her to come back safely.

The Archmage Ellen had set aside her silken robes in favour of a rather homely green gown, with a russet shawl flung around her shoulders and her hair pinned up at the back. Hrugaar had also changed out of his borrowed robes, and was clad in his familiar shirt and breeches of grey green. He had a coil of rope slung over one shoulder, and a knife tucked under his belt.

Morvaan wore his battered old satchel over his robes, stocked afresh with food by the helpful *chaedar*. Dhûghaúr had a larger pack, hung about with four waterskins, and carried a black staff in his hands. At Rhysana's questioning look, he explained that the pack contained more food, a blanket, bandages, and the usual travelling gear that he took with him on journeys. Ellen observed that she hoped that this journey would not last so long that it would be needed.

Rhysana herself had put on a dark blue gown with divided skirts, with her silver fair hair braided into a double crown about her head. The gown was a little too heavy and warm in the heat of the afternoon, but she knew that she would feel the benefit of it in the underground halls of Illana's fortress. She also carried a satchel, with the Warden's codex wrapped in a silken napkin safely inside.

She made the *leap* to the rocky shore, close to the cliffs. The first thing that they noticed was the rushing roar of the river, and then the coolness of the air. The sun had now gone well round to the west, and the whole of this side of the headland spur lay in shadow. A strong breeze eddied around them, so close to the cliffs and the water's edge. Rhysana shivered, and the Archmage Ellen pulled her shawl more snugly about her shoulders.

The cliffs seemed taller and more weathered than Rhysana remembered them from the mirror, and drab and dreary compared to the sunlit hills of the Sêchral lands away east beyond the river. Only a few straggling bushes and scrub creepers clung to the narrow ledges, with here and there the darker shapes of ravens perched among the branches or swooping out across the water. Though the Council – or perhaps the Warden himself – kept careful watch here, the place had an air of neglect about it. Of the staggering sense of power which she had felt through the mirror there was no outward sign, save for a faint whisper like a chill breeze across the back of her neck.

'I can see no one else around,' said Hrugaar, coming back from the river's edge; 'other than the birds. They do not seem to mind our being here.'

'Have we come to the right place?' Dhûghaúr asked. 'I mean, I can feel the power at work within the stone. But is this not a bit out of the way for a gate to a great fortress?'

'Perhaps it was always a hidden way,' said Hrugaar.

'It was not hidden,' Rhysana told them. 'There was a landing here. But there were other doors, Dhûghaúr. The main gate was on the other side, to the northwest. The Council blocked that way, and the doors have long been buried deep. The Enchantress Dukhoi also made mention of closing a river gate – though that was lower down I think, perhaps underwater. This is the only door left open for us.'

'If Ellen can get you in,' said Morvaan.

The Archmage Ellen stood facing the cliff, the white steel rod of the Prime Councillor now unwrapped and held lightly in her hands. Her bronzed brows were furrowed in thought.

'I may need your help,' she said aloud. 'Look.'

Ellen shifted the rod in to one hand and drew a wide circle in the air before her. The rocky surface of the cliff began to blur and fade, until it seemed no more than a fine curtain veil lit from behind. Beyond, now plain for all of them to see, was the narrow cleft with its smooth steps leading up to the stone doors. The medallion seal upon the doors shone bright as the full moon; and the cleft was filled – even as Rhysana had seen it before – with a web of power that seemed to be spun with strands of finest crystal, polished and glittering with every hue imaginable.

The change upon the air was truly staggering. To Rhysana's trained senses it felt as though a furnace door had been opened, or rather that she had stepped from a furnace into an ice house; and mingled with that sense of power was simple mortal terror. It seemed to her that the crystal was almost a living thing, watching. She wondered, in some detached part of her academic mind, whether that was what Ellen and Imarra had meant when they spoke of dealing with the defence matrix in Arrandin as if it were a living creature.

Dhûghaúr gasped, and Hrugaar cried out in delight. Rhysana felt the need to sit down, and accepted Morvaan's proffered arm gratefully. Ellen beckoned for them to come closer.

'Tell me, Hrugaar,' she said in her deep, handsome voice, without looking away from the cleft, 'what do you see on the seal?'

They all looked. To Rhysana's eyes it seemed to be a disc of mother-of-pearl, pulsing and swirling with light in a pattern that eluded her.

'There are seven rings of power,' said Hrugaar, 'bound by a star of eight rays – no, sixteen.'

'Good,' said Ellen. 'I thought that I might have been mistaken. That will make this easier.'

'Shrewd are the eyes of the Fay,' Morvaan murmured.

'Or perhaps I shall yet be an Archmage,' said Hrugaar.

Ellen snorted. 'Now I should be grateful for a little peace while I work,' she said.

She stepped forward until she was all but touching the outer veil of power. The other magi hung back, holding themselves ready in case she had sudden need of them. Ellen held the rod upright before her in both hands.

For several heartbeats nothing happened. Then the seal grew brighter, turning to pure white, and all colour fled from the crystal web. Ellen spun the rod slowly through a half turn. The web of power faded and shrank back upon itself, vanishing into the seal; and then the seal flared and went dim, and the stone doors parted and ground inward. Darkness seemed to flood out from the open doorway, plunging the narrow cleft into shadow.

Hrugaar whistled.

'That will hold for a little while,' said Ellen, allowing herself a small smile of satisfaction as she turned back to them. She waved aside their praise and thanks, and began to wrap the rod in its golden silk covering. 'I may need to do it again when we come back.'

'You shall,' Morvaan nodded.

Rhysana looked at him. 'You have been here before,' she said accusingly.

'Of course,' he said. '*Once in every generation the seal shall be renewed*, remember? I came here with Herusen and the High Council, many years ago now. We took a quick look inside.'

There had been no mention of such a visit in the Warden's codex. Rhysana wondered whether the Warden had omitted to mention it because some of those magi – like Morvaan himself – were still alive, and he would have considered it a breach of their personal privacy.

'Why did you not say so before?' she demanded.

'Because this was a little test of my own, if you like,' he told her. 'Not that I have any great doubts about the Archmage Ellen's ability. But I happen to be rather fond of you all; and like Torkhaal I hesitated to let you take the risk of going in there, no matter how important you believed it to be. So I decided that if Ellen could manage to open the seal, then I would take that as a sign from the gods that you were doing the right thing.'

'Is that not tempting the gods?' Ellen asked him.

Morvaan shrugged sheepishly. 'Allow an old man his follies.'

'So what did you find inside?' asked Rhysana.

'And shall you not come with us?' added Hrugaar.

'Our errand was different from yours,' replied Morvaan. 'Had we found anything to do with the demon captain or Illana's work, I should have told you well before now. And no, Hrugaar, I am not about to come with you. But I can do a little better than that, perhaps. I shall give you my memories of the place, such as they are.'

Hrugaar's face brightened, and then clouded with sudden guilt. 'Perhaps you should give them to Rhysana,' he said.

'You have the mental gifts to take them more readily,' Morvaan returned. 'And besides, if I give them to you then the two of you will have to stay together and look after one another, if you wish to make use of them. I promised Torkhaal no less.'

'It smacks of conspiracy,' sighed Rhysana, though in truth she did not greatly mind. She was too grateful for the gift of extra knowledge of the fortress. Without Morvaan there himself, his memories would be the next best thing.

Morvaan and Hrugaar joined hands, and whatever passed between them could not have lasted for much more than a minute. Hrugaar's eyes flared wide and bright green at one point; but since they were obviously talking mind to mind, Rhysana had no idea what had prompted it.

Ellen had stowed the rod in Dhûghaúr's pack, and the two of them had gone on to the outer edge of the cleft for a closer look at where the magic of the seal had been. The other magi picked their way over the rocks to join them. Morvaan wished them all good luck.

'We should move inside soon,' said Ellen.

Rhysana needed no second bidding. She kindled a ball of her silver-blue magelight in her hand, and led the way up the stone stair to the open doors. A cold wind buffeted around them. Though she now knew that it was not entirely true that no one had come here in the last thousand years, she still had the fanciful notion that her footsteps were somehow taking her back through time, to the days of the First Council and the dawn of the Golden Age.

She paused on the topmost step. The two half moons of the seal glowed soft as pewter in her magical light, their power briefly sleeping. The tall hallway beyond led straight into the hillside.

The Archmage Morvaan was still standing beyond the mouth of the cleft, his grey robes fluttering in the wind. She waved down to him, and he waved half a muffin in answer. Then she smiled to the three magi with her, and led them into the darkness.

Kellarn did not see the Guardian again until that evening. The fauns had left before dawn – taking almost nothing from the horses' saddlebags – and the tree-spirits had kept themselves hidden. The three humans stayed close to the stream at the foot of the hill, watching the cloud shadows scud across the lake of Alvinaah and the life of the woods going on around them. By unspoken agreement they did not venture further away along the shore, though they had not been expressly forbidden from doing so.

In the middle morning Mellin had offered to walk the horses for a while, giving Kellarn and Corollin the chance to speak privately. They had sat down together in the shade of the birches, and Kellarn repeated what Dyrnalv had told him about facing the Dead, as far as he could remember it. Corollin frowned thoughtfully.

'This is not quite as I had expected,' she said. 'Losithlîn told us that the Guardian of Telbray Woods could discover whether any of the old Kings of Farodh have been reborn into the waking world at this time; and thereafter we had begun to consider how we might gain access to the memories of the Dead. But this sounds as if the Guardian intends that you should visit the Realms of the Dead – or that some of the Dead should be called here to speak with you.'

'I had thought before that we might have to speak with them,' said Kellarn. 'There was mention of it at the Sun Temple, I think. But I had also thought that you would be the one to do it – or perhaps the two of us together, with you leading.'

'So had I,' she agreed.

'So what am I to ask?' demanded Kellarn.

Corollin shrugged, her hands raised in an open gesture. 'If the Kings of Farodh made their own bar, and where it is now. But it depends on what exactly the Guardian plans for you to do. Did she tell you nothing more.'

'Only that I was free to choose,' he said, 'whether to do it or not.'

'Then we must try to find out more from her,' said Corollin.

But the chance to question Dyrnalv did not arise. They had spent the rest of the morning practising tumbling rolls on the grass; and then they ate their noon meal and dozed a little in the sun. Then one of the male tree-spirits came and spoke with Corollin in the elven tongue – or at least Corollin spoke, and the tree-spirit seemed more to hum and sing in musical exchanges. He bade them bathe and swim in the lake, to cleanse themselves before evening. They also took the chance to wash some of their clothes, and let them dry spread out in the heat of the afternoon.

The sun had dipped down behind the Black Mountains, and the pale crescent of the new moon hung close behind the snowy peaks, when the Guardian at last returned. She came down the hill and through the trees, robed in black over white, with a heavy stole of scarlet overworked with gold. Her coppery head was bare, and a curved blade like the crescent moon was slid naked beneath her girdle. A gold ring set with a large red stone glowed softly on her left hand. The tree-spirits burst into song as she passed by.

She stopped by the first birch tree, on the far side of the stream, and beckoned for them to cross. Kellarn glanced at the other two and moved forward. At Corollin's suggestion he was still barefoot, and had left off his mailshirt; but he had his sword and shield with him. The stream was icy cold about his feet.

Corollin followed behind him. The Guardian seemed not to mind.

'And you, Mellin Carfinn?' she asked.

'I have made my own peace with the Dead,' Mellin answered. 'And someone has to stay with the horses.'

The Guardian nodded, accepting. Then she turned and led the way back toward the hill. The smell of rose petals and sweet incense trailed on the air behind her – the smell of a funeral pyre.

Beyond the trees they turned to the left, circling the hill even as they climbed, making a spiral path toward the top. The wind had died down, and the sounds of the settling forest grew dim and distant as they mounted higher. When they reached the bare, grassy crown of the hill, they arrived from the south, and the lake and the rolling heartland of the Telbray Woods were spread out before them. The Guardian turned around.

'You wonder what I plan to do,' she said to both of them. 'That is as it should be. To learn, you must take the path of unknowing.

'Besides,' she added with a wry smile, 'I am not entirely sure myself, yet.'

Kellarn found himself grinning. He glanced sideways at Corollin; but she was watching Dyrnalv, as quietly serious as ever. He turned his attention back to what they were doing.

The Guardian swept her arms wide and up above her head. Tiny specks of light trailed in their wake, like clouds of stars or drifting feathers. She brought her hands down again, and the trailing light grew stronger, streaming in pale ribands. She began to move.

He gazed, spellbound, as she danced and spun in circling motions around the hilltop. At first he watched the Guardian herself – the grace of her lithe form beneath the flowing robes, her strength of control, the flick of her red gold hair in the twilight. But his gaze was drawn to the ribands of light streaming from her hands, weaving into whorls and spirals on the twilight air in a pattern he could not grasp, but only follow. She began to hum, and then to sing softly, though the words of her song eluded him. The silence deepened behind her voice into profound stillness.

At last she stood before them again with hands upraised, and finished her song on one long, high note. The light of her power was all around them in a filigree dome. She brought her hands down, and the dome scattered and drifted down with them in a shimmering cloud, bringing all the stars of the summer sky with it, fading just before it touched the grass. And then they stood in darkness beneath an empty void, and the only light was the Guardian herself.

'Come now,' she said. 'We shall pass beyond the measure of time and gaze into the Well of Life, wherein the memories of all things may be glimpsed as reflections in a pool, for those with eyes to see.'

She turned and moved away, and a path of light unfurled from beneath her feet and ran away ahead of them, straight down the hillside. Corollin followed at once, and Kellarn came behind.

They went down the slope, and through a closer darkness that might have been the shadow of the trees; and so came to the shore of the lake, which rippled soft and silver in its own light. The shining pathway ran straight on down beneath the waters, and the Guardian followed it without pause. Corollin and Kellarn looked at one another, and held hands as they ventured in behind her.

The lake had the feel of water about his legs and chest as

he waded in, though it was neither hot nor cold. But as his head passed beneath the surface, Kellarn found that he could breathe as easily as in air, and keep his eyes open with little difficulty; and it was easier to see things in the silvery light.

They passed across a lake floor of glittering pebbles, clouded with drifting sand, and came presently to a pair of standing stones, capped with a heavy lintel just higher than Kellarn could reach. The shining path ended between the stones' feet.

The Guardian reached within her robes and drew out a cube of ivory, about the size of a man's fist, inlaid with golden patterns on all sides. She held it out before her, and Kellarn saw that the nearest side to him had the familiar symbol of Fire and the Sun. There seemed to be other symbols of the *Aeshtar* on the other sides. Dyrnalv smiled at him, and twisted the cube between her hands. The sides turned and slid and turned again beneath her fingers like a puzzle-box – though one more complex than Kellarn himself had ever seen – and then a shadow appeared between the two pillars, and became a passageway beyond, and they passed through swiftly.

The passage was dark after the silver light of the lake, and felt closed and stifling. The sides and roof were made of huge rough slabs of stone, like the black stone of the mountains. The only light came from the Guardian, a soft glow of ruddy gold that drifted about her hair and reflected dimly here and there in winking sparks from the faces of the stones. The brush of their bare feet upon the floor echoed like furtive whispers ahead and behind them.

They pressed on along the tunnel, with the feeling that they were going down deeper, now passing low-lintelled doorways on either side that opened into darkness. Kellarn rested his hand on his sword, though he did not draw it. Corollin seemed uneasy too, holding her staff at the ready as she looked about her.

At last they came to a taller chamber, fashioned of the same stones. In the midst of the floor was a small pool, roughly oval, bordered only by the uneven bed-rock. The Guardian led them round to the far side. The surface of the water shone softly, lighting their faces with clear light; and the air seemed suddenly sweeter and easier to breathe. Kellarn looked up, and saw that the chamber opened above them into a ragged shaft, filled with jutting spurs of rock and dripping with moisture. He felt that he was gazing up through the heart of a mountain.

'Here is the Well of Life,' said Dyrnalv; 'though it has other names, and other guises. Here you may seek any of those who have been born into our waking world. Son of Dortrean, whom do you seek?'

Kellarn looked at Corollin, and she nodded.

'The First King of Farodh,' he answered. It was the First Kings who had made the bars of the artefact; and their knowledge was supposed to have died with them.

'Morvargh, First King of Farodh,' said the Guardian, her voice echoing from the stones around them.

She stepped forward to the brink of the pool. Kellarn and Corollin edged forward on either side of her.

The surface of the pool shimmered and went dark. Then, one by one, pinpoints of light began to float up from the depths, like stars appearing in the evening sky. For a time, nothing more than that seemed to happen. But then Kellarn realised that the stars were gathering to form an image, like a reflection in a dark mirror.

A man's face was looking up at him, strong-jawed and determined, with eyes deep set beneath straight brows. A helm of sorts crowned his head, with skirted panels hanging down on either side, and the knotted ends of a heavy torc sat before his throat. Behind him, as if at a distance, Kellarn could make out the shapes of swans in circling flight.

'Hail Morvargh, King that was,' said Dyrnalv softly. The image rippled and faded again, and their own reflections stared back at them.

'Is that it?' asked Kellarn. He felt suddenly disappointed.

'You have seen what you sought to know,' said Dyrnalv. 'He

who was once Morvargh is now with the Dead. Had he been reborn into another life in our own time, now in the waking world, the water would have shown it.'

'Oh,' said Kellarn.

'But can we still reach him?' Corollin asked. 'Or must we go through all the other Kings of Farodh, until we find one who is reborn?'

The Guardian turned to Kellarn. 'What do you wish to do?' she asked him.

Kellarn felt uncomfortable at being singled out, especially since he thought the quest to be more truly Corollin's than his. 'Asking Morvargh seems to be our best chance,' he said, looking to Corollin for her agreement.

'Then we shall attempt it,' said the Guardian. She nodded to Corollin, as if in apology, and led the way back from the edge of the pool.

At the far end of the chamber was a lintelled doorway which Kellarn did not remember having seen when they came in. Dyrnalv now led them through, and they found themselves in another stone passage sloping up. Before long it became a rough-hewn stair, snaking from side to side as it led them higher. But there were no side passages leading off, and they felt no sense of present danger as they had before.

The stair ended abruptly, and they came out on to a wide shelf of rock open to the empty sky above. Sheer cliff walls rose up behind them, and stretched ahead to left and right; and beyond the shelf Kellarn could see the tops of many trees, glowing deep green in an otherworldly twilight. At the very edge of the shelf sat two great statues, fully three times their own height, each carved in the likeness of an ox with curved horns balancing an orbed moon upon its head; and one was all of pale silver, and the other had the deep lustre of black opal.

Between the statues, and apparently barring their way, was a shorter mound of shadow. As they stepped out on to the shelf the shadow stirred and uncoiled, spreading huge wings to left and right to veil the oxen's faces, and a head of horn and scale reared up upon a serpent's neck. The memory of a black wyrm's eyes glared down at them from beneath ridged brows. Kellarn's hand went back to his sword.

Dyrnalv walked forward across the shelf, as calm as ever.

'None shall pass,' came the voice of the dragon – a voice so deep that it shook the air around them, and the stone shelf trembled beneath their feet.

'We may pass,' said Dyrnalv in the stillness that followed. 'We come to speak with the Dead at Rest, with he who was once Morvargh, First King of Farodh.'

'Morvargh is long gone,' said the dragon, sounding almost bored. 'Run away, or I shall have to eat you.'

'I have looked into the Well of Life,' she challenged. 'He is not gone, and we must speak with him.'

'Well there's a pity, because you can't.'

Dyrnalv stood still before him, dwarfed by his shadow. She raised her left hand, and a cone of light streamed down around her, so that she seemed wreathed in living flames.

'I am the Guardian of the Western Woods, and I bear the Ring of Red-Golden Dragons,' she sang. 'I deem the need is great. With Morvargh we must speak.'

'Very pretty,' the dragon snorted, flexing his claws against the stone. 'But still you may not pass. Not even if the Father of All Dragons himself sent you. You're only a Guardian, my dear. Where Morvargh has gone, you may not go – not as you are.'

Dyrnalv let her hand fall, and the flames died. She turned back to Kellarn and Corollin.

'He is right,' she said. 'As a Guardian I have power in the dance of life and death. But Morvargh – or the one who was once Morvargh – has gone beyond, with those who do not need to be reborn into the waking world, unless they so choose. We may not follow him there now.'

'But if you knew that, then why did you bring us here?' asked Kellarn.

'You said that you wanted to speak with him.'

Kellarn swore. He did not know whether to feel stupid or angry, or just frustrated.

Corollin looked at the two of them, and then walked toward the dragon.

'We can't go there,' she said to him, 'but can you call Morvargh to us?'

For answer the dragon reared its head and spat down a ball of shadow at her. Corollin whirled her staff with blinding speed, raising a shield of golden power about herself. The shadow seethed against the gold like a swarm of bees. She staggered and fell.

Kellarn was already moving, drawing his sword as he sprang past Dyrnalv. Crimson fire roared into life along the blade.

'Hold!' the Guardian commanded.

Kellarn skidded to a halt, still grasping his sword furiously. The dragon sat back on its haunches, ruffling its wings as it stared down at him. Corollin stood up again in the silence.

'You didn't tell me about the sword,' the dragon grumbled.

'I do hope it makes a difference,' said Kellarn dangerously.

'I'm sure you do.' The great beast dropped his head a little closer. 'Perhaps you should tell me *why* you want to see this Morvargh?'

Kellarn kept his sword raised in warning, though the flames had died away. Thus far they had kept their quest as secret as they could; and even here – wherever *here* was – he was loth to speak of it, especially to an unknown dragon such as this. Neither Corollin nor the Guardian offered him any help, and he was not about to risk turning around to signal to them.

'There is something only he can tell us,' he replied.

'I see,' said the dragon. 'Would it help if I told you that what you really seek is in the waking world, and not here?'

'Not much,' said Kellarn. 'I mean – well no, that's not the point. What we need to know, only Morvargh can really tell us.'

'Dear dear,' the great wyrm sighed. 'Well, you can put

your sword away now. My death won't be of any help to you.'

'What do you mean?'

'What I said.'

Kellarn frowned. He was better at killing dragons than riddling with them. He did not know whether to trust the creature or not. He no longer knew what he was doing here.

And then he remembered what Dyrnalv herself had told them, back on the hilltop. *To learn, you must take the path of unknowing.* Perhaps that was what he should be doing here – asking questions, not suggesting answers.

He lowered his sword a few inches.

'If your death will not help,' he said, 'what will?'

The dragon relaxed visibly. The Guardian came forward to stand between them, facing Kellarn.

'Why Morvargh in particular?' she asked.

Kellarn risked a quick glance at Corollin. She nodded at once.

'He made something, and then hid it,' he explained. 'Very secretly. No one else may ever have known where it was hidden. And it is very important that we find it. But if Losithlîn told you we sought the dead Kings, did she not tell you about it?'

'No. But things rarely stay hidden for fifteen hundred years. Someone usually knows something about them.'

Kellarn frowned. Of the four bars that they had found, three had remained undisturbed in their original hiding places; but they had had guides – of one sort or another – to all four. He felt that he was missing something.

'I don't know where else to start looking,' he said. 'Morvargh was our best choice. Or if not him, then one of the other dead Kings. Can you not help me to reach him?'

The Guardian looked up at the dragon. He bowed his great head and shrank down. A moment later his shadow flowed up and over her shoulders, and her robes of red and black became a cloak of countless feathers. A dark hood now covered the glory of her hair. Kellarn took a step back.

'There is another way that you may take,' she said. 'If you so choose.'

She reached beneath her cloak and drew out a round fruit, like a small peach, its smooth skin all of silver shaded with gold.

'This was called a moon apple by the people of Farodh,' she told him; 'though it has other names in other kingdoms, and its virtues have many uses. Were you to eat of it now, it would bear you to the Realms of the Dead for a while. You would move among the Dead, as one of the Dead, while your body remained here with us; and we would watch over you, and be sure to bring you back to life within the proper time. It is a perilous fruit, for a perilous journey. But if I did not think that you had the courage to do it, I would not offer it to you now.'

Kellarn stared at the fruit uneasily. Corollin came forward beside him.

'Do you advise me to take it?' he asked the Guardian.

'It is a way that is offered to you,' she said. 'In the Realms of the Dead you may find the help that you seek, or you may not; and there may be those among the Dead who will seek to hinder or harm you. You must go alone, for we may not come with you. It is not for me to counsel you in this, Son of Dortrean. It is for you to choose.'

'Can we not go that way?' asked Corollin, nodding toward the two statues and the treetops beyond.

The Guardian shook her head. 'We have not the right to pass.'

Kellarn looked down at the fruit again.

'If I don't eat it,' he said, 'what happens then?'

'Then you do not,' she answered simply. 'There is no one who will blame you, and it does not mean the end of your quest.'

Kellarn thought that he might well blame himself, even

if no one else did. It seemed pointless not to do it, having come this far; and if a short journey to the Realms of the Dead could save them months of searching in the waking world, then it was worth every bit of the risk. With the enemy so close to returning, they might not even have many months left.

'Do I really have a choice?' he said, forcing a grin for Corollin's sake. She shook her head and smiled wanly.

He sheathed his sword, and took the silver moon apple from the Guardian.

'I just eat it?' he said.

She nodded. 'You were best to sit down.'

He sat cross-legged upon the ground, swinging his sword sheath around so that it lay across his knees. Corollin knelt down anxiously beside him.

The first bite burst in his mouth with all the sweetness of the ripest peach, and juice trickled down his chin. He tasted the sharper tang of lemon as he chewed and swallowed, and his eyes watered and crinkled in pleasure.

'Remember, Kellarn,' came Dyrnalv's voice. 'The answers of the Dead may rebound upon the living.'

The second bite seemed sweeter than the first, and edged with a little salt; so that his breath became uneven, and a warmth of passion quickened in his blood.

His hand trembled as he bit again, and he swallowed without chewing. Then sudden pain exploded within him; and he doubled forward, and pitched headfirst through the stone and on into an endless falling.

Kellarn woke to find himself lying on his back amid tall grass, with a grey pall of cloud high overhead. The pain had gone, and he felt only the dullness of having been too long asleep. The air was hushed all around him. He flexed his stomach once, testing, and sat up.

The grass was so tall that still he could not see over it. He pulled in his bare feet and stood up.

The first thing he realised was that the grass was razor sharp, cutting painfully into his feet as he moved.

The second thing was that he had no memory of where he was at all.

He was standing in the midst of a wide open plain, with no trees or buildings to break the endless sweep of the grass. The land lay quiet, as if under bright moonlight, yet the sky overhead was a uniform silver grey with no sign of the moon herself. Away to his left, and stretching for perhaps a third of the way along the horizon, was a ridge of low hills, and the sky seemed brighter beyond them. To the left of the hills the horizon blurred into a duller, misty shadow.

As he looked about him, Kellarn saw that there was movement here and there upon the plain – tiny sparks of colour, or darker specks of shadow, moving with no pattern or purpose that he could fathom.

Then memory stirred within him, and he knew that he was in the First Realm of the Dead.

The knowledge held no great terror for Kellarn. For one thing, the Guardian had told him that he would not be here for long, and he had no reason to doubt her words. For another, the prospect of death itself did not frighten him – the painful moment of dying, perhaps, but not being dead thereafter. As a son of the *Aeshta* faith, he knew that it was but one more step in the great journey of the soul, the dance of life and death and rebirth. And besides, he was not so much in love with his present life that he feared greatly to lose it. The release of death was something that he had longed for many a time.

What struck him now was more a feeling of foolishness, for having come here ill prepared. They had pinned most of their hopes on finding the First King of Farodh; but Morvargh would be nowhere near here, and it might prove a long and difficult journey to find him – too long, perhaps, for the time that Kellarn had here. It occurred to him that before he had eaten the moon apple he should have asked the Guardian if there might be other former Kings and Queens of Farodh here in the First Realm who might be able to help him; though he supposed that he could still try looking for them.

Then there was the warning that the panthress had given, that the Dead might also be seeking him. Since he was now in the Realms of the Dead, Kellarn thought that that might not prove so much of a problem. After all, if he counted as being dead already, what more could they do to him? He checked at his side, and found that he still had his sword with him. That was an added comfort.

Kellarn looked at his feet. Though the grass still cut them, there was no blood. The pain was something he would have to endure. He glanced around him once more, and then set off toward the hills.

As he waded through the long grass, he fell to wondering who among the Dead might be looking for him. With the recent war, he had made enemies enough among the Easterners and Southers who had died, though few of them might have had much idea who he was. He had some enemies from among the Court Noble, of course, and among the Emperor's followers, who might now also be dead. From what the panthress had said, he did not suppose that whoever sought him would be friendly.

The revenge of dead enemies did not greatly trouble him. What he dreaded more, he thought, was that he might meet here the shades of those who had once been his friends – Takshar of Dregharis, who had followed him to Herghin and been slain, and his brother Solban. The guilt of their deaths still weighed in his heart. Mellin Carfinn, he remembered, had said that she had made her own peace with the Dead. That was something that Kellarn had not yet done, and which to him seemed more daunting than fighting them.

Whether much of Solban's memory would now remain, even in death, Kellarn did not know; but he could not imagine what he would say to him if they met. He knew what Solban had meant by *Kellarn was right.* He knew that Rhydden was responsible for his brother's death, whatever demon had killed him. Nor could he bring himself to say farewell, nor ask forgiveness, until he had avenged him.

'No hurry then, laddie,' called a deep voice from nearby.

Kellarn stopped and turned. One of the Dead came toward him. He was taller and broader than Kellarn, with dark hair tied back and a full beard, and wearing a simple baggy shirt; but he was somehow less solid and real than the grass around him.

'Durlan, from Port of Farran,' said the man. 'So you ended up here too then.'

'Yes,' said Kellarn. The name was familiar, more so than the face. Durlan had been a slave with him on the Souther warship.

'I thought you'd lost an eye,' he said, remembering.

'Did I, laddie?' Durlan frowned. 'Well, perhaps I did. But you can stay a bit and have some fun, I'm thinking.'

He was standing almost within arm's reach. His voice was less slurred than Kellarn remembered; though when they had known one another in life they had been weary for much of the time, and Durlan had been half drugged and worn out by the Southers in other ways.

Kellarn realised that the borderlander had undone his belt and had one hand down the front of his breeches.

'There's not much else to do here, and no hurry to be doing it,' Durlan grinned.

'I have to be going,' said Kellarn.

Durlan reached out and grabbed his arm. But in spite of his remembered strength, Kellarn was too solid for him to hold. He sprang away easily, and set off at a run through the grass.

'When you grow bored, I'll be waiting then,' the borderlander called after him.

Kellarn did not bother to look back. Durlan had been an unsavoury ally at best, and treacherously selfish at the last, and he had no desire to dally with him, now or ever. He might have pitied him, but felt more inclined to laugh now that the moment had passed.

There was more movement on the plain around him, and

he realised that the tiny specks of colour which he had seen before were in fact other people and creatures – some as dim and misty as Durlan, and others more bright and real. A great destrier, bright as a tawny flame, galloped by just ahead of him, riderless and joyful. He called after it, but it ran on toward the hills and paid him no heed. Then from away to his left, perhaps a mile or more distant, another horse seemed to be heading toward him.

Kellarn jogged on through the grass, gritting his teeth against the sharp blades that slashed at his feet and hands. The hills seemed hardly any nearer.

With a start of surprise, he realised that another of the Dead was now just ahead of him, and coming toward him on foot. He had dark shoulder length hair and a tunic that glimmered with fallow gold. Kellarn stopped short, fearing at first that it might be Solban. But as the shadowy figure drew closer, he saw that it was not so. It appeared to be a boy of his own age, or slightly younger, with dark eyes and a sulking look. His ghostly image was dimmer than Durlan's had been, which was perhaps why Kellarn had not noticed him before; and although the face was faintly familiar, Kellarn could not yet put a name to him.

'What are you doing here?' the boy asked, coming to a halt several paces ahead. His voice was soft and mournful, and tinged with irritation.

'Do I know you?' Kellarn countered.

The boy frowned, as if trying to remember. 'Goshaún,' he said at last. He seemed to grow a little more solid as he spoke the name. 'I thought you were supposed to be a great war hero. Rhydden hated that, you know. I suppose he had you killed?'

'Not exactly,' said Kellarn.

He remembered the face now. Goshaún had been the youngest of the Sêchral children, the brother of Rhydden's new Empress. Kellarn had not heard that he was dead.

'Well you're here aren't you?' Goshaún sneered. 'The bastard killed me too, you know. And your brother. There was quite a fuss about that when I first got here.'

'What do you mean?' Kellarn demanded.

Goshaún looked down at his feet.

'They shredded him,' he said. 'Well not they, but that damned demon they all serve. Some woman I met said he was like wildfire when he came here, right out of control. He didn't stay long.'

'Who are *they*?'

'What does it matter?' Goshaún sneered again. 'The Emperor, that arsehole Rinnekh, half his damned Destriers. A couple of the Magi. Oh, and Tighaún,' he said, jerking his head toward the horseman who was now fast approaching. 'He doesn't like you either.'

Kellarn glanced to his left. The horse – a rich chestnut – was less than a furlong distant. Its rider was a tall man in grey and brown, with the classic build and bearing of the nobles of the Lautun Houses. He guessed at once that it was the imperial spy who had followed him to the edge of the Wasted Hills.

'Do you mean,' he said, holding his thoughts together with an effort, 'that the Emperor summoned the demon that killed my brother?'

'Most likely,' Goshaún shrugged. 'I wasn't there. But what does it matter? That's the price he paid for serving the bastard. We all paid the price, one way or another.'

Kellarn swore. 'I should have been in Ellanguan.'

'And come here with him?' Goshaún gave a mocking laugh. 'Not everything happens because of you, even if you are a great warrior. Solban made his own choices, like the rest of us. But I must admit, when I heard about you, I had hoped that you might teach Rhydden a lesson. I guess it's too late for that now.'

'It's not too late,' said Kellarn. 'I'm only here for a short time.'

Goshaún looked at him strangely.

'Ah, your heathen belief that you can be reborn,' he said. 'I haven't seen any sign of that here.'

'No,' said Kellarn. 'I'm not dead yet. I shall return to my living body very soon.'

A flicker of light kindled in Goshaún's dark eyes, and he became brighter and more solid still. But at that moment there was a thrashing in the grass nearby, and Tighaún reined in his horse beside them.

'So you came here in the end,' the horseman said; 'though not because of me.'

'All men come here when they die,' Kellarn answered, 'but not all linger in this first Realm. Do not hinder me from my way.' He rested his hand on his sword.

'Get lost, Tighaún,' said Goshaún. 'We don't need your meddling.'

'I have a score to settle here,' said Tighaún smoothly. 'And there are some loyalties that bind the soul, even in death.'

He drew his own sword and held it up. No light reflected from the blade at all, so that it cut a line of empty darkness against the grey pall of the sky.

Kellarn drew his sword in answer, and red flame rippled into life from hilt to tip.

'Stand back and let me pass,' he said steadily. 'I shall not ask again.'

Tighaún laughed. Then he tossed his sword high into the air, shouting something in an ugly tongue. The dark blade winked and vanished; and then a deeper shadow rushed into the sky.

Goshaún was the first to move, snatching a short blade from his side and driving it deep into the horse's flank. The creature reared and screamed; and faced by both the boy's attack and by the gathering darkness overhead, it wheeled and bore its master far away.

'If you are what you say,' cried Goshaún, 'then go! And strike a blow for me!' He turned and vanished into the grass.

Kellarn looked up. An empty shadow blotted out the sky, spreading vast wings as it descended. The air about him grew thick and dark as smoke, and stifling in his throat. He raised his sword in challenge, swinging in wide arcs as if to drive back the darkness with its holy fire. The patterned blade shone bright with molten gold.

'*You shall burn the illness that blights the land,*' he cried, remembering the words that were there. This was the task of the Sun: to drive out sickness and darkness, and to bring healing and light; and to guard the threshold between the living and the dead.

But it was not enough. And there was something more, beyond the words, if only he could remember.

Tighaún had said that there were loyalties which bound the soul beyond death. In life, he had been allied with the shadowfay. This darkness had not the feel of the shadowfay, nor even of the demon of the *Ulhennar* that they had fought near the Wasted Hills. But Tighaún had also served the Emperor, and the Emperor served a demon; and he had summoned that demon to destroy Solban. The great demon. Lo-Khuma.

The blackness was now all around him, and only the sword of Fire held it back. His throat was full of earth. His strength was failing.

Lo-Khuma could not enter the waking world, but was he barred from the Realms of the Dead? Kellarn did not know. The First Kings had driven the demon back, but no mortal man could destroy him. Not even Halgan, the great priest of Fire and the Sun. Few even of the greatest creatures from the ancient strife of the gods could have done so, the moon fay had said.

Kellarn sank to his knees, crushed by the weight of the falling darkness. The light of the sword dissolved into countless sparks, and his head reeled. The battle seemed beyond him. And yet he knew that there was a way, another answer, if only he could find it. He turned inward, chasing the thought back down into the elusive well of memory.

A pair of enormous eyes was waiting for him, and Kellarn knew that he was right. With that last thought he plunged into their starlit depths, and all other senses fled.

II FIRE IN THE EARTH

Chapter Seven

Rhysana gazed about her in the dim glow of her magelight, the Warden's codex open in her hands. She had come to her first real check. Before her feet the paved floor broke apart into a jumbled ruin, on the brink of a drop into emptiness.

Hrugaar crouched down beside her, peering into the dark with his keen eyes. Dhûghaúr, still puffing from the climb of the last stair behind them, was picking his way up on to the tumbled stone to her right. The Archmage Ellen was looking over her shoulder.

'Is there another way that we could take?' Ellen asked.

'Oh, several,' said Rhysana absently. 'The main stair is farther over to the west. But that was well defended, and we should run into all kinds of fun if we tried to go that way. I was hoping to follow a quieter route.'

Thus far her plan had succeeded. The tunnel from the riverside had led straight to the eastern edge of the underground fortress; and from there they had passed the dart traps and sliding blocks of the *noghru* defences – all disabled long ago by the First Council – and made their way round without mishap to the triple tiered Hall of Earth, with its many stairs and galleries and carved stone dragons with shaggy manes and jewelled eyes. Torkhaal, she thought, would be sorry to have missed the dragons.

From the Hall of Earth they had climbed up through the heart of the citadel, the physical centre of the mystical cube of nine which Rhysana knew had governed its construction. From her first reading of the Warden's codex she had perceived that there were nine principal levels within the citadel, and that each level could be seen as the magical square of nine by nine proper to its sequence within the cube, with the larger halls positioned where the principal mystic numbers on that level should be found. Thus the great Hall of Earth had been on the fourth level – that number being held holy to the *Aeshta* Lords of Earth – which had been the same level as the riverside gate through which they had entered the fortress; and from there they had climbed up safely through the centre of the fifth to reach the sixth level, where still they were.

The fifth level – being the number of conflict, and separating the lower fortress from the upper – had been Rhysana's greatest fear when she had planned their journey. At the time of the taking of Whitespear Head it had been filled with dark magic, with seals binding guardians and demonic creatures from other Realms, and vicious enchantments long since proscribed or forgotten by the Council. Had she even told the other magi what had once been there, she doubted that they would ever have agreed to let her come. But from the descriptions in the Warden's codex she had learned of the safe route that the First Council had found.

Having thus bypassed the worst of the defences they had come to the more orderly part of the citadel, where it was known that Illana's allies from among the Blackbeard dwarves of the *noghru* had dwelt. It had been an easy task to follow the straight passages eastward, with their carved square doorways at regular intervals on either side, and so on up the last stair which had brought them here, to the edge of the Hall of Fire.

Dhûghaúr gasped in the shadows. Hrugaar sprang to his feet.

'What is it?' he called softly.

'Just a stitch, nothing worse,' Dhûghaúr replied. 'I think that we could do with some better light.'

'I like not the feel of this place,' said Hrugaar. 'Something evil has happened here.'

The mellow bronze glow of Dhûghaúr's power blossomed

into life, driving back the shadow as it spread up and out around them. The magi shielded their eyes against the sudden light.

The hall before them was perhaps some seventy feet across, and about the same in height. It had six sides of equal length; and where those sides met, six towering serpent statues upheld the vaulted ceiling with their outspread wings. Once, Rhysana knew, these winged serpents of Hýriel had been adorned with carved and gilded feathers, and their eyes had flickered with magical flame. But now the gold was gone, and the ruddy stone of the hall and statues had been melted and twisted like wax set too near to the fire, as though from a great burning. A large forked crack was torn across the vault. The floor had collapsed away into a yawning pit, stretching down into shadow beyond the reach of Dhûghaúr's light.

'There,' said Rhysana triumphantly. She pointed to an open archway high up on the second wall to their right. The shattered fragments of steps and balustrade clung to its lower edges; but from what she could see at this angle, the stair beyond the hall looked sound enough.

'Was there a battle here?' asked Dhûghaúr, clambering back down to join them.

'Not in the First Council's time,' said Rhysana. She closed up the Warden's codex, and tucked it away safely again inside her satchel.

'This damage is more recent,' said Ellen, 'or I am no judge. Did Morvaan come here, Ru?'

Hrugaar had crouched down again, looking over the edge into the darkness.

'No,' he said quietly. 'They did not come up this high. I thought that I heard something.'

'What?' asked Rhysana and Dhûghaúr together.

Hrugaar shrugged. 'I do not know. I can *feel* something down there, among the rocks. Yet there is nothing that I can see.'

He moved back and stood up again quietly.

'Let me look at that stitch,' he offered to Dhûghaúr.

'I am fine,' said the little mage, waving him away shyly. 'It is easier already. Will whatever Ru can sense attack us, do you think?'

'It will if we stay here,' said Ellen. 'We ought to keep moving. Shall I make the *leap* there for us?'

'Better not, I think,' said Rhysana. 'The edge of the stair is unsafe, and we do not know what we might bump into farther up. A more cautious approach might be sensible.'

'Do you intend to fly?' Ellen wondered.

'No, to ride,' said Rhysana. 'Gather close to me – and Ru, keep your eyes open for signs of trouble.'

The three magi moved obediently to form an arc behind her. Rhysana drew a deep breath, and then let it out slowly to steady herself as she concentrated on her spell. The air of the hall was stale and bitter, with a chill edge of dampness; and like Hrugaar, she could sense a whisper of malice from somewhere far below. But the air would serve her purpose.

She drew another deep breath, and then blew it out down the front of her gown, charging it with the power of her spell. The breath misted and glittered as it swept down around their feet; and she took it and wove it with her thought into a platform beneath them, curling up into a protective wall about their legs, like a carriage or a coracle boat.

'It tickles,' murmured Dhûghaúr.

Rhysana fastened off her spell, checking twice to satisfy herself that it would hold. Then she glanced around the hall again.

'You may wish to hold on to me,' she told them. Dhûghaúr and Ellen did so. Hrugaar rested one hand on her shoulder, but as though he were more concerned for her than for himself.

Rhysana smiled, and focused her attention on the archway where she wished to go. The misty coracle of her spell lifted and sailed slowly forward out across the pit. Dhûghaúr clung tightly to her.

They were perhaps two thirds of the way there when Hrugaar pointed with his free hand, and sparkling drops of silver-green power flew down and flared in the darkness far below.

'What is it?' Ellen demanded.

Rhysana held to her purpose, willing them forward more swiftly and resisting the urge to look down.

'I thought that there was something there,' said Hrugaar. 'In one of the tunnel openings.'

'There are tunnels?' gasped Dhûghaúr.

'Of course there would be,' said Ellen practically. 'There must have been rooms and passages on the levels below.'

Rhysana guided them in through the archway, and set them down a short way up the stair. Hrugaar sprang out at once and clambered back down toward the hall.

'Take care!' Ellen warned.

Rhysana unwove her spell and turned around. The bronze light was dimmer here, and the stair ahead climbed up into deeper shadow. Hrugaar was crouched down perilously close to the broken edge. He seemed to be listening as much as looking. At last he scampered back up to join them.

'Whatever it was, it seems to have gone now,' he said. 'It reminds me of something.'

'Can it reach us by another way?' Ellen asked.

'There are other stairs,' Rhysana allowed uneasily. 'But none too near. And it would have to know its way around, and be able to get past the defences. It could take some time to find us.'

'We were best to move quickly then,' said Hrugaar.

Rhysana kindled the silver-blue ball of her magelight again, and they set off up the stair. Before long they came to a small landing where the stairway turned to the right.

Dhûghaúr gasped and staggered as he came up behind her. He sank down against the wall, clutching his chest. His staff clattered loudly to the floor.

Rhysana turned back to him in concern. Hrugaar came bounding forward. Dhûghaúr lifted his pale face toward her, his dark eyes wide with terror. He lifted his hand from his chest, and the palm was black and moving. And then his body jerked in spasm, and a hundred black *things* spewed out from his mouth and nose, like lice and earwigs scuttling and leaping.

Rhysana heard herself screaming. The landing whirled with light and shadow. Hrugaar and Ellen were shouting. And then a wave of panic swept through her, choking the air from her throat and scattering her senses into darkness.

Torkhaal was at the opening ball when the warning came. He had lingered with his son in the Telún apartment, and arrived at the ball only a short while before the Archmage Morvaan. Taillan had been restless and fretful in the late afternoon heat, perhaps picking up on his father's own uneasiness over Rhysana's errand. In the end Nereïs had shooed Torkhaal away with Lavan and the twins, sending them on ahead of her so that she could settle the younger children to bed.

The formal opening of the Summer Court was held in the huge ballroom of the river wing on the eastern side of the imperial citadel. The ballroom – as Mellin Carfinn had once observed – seemed as long as a racecourse, with tall mirrors on the landward side that stretched from the floor to the high vaulted ceiling. Along the length of the river side a row of pillared arches gave on to a raised gallery with windows looking out over the estuary. The hall, like much of the river wing, was lined throughout with the white marble so favoured by the imperial nobles – except for the mirrors and for the floor, which was flagged with polished squares of marble and jasper of every hue. At previous balls, Torkhaal had seen the hall decorated in many fanciful and even magical ways; but that evening the Emperor's household had confined themselves to rather modest garlands of fresh greenery and summer flowers.

More than a hundred people had arrived there before them, arrayed in all their colourful finery, but the size of the ballroom prevented it from feeling either too crowded or too hot. The Emperor himself was not expected for at least another half an hour, and the opening ceremony itself would be an hour after that. The Telún twins had run off with some of the younger nobles, to explore the hall and to peek through the panelled doors of the antechambers where the food for the later feast was being laid out. Lavan steered a course up on to the raised gallery to join Nereïs' cousin, the flame haired Lady Lauraï Raudhar of Renza.

Lauraï wore a flowing gown of a deep sea green, which suited her pale beauty well. Escorting her that evening was her kinsman by marriage the Lord Aúrun of Renza, tall and fair like most of the men of the Watchful Isle, clad all in pale blue. Torkhaal and Aúrun had been bridegrooms together at their double wedding, when Aúrun had married the Lady Broneïs of Renza, and there was something about him that always reminded Torkhaal of Hrugaar. But then it was said that the Lords of Renza had sea fay blood somewhere in their veins.

Aúrun was cheerful as ever, and the more so when Torkhaal came up to greet them. Lauraï smiled, but with an air of distraction; and it was soon clear from her conversation that she was disturbed by the recent events in Ellanguan. Nor was she alone in that regard. Though there was music in the ballroom, few of the nobles present had yet begun to dance. Most were talking in small groups, or circling from one to another. There was little laughter, and what merriment there was seemed somewhat strained. High Councillor Sollonaal was down at the far end, his dark head bobbing above his distinctive robes of turquoise and gold; and Lirinal of Dregharis was with him, and there were one or two other magi around. The Lords of the *Aeshta* Orders were more notable than usual by their absence.

The Archmage the Lord Morvaan of Braedun was announced a few minutes later. He had changed into his familiar robes of purple and grey, and perhaps looked more businesslike than festive as he came in. But he seemed as relaxed as ever as he ambled across the coloured floor, stopping here and there to greet one person or another, making his way slowly toward the raised gallery with no sense of undue haste or alarm. Torkhaal himself relaxed, reading from Morvaan's untroubled manner that thus far, at least, Rhysana's journey to Whitespear Head had been successful.

It was not possible to talk of it openly in the ballroom, and even a discussion mind to mind might have attracted unwanted attention from the inquisitive. But as Morvaan grasped Torkhaal's arm in friendly greeting, he sent a swift burst of reassurance that all was going well. It was the best that they could hope for at that stage.

Following Morvaan up the steps on to the gallery came Torkhaal's friend Gravhan, dressed in tunic and breeches of dark green as a knight of the Môshári Order. At his elbow was a younger woman of about Torkhaal's own age, with dark brown hair coiled and braided very fetchingly about her face. She wore a full skirted gown of silver-grey silk, with a black sash fastened with a diamond brooch in the shape of a bear's paw. Torkhaal felt at once that he should have recognised her, but Gravhan saved him the embarrassment by introducing her as his niece by marriage, the Lady Camarra Kelmaar of Dârghûn – Miranda's younger sister, and wife to the Lord Haldrin Dârghûn, Herusen's heir.

'You grow more beautiful with every passing moon, my Lady,' Torkhaal told her, bowing deeply. 'I trust that we may still hope to see you on the Council before too long?'

'Perhaps sooner than you think,' Camarra laughed, offering him her hand to kiss. 'I am to prepare for my trials as soon as this Court is done.'

'You can't keep Darghûn off the Council for long,' chuckled Morvaan. 'Is your husband here, my Lady?'

'He is expected at Court any day now,' she replied. 'He wished first to see his troops safe home. Lord Gravhan has kindly agreed to be my escort until Haldrin arrives.'

'Where were you hiding then?' Torkhaal asked Gravhan. 'I did not hear the heralds announce you.'

Gravhan grinned and waved the question aside, and the conversation turned to other things.

The four of them talked for several minutes, chiefly about

Dârghûn and Herusen's extended family, and how well Camarra liked them; and of her early difficulties with Haldrin's mother, the Lady Rogheïn Aartaús of Dârghûn – whom Camarra liked very much, but who had for many years been the chatelaine of the Dârghûn manor house and had her own opinions on how things should be done. Yet through it all, Torkhaal gathered that Camarra was here as much on behalf of Kelmaar as Dârghûn; and that Gravhan, of course, was here on guard as a knight of the Môshári; and that apart from the tide of events in Ellanguan, the *Aeshta* Orders had found a new cause for concern.

'Something has changed with the birth of this new moon,' Camarra told them, so softly that the three men had to lean closer to her to hear. 'Or perhaps something happened last night, while our eyes were turned elsewhere.'

'The Enemy has drawn closer to the waking world,' agreed Gravhan. 'His feet are on the very threshold. Imarra has felt it.'

'The priestesses of Aranara have foretold that this will be a Moon of Calling,' said Camarra; 'though I have not the skill to see that for myself.'

Torkhaal was about to ask what a Moon of Calling was, and how one might hope to see it. But at that moment his stomach turned to ice, and he felt the faint rush of distant panic. He gasped and clutched at Gravhan's arm.

'What—' Gravhan began.

'Rhysana,' said Morvaan.

Torkhaal nodded, mastering himself. There was nowhere private for him to go, except the antechambers on the far side of the ballroom floor, and he hesitated to draw attention by disappearing in a magical *leap*.

Camarra led him aside swiftly, and sat him down on the nearest of the cushioned window seats. Gravhan sat with him, and Morvaan and Camarra positioned themselves to mask them from the view of the crowd. The window behind was open, and a cool breeze blew in from the estuary far below. Torkhaal shivered within his robes.

Gravhan held out his hand palm upward, not touching him. 'Where is she?' he asked.

Torkhaal shook his head.

'Can you find her?'

Torkhaal closed his eyes briefly, steadying himself. He knew that she was not dead. He could feel it. But that was all. Hrugaar should still be with her; but they might need his help. He had to find out.

He nodded to Gravhan without looking at him, and took hold of the proffered hand. He felt the strength of the knight flowing into him, supporting him. He knew that he could trust Gravhan to look after him.

Torkhaal closed his eyes again and turned his thought inward. He focused on that part of himself where Rhysana was, that *was* Rhysana, and quested through it to touch her mind.

Darkness blocked him.

He tried again, more slowly and with more strength. Shadow and distance still conspired against him, slipping and sliding beneath his touch. He could sense that she was there, but could not reach her. It did not help that she had not the mental gifts that he and Hrugaar had.

But Hrugaar had them.

Torkhaal shifted back, brushed minds fleetingly with Gravhan, and turned to hunt for Hrugaar.

Again he met with shadows and confusion; and then, almost in surprise, Torkhaal remembered the rock and magic of Whitespear Head itself, which must be working against him. Or at least, the magic would do so. As a mage of Earth, the rock might help him. He shifted his thought, pushing less strongly and letting himself drift along course and vein of imagined stone. And then suddenly he was through, and facing a wall of silver-green water. Torkhaal rushed forward. The water drove him back.

Hrugaar! His voice seemed empty, powerless. *Hrugaar!*

The face of the water darkened. A single wave lapped out

and swirled around him drawing him closer in; but he did not let him inside.

Hrugaar!

The wave swirled higher and slapped his face in a spray of icy foam. Then he was drawn further in, and the green water was all around him.

Not now, he heard his friend's thought, oddly distant. *Rhysana needs me.*

Rhysana?

She is well, Hrugaar assured him. *But this linking of minds may bring danger to us here. You should go.*

I felt something, Torkhaal told him.

We were frightened. It has passed.

There was a stirring in the water around him, a troubled blend of shadow and silver light; and then he glimpsed Rhysana's face, as through Hrugaar's eyes. Her head was resting on a bundled pillow, and shining softly golden with reflected light. Her eyes fluttered open and looked up at him, and she smiled.

Torkhaal? she said in her clear, sweet voice.

And then the vision faded into green, and the water washed him back again.

Go now, said Hrugaar. *We shall return.*

Torkhaal withdrew, feeling the world around him grow lighter and clearer again as he surfaced into himself. There was a coolness on his brow, as though Hrugaar had given him a parting kiss there; and the warm strength of Gravhan of Môshári still flowed into him through their joined hands.

He opened his eyes, feeling relieved but a little self conscious. The noise of the ball was still going on, and no one seemed to have noticed him.

Camarra shielded us, sent Gravhan. *You went very deep for a while.*

Yes, answered Torkhaal. *But Rhysana is safe – for now. I shall be happier when they have returned home.*

They?

Hrugaar is with her. Torkhaal squeezed Gravhan's hand in thanks, and then released it, gently breaking the link between them.

Rhysana woke as though from a deep sleep, with the feeling that she was safe at home in her own bed, yet with the faintly nagging doubt that she ought to be doing something else. She could feel her husband's *presence* close by. She opened her eyes, blinking in the golden light, and half imagined that she saw his handsome face looking down at her. She smiled.

'Torkhaal?' she murmured.

Then her vision cleared, and she saw that it was Hrugaar leaning over her. His fair face was grubby and tear-stained, but he managed a weary smile.

Torkhaal was with us in thought, his voice whispered within her mind. *He has gone now.*

He sat back on his heels, moving away from her. Rhysana felt his *presence* fading from her, like the tide going out. The floor was hard and uncomfortable beneath her, and the stone vaulting overhead did not belong to her own chambers. She struggled to sit up.

Hrugaar moved at once to help her. The Archmage Ellen came toward her from her right, the white steel rod of the Prime Councillor now cradled in her arm. Rhysana took in the small stone chamber around them, and remembered where she was.

'Dhûghaúr—' she began.

A memory of writhing darkness and horror fluttered at the edges of her mind – but somehow remote, as if blurred or already half forgotten.

'He is gone,' said Ellen flatly.

Hrugaar turned his face away. Rhysana moved to rest her hand on his arm, but then thought the better of it.

'Hrugaar wanted to *leap* out with you at once,' Ellen told her. 'He was worried for your health – and for your child. I am still half minded to agree with him. But I thought that you had the right to make that decision for yourself, if he could bring you out of shock in time, and have you well enough to go on.'

Ellen's face was grim and set, even in the tawny glow of her own magelight, and she was hugging her arms about herself tightly. Rhysana realised that she had been using Ellen's shawl as a pillow.

'What happened?' she asked.

'Do not dwell upon it just now,' Ellen warned.

'I need to know,' said Rhysana. 'It may affect whether I decide to go on.' She picked up the russet shawl and shook it out, to give herself something simple to focus on. It was more damp than dusty from the stone.

'It was *shadowshot*,' said Hrugaar. 'A dart of the shadowfay, wrought with malice and power to turn human flesh into crawling carrion. I should have known.'

Rhysana closed her mind against the burgeoning thought, schooling herself to calm.

'You could not have known,' said Ellen firmly.

'I should have known,' Hrugaar repeated. 'I sensed their presence. I should have known that he had been shot.'

'And what then?' Ellen countered. 'I have heard of the legends of *shadowshot*, Hrugaar. Even Imarra of Môshári might not have saved him, had she been here.'

'It is not your fault, Ru,' said Rhysana gently, reaching out to touch him now. 'It is rather my fault, for letting him come here.'

'Do not you start,' said Ellen. 'It is no one's fault but the damned shadowfay.'

Hrugaar turned to hug Rhysana tightly, his body wracked by heavy sobs.

'I was too late to save him,' he wept. 'And I had to save you. Ellen—'

He left the words unspoken, but Rhysana could guess the rest. Hrugaar had used his healing gifts to save herself and her unborn child, for fear the shock should cause her to miscarry. Ellen had been left to deal with what was left of poor Dhûghaúr.

She held him close, crooning softly to quieten him, and mourning the loss of the little mage and the sorrow that she had brought to her friends. Later, when she was alone, she would weep for Dhûghaúr. And later, when Ellen was ready, she would talk to her about it. For now, she needed to keep moving – and, if she could, to bring some good out of Dhûghaúr's death.

'Where are we, and how long have we been here?' she asked Ellen, once Hrugaar had mastered himself again.

'You were only out for a short while,' Ellen answered. 'The landing where it happened is just there. Ten minutes, at most.'

She pointed to the doorway just beyond Hrugaar, where a flight of steps led down. A barrier of bronze power sealed the stairway a short distance from the top, no doubt set there by the Archmage Ellen herself.

Rhysana nodded. 'Ru,' she said gently, 'how great a danger are the shadowfay really likely to be here, now that we are aware of them?'

Hrugaar sat back and blew his nose in his handkerchief, and then wiped his eyes.

'They are always a danger,' he replied.

Ellen tapped her fingers against the rod. Rhysana passed her her shawl.

'But how dangerous?' she pursued.

'Were one of the greater shadowfay here,' said Hrugaar, 'they would be upon us already. But I have not sensed the presence of anything so terrible. Not yet.

'I think,' he went on slowly, 'that we must have surprised one of the lesser of their kind. They fear light, and flee from it. What other evils that one may find to send against us, I do not know. Yet against the three of us, forewarned, he may prove no great threat.'

'And he would have to find his way up through Illana's defences,' said Rhysana.

She rolled sideways on to her hands and knees and stood up. Hrugaar was swiftly on his feet to help her.

'I think that we should try to carry on, while we still may,' she told them.

'And if we should meet the shadowfay again?' demanded Ellen.

Rhysana checked that she still had the Warden's codex, and tugged her satchel back into place.

'There is a connection between Illana's lore and the demon captain,' she said. 'There may be something here that can help us. The shadowfay served the demon in ages past. Can we risk letting them find it before us?'

'Put like that,' said Ellen, 'I suppose not.'

Rhysana called up her silver-blue magelight again, making it brighter than before to please Hrugaar. Then she stood with her back to the stair whence they had come, to regain her sense of where she was going. The chamber they were in was square, with a doorway leading out on each side. She took the passage straight ahead, to the west.

The passage continued for some time, without any doorways on either side. Hrugaar and Ellen kept close behind her, Hrugaar now carrying Dhûghaúr's black staff in his right hand. Then a short flight of steps led them down into a long pillared hall, with tiered galleries above to left and right, and a high ceiling lost in shadow. The hall had been carved from the rock of the Whitespear Head promontory, and was partly lined with the blue-grey stone of the Blue Mountains far to the east. There were still piles of the same blue-grey stone stacked at intervals around the floor, and the remains of timbered structures around some of the pillars at the nearer end. It was clearly a part of the fortress that had been unfinished at the time of Illana's defeat.

They picked their way carefully across the debris on the floor, keeping a watch on the shifting shadows of pillars and timbers to either side. But nothing sprang out to attack them. At the far end of the hall was another short flight of steps leading up into another passage; and beyond that a similar hall to the one through which they had just passed. This second hall, however, was more nearly complete. There were three long fountain pools sunk end to end along the centre of the floor, and the pillars had been carved with the likeness of climbing vines. There were no furnishings of any kind; but flanking the steps and doorway at the far end were what seemed to be two huge tusks, nearly twice Rhysana's height, standing propped against the wall.

'Are those dragon bones?' whispered Hrugaar.

'Whale bones, more like,' said Ellen thoughtfully.

They passed to the left of the empty pools, once again alert for signs of danger. Unlike the first hall, there were now tunnels leading off beneath the galleries on either side, and the sound of their own quiet footsteps ran away in most unsettling echoes. Rhysana quickened their pace.

As they rounded the end of the third pool and headed for the steps, Hrugaar caught her arm and pulled her back.

'There is a light ahead,' he whispered urgently.

'What kind?' Ellen asked.

Hrugaar motioned them to move back, and scooted forward a short way, crouching low, to risk a second look. Rhysana frowned, thinking of what lay ahead; and then she smiled.

'There is another chamber like this,' said Hrugaar, coming back; 'and a light like ours.'

'It *is* ours, Ru,' Rhysana laughed. 'Good. I am glad that that has survived – and it means that we have come the right way.'

'What has survived?' he asked, trying not to look foolish.

'One of the more interesting defences, to my mind,' she told him. 'Come and see!'

She led the way on up the steps, pausing for a moment to look at the huge bones on either side of the doorway. The Warden's codex had referred to them as *tusks of some unknown underground beast*, but she would leave Ellen to debate that with him later. Then she went on into the passageway, with Hrugaar and Ellen following warily behind.

The passage ran for scarcely a dozen paces before it ended in three mirrors of equal width, which stretched from floor to ceiling and were bordered with white marble on all sides. The middle of the three faced straight down the passage toward them, and it was in this that Hrugaar would have seen the reflection of her magelight when they were out in the hall. They could all see themselves clearly now as they approached. The two side mirrors were set at matching angles, so that the passage seemed to end in a lantern bay.

Rhysana stopped to look at her three reflections, and smiled.

'I can sense that there is magic here,' said Hrugaar, 'but how is it a defence?'

'It is quite simple,' she explained. 'The mirrors are only a *glamouring*. One may pass through them quite safely.'

Four Hrugaars shrugged. 'Then what difference would that make in the dark?'

'That is the other part of the spell,' said Rhysana. 'It sends you the opposite way. We wish to turn right here, so we have to go through the left mirror.'

'Is that not a little too simple to stay secret for long?' he wondered.

'Perhaps,' Rhysana smiled. 'But it is a remarkably early example of its kind, and it has stood the test of time for a thousand years.'

'We have not tested it yet,' Ellen reminded her.

Rhysana sighed and breathed out, focusing her trained senses to study the balanced energies of the spell. There was no sign that it had begun to fall apart.

'I think that all is as it should be,' she said aloud. 'Do you want me to go through alone, or shall we brave it together?'

The three of them held hands, and Rhysana led the way through. She felt only the lightest brush of power across her face, as if a soap bubble had bumped against her nose and burst. They found themselves standing in another passage, with a lantern bay of three mirrors behind them.

'So which is the way back?' asked Hrugaar.

'The right-hand mirror,' she said. 'But I do not plan to come back this way. I hope that we may make the *leap* straight home, once we have found what we are looking for.'

'Morvaan seemed to think that we would have to leave by the way we came in,' said Ellen. 'But I must agree that under the circumstances I should like to prove him wrong.'

They set off quickly along the passage, and came to a small round chamber. There were openings to left and right and a wider stair straight ahead of them.

'How far are we from where we have to go, anyway?' Ellen asked.

'Not far,' said Rhysana. 'Illana's private chambers should be a little way ahead and above us. We have three more stairs to climb.'

'There is trouble on the air here,' said Hrugaar, glancing around.

'The shadowfay?' asked Rhysana.

'No,' he said. 'There is power of some sort. Look!'

He pointed to the tip of the rod in Ellen's hands, which seemed to be glowing more brightly than with mere reflected light. Rhysana dimmed the power in her magelight until it was no more than a pale blue candle flame hovering in the gloom. As their eyes attuned to the change in light, they could see tiny sparks and flickers of energy playing up and down the length of the white steel rod – and not only along the rod, but upon Dhûghaúr's black staff and around the bobbing magelight itself.

'Bugger,' said Rhysana. She focused her trained senses again, as she had done back at the mirror defence; and then she could see that faint wisps of pale energy drifted around their bodies, and trailed in lazy curls on the shadowed air.

'What is causing this, Rhysana?' asked Ellen. 'Was it the *glamouring* spell that we passed through?'

'No,' Rhysana answered. 'Some other magic near here must have faded or become unsound over the years, and traces of the energy still remain. It does not seem to be too dangerous.'

'It is worse upon the stair,' said Hrugaar. 'Is that the way we must go?'

'Yes,' she nodded.

'I think that we were best to try to earth it as we go,' said Ellen. 'Give me the staff Ru – it is more suited to this kind of work.'

She handed him the rod in exchange for Dhûghaúr's staff, and held it upright before her with the heel planted firmly on the stone floor. She breathed deeply in, and then out. The glitter of energy faded all around them, and the air felt suddenly dull and lifeless.

Rhysana made her magelight brighter with a thought, and led the way up the stair. She had not gone far before the globe of light began to sparkle and flash quite visibly. She felt her skin beginning to prickle.

'Let me go first,' Ellen offered.

The stair was wide enough for Rhysana and Hrugaar to stand on either side, with Ellen one step ahead of them. The Archmage repeated her earthing spell with the staff; but this time the air did not wholly clear, and a firefly flicker danced briefly around Ellen's head.

Ellen swore beneath her breath, but the tunnelled stair made her voice echo more loudly. 'The power is getting stronger,' she told them. 'Or we are getting closer. And I fear that we are making it worse, just by being here.'

'Do you mean that we have awoken it?' asked Hrugaar.

'I suppose that the Fay might put it thus,' Ellen nodded. 'Other power draws it – the rod, the staff, Rhysana's magelight, indeed the very energy of life within our own bodies. Even my simple spell began to make it worse, in an effort to counter it. If I could find the source of the original spell, I might be able to put a stop to it. I presume that there was another defence up ahead?'

'Not exactly,' said Rhysana. 'This stair should lead to the Hall of Water, which was one of the wonders of Whitespear Head.'

'The magical wonders,' said Ellen grimly. 'That is just what we needed, for one of those to go wild on us.'

'It has not harmed us yet,' Hrugaar pointed out. 'If we keep our light low, and stay calm and quiet without use of magic, could we pass safely through?'

Ellen looked doubtful.

'It is worth a try, since we are here,' said Rhysana. 'We can turn back if the danger grows too great.'

Ellen gave in, though she insisted that she should take the lead and that Rhysana should keep her light as dim as possible. They moved on slowly up the stair, hampered both by the lack of light and by the growing weight of power on the air around them. Rhysana felt her skin crawling, and the back of her neck prickled as though she were about to come under attack; and it was like trying to breathe in a thick sea mist. It became harder to stay calm and patient – and not to smile, in spite of herself, at the sight of Hrugaar, whose fair hair now bristled like the tail of a startled squirrel.

After what seemed an age, though it was probably not much more than two minutes, the stair ended in a square vaulted landing. Before them were double doors of grey oak, silvered with age, carved with interwoven sea serpents and set with ring handles and hinges of grey steel.

'Let me,' murmured Hrugaar.

He crept forward to the doors, and rested one hand gently against the carved wood. A whisper of green light played up and down his arm, and then faded. After a few more moments he thrust the white steel rod beneath his belt, placed both hands on the ring to the right, and pulled. The door opened with a growl of protest, which echoed alarmingly ahead and behind, and stuck fast when it reach a gap of about an arm's length. There was a brief flare of light from the hall beyond, and then a sound like breaking glass.

The three magi froze, listening intently. Rhysana found that she had been holding her breath for some time.

Hrugaar was the first to move, tiptoeing silently to the edge of the open door to peep round in to the hall. Then he beckoned them forward to look.

The Hall of Water was circular, a little smaller than the Hall of Fire had been and with a lower, domed ceiling; and even at the time of its construction it might hardly have been considered to be a chamber on a grand scale. In Illana's day the dome had been lined with clear glass or crystal, enchanted to throw down endless dancing rainbows and drops of silver light like rain. There had been mirrors on the walls and doors too, between pillars of white stone; and the floor had been a spiralled water pattern of blue and grey.

But now the hall lay in ruin. Much of the dome had shattered or fallen, revealing the dark rock behind, and only a few small patches glowed fitfully here and there with a dull, sickly pallor. The floor was cracked and blackened in many places, and strewn with the wreckage of the dome and the mirrored walls; and one set of doors on the far side hung twisted on broken hinges. Over all, the remnant energies of the shattered spells drifted and flickered with many colours, in mockery of the rainbows they once had been. The air seemed tense and heavy as the stillness before a storm.

Hrugaar laid one finger to his lips, but Rhysana did not need the warning. The noise from the door must have been enough to dislodge one or other of the mirror fragments in the hall, which they had heard fall. There was no knowing how much more of the dome might come down around their ears at any moment. She drew Ellen and Hrugaar back from the door to the far side of the landing.

'We need the first passage to the left,' she whispered slowly. 'There may be a mirror hiding it.'

The other two magi nodded. There was no question of Ellen attempting to earth all of the energies left in the hall. Even though she might have achieved it, given sufficient time, effort and support, they could afford neither the risk nor the delay.

'I shall go first,' whispered Hrugaar. 'My senses are keener than yours.'

He glanced pointedly at Rhysana's magelight. She nodded, and let it fade and go out. A flicker of orange light played across the vault above them.

They waited a few more moments to let their eyes adjust to the darkness, then he led the way back to the doors. The baleful glow from the dome of the hall seemed to have grown stronger, more awake.

Hrugaar left Rhysana standing in the doorway, with Ellen just behind her, and moved slowly to the left across the floor. His booted feet made no sound as he picked his way between the shards of broken glass. From her vantage, Rhysana could now see that there was a wall of white stone beyond the door, and then an open archway beyond that leading off into a wide passage no more than twenty feet from where she stood.

Hrugaar had covered only half the distance when the drifting energies overhead swirled suddenly together and arced down through the air toward him.

Rhysana was powerless to cry out. But Hrugaar had his wits about him. He sprang forward, leaping headlong toward the open doorway ahead. The bolt of power slammed into the floor where he had stood a moment before, shattering the stone where it struck. The noise of impact echoed around the hall, bringing down a rain of glittering glass. Then Hrugaar reached the threshold, and a sheet of bright green flame filled the doorway around him. He hung there like a puppet, dangling in mid-air.

For a long moment the whole hall was flooded with green light, bouncing wildly between glass and stone. Rhysana shrank back against the door. Then the light went out, and the noise faded; and there was only the pallid, moonlit glow of the dying patches of the dome. The air seemed suddenly clearer.

'Quick!' said Rhysana, grabbing hold of Ellen's arm. 'While it has burned itself out.'

She hurried forward across the floor, dragging Ellen after her, heedless of the crackling glass beneath her feet. She braced herself as she passed through the next doorway; but her guess had proved correct, and there was no barrier there to stop them.

'Ow,' muttered Hrugaar, dragging himself to his knees as they came through.

Rhysana bent down to look at him, though there was little enough light to see by.

'I am all right,' he told her. 'Just a little wobbly.'

'You have no business to be alive at all,' said Ellen.

The two women helped him to his feet, and they moved off again along the passage. Since there were no telltale glimmers of power anywhere near, Ellen risked kindling a deep bronze ball of magelight to guide their way.

The passage brought them to another stair, which led up into a high square lobby all of black stone. Away to their left began a grander staircase, sweeping up around the walls and back above their heads. There were crystal lamps set at intervals along the stair, though none were lit; and at the foot of the stair the stone rail ended in a small carved dragon.

'This will take us up into Illana's own part of the citadel,' said Rhysana, her voice hushed in awe. 'We should be safer there.'

'Safer, but not safe,' said Ellen.

Rhysana ignored her. 'Are you sure that you are all right, Ru?' she asked.

'Well enough,' he said, ruffling his fingers through his hair. 'I think that it looked worse than it was.'

Rhysana frowned, not entirely convinced. But he had taken no great hurt that she could see, and the excitement of being so close to Illana's own chambers would not let her worry about him for long.

She led the way up the long stair, puffing a little with the extra weight that she carried. Hrugaar kept pace beside her, holding Dhûghaúr's staff once more. Ellen came behind with the white steel rod, climbing at a gentler pace, like a mother keeping an eye on her adventurous children.

At the top of the staircase they came to a landing of the same black stone, with closed doors on either side. Rhysana called up her silver-blue magelight and headed straight for a pair of larger ebon doors at the far end. With Hrugaar's help she thrust them open; and then she paused to regain her breath and to look about her, while Ellen caught up with them.

No account in the Warden's codex had prepared her for the terrible splendour of this next hall. It was a vaulted cube of pale stone, more than fifty feet across, and all around the walls was a wide carved frieze of life-sized figures engaged in battle. They had entered at the centre of the south wall, and there were matching doors to the north and west. In the east stood a great panelled chair like a throne. There were a number of heavy stools around the borders of the hall; but the central part of the floor was clear, and chequered like a huge *sherunuresh* board made up of flagstones each fully a yard square. The great lamp of silver and crystal, which had once floated high overhead, had long since fallen and shattered among the dust of ages upon the floor, and its light had gone out.

Rhysana shivered, from more than just the cold. The pale blue of her magelight, drifting just above her head, threw the carved figures of the frieze into deeper relief of light and shadow, so that they seemed almost to move with a life of their own. The vault overhead was all but hidden in darkness. It struck her as not a comfortable place to be; and Hrugaar must have thought so too, for after only a brief glance around he moved protectively to Rhysana's side, holding the black staff ready with both hands.

'Where now?' asked Ellen as she joined them.

'Straight ahead, I think,' said Rhysana quietly. 'The doors on the left lead through some other chambers and round to the great stair that comes up from the west. We may have to try that way later. The other doors should take us toward Illana's library and study rooms, which I think are the best place to start.'

Though she had said straight ahead she led off to the left across the floor, moving around the edge of the chequered pattern. The magi who had come here before had found no trace of magic in the floor, but Rhysana was not minded to tempt the gods upon that point. None of them felt like closing the doors behind them. The drawback to her chosen route was that they had to keep closer to the carved frieze, beneath the hostile gaze of countless dust clogged eyes.

At first she had thought that they were mostly men and women, with a few beasts of war and an uglier figure here and there that more resembled some of the goblinkind. But as they moved around the hall she saw that there were the stockier shapes of armoured *noghru* with their square shields, and taller warriors that might have been some of the Fay; and there were trolls and ogres and evil creatures from other Realms, and winged beasts flew above them higher up in the dimmer light.

'This chamber gives me the creeps,' Ellen muttered as they neared the far corner.

'The carvings show a battle of the Bright Alliance,' said Hrugaar.

'Yes, that would seem to fit,' said Rhysana. 'You don't suppose—'

She paused to look around, letting her voice trail away. If that were so, then there might be a carved likeness of the enemy captain himself among his battling hordes. She was not sure whether she wanted to see an image of Lo-Khuma in this unfriendly place.

'Behind the throne,' said Hrugaar, catching her thought.

It was too far away for Rhysana to see clearly in the gloom. But her curiosity got the better of her, and she sent her magelight sailing ahead toward it as they made for the northern doors.

How she could have missed him before, Rhysana could not imagine; for the carved image of Lo-Khuma dwarfed all other figures within the frieze. He must have been three or four times the height of the human warriors. In form he was like a man, powerfully built and clad only in a simple kilt; but his face had a cruel, feral beauty, far beyond humankind. At his back, and seeming to hover above him, were demons with horses' skulls such as they had seen at the siege of Arrandin. To either side of him were two tall men who stood head and shoulders above the rest, with great swords in their hands and jewelled circlets instead of helms.

'Ferrughôr and Falladan, one would assume,' said Ellen. 'The one on the right bears a strong resemblance to the statue of Falladan in Ellanguan.'

'I wonder if the other Kings are shown here,' said Hrugaar. But none of them seemed minded to tarry to find out. They dragged open one of the heavy doors to leave.

The grinding of the door echoed dully around the hall. It was followed a moment later by a deeper rumble from farther off, like thunder in the distance. The three magi looked at one another anxiously.

'The Hall of Water?' asked Ellen.

'No,' said Hrugaar, 'that lies below us. We should have felt it through the floor.'

'The great stair, then?' Ellen offered.

'Perhaps,' Rhysana allowed uncertainly. 'But it did not seem to come from ahead. Quick! While we have time!'

They hurried through the open doorway, Rhysana's magelight whipping in behind them and over their heads, and pulled the door shut. The dark stone walls of the passage seemed suddenly oppressive, as though a trap were closing around them.

Rhysana led the way ahead, with Ellen following just to her right and Hrugaar keeping a rearguard. She tried to block the imagined thought of the carved figures clambering down from the frieze to lumber after them.

They passed a couple of smaller rooms, and the passage on

the right which led off to the chambers where Illana had slept, and turned left into a low rectangular hall. The hangings and settles of the hall had been destroyed by fire at the time of the taking of Whitespear Head, and the hearth was choked with rubble and dust; but it might once have made rather a homely room. In the far corner was a stone stair up to an open door, and beyond that a short passage took them straight into a larger hall lined in grey stone. The Warden's codex had referred to this as a *study chamber*, but it struck Rhysana that *classroom* or *practice hall* might have been nearer the mark. It was fully twenty paces long and ten broad, and at the far end away to their left were three long stone tables. There were three low doors along the far wall, covered in a silvery metal that had once been polished to mirror brightness, but which was now tarnished and dull and bereft of its former glory. To the nearer end on their right were tall double doors of grey stone that stood wide open.

'So where are we?' asked Hrugaar.

'The study rooms,' said Rhysana. 'Two of the silver doors lead to store rooms, the middle one to a smaller work room or study. Through the stone doors are the vaults where a few magical treasures were found; and beyond those, the library. If my guess proves correct, then what we are looking for may be somewhere around here.'

'And what are we looking for, exactly?' Ellen demanded.

Rhysana winced inwardly. That was the heart of the problem. She really had no clear idea of what she had expected to find here, only the hope that she would know it when – and if – she found it. And some of the finest minds of the First Council had been here before her.

'Something so well hidden,' she said, 'that even the First Council could not find it; or else so obvious that they overlooked it. I think that there must have been another vault, or somewhere where Illana kept her most secret work or wealth.'

'And why here?' asked Ellen.

'It fits with the magical cube of nine,' said Rhysana. 'The

library is perhaps the most likely place on this level, because it takes the position of sixty-four – the square of eight, the number of Air and Intelligence, and this is the eighth level of nine. There was a way up from there to the top level, but that whole area was either poorly mapped or never finished, and could take far longer to explore.'

'And time we may not have,' said Hrugaar. 'Shall we try the library first?'

Rhysana nodded and led the way.

Beyond the tall doors was a wide corridor of smooth black stone, with statues of hawk-headed men standing on raised plinths in a row down either side. There were eight plinths, but the third one on the right was empty and the shattered remains of that statue were now scattered across the floor. Hrugaar grabbed Rhysana's arm, pulling her back.

'There is power in the stone,' he warned. 'The statues watch us.'

'I know,' she said, patting his hand and then removing it. 'They are here to guard the vaults. The doors are halfway down on either side, but hidden by the craft of the *noghru*. The statues will not harm us unless we try to open the doors. That one was destroyed by the First Council.' She set off again at a brisk pace, trying to ignore the prickling of her skin as she passed beneath the gaze of those eyes.

'I trust that you are not thinking of searching the vaults?' said Ellen, hurrying beside her. Rhysana did not answer.

They went down a flight of steps at the far end, and through another pair of open stone doors into the library.

'Is it safe to risk some real light here, Ru?' Rhysana asked.

He sniffed the air, and then cocked his head as if listening. He frowned, and then nodded. Rhysana sent her magelight out in to the middle of the chamber, and let it shine out as bright as a spring morning.

The library stretched to left and right, and was of a size with the practice hall that they had left behind them and faced with the same grey stone. But unlike the hall it had two great square pillars stretching up into a ribbed vault; and both the walls and the pillars held row upon row of deep stone shelves. At the far end to the left, another pair of doors had been flung wide open and piled stone and rubble had spewed out across the flagged stone floor, blocking that way entirely. There was nothing to be seen on the shelves, other than the faded scars of ancient burning, and layers of mould and dust.

The three magi moved out into the room, picking their way carefully across the dusty floor as they spread apart to speed their search. Rhysana focused her senses intently, but there seemed to be no trace of magic here that she could find. She pictured to herself how the place might have looked in Illana's time, with books and scrolls stacked neatly on the shelves, and perhaps cunning objects of wood or stone or precious metal displayed in between, or treasures looted from the Wasted Hills of Lautun; for even Illana herself would have been hard put to gather so many manuscripts that she could fill every shelf in this library. There had been lamps here then, too – crystal orbs that floated free in the air and followed one about. The magi had taken them for study, but none now remained in the keeping of the Colleges.

Hrugaar was searching around the central pillars, wrinkling his nose as he probed the carved stone with clever fingers. Eventually Ellen came over to join Rhysana, holding one corner of her russet shawl to her face against the dust.

'Was the stair to the upper level beyond there?' she asked, gesturing toward the doorway filled with rubble.

'Yes,' Rhysana sighed. 'There might even have been a way up to the surface beyond, though that part was unclear. But the main rooms shown on the upper level – the Halls of the Sun and Moon, and an observatory of some kind – were all farther to the south and east. We could still reach them, were we to brave the great stair. Perhaps we shall have to do so.'

'Well there seems to be nothing here,' said Ellen. Rhysana reluctantly agreed.

They fetched Hrugaar and went back out into the black

stone passage. Rhysana dimmed her magelight again. They hurried past the hawk-headed statues, and reached the safety of the long practice hall. Rhysana made straight for the middle door on the right. After the library, this was her next best choice in this part of the fortress. The few scattered papers of Illana's work that had been found had been in the small study room that lay beyond.

The silvery metal that covered the door was so dull and patchy that even close to it gave little in the way of reflection, save for a few blurred smears of blue and green from her own and Ellen's gowns. Across the low lintel above, and up and down the length of the stone posts on either side, were carved many Old Kingdoms runes and several discs of the moon in her changing phases.

'There is a series of pressure points to open this door,' she said, pulling on her gloves before she took out the Warden's codex. 'They have to be pushed in the correct order to release the nine tumblers of the lock.'

'Might one not just make use of an opening spell?' asked Ellen.

'Provided that you knew the correct order to release the tumblers,' said Rhysana absently. 'I have a drawing of it here.'

She flicked her way through the pages. She was almost certain that she remembered the sequence, but she needed to reassure herself that she was right. The last thing that Rhysana wanted to do was to jam the mechanism by making an error in haste. And given the state of the metal surface of the door, it was by no means certain that the tumblers were not already ruined beyond use.

Hrugaar had moved away to look around the hall while Rhysana searched through the codex. He came back looking unsettled.

'The air is changing,' he told them. 'Something evil is coming nearer – the shadowfay, I think. We should leave very soon.'

'Two minutes, Ru,' Rhysana pleaded. 'I need to check this room if I can.'

'If we can not make the *leap* from here, we shall likely have to fight our way out anyway,' said Ellen practically. 'Tell me where to push, Rhysana, while you hold the book.'

'The full moon disc first,' said Rhysana. 'Shoulder height on the left.'

Ellen found and pushed it. For a moment nothing seemed to happen. Then Ellen pushed harder, and the stone disc slid inward beneath her fingers. There was a whisper of movement within the door, and then a soft click.

'Now the crescent moon, right of centre on the lintel,' Rhysana told her.

'What do the runes say?' asked Hrugaar.

There was a second click from the door.

'They are here in the picture, Ru,' said Rhysana. 'Something about moonlight and moon shadow, I think. Now the waning moon, about halfway down on the right.'

Hrugaar looked over her shoulder at the drawing of the doorway on the page, while Rhysana went on relaying the sequence to Ellen. The runes were of a kind that had been in common usage during the Wars of Power, and the inscription was in the scholarly language of Illana's day, so that there was little difficulty in translating them. But they seemed to have little to do with the method for opening the door, so Rhysana had not taken much notice of them.

The sixth tumbler gave Ellen the greatest difficulty, until it gave way with a loud thunk. For a few anxious moments they feared that the lock would be unusable; but the seventh and eighth discs slid and clicked quite happily.

'*To see the face you know, and know it not,*' quoted Hrugaar, translating from the open page. '*To laugh behind a smile's shadow. To find the moon's light by stepping into her shadow, and watching the world change.*'

'Or *walking within her shadow*, perhaps,' said Rhysana. 'And finally the full moon, left of centre on the lintel.'

The Archmage Ellen was already there before her, though she had waited for Rhysana to speak before she pushed. The last disc slid in, and there was a more musical sound like the faint ring of a bell, and then the door swung inward. A wave of heavier, cloying air rolled out to greet them.

Chapter Eight

Rhysana swiftly tucked her codex and gloves back into her satchel. Hrugaar crouched down to peer through the doorway in to the shadowed room beyond.

'There seems to be another mirror in there,' he told her.

'Yes, that would be right,' she said. 'It was enchanted, but those who came here could not fathom its power or purpose. Nor were they able to remove it.' She sent her magelight ahead of her, and led the way forward.

The doorway was low enough that even Rhysana had to stoop to go through. There was a short passage just a few paces long, and then a single step up into the study room itself.

The chamber was quite small – perhaps a third of the length and width of the practice hall behind them, and of the same grey stone – but a comfortable size for its purpose. The passage entered well to the right of centre. A long stone table stood against the left hand wall, and a tall panelled chair of silver-grey oak had been set back to the right hand side of the chamber, facing it. There were deep recessed cupboard shelves let in to the walls on either side at the corners. The far end of the chamber was dominated by a large round mirror, in a carved stone frame the size of a cartwheel.

Though there was much less dust here than in the other parts of the fortress, the air was so thick that it was becoming difficult to breathe. Rhysana risked a quick freshening spell to clear it, so that they might look around without fear of choking. If there were any creatures nearby that could sense the use of power, as Hrugaar had warned, they would have been aware of the magi's presence anyway by now.

The table and shelves drew her like lodestones, but she moved first to her near left. There on the floor was a patterned square, on a much smaller scale than the one that had been in the hall with the carved wall frieze, perhaps about four feet across. It was made up of square tiles of black and white marble, nine squares by nine, with a narrow border of lozenges upon smaller alternating squares. Of all the fabled treasures of Whitespear Head, this was the one that Rhysana had privately most wanted to see.

'It is not a true *sherunuresh* board,' said Hrugaar, bending over her shoulder as she went down on one knee to study it more closely. 'The colours on that end row are the wrong way round.'

'Is it some form of matrix defence, such as we found in Arrandin?' Ellen wondered.

'It was more than that,' said Rhysana. 'Squares such as these were once used to make magical *leaps*, from one to another – much like the spell that we still have, but requiring less energy and skill. You must have heard tales of them from the days of the Golden Age.'

She rested one hand lightly on a white square, searching through her fingertips. She half fancied that she could sense a faint stirring of energy within the stone.

Hrugaar gave a low whistle and hunkered down beside her, pressing his own hand on to the patterned square. 'There is still some enchantment within it,' he said softly. 'Moon magic, I think.'

Rhysana sighed and stood up. Under less pressing circumstances she could have lingered here for hours, exploring the forgotten ways of the matrix energies. She promised herself that she would return one day to study it more thoroughly. But for now time was running short. Ellen had already gone on to look at the mirror. Rhysana glanced at the empty shelves in the corner, and then took two quick steps to the near end of the stone table.

The outer half of the tabletop had been left clear; but toward the rear, where it butted up against the wall, were gathered the familiar oddments and paraphernalia that one might expect to find on the desk of any scholarly mage. There were quill pens and brushes and a stubby lead stylus, small bladed knives, a ruler and dividers, a wooden stretching frame like a book-rest for holding a parchment sheet for work, and an assortment of stained pots and bowls and scraps of perished cloth and discarded parchment, and the remains of what must once have been a hare's paw. At the near end was a small casket, its lid left open, with several small compartments holding chips of precious stones – lapis and red jasper, and what looked like serpentine – which Illana would have ground down to use for her coloured inks; and beside the casket was a curled drinking horn with a golden stand. On the shelves in the far corner, beyond the table from where Rhysana stood, were many more pots made of stoneware or glass, and pestles and mortars of marble and bronze. There were no books or scrolls anywhere to be seen.

'Curious,' said Ellen. 'The mirror shows the chamber, just as we see it, but the three of us have no reflection at all.'

'The frame seems to be part of the wall,' said Hrugaar, his head pressed close in to one side in an effort to see behind.

'Small wonder that the First Council did not move it,' said Ellen. 'I wonder if the runes on the doorway referred to this mirror, since they spoke about seeing and shadows.'

Rhysana thought back to the three large mirrors in the Warden's secret chamber, in the library building of the Lautun College.

'Look for pressure points in the carvings on the frame,' she told them. 'There may be another door.'

She took one last glance at the tabletop. The sight of the drinking horn had made her thirsty again. It seemed an age ago that Dhûghaúr had offered her one of his waterskins, when they had first reached the Hall of Fire; and the thought of finding a hidden door by using the mirror served only to make her throat drier with excitement.

A small wooden object, half hidden behind the goblet and the open casket, caught her attention. Rhysana leaned over and picked it up. It was about the length of her hand, and shaped like a horse sitting up on its haunches, and reminded her at once of a *sherunuresh* piece – or of the seated horse statues all along the eastern bank of the Rolling River outside, which had once guarded the border between the kingdoms of Dortrean and Lautun. Though the workmanship was simple, and the wood dried and cracked with age, its scholarly value as a possible gaming piece from such an early date was beyond question. And besides, it struck her that her son Taillan might like to see it.

There was a soft click from somewhere behind her, and then a sense of movement from the outer passageway and a sudden chill of fear. Rhysana whirled around, hiding her hands swiftly behind her skirt like a guilty student caught where she should not be.

Two small figures stood poised just inside the chamber, blocking the way out. Rhysana could not doubt but that they were shadowfay. Their faces were pale and achingly beautiful, with huge dark eyes beneath elegant brows that frowned against the light; and their long hair and garments were all black, with the sheen of ravens' wings. Their hands were wreathed in tiny clouds of seething darkness.

In the middle of the room, almost within arm's reach of her, stood a taller figure. His face and hands were wholly hidden beneath hooded robes of rich black velvet; but there was no mistaking the malice of his unseen gaze, and the sensation of sliding coils closing about her throat.

The Imperial Counsellor.

'What are you doing here, Eminence?' Ellen challenged him.

The Archmage Merrech hissed a command to the shadowfay,

in what Rhysana guessed must be their own tongue. From Hrugaar's set expression, and the waiting poise of the two shadowfay themselves, the sense of it seemed plain: *if they try anything, kill them.*

'The Archmage the Lady Ellen of Raudhar,' Merrech purred with mocking courtesy; 'and our golden boy Secretary, and of course the inestimable High Councillor Rhysana. I might ask the same of you. I do not recall a High Council assembly to grant permission for you to come here. Nor,' he added, nodding toward the white steel rod clasped in her hands, 'do I recall a formal election having taken place today. Or am I in error, and should congratulations be in order?'

'You may be in error upon many points, Eminence,' said Ellen, 'but that is not one of them.'

'Good,' he nodded. 'Then we are agreed. We have all played truant from the opening ceremony of His Imperial Highness' Summer Court to witness history in the making, as High Councillor Rhysana at last unlocks the hidden mysteries of Illana's lore.'

He had turned his attention back to Rhysana as he spoke, and the sensation of sliding coils grew worse, so that she was finding it difficult to breathe. She inched away from him along the edge of the table, all too aware that it was putting her farther away from Ellen and Hrugaar and closer to the watching shadowfay.

'How did you get here?' she managed to ask.

'The shadowfay came here many years ago,' he answered. 'They were kind enough to show me the way in. I am sorry about the fate of your little colleague, by the way. They are mischievous creatures, the shadowfay; and since you neglected to tell me that you were coming here, I arrived too late to prevent them from harming you.'

Hrugaar was restraining himself with difficulty. Rhysana worked her way clear of the table corner. She still felt acutely vulnerable, but less hemmed in.

'I might add that you found your way remarkably swiftly,'

Merrech went on. 'But then perhaps you had more help from the Warden of the College libraries than did I?'

'Herusen told me,' said Rhysana. It was only one part of the truth, but she did not want to put the Warden in danger – though whether even the Archmage Merrech was capable of causing the Warden harm might have been a debatable point. 'He came here to renew the seal, as the Prime Councillor of his generation.'

'I do not recall that he came this far up,' Merrech observed with silken smoothness. 'What was it that you hoped to find?'

'I do not know, exactly,' Rhysana demurred.

The Archmage snickered beneath his hood – a curious sound that echoed around the walls like the rustle of running beetles.

'You shall have to do better than that,' he said, drifting a step closer to her. Rhysana took another step back.

'You are the expert on Illana, Archmage,' she said. 'Do you tell me.'

He turned his hooded head toward Hrugaar and Ellen, and then back toward herself.

'I imagine,' he said, 'that you came hither in the hope of finding a hidden vault, wherein would lie volumes of ancient lore long forgotten by the Magi, and perhaps Illana's own notebooks, from among which the missing pieces of the puzzle of the *Argument of Command* could finally be found. It is every scholar's dream, and one that has been shared by almost every mage who has studied Illana's work in the last one thousand years – though few, of course, have ever followed the dream thus far. I must confess to being almost disappointed in you.'

Rhysana had let her gaze shift focus while he was talking, to exchange glances with Hrugaar. Hrugaar returned the look, and then glanced pointedly down and back again with his eyes, as if he were trying to tell her something. She realised that she must be standing at the edge of the chequered pattern on the floor.

'Do you not then believe that there is anything to find here?' she asked Merrech.

The beginnings of a plan had stirred within her mind, and she needed to keep it hidden from him. She began to edge very slowly toward the centre of the patterned square, keeping her eyes focused on his faceless hood as though she were giving him her full attention.

'Not even Illana could have owned copies of every book or scroll of lore that she ever studied,' the Archmage replied; 'and no doubt some of her sources came by word of mouth, from oral traditions that were never written down. I therefore think it likely that Caraan and his folk took whatever was to be found here; and that whatever other written sources Illana might have had to work from were simply held by others, and met with other fates over the years. As for Illana's personal notes, I imagine that either they were destroyed or that she took them with her when she disappeared. I doubt that she would have left them here for Caraan – or for you – to find.'

Rhysana silently upbraided herself. How could she have been so foolish as to overlook the possibility that Illana had taken her research with her? And yet her instincts told her that his explanation did not quite seem to fit.

'Then why are you here at all,' she countered, 'if you believe that my search will prove fruitless?'

'An interesting question,' he nodded. 'Let us say that you have shown a talent for surprising me in the past, on more than one occasion. Your resourcefulness intrigues me. And our Prime Councillor Elect is not such a fool that she would risk the wrath of the High Council to follow you here, unless you had found a most convincing argument to persuade her. So perhaps I should ask again: what was it that you hoped to find here, Rhysana?'

She was standing now, as near as she could guess, in the centre part of the patterned square. From her studies she knew that such squares were designed for travel from one to another, and that the spell to work them had been considered relatively simple. The drawback to that, Rhysana supposed, was that one had to know where the other squares were to be able to *leap* to them; and the only other possible floor pattern she could think of that might have been used for such a purpose was one on the Monastery Isle of Telúmachel – which, at the time that she had studied it a few years before, she had concluded was designed for quite another purpose. But that mattered little. The more important question was how much the Archmage Merrech knew of them.

She could, of course, simply have tried to make her own *leap* to safety, in the hope that Hrugaar and Ellen would be quick enough to follow her. The drawback to that was that even her own *leap* required vital seconds of preparation; and if the shadowfay at the door should sense the building of power within her, as most likely they would, they might be swift enough to hurl whatever it was that they held at either herself or her friends. The memory of how their *shadowshot* had destroyed Dhûghaúr – though blurred and made distant to her mind by Hrugaar's healing gifts – was enough to persuade her against taking such a risk. Yet it had occurred to her that if she could at least waken the energy within the patterned square, she might hold Merrech's attention and persuade him to tell the shadowfay to hold their fire; which in turn could buy Rhysana and her friends the few vital seconds that they needed to make their escape.

The drawback to that was that she had to find out how to use the square. She needed to keep the Toad talking – and to give him something else to think about.

'Your guess was not entirely correct, Archmage,' she told him. 'I do believe that there is something here still to find. But we have not come to solve the riddle of the *Argument of Command* itself. From my studies, I believe that there is a connection between Illana's work and the Easterners' foretellings of the demon captain's return, of which I have no doubt that you have heard. We came hither to discover what else she knew of Lo-Khuma – or at least the source of her knowledge, if it was still hidden here – in the hope that it might help the *Aeshta* Orders to defeat him.'

The shadowfay screamed in fury, and one of them spat out a mouthful of strange words. The hooded Archmage raised one long, pale hand to silence them.

'They understand you, even if they refuse to speak your tongue,' he warned. 'They demand that I kill you at once. I can test their patience only a little longer. What exactly have you discovered?'

'Illana clearly knew something of the lore about him,' she said. 'There are lines in the *Passing of Lordship* which echo very closely the words of the Easterner wizard during the parley at Khôrland.'

Rhysana was trying to picture the patterned square in her mind, to determine where she must begin to pick up the energy that it held and the sequence of tiles that she should follow. It was typical of Illana, she thought, to choose something as elaborate as a square of nine. Nor was it a standard square, as Hrugaar had observed. The reversal of the coloured tiles along one side suggested to her that it signified one of the tiered levels of a magical cube of nine. Yet since it occurred along the side, it should reflect the second or ninth level; whereas here, in terms of the magical cube of the fortress structure itself, they were still on the eighth.

'Whichever way the influence passed,' she went on, 'from the East to Illana, or from Illana to the East, there is clearly a connection. And then there is the carving of the demon in the square hall. And something brought *them* here.' She gave a slight nod of her head toward the shadowfay. 'And I guessed that that connection was where you found out more about him.'

The words had slipped out almost without thinking, she was so preoccupied with the riddle of the square. The Archmage gave another chuckle.

'Alas, no,' he said. 'The shadowfay told me. But if you thought that Illana's lore drew upon Easterner tradition,

Rhysana, I should have thought that you might have approached the wizards themselves. There is something else that you have not told me – something about that mirror, perhaps, since you seem to be so determined to draw me away from it.'

Rhysana glanced past him at the mirror, and remembered the carved runes upon the doorway outside. And suddenly she understood.

'Very well then,' she said, 'there is another place, a hidden place that the First Council never found. Come with me and I shall show you.'

She had startled everyone in the chamber. She had even startled herself. But she did not doubt her guess. The carved runes, or at least some of them, referred not to the mirror but to the patterned square beneath her feet.

Illana's secret chamber was upon the ninth level of the fortress – probably, Rhysana thought, in the mystical position of eighty-one upon that level, though its precise location was not important now. The square beneath her feet signified the ninth level, and so counted as a reflection or shadow of it here upon the eighth. If she could but waken the energy of the matrix pattern, it should take her straight to where she had to go. Or as the runes had put it, *to find the moon's light by stepping into her shadow, and watching the world change*.

Taking the Toad Archmage with her might not have been Rhysana's preferred choice, but it seemed to be her best choice at this stage in the game. She was not about to risk the lives of her friends any further by trying to outwit Merrech, so she had to play into his hands. It was, a distant part of her mind reflected, curiously in keeping with the theory of *playing to lose* – the very theory which she had proposed to him on a number of occasions as a possible solution to the *Argument of Command*.

The hooded Archmage forced a laugh – a tight, hissing sound that belied his outward poise.

'Remarkable,' he observed. 'I am almost tempted to doubt you, so confident do you appear in your readiness to show the proof. You shall forgive me the discourtesy of asking, but how far do you expect me to follow you on this wild goose chase for a hidden place? And what enchantments or trickery will there be upon the way? The shadowfay grow impatient.'

'There is no trickery,' Rhysana said steadily. 'I am standing on a magic square. Let me work its power, and it will transport us there in a single *leap*.'

The shadowfay sniggered in mocking contempt. Merrech silenced them again. He loomed over her, taut as a bowstring, and she felt his hidden gaze boring into her with the sharpness of serpent's fangs. It was all that she could do not to cry out.

'Betray me, and your friends are dead,' he hissed.

Rhysana nodded, disciplining herself to calm. The shadowfay were watching her, like gloating carrion birds waiting to feed. Ellen looked anxious. Hrugaar's eyes were wide and bright with excitement and readiness. The Toad seemed to be daring her to try, and to fail.

She gathered her skirts and crouched down, counting quickly across the rows to find the first square tile that she needed. It was a white one. She laid her palm flat upon the surface and focused downward with her trained senses, hunting for the tickle of energy that she had felt before. It seemed to leap up into her hand.

If Rhysana had feared that it might prove similar to the matrix in Arrandin – or even the floor pattern of the great assembly chamber – she was relieved to discover that only a small fraction of that amount of energy was involved. When she stood up, a slender riband of pale moonlight spun out between the tile and her hand.

The shadowfay snarled a warning. Merrech snapped back at them in command.

The spell was so simple that Rhysana did not even have to touch each of the tiles in turn with hand or foot; she could just stand there and follow through the numbered sequence of the magical square of nine within her head, watching in her mind's eye as the power leaped from square to square, spinning a web of moonlight around her.

As she came to the last run of tiles, the patience of the shadowfay failed.

A black dart skittered past her shoulder and vanished into the cupboard shelves beyond. Hrugaar was suddenly gone. The Archmage Ellen shone bright as the sun, wrapped in an aureole of golden power. The shadowfay wailed.

Rhysana finished her spell, feeling the energies sing as they knotted into place. The Toad wavered visibly, but then he lunged forward to grab her by the wrist. The chill vice of his grip made her gasp aloud in pain. And then the moonlight flared bright around them, and she felt the familiar swoop in her stomach as the *leap* carried them elsewhere.

Her first impression was of darkness again, after the brightness of the spell, and then the scent of Merrech's freshly laundered robes. He was still holding on to her, breathing heavily. And then the darkness burst into a flood of deep opalescent green as he conjured a ball of magelight, away to their right. She kindled a silver-blue ball of her own upon their left.

They were in a cave rather than a chamber, with rough walls that reflected their lights in dull scattered fragments like shards of slate. Ahead of them was a large stone block, which seemed to have been shaped from a raised part of the floor to serve as a table. Its faces had been cut smooth and carved with intricate borders and runes; and resting side by side upon its surface were three large tomes and a number of scrolls and piled papers, and two splintered shafts of dark red wood that looked to be the remains of a broken staff.

It was, as Rhysana told herself afterward, the finding that mattered. For from the moment that she laid eyes upon the gathered treasures she knew that she had already lost them.

The Toad moved forward to the table, dragging her with him. She made no effort to break free.

From close to she could see that the tomes were bound in

a dark scaled hide, and that the scrolls were tied with cords of golden thread. The stacked papers were held down with a weight of rose quartz, carved and polished into the likeness of a seashell; and the first sheet beneath it was crammed full of writing in black ink, in a tiny, precise script typical of the scholarly style of the early sixth century. There was no sign of age or damage upon anything there, except for the broken staff; and a glimmering of enchantment played over the surface of the carved table, and seemed to spread out to fill all the cave around them.

'Truly remarkable,' said Merrech, breaking the silence.

Rhysana prised her wrist free of his grip. 'They are yours to take, Eminence,' she said.

He turned his hooded head toward her.

'Noble and generous to the last,' he mocked. 'But the gesture is meaningless. Surely you do not imagine that I shall allow you to leave here alive, knowing even what little you do? Or are you still pursuing your charming notion of *playing to lose*, in the vain hope that you might yet survive?'

It was closer to the truth than Rhysana might have wished to admit, but she had more practical arguments to persuade him.

'You are not about to kill me,' she said.

'Do not be so sure of that,' he hissed. 'I have tried do so before – and damned near succeeded, if you remember. There is none here who will save you now.'

'Illana's work has been found.' She could not quite keep the tremor of awe from her voice. Her whole body seemed to be trembling. 'But it has not yet been read. The text may prove as riddling as the *Argument of Command.* It may not hold the answers that you seek. Until you have studied what is here, Eminence, you are not such a fool that you would risk losing me. You have said yourself that you believe that my own insights may prove to be the key.'

Aranur of the golden fay had said much the same thing. Or, to be more precise, she had said that Rhysana herself was the key. That had been her wedding gift to Torkhaal and Rhysana, nearly three years ago now. At the time, Torkhaal had surmised that Aranur had referred to her deepest passions, born of her inmost self, which in Rhysana were made manifest in selfless love and commitment – though he too often embarrassed her with such words of adoration. Yet Aranur's lessons to them had been more about choice, and understanding the desires of your heart before choosing; all of which seemed to have little enough to do with the cruel irony and malice of the *Argument of Command.*

'I think that you over-estimate your own worth,' the hooded Archmage returned. 'Your studies may once have shown promise, but your understanding has become flawed. Illana was not playing to lose. She writes of command and control – or *rulership*, if you prefer a single word for it.'

'The text shows certain attitudes,' Rhysana allowed, 'perhaps even a sense of strategy, in *sherunuresh* terms. But though we may differ on Illana's political theories, I think that we do agree upon the fundamental magical theory involved: the principle of need and fulfilment.'

'*Eann'o*,' Merrech opposed, as though in formal debate. 'You argue that Illana let her enemies grow strong, and herself grow weak, in the hope that their strength would pass to her. I find no proof of that in the text. Nor do I think that she played her enemies off, one against another. The *Argument of Command* more resembles the old fashioned name magic – the theory that knowing a creature's true name gives you power to control it.'

'I have heard of the theory, Eminence,' said Rhysana.

'Illana understood,' he went on, 'that knowing a great deal about someone, or something, also gives you power over them. By understanding how things will act and react, one can make the smallest changes to bring them together; knowing – and thus effectively controlling – how events are most likely to unfold thereafter.'

'So you knew all along that I would bring you here?' she demanded.

'Oh no,' he said smoothly, waving one velvet sleeve in affected modesty. 'As I have said, Rhysana, you have a talent for surprising me. Yet you display an almost reckless passion in your pursuit of academic excellence, quite outstanding in your generation. It intrigued me to see how far that might take you in the study of Illana's lore.'

Rhysana blushed faintly at the praise, which under the circumstances could hardly be passed off as flattery. Yet it struck her that Merrech, like Torkhaal, had seen her selfless passion as the key to the *Argument of Command*.

'So it is not a magical treatise at all?' she ventured, bringing him back to the text.

'On the contrary,' he answered. 'Illana shows plainly in the *Mazes and Psychic Constructs* that precise knowledge of a pattern enables one to make of it a matrix of power. With the *Argument of Command* she took that principle and translated it to the greater patterns of life itself.'

'She mentions the mastery of beasts, and the beguiling of the mind,' Rhysana allowed. 'Do you then believe that the text contains greater enchantments to enslave and control?' It was something that she could well imagine would have appealed to Illana's twisted genius.

'Perhaps,' said the Archmage dismissively. 'But more than that, Illana aimed at the highest goal of all our Art. I think that she discovered the power to behold the patterns of life itself, and to shape and command them at will – to take whatever the heart desires, and to have the knowledge and power to make it so.'

Rhysana stood thunderstruck as the full import of his words sunk in. In that moment he could have killed her with a thought. And then she knew that she had gone beyond him.

'But Illana failed,' she said.

'In some respects,' he nodded. 'Through mischance, or human error perhaps. Yet her knowledge has been preserved here for us.'

Rhysana was only half listening to him. That was not what

she had meant. The first moment of insight was fading, and she was striving to hold on to it, to follow through the thought.

The *Argument of Command* was merely that – an argument, filled with all the frustration and fury of a mage proposing the theory of a spell that she had not been able to work.

The true theory, which Illana seemed to have misunderstood, was simple. Any child who had ever stood with their hand upon a blackthorn tree, and made a wish for the gods or the Fay to grant, would grasp the idea. But it might take an Archmage or the greatest of the *Aeshta* priests to achieve it; *presenting themselves*, as the Warden would have put it, *with humility – or arrogance – to shape the raw power contained within the fabric of all that is*.

Aranur had known, as surely all the great Guardians would once have known; and indeed, as one of the noble golden fay it might have been part of her natural power. The *Argument of Command*, Rhysana remembered, made scant mention of the elvenfolk of the Fay. And so Aranur had taught her about understanding the desires of her own heart, and the strength of her own passion, and the choices that she made. That understanding and passion, harnessed with her magical training to perceive the power within the world around her and to call to it, was all that she needed to succeed where Illana had failed.

The rest was the endless learning of wisdom – to know when to act, and to understand how one's choices could rebound upon the lives of all – for it was a wild power, cutting across the spiralling patterns of the dances of the gods. Whether the gods themselves could foresee its use, and weave it into the greater patterns of the dance of life, Rhysana was in no position to debate. As the daughter of a thousand years of Council tradition, the thought of such power in the hands of someone like Illana or Merrech filled her with no little alarm.

The *Argument of Command* showed great insight into the patterns of life – the legends and histories, and the lore of many creatures and races – albeit slanted from Illana's scathing viewpoint. But from her memory of the text, Rhysana was sure that Illana had not perceived the simple truth of the spell that she had laboured to find. Whether in later years – between the writing of the treatise and the fall of Whitespear Head – Illana had guessed that truth, and recorded it somewhere among the papers on the stone table next to her, Rhysana was less than certain. Given Illana's apparent obsession with the study of every pattern and outward form, she considered it unlikely.

Whether the Toad Archmage next to her would perceive the truth, or find the answer staring up at him from Illana's writings, was even less certain. Given his long habit of manipulating others, of being the shadowed power behind the Emperor's throne, she doubted that he would solve the riddle for himself. It was a chance that she would have to give him, a risk that she would have to take.

Again she found herself playing to lose.

'Do you understand now,' Merrech sneered, 'why I found your interpretation somewhat flawed?'

Rhysana permitted herself a soft, fluttering laugh, which he might take for sign of nervousness or embarrassment if he would.

'You propose a remarkable theory, Archmage,' she said. 'I shall be fascinated to hear the proofs – when you find them amongst these manuscripts.'

'And still you do not challenge me for them.'

'I do not,' she said. 'They will be safer in your care than with any other mage in the Empire; and when you are done with them, you will give them into the care of the College libraries.'

'Even as you were to present your findings concerning the Arrandin matrix to the High Council?'

Rhysana conceded the point with a nod. 'Whatever you may think of the present Council,' she returned, 'you believe in the Magi and their learning. You will not suffer this knowledge to be lost. And if it be preserved for those who come after us, then I may comfort myself that my efforts have not been entirely in vain.'

'Perhaps I should just destroy them now,' he said.

'No!' she cried at once.

The Archmage Merrech laughed. For the first time, Rhysana realised that there were no echoes in the cave.

'So you do care, after all,' he purred.

'I have never stopped caring,' she told him.

She stepped back from the carved table – not without a shiver of regret – and made her way across the floor. He made no move to prevent her. There was another squared pattern there, where they had arrived, conforming to the eighth tier of a magical cube of nine. Rhysana knew that it would take her back. But there was one more move that she must make.

'You may find, Eminence,' she said, 'that some of the information there is about five hundred years out of date.'

The Archmage sighed. 'Do you not mean one thousand?'

'No,' she said. 'The wars of the Bright Alliance were fought five centuries before Illana came here. That is where we are heading, is it not?'

He turned his back to her, looking down at the gathered treasures.

'I can no longer guarantee your safety at Court,' he warned.

'Perhaps you never really could,' she said. 'Your Rhydden must be quite as much of a handful as my son.'

He gave no sign that he had heard her.

'You may find,' his voice hissed on the air around her, 'that you have to make use of the floor pattern. A seal of power keeps this cave from the world outside.'

Rhysana had guessed as much for herself, but she had already determined that she would go this way. She could not leave Whitespear Head until she was certain that her friends were safe. She stepped upon the patterned square, found and picked up the thread of moonlight power within, and wove the simple spell to take her back.

The pallid flare of the spell gave way to a bright golden light, so that Rhysana had to squint for a few moments. The

Archmage Ellen was standing nearby, still radiant with the tawny aureole of her own power. Hrugaar was hunkered down before Rhysana's feet, at the edge of the chequered square. He sprang up to hug her in delight.

'But what did you find?' he asked.

'And where is His Eminence?' demanded Ellen.

'He is coming,' said Rhysana. 'We had better leave at once. Where are the shadowfay?'

Ellen pointed toward a new statue of grey stone beside the door passage, its left arm cocked back as if to hurl something.

'Ru *leaped* outside the door when you went,' she explained. 'Between us we finished them off.'

There was no sign of a second body; but Rhysana noticed that the air was now thick with a smell like boiled giblets or offal, which made her stomach queasy. She was beginning to feel the shock of her encounter with Merrech, now that the worst danger was past.

'I think that we may *leap* straight from here,' she said, 'if Ru managed it before.'

'I stayed within the fortress,' he reminded her. 'We may not be able to pass outside.'

'The High Council warded the place to keep people out, not in,' said Ellen. 'But if we fail, then we can leap straight down to the river gate passage and I can open the doors to let us out.'

Rhysana nodded. 'What is the time?' she asked. 'I seem to have lost track.'

'You were only gone for a few minutes,' said Ellen.

'The sun has not yet set in the world outside,' said Hrugaar. 'Torkhaal should still be at the opening ball.'

'I was thinking of Taillan,' said Rhysana. 'Perhaps we should go straight to the palace to fetch him.'

'Dressed like this?' Ellen countered. 'We might as well tell the whole Court where we have been.'

'Torkhaal will bring him home safely,' said Hrugaar.

'The Toad knew we were here,' Rhysana objected.

She did not trust Merrech. Nor did she trust what Rhydden might do in his absence, while the eyes of the Court were turned toward the spectacle of the opening ball. Torkhaal was among friends and could look after himself, but her young son could not.

'Then I shall fetch him for you,' said Hrugaar. 'I can pass through the citadel unseen.'

'We shall go first to the College,' said Ellen, taking control. 'You can go on from there, Ru. I had better make the *leap* for all three of us, I think – unless we are waiting for His Eminence to join us?'

'No,' said Rhysana and Hrugaar together.

They each rested a hand on Ellen's arm. There was a moment of darkness, with the summer stars wheeling wildly overhead, and then they stood on the flagged stone floor of one of the visitors' landings in the College of Magi in Lautun. Rhysana savoured the sweet, slightly musty air of the familiar surroundings, and sighed in relief.

The landing had no windows, so Ellen exchanged her bright aureole for a more practical ball of tawny magelight. Hrugaar presented Rhysana with the small casket and curled drinking horn from Illana's study chamber.

'I thought that you might give these to the Warden,' he told her. 'We had to bring him something back.'

'How did you know he knew?' she asked.

'How could he not have known, with all the hard work of research that you have done?' He handed Dhûghaúr's black staff to Ellen. 'I shall be back soon, bringing Taillan safe with me.'

'I know,' she said. 'I am sorry, Ru.'

'We slew the shadowfay,' he said. 'Killing the Toad would not have brought him back. And it would have been harder still to lose either of you.'

He managed a wry smile, and then vanished. Rhysana blinked at the sting of gathering tears. She was suddenly very tired.

'I must return the Prime Councillor's rod,' said Ellen. 'Shall I walk you back to your apartment first?'

'I shall be all right, thank you,' Rhysana assured her.

'Well I shall come with you as far as the cloister,' said Ellen. 'It is on my way. And then I shall join you afterward, if I may? I think that we need to talk.'

'Of course,' said Rhysana.

They walked together in silence through the deserted hallways and stairs of the College buildings, and out into the early evening of the cloister garden. The colonnades were deep in shadow, but the air was much warmer here than it had been in the halls of Whitespear Head, and heady with the scent of honeysuckle, and the sky above them was a haze of indigo and blue. There were also the everyday sounds – the chattering of the finches and sparrows, and the carolling of the College martlets beneath the eaves.

Ellen went away to the right, toward the tall bronze doors of the library. Rhysana took a short cut across the lawn toward the low door which led to the stairway to her apartment. She might have been tempted to linger here for a while, enjoying the colours and scents of the garden and the antics of the birds after the chill and the dust of Illana's fortress. But she was too tired and thirsty, and Ellen would not be gone long.

When she reached her apartment she set the casket and drinking horn down on the table, and went straight through into her bedchamber. She could have wished for a long bath, and something to eat; and then a long sleep afterward, while her mind took in all that she had seen and learned that day. But bath and sleep would have to wait. Hrugaar would be bringing Taillan back, and probably Torkhaal with him, and Ellen would be here; and they would all want to know what had passed between her and the Toad Archmage.

Rhysana clapped her hands to summon the *chaedar*, and sent them off to fetch tea and pastries. Then she took off her satchel, and changed out of her heavy clothes before having a quick wash to freshen herself.

As she stepped out of the divided skirts of her dark blue gown, she heard the muffled thud of something solid striking the floor. Rhysana frowned, and felt around in the bundled cloth. There was something long and hard in one of the pockets. She sat down on the side of the bed, holding the gown on her lap, and focused her senses. There seemed to be nothing magical there. She reached carefully into the pocket with one hand, and pulled the object out. It was the carved wooden horse that she had found in Illana's study chamber.

Rhysana smiled. She had forgotten about it until that moment. She guessed that she had been holding it when Merrech surprised them, and she must have slipped it into her pocket without thinking.

She turned the piece briefly in her hand. It felt oddly weighted, as though it had been carved of a very solid kind of wood. Rhysana held it higher, to get the benefit of the light from the window behind her; and then she caught a flash of reflected light from one of the deeper cracks across the horse's back. There seemed to be something made of metal inside.

Rhysana looked at the piece more closely, intrigued. There was no seam or join that she could see in the wood itself, to show how the metal had found its way in there. But if, as she supposed, this was an early *sherunuresh* playing piece, she did not want to risk damaging it by trying to find out now. And besides, she had not the time to spare. She decided to show it to Torkhaal later, to see what he could make of it. She tucked the little horse safely away inside her satchel, next to the Warden's codex, and moved as swiftly as she could to get washed and dressed.

As it turned out, Rhysana need not have hurried herself. Ellen seemed to have had the same idea about washing and changing, for she arrived fully half an hour later in light silk robes of bright meadow green. Hrugaar came in behind her, with Torkhaal carrying a sleepy Taillan. By that time Rhysana had drunk four tumblers of tea, finished all the applemince pastries, and was just wondering whether to call for supper without waiting for the rest of them. She had also had time to put her thoughts in slightly better order.

She left Ellen to speak to the *chaedar* about food while she settled Taillan to sleep in his own cot, and sent Hrugaar off to wash his face and hands. Torkhaal came through into the bedchamber with her. It was soon clear that Hrugaar had told him most of what had happened, and he seemed to be more concerned with reassuring himself of her own well being. Rhysana found out by asking that Morvaan had stayed behind at the ball with Gravhan and the Lady Camarra.

When they went back out into the living chamber, the *chaedar* had already brought a huge jug of chilled cordial and two baskets piled high with milk rolls and raisin breads, and half a round of yellow Raudhar cheese. A plate of fresh sardines soared through the air, carried on unseen hands. Ellen had sat down at one end of the long table, while Hrugaar poured drinks for them all.

'So where did you go?' he asked, as soon as she came in. 'And how did you escape the Toad?'

'I told you at the time,' Rhysana said calmly, going to sit next to Ellen. 'Illana did have a hidden chamber – a sealed cave – and the matrix pattern took us there.'

'But how did you know where to go?' Ellen demanded. 'I know that you said that it was possible to *leap* from one such square to another. Yet surely you would have needed to know where the other square was, in order to get there?'

Rhysana shook her head, reaching for a milk roll. Torkhaal sat down beside her.

'The matrix patterns were a little different from what I had expected,' she said. 'The two squares were keyed specifically to one another. I do not think that you could use them to *leap* to any other square.'

Ellen passed her the butter. 'That does not quite answer my question.'

'Normally when you make a *leap*,' Rhysana explained, 'you picture in your mind the place that you wish to go, and then work the spell to take you there. With the matrix pattern in the study chamber, it worked the other way around. The pattern belonged to another place within the fortress; so when you triggered the spell within it, it took you there to where it belonged. That was what the runes on the door meant, about stepping into the shadow to find the light. And then the other square belonged to the study chamber, to bring you back.'

'So wherever you are, there you go,' Hrugaar grinned.

Torkhaal tossed a bread roll at him. 'So what did you find in the hidden chamber?' he asked.

Rhysana blushed, and reached for her tumbler of cordial. To declare what she had found was one thing; but to explain, even to her husband and friends, why she had lost it was quite another. She took a slow, deliberate sip, and set the tumbler down again.

'Illana's study notes,' she said steadily; 'and some books and scrolls – probably her own, I think.'

Torkhaal let out a whoop of delight, and leaned over to kiss her with a mouthful of sardine. Ellen swore beneath her breath. Hrugaar was grinning broadly, his eyes bright with tears of joy.

'His Eminence has them,' Rhysana told them.

Torkhaal's exuberance faded. Ellen studied her tumbler, as though wishing that it held something much stronger than cordial.

'What?' cried Hrugaar.

'He would have killed you, had you tried to stop him,' said Torkhaal.

'Perhaps,' said Rhysana. 'Though that would not have stopped me from trying, had I thought it the right thing to do. I chose to let him win on this occasion.'

'Is that not taking the idea of playing to lose a bit too far?' Hrugaar wondered.

'Not really,' she said. 'He only thinks that he has won.'

'The Toad took the prize,' he reminded her. 'To most people that counts as winning.'

'He will keep the manuscripts safe,' said Rhysana. 'Better than anyone else in the Six Kingdoms, perhaps, except for the Warden himself. And in the end they will come to the College libraries, and not be lost. But it will take him many hours to go through everything that was there, and even then he may come no nearer to understanding the *Argument of Command.* I persuaded him that he had to let me live, in case he might have need of my help again.'

'I trust that you will consult with at least one of us before you do so?' said Ellen.

Rhysana nodded humbly, and took a bite of her milk roll.

'I hate to be the one to point this out,' said Torkhaal, 'but if the demon captain returns, there may be no one left to study the manuscripts anyway.'

'Have you heard something at Court?' Ellen demanded.

'Yes and no,' Torkhaal sighed. 'The *Aeshta* priests believe that something has changed with the birth of this new moon, and that the Enemy now stands on the threshold of the waking world. Camarra said something about it being a Moon of Calling, whatever that may mean.'

'That is a time when the gods call to a new hero or servant,' Hrugaar supplied. 'Or so it is said among the moon fay. It is seldom the time when that hero is openly revealed, nor the time when great deeds are done; but it is a crossing point in the patterns of the dances of the gods.'

'I do not see His Eminence as a new hero,' said Ellen drily. 'But if what the *Aeshta* priests have said is true, I could wish that Illana's manuscripts had come to us rather than to him.'

'We have no need of them,' said Rhysana.

Ellen looked at her sharply. Hrugaar made as if to speak, but Rhysana frowned at him in warning and he closed his mouth again with a snap.

'Not for the moment,' she explained. 'We have already learned what we needed to know. We have seen for ourselves that the Toad has dealings with the shadowfay, and that he can command them; and that he has learned more of Lo-Khuma from their ancient lore, not from Illana.

'The Toad suggested looking at Easterner traditions. But it seems to me that we have no need to look for them now. We already know from their Wizards – and from the *Argument of Command* – that they believe that the Enemy will arise in the very heart of our own Empire. That is why they brought war to our borders less than two months since – and why they will return when they judge that the time for his coming is at hand. Together with the *Aeshta* priests, they will be our weather vane to warn of the approaching storm.'

'Kata Aghaira,' said Torkhaal. 'The Easterner loremaster. She was in Arrandin when the war began. She knew that something was going to happen, if not exactly when. Aghaira will be watching for signs of the next attack; and she is bound to come here ahead of them to witness the great events for herself, to add to her collection of stories.'

'Precisely,' said Rhysana. 'And if Easterner lore makes any mention of how to defeat Lo-Khuma, then Aghaira is the most likely person to know of it.'

'Aghaira spoke of the worship of the demon spreading like a sickness among the clans,' Hrugaar offered. 'Yet she said nothing of how it might be cured.'

'Perhaps the Easterners have no lore for his defeat,' said Ellen. 'Only the First Kings of our own Kingdoms seem to have achieved it – once he was fully in the waking world, that is, since there do seem to have been other occasions when he has been driven back from the threshold. But the First Kings do not appear to have left any written records that survive, nor has their knowledge been handed down to us through the *Aeshta* Orders – unless Illana's manuscripts make mention of it.'

'The Toad believes,' said Rhysana, 'like many others before him, that the *Argument of Command* is all about the power to command and to control. There is considerable support within the text for that interpretation. Had Illana known, at the time of writing, of a way to control or defeat the demon, it seems most likely that she would have mentioned it. Yet even in the historical sections, her detail of Lo-Khuma himself is sparse. If she discovered more in her later work, then the Toad is now better placed to find and to use it than any of us.'

'Hardly a comforting thought,' Torkhaal growled.

'Perhaps not,' she allowed ruefully, helping herself to another roll. 'But I do not believe that he wants the demon to return, to destroy everything that he has worked for. I think that he is more likely to be looking for a way to control or to prevent him. And to that limited extent, I am afraid that we may have to regard him as an ally.'

'And Rhydden?' Ellen asked.

'I do not know,' Rhysana sighed. 'It seems clear that there are followers of Lo-Khuma among his household, and that the Toad is aware of them and trying to keep control of what is happening. Rhydden himself must know of this. But how far he may agree with the Toad, or be ruled by him, I do not know. I have a feeling that Merrech's power over Rhydden is waning.'

'So the Emperor is still our enemy?' demanded Hrugaar.

'Put like that, Ru, I suppose that he is,' she said. 'The question is, is he more or less dangerous without the Toad's control? They have worked together for so many years, it is difficult to tell them apart.'

'If Rhydden even permits the servants of Lo-Khuma within his household,' said Ellen, 'and dealings with the shadowfay, then he has betrayed us all and is no longer fit to rule.'

There was silence around the table. The *chaedar* brought in a plate of steaming sausages and grilled gammon. Rhysana accepted a sausage absent-mindedly, but found that her appetite was failing.

'What about the Southers?' asked Hrugaar. 'The Souther woman Mijal said that some of them – the K'tarim, I think – were servants of the Enemy. If Rhydden and the Toad have dealings with the followers of Lo-Khuma, then I should lay odds that so does their precious puppet Rinnekh. He could have commanded the burning of the Kelmaar School in Ellanguan.'

'Kellarn blamed the Emperor for Solban's death,' said Rhysana, 'but Rhydden might have used Rinnekh's contacts with the Southers to achieve it. Either way, the line of command holds true.'

'But Mijal said that Ambassador T'Loi and his people are not of the K'tarim,' said Ellen. 'And T'Loi commands the Souther forces, does he not?'

'He does,' Hrugaar allowed. 'Yet though he has made his own alliance with Rinnekh, Rinnekh is still the Emperor's whipping boy.'

'And Erkal Dortrean has been sent down to Braedun,' said Torkhaal, 'to make sure that the Southers there behave themselves and do the Emperor's bidding. Either way, Rhydden ends up with control of all of the Souther forces within the Empire.'

'But will he use them to drive the Easterners back,' Ellen asked, 'or to enforce his imperial will upon his own people, as appears to be the case in Ellanguan?'

'Or both?' Torkhaal countered.

'Ellanguan may have been Rinnekh's doing, rather than the Emperor's,' said Hrugaar.

'But Ellanguan under tighter control, without the disruptive presence of the *Aeshta* orders, is just what Rhydden wants,' Rhysana pointed out. 'That is the way in which the Toad and Rhydden work, remember? They manipulate people by putting them into a position where of their own free will they will make the choices that bring about the desired effect.'

'And how are they manipulating you – or us?' Ellen wondered.

'The Toad has Illana's manuscripts,' said Hrugaar. 'Dhûghaúr's bravery in wanting to help us led to his own death.'

Rhysana took another sip from her cordial, remembering her conversation with Merrech in the cave.

'No,' she said. 'Merrech is still bound by the patterns of life, the dances of the gods; and the foresight of the gods is greater than his. He did not expect me to find any more of Illana's work at Whitespear Head. I think that that discovery has put him out of reckoning.

'I think,' she went on, 'that Dhûghaúr's bravery was part of the pattern that the Toad did not see – a pattern in which he himself had to play a part. The shadowfay must have warned him that we were there, after they shot Dhûghaúr. Had the Toad not come after us, we might have fled the shadowfay and never discovered how to use the matrix square to reach the hidden cave. And had Dhûghaúr not come with us, then one or other of us might have died in the Hall of Fire, and there would not have been the two of you left to overcome the shadowfay. None of us might have escaped alive.

'Yet we are here, and much of that which we could only guess at before has now become more plain. I think that the gods have given Illana's manuscripts to the Toad for a reason – whether to help in the fight against Lo-Khuma, or simply to keep him occupied and out of our way.

'And I think,' she added tentatively, 'that I might at last have unlocked the riddle of the *Argument of Command*.'

Torkhaal choked on a mouthful of cordial.

'What?' gasped Hrugaar, his eyes bright with excitement and unshed tears.

'I only said that I might,' Rhysana told him, glancing anxiously at her husband. 'I shall have to sleep on it. But if my guess proves correct, I doubt that the Toad will ever fathom it.'

'And hence you would not need Illana's manuscripts,' Ellen nodded.

Chapter Nine

Rhysana slept soundly that night, and if she dreamed she did not remember it. She awoke with a heavy head and the feeling that there was something that she had left unfinished. For once her husband and son were up before her.

She rose and dressed slowly, allowing herself the luxury of another bath, and put on a loose fitting gown of pale blue silk. The *chaedar* came to brush out her hair and pin it up with ivory combs. Rhysana would have sent them away and managed it for herself; but then she remembered that there was to be a High Council meeting that morning, and she had to allow that they would probably make a better job of it. The presence of their unseen bodies around her was something of a trial, for her head still felt heavy and dull, and the air was already warm and humid with the threat of a coming storm. The warmth of the air she countered with a cooling spell, which helped to clear her head a little. But much as she loved the *chaedar*, she found that she wished to be alone for a while.

When they were done she fetched the Warden's codex from her satchel, inspecting it critically for signs of damage before wrapping it up again in its silken napkin. Then she took it with her and went out into the living chamber of their apartment.

Torkhaal and Taillan were sitting reading together by one of the open casement windows.

'Am I dreadfully late?' she asked, going across to kiss them.

'Not really,' Torkhaal grinned. 'We were waiting breakfast until the others arrived, anyway.'

'Good,' said Rhysana. 'I just need to visit the Warden briefly.'

'What about those?' he asked, nodding toward the long table. Illana's casket and curled drinking horn were still there from the night before. 'Shall we bring them for you? Small hands have been itching to play with them.'

'No,' she said. 'You had better stay, in case Ru arrives, or Ellen. The *chaedar* can carry them for me. I shall not be gone for long.'

She clapped her hands lightly, and there was the familiar thrill upon the air as the *chaedar* returned.

'Breakfast?' Taillan demanded.

'Soon,' Torkhaal promised him.

'*Limminn'æm,*' instructed Rhysana, pointing to the tabletop. The casket and drinking horn rose into the air, and followed behind her as she went out.

The other magi all arrived before Rhysana returned, so Torkhaal did not wait breakfast for her. He sat Taillan next to him at the end of the table, with Hrugaar and the Archmage Morvaan upon his left, and Ellen facing them. Morvaan had arranged a High Council meeting in little less than an hour's time, and had come to tell Rhysana personally. He also wished to hear of their adventures at Whitespear Head for himself, and was seldom averse to accepting another meal when it was offered to him.

Hrugaar had spent the night alone in one of the guest chambers set aside for visiting magi on the south side of the cloister, and had arrived soon after Rhysana left, looking rested but a little subdued. He had once again borrowed Torkhaal's black councillor's robes, both as a sign of mourning for Dhûghaúr and because he was not sure whether he would be needed for the High Council assembly.

Torkhaal had linked mind to mind with him in greeting when he came in, concerned for his friend's well being. But apart from a sense of emptiness where he had lost Dhûghaúr, and a lingering sense of self blame that he had not been able to save him, Hrugaar did not seem to have suffered any greater hurt. His deep love for Torkhaal and Rhysana and their son remained, and his hatred for the Toad had grown keener; so that if he appeared subdued, it was less to do with his own private grief, and more a sign of his determination to meet the challenges that lay ahead. He was also greatly curious to learn what Rhysana had discovered about the *Argument of Command*, and whether it would be of use to them against Lo-Khuma – and he half expected a battle of wits to prise the secret out of her.

It was partly a measure of Hrugaar's mood that he took Ellen and Morvaan to task about the coming election almost as soon as they were seated at the breakfast table.

'You shall be Prime Councillor, shall you not?' he asked Ellen.

'Perhaps,' she said tightly.

'You shall not be there to persuade us,' Morvaan told Hrugaar. 'Only the High Council may be present.'

Hrugaar looked indignant.

'I do not like the idea of it at all,' said Ellen, allowing the *chaedar* to pour her tea. 'I only agreed to stand because I liked the idea of Sollonaal's election even less, and we were running short on suitable candidates to oppose him. High Councillor Ferghaal lost ground on the question of dealing with the Southers—'

'That was mostly Merrech's doing,' Morvaan put in. 'Ferghaal is a strong leader. He may have better support this morning.'

'I hope so,' Ellen sighed. 'He is perhaps our best hope. Asharka of Braedun is a worthy woman, but more concerned with the Colleges than with the world outside. Trialmasters Ekraan and Foghlaar are wholly committed to their academic work, as is High Councillor Rikkarn to his research. Lirinal of Dregharis has a fine mind, but I fear that politicially he would just become Sollonaal's puppet. And Drôshiin of

Sêchral would probably turn the Colleges into bawdy houses for his amusement.'

'Another fine mind turned rotten,' said Morvaan sadly.

'But either one of you two would make a very good Prime Councillor,' Hrugaar objected.

Ellen shook her head. 'We have been through this before, Ru. Archmagi are less suited to the role.'

'Yet better suited than Sollonaal,' he countered.

Ellen looked to Morvaan for support.

'That very touch of brilliance,' the old mage sighed, 'which sets us apart from the rest of the Council, is also a touch of madness or of folly. I should perhaps be too irrepressible, or mischievous like yourself.'

'And I fear that I should be too severe,' said Ellen. 'I lack Herusen's patience and humanity.'

'Do you mean that I may become an Archmage, too?' Hrugaar asked Morvaan eagerly.

'Archmagi often turn to folly,' said Morvaan. 'Not all fools turn into Archmagi.'

'Foolish Ru!' laughed Taillan, banging his porridge spoon on the table. 'Foolish!'

Torkhaal chuckled as he hushed him.

'Archmagery can only be caught, not taught,' said Ellen cryptically.

'Then how do I catch it?' Hrugaar returned, undaunted.

Morvaan helped himself to more porridge. 'Any journeyman,' he answered, 'who gains sufficient experience and mastery of their art may brave the ordeals to become a mage councillor. Of those who join the Council, some few – such as yourselves – will show the courage and insight to make an outstanding contribution to our work, and in time earn a place among the High Council.'

'The Archmage Morvaan has proposed that both of you should be considered for admission to the High Council,' Ellen explained. 'This is based on all your efforts over the past few years, and especially your contribution to the defence of Arrandin. Torkhaal clinched it, I think, with his destruction of the *ghomughr*. Why you were proposed, Ru, I can not imagine – unless it were for your stubborn recklessness in the face of common sense.'

Torkhaal blushed, and busied himself with scraping together the last of the porridge in his son's wooden bowl. He was grinning so broadly that he felt that the corners of his mouth must be reaching his ears. Hrugaar squeezed his leg beneath the table, sharing his joy and excitement.

'Insight and self sacrifice, actually,' said Morvaan absently. 'But to continue. From among the High Council, one person is chosen to act as Prime Councillor over all; one who hopefully has the wisdom and experience to guide us, and to represent us as a figurehead to the world outside – in particular to the Lords of the Court Noble.

'The Archmagi, Hrugaar, are a breed apart. Some among the High Council come in time to gain an extraordinary insight or mastery within their chosen field, that touch of brilliance or folly which I mentioned before. It is perhaps as much a gift from the gods as an achievement of long study, and both must come together. For myself, it came with my intuitive grasp of the power of the Sun, in all its many forms. For the Archmage Ellen it was her insight into the very pulse of life within all living things. Her presentation to the High Council on shape-changing and the nature of magical creatures was quite outstanding – though I dare say that the Lady is too modest to have made mention of it to either of you.'

'Nor is there time for that now,' said Ellen firmly. 'The High Council is a big enough step for you to take – if your admission is approved. And we have the election to contend with before then.'

'Yet you do believe that I shall be an Archmage, ere long?' pressed Hrugaar.

Ellen picked up a peach from the fruit bowl, stroking the smooth fur of its skin.

'Both of you, perhaps,' she allowed. 'If you can catch archmagery, then you can catch this.'

She tossed the fruit across the table. Hrugaar dropped his spoon to catch it. The peach slipped past his fingers and rolled round to hover at the back of his hand. He laughed, and whipped his hand around to grasp it. Again the fruit eluded him.

'Not yet, apparently,' Ellen smiled.

Taillan chuckled in delight, reaching out with both arms. 'Mine!' he said.

Ellen picked another peach from the bowl. 'You shall have your own,' she said, and began to slice it down for him.

Hrugaar frowned in concentration. His third attempt to catch the fruit was no more successful than the first.

At that moment Rhysana swept in from the outer hall, the scent of honeysuckle still drifting about her from her walk through the cloister garden.

'Do not play with the fruit, Ru,' she said absently, plucking the peach from the back of his hand and taking it with her to the far end of the table. 'You shall only be giving Taillan ideas.'

Everyone turned to look at her as she sat down.

'What is it?' she demanded, surprised.

'Good morning, High Councillor Rhysana,' said Ellen. 'I trust that you slept well?'

'Yes, thank you, Archmage,' she answered. 'Good morning – Morvaan, Ru. Forgive me, have I interrupted something?' She signalled for the *chaedar* to bring her some tea.

'Not at all, said Morvaan easily, passing her a bowl and spoon. 'We were just discussing the High Council assembly, which the three of us shall be attending shortly. If you feel up to it, that is.'

'Of course,' said Rhysana. 'Just as soon as I have had something to eat.'

'A lady after my own heart,' he winked at her.

'And then you can tell us about the *Argument of Command*,' said Hrugaar.

'Later, Ru,' she said. 'The High Council is enough for me to think about for the moment.'

'Now you sound just like the Archmage Ellen,' he sighed.

Erkal Dortrean stood back from the rail, giving the Braedun sailors room to work while they brought the ship alongside the wharf. The morning air was filled with shouts and whistles and bursts of song, and the cries of the gulls that seemed to have followed them all the way upriver from the coast.

The Braedun *commanderie*, whither Erkal was bound, was still the best part of a league ahead at the upper end of this part of the river valley. From where he stood he could see the eight white towers of the ancient keep, set in a circle on a hilltop perhaps a quarter of a mile back from the northern shore; and gathered around the keep were cloistered buildings and towers of the blue-grey stone of the Blue Mountains. At their feet, and stretching west down the hill toward him, were the cottages and barns and workshops of the *commanderie* village. To the south the hill slopes ran out into a broad apron of lush meadowland, still half hidden beneath pale plumes of lingering mist.

The Galloppi River, Erkal knew, came down in a fall on the far side of the *commanderie* hill, and flowed in a curve around the meadow apron before winding its way west through the wide valley to the trading village of Reddit, where they were about to put ashore. The village was said to be as old as the *commanderie* itself, and boasted several fine houses and towers of stone that belonged to the local merchant families; and an old paved road climbed from here to the keep along the northern hill slopes. Beyond Reddit, the Galloppi turned south again, through a narrower valley gorge with wooded hills on either side, and then west and south toward the distant sea.

Such was the *commanderie* vale as Erkal had heard of it all his life, the principal seat of the Braedun Order and their private domain. What spoiled the sight for him that morning was that this tranquil valley was now a camp of war. From the *commanderie* village down to the river, and reaching south toward the meadowland and west a good way toward him, were the tents and banners, wagons and cooking fires of the Souther hosts. Three of their smaller ships were moored there, up by the meadows, their sails furled and dark with the sunlight behind them, and their gilded rails gleaming fitfully through the shrouding mist.

From what Erkal could guess, there must have been close on five thousand people gathered in the vale, warriors and camp followers and slaves, and perhaps another four hundred now marching upriver to join them. That was far more than he had been led to expect, and far more than the *commanderie* itself could ever comfortably have housed – at least, as far as the Six Kingdoms' need for personal space was concerned. From their many banners of mulberry and scarlet, purple and ochre and black, he could tell that there was a mix of warriors from several of the Souther lands. All were notionally under the rule of Ambassador T'Loi, far away in Ellanguan; but there would undoubtedly be other commanders here to keep the peace between them.

More than half of the banners here, so the priests of Braedun had told him, belonged to the lords of the K'tarim – or *Kentorim*, as they named themselves. It was their leader, Talarkan, who had so far acted on all the Southers' behalf in dealings with the *commanderie*. The K'tarim, like the God-King's people of the Su'lorim, were tall and elegant folk from the coastal regions of the Souther empire; and both peoples produced many powerful warriors and sorcerors, and laid claim to a wealth far beyond the greediest dreams of any merchant or noble within the Six Kingdoms. Ambassador T'Loi himself was of the Su'lorim, and close kinsman to the new God-King; but his people – those with the banners of purple or ochre-gold – numbered well less than a thousand here, and Erkal had yet to learn who commanded them in T'Loi's absence.

And then there were the Islanders, the *ilionin*, the lesser folk from the scattered islands off the Souther shore, looked down upon by all the Souther races that Erkal had ever met. They were sallow skinned and shorter of stature, cunning and wilful as runaway children, excellent sailors and fishermen, and pirates and thieves. Many of them would serve as slaves or crewmen for the more rich and powerful of the Souther peoples. Theirs were the smaller ships, swift and nimble, moored further up the river; and no doubt the *ilionin* had been tasked with bringing the barrels and crates of supplies now stacked along the Reddit hythe, and being carried in wagons along the road.

What other people might be here, Erkal did not yet know; though he guessed that they would be fewer in number and serving as warriors or slaves under the Su'lorim and K'tarim. But he found himself relieved to see no sign of the mounted archers of the T'gaim and their swift horses, who alone could make serious challenge to the might of the heavy cavalry of Lautun.

'Boldrin of Levrin,' said Kierran's voice beside him. 'Thank all the gods!'

Erkal turned to look down at the wharf. There were perhaps half a dozen men and women among the busy crowd there dressed in the grey-blue of Braedun; but there was no mistaking the holy knight, with his handsome face and bright blue eyes beneath thick brown Levrin hair. He mounted the steps three at a time to the raised platform where the gangplank had now been set. Two of the ship's crew lifted back the bar of the side rail, and stood to attention for Erkal to go ashore.

The Earl gathered his scarlet cloak about him, and thanked the men before crossing over. Boldrin grasped his arm in welcome, and then they turned to see the other members of Erkal's party safely ashore. The priestess Hannaï of Braedun came first, treading lightly across the plank in spite of her many years, and making the sign of *Aeshta* blessing to the two men before going on ahead down the steps. Behind her came the *noghr* priest Dharagh, using his temper to outface the fear of the narrow drop to the water below. And then behind him came the young Lord Kierran of Arrand, who was only too glad to accept Erkal's helping hand.

'So why are you here?' Erkal asked Boldrin, as they went down the steps to the wharf.

'I have come to escort the last of our Order back to Arrandin, your Grace,' the knight told him. 'At least, those who are leaving. Some few will remain behind.'

'I see,' said Erkal carefully.

He had to admit to himself that he was much comforted by the thought. He had not liked the business of handing over the *commanderie* from the start, and was only too willing to uphold the right of the Braedun Order to leave certain of their members to keep an eye on the place. Beyond that, he had also found himself strangely relieved to see Boldrin's friendly face among the crowd. Though Hannaï and the ship's crew had been kindly enough, there had been a slight wariness in their dealings with him; as though they wondered how far he had the interests of their Order at heart, or how far he was now the Emperor's man. The great number of Souther troops also disturbed him. Mindful of Captain A'lil's warning the day before, Erkal had the unpleasant feeling that he might soon be held here as hostage, much like Ambassador T'Loi in Ellanguan.

He had no time to talk further with Boldrin just then, for there was a sudden commotion among the crowd and a group of Southers came down the stone steps from the village square. Their leader was very tall, and they were all clad in black, trimmed with murrey and gold; and two of them had large mastiffs, black and tan, held on tight chains. The villagers hurried aside. The dogs bounded toward the *noghr*, jaws grinning wide, dragging their handlers behind them. The beasts stood fully as high as the dwarf's shoulder.

'Down!' Dharagh told them firmly.

The dogs skidded to a halt on the timbered wharf, sat down,

and then lay down on all fours. The *noghr* went down on his knees, still swaying a little, and patted their great heads. The Souther leader laughed.

'The Most Worthy Talarkan of the K'tarim,' Boldrin introduced him. 'His Grace, the Earl of Dortrean.'

The two men bowed in greeting.

Talarkan was nearly a head taller than the Earl, with long black hair swept forward over his left shoulder and reaching down nearly to his waist. He wore a long black tunic with a split panelled skirt that came down to below his knees, over heavy breeches and boots. His face had a paler olive tan than was usual among the K'tarim, with dark eyes, and a single pale blue gem hung from a silver chain upon his brow.

His daughter Ellaïn, Erkal thought, would have swooned at the sensuous grace of this handsome Souther. For his own part, he found the man faintly irritating.

'Perhaps your dwarf would care to ride my dogs through the village,' said Talarkan, after several more bows had been exchanged.

One of the hounds had now rolled over on to his back, his tongue lolling in contentment as the *noghr* made a fuss of him.

'He is not one of your household dwarves,' said Erkal, 'such as those kept by your own people for amusement. Father Dharagh comes from a folk called the *noghru*, and he is held in honour as a Chosen Priest among our people. He is also, I should point out, a most skilful warrior with that axe of his – enough to make a good dint in your family jewels, should you offend him.'

Talarkan's men put their hands to their swords. Kierran moved closer to Erkal's side.

'Is this the poor manner you use for all your guests?' Talarkan sneered. 'To offer insults and threats in return for kindness?'

'Perhaps you misheard me, Most Worthy,' the Earl said calmly, resting his hand upon Kierran's arm to stay him. 'Among the K'tarim, I believe, it is a deep insult to speak ill of one of your anointed priests; and better men than either of us have died slow and painful deaths in payment for it. Perhaps it would be wise for us to say that we never had this conversation?'

Dharagh hauled himself to his feet, and straightened his axe beneath his belt. The dogs scrabbled up beside him.

'Welcome, your Grace of Dortrean,' said Talarkan, bowing. 'You honour us with your presence.'

'Your honour is my honour,' Erkal returned, bowing again.

The Souther nodded, signalling to his men. 'Your knights have sent horses to bear you,' he said.

Erkal gestured for Talarkan to precede him up the steps. There was another exchange of bows before he did so. The Southers and the dogs cleared the way before him.

'Wonderful beasts,' said Dharagh, falling in beside Kierran. 'But are we not wasting our time with that fool?'

'What is a Most Worthy, anyway?' Kierran asked.

'About one step up from a captain,' Erkal explained quietly. 'And no, we are not wholly wasting our time with him. Talarkan speaks for the K'tarim, and so we have to work with him – or work around him. As with most armies, it is more likely the case that those at the top, or those at the lowest level of the chain of command, are the ones who will get things done. Talarkan appears to be a middle ranker.'

'That makes him a more dangerous man to cross,' said Boldrin.

'On a personal level, yes,' Erkal agreed. 'But it is who commands him that is of interest to me. And in the short term, it is the leaders of the rank and file below him who will keep his men under control and prevent wanton harm to the *commanderie* lands and villages.'

'So what are we going to do?' asked Kierran.

'Keep making friends with the hounds,' Erkal answered.

The High Council meeting took fully as long as Rhysana had expected, though with one or two unforeseen twists and turns along the way. Her main consolation was that the air was cooler in the great assembly chamber than elsewhere, which left her head a little clearer to think.

All twelve remaining members of the High Council were present that morning. The Archmage Morvaan had managed to drag High Councillor Rikkarn away from his work, and he was seated in the southwest to Sollonaal's left, arrayed in his robes of red and grey. The High Councillor the Lord Drôshiin of Sêchral had arrived in sumptuous robes of cinnamon silk, bordered with red and gold and embroidered with circling doves and ravens. Like Rikkarn, Drôshiin was now well past his three score years, but Rhysana thought that he looked healthier than when she had last seen him. His round face had a better colour, and his thinning hair was darker again as if it had been dyed. He had greeted her warmly in a cloud of perfume as he circled round the chamber, his dark eyes flicking across her rounded belly with a saucy familiarity that brought a flush of heat to her cheeks. He sat down across the chamber from her in the northwest, to the left of the Archmage Merrech.

When Morvaan called for an initial vote, to test the waters before the election debate began in earnest, the High Council's opinion was divided fairly equally between Ellen, Ferghaal and Sollonaal. Rikkarn offered to propose High Councillor Asharka, but she declined to stand upon this occasion, saying that she felt unequal to the role within the Court Noble that was clearly expected of their new leader by the greater Council. Ellen then repeated her own belief that Archmagi were not the best suited to the role of Prime Councillor, but she did not formally withdraw from the running. Given the uncertainty of Ferghaal's strength of support in a challenge against Sollonaal, Rhysana could well understand why Ellen was unwilling to stand down at this stage.

The debate itself took the better part of an hour, though there was little in it that Rhysana had not already heard. Within the closed circle of the High Council, Sollonaal now admitted that it was more than likely that the remnant of the Kelmaar Order would be asked to withdraw from the city of

Ellanguan until the present crisis had passed, and that the members of the other *Aeshta* Orders within the city might also be asked to remove themselves for the time being. Sollonaal assured the anxious magi that he was making every effort to argue the case against it with the Lord Steward Rinnekh; but it appeared that Rhysana was not the only one present who found herself unwilling or unable to believe him.

High Councillor Ferghaal reported that the Earl of Dortrean was arriving at the Braedun *commanderie* that morning, and that the formal hand-over would soon be complete. The Souther forces had behaved remarkably well, whatever the feelings of the people of the Six Kingdoms toward them. Ferghaal seemed to have resigned himself, at least, to the reality of their presence there. Rhysana wondered whether he might have had more to say on the subject had the Emperor's Archmage not been listening.

Merrech's silent presence in the assembly chamber had not so far greatly unsettled her. Whatever his opinion of the Council, she would not have expected him to miss so important an event as the election of a new Prime Councillor. Nor was she much surprised that he had declined to acknowledge her, given that they had said all that they needed to say to one another, for the moment, the previous evening. His very presence there in the assembly chamber – a stark black shadow against the cushioned white silk of his High Council seat – was enough to remind her that he believed that he had won.

It was only when he raised his hands and began to speak, fairly late on in the debate, that Rhysana realised that he was playing a different game.

'Fellow councillors,' he said in a voice as smooth and soft as silk; 'before this debate goes any further, it is with some reluctance that I feel that I should present one or two more points for your consideration. The first is that I must agree with the Archmage the Lady Ellen of Raudhar that she might be unsuitable in the role of Prime Councillor. It has come to my attention that only yesterday she took the white steel rod of the Prime Councillor's office and used it to gain entry to the sealed fortress of Illana at Whitespear Head, with neither the knowledge nor the authority of this Council.'

Several of the assembled magi appeared shocked at this news. Morvaan sent a comment to Rhysana, mind to mind, but she was intent on watching for Ellen's reaction and failed to catch it.

'I understand,' Merrech went on, 'that at least one of our members did go with her, namely High Councillor Rhysana; and also two rag-tag members of the greater Council – one of whom, alas, met with his death as a result of the inherent dangers of such a journey. While I should not wish to intrude on any mage's right to personal privacy, I feel that in the circumstances such wilful disregard for High Council procedure, and the resultant death of one of our own magi, must be taken into account when considering that mage's suitability to be chosen as our next Prime Councillor.'

'Is this true, Archmage Ellen?' asked Trialmaster Foghlaar.

'It is,' she replied calmly. 'I need not remind this Council of the present threat of the demon Lo-Khuma's return. We believed that there might be lore still hidden within Whitespear Head, from the time of the Old Kingdoms, which could help us to prevent it. With Iorlaas gone, the need was too pressing to wait while this Council debated the election of his successor and then squabbled at length over the risks involved in entering Illana's fortress.'

'I knew of this also,' Morvaan put in. 'I judged that if the Archmage Ellen was capable of passing the seals in safety, then the time was ripe for her to do so.'

'That judgement was not yours alone to make,' said Drôshiin of Sêchral; 'no matter how great you felt the need to be.'

'The late Mage Councillor Dhûghaúr of Moraan came with us of his own asking,' Ellen continued. 'He was slain by the cruel arts of the shadowfay, and not by any magic left by Illana herself. I should add that His Eminence the Archmage Merrech was also there at Whitespear Head, in company with the shadowfay; and that had it not been for the wisdom of High Councillor Rhysana, and the quick wits of Mage Councillor Hrugaar, I doubt that he would have suffered us to leave there alive.'

'This is all very interesting,' said Sollonaal, above the murmurs from around the chamber; 'and I fear that it may indeed call into question the judgement of some of our worthy colleagues. But there seems to be a private disagreement here, which has little bearing on the due process of election.'

'But knowledge that may defeat the demon captain is very much this Council's business,' said High Councillor Ferghaal. 'Archmage Ellen, did you find what you sought?'

Ellen gestured for Rhysana to make answer.

Rhysana found herself suddenly trapped. She had no intention of lying to the High Council; but she was uncertain how much of the truth should yet be told.

'Not as such,' she said carefully; 'or not that I am aware. We did find some papers, which may or may not be in Illana's hand. Those are now in the care of the Archmage Merrech, as the foremost scholar of Illana's work within our time, and I trust that he will present his findings to the High Council in due course.'

There was far greater outcry at this latest news, both of excitement over the find and indignation that it should have passed so swiftly into the clutches of the Emperor's Archmage.

Morvaan clapped his hands together for silence, and then raised them palm outward on either side of his white head in the prescribed manner for speech.

'One might wonder,' he ventured, 'what business the Archmage Merrech had with the shadowfay, that took him to Whitespear Head? And since the shadowfay of old worshipped Lo-Khuma, and it has been rumoured over the past several weeks that the demon has servants within the Imperial Household, where indeed he may stand upon the question of Lo-Khuma's return?'

'Wonder away,' said Sollonaal 'but not in the Council's time. These are matters of personal or religious persuasion; and since the Archmage does not stand as a candidate for election they have no part in this debate.'

'*Eann'o*,' said Merrech. *I oppose*. 'I imagine that these questions are indeed of concern to many gathered here, and they bring me to the second point that I wished to make. It is therefore relevant to this debate.'

This should be good, Morvaan's thought whispered in Rhysana's mind. The prospect of what Merrech might say next had set her on edge; but she returned his wry humour with a soft smile.

'It has been known for some time,' Merrech sighed, 'among His Highness' closest circle of advisers, that there are servants of the demon within the Imperial Household. It was judged wisest to keep them there, rather than to drive them out, so that they could be watched and controlled, and in some measure prevented. Since their natural allies were the shadowfay, I took upon myself the unpleasant and highly dangerous task of gaining the shadowfay's confidence, so that as much could be learned from them as possible for the sake of the Empire.'

'Better the demon you know than the unknown demon you fear,' quipped Trialmaster Foghlaar.

'Precisely,' Merrech hissed. 'There are those among the followers of the old gods who hold that all of the *Vashtar* are demons; and the same is said in turn of the Lords of the *Aeshtar* and of many of their great creatures by the servants of the imperial gods. Different faiths, different beliefs. For the safe rule of the Empire, such matters of personal faith have at times to be set aside; and since the Easterner clans – and some of the Souther peoples, by report – are servants of the demon, this passed beyond the bounds of faith into the realm of politics and rulership.

'It would appear that I must remind this Council yet again that, as a body, we should not intervene in matters of politics or religious persuasion, both of which are here clearly the case – even though, as High Councillor Ferghaal is most anxious to remind me, this particular demon might bring an end to all life as we know it. I am not proposing that individual magi should do nothing, that of course is their free choice. But in this case, until and unless the servants of the demon abuse power beyond their control, it will not be the Prime Councillor's place to lead this Council against them. And for that reason, I doubt that High Councillor Ferghaal's proven and passionate faith in the Lords of the *Aeshtar* would allow him to sit easily on the Prime Councillor's throne.

'However, before the worthy High Councillor Sollonaal pats himself too heartily on the back, I should complete my second point. As an individual, every mage has a right to make political alliance as he may choose. But when, as in Sollonaal's case, he drags an entire College and most of the Ellanguan Magi into an obvious alliance with the Lord Steward Rinnekh, one must view his possible ability to lead the neutral Council of All Magi safely through the political arena of the Court Noble with the deepest of misgivings.'

'And who better than you to speak of obvious political alliance,' snapped Sollonaal.

'I did not present myself as a candidate for election,' Merrech returned smoothly.

There was some scattered laughter around the assembly chamber. Sollonaal looked furious.

'Well, now that you have discredited us all, Archmage,' said Ellen, 'have you another proposal to make?'

'Personally, I think that High Councillor Rhysana would be our best choice,' he replied, 'as and when she stops breeding. She has a better understanding of the Emperor than any of you.'

Trialmaster Foghlaar leaned over in his seat toward Rhysana. 'Do you wish to stand, my dear?' he asked.

Rhysana smiled and shook her head. She had guessed whom the Toad Archmage would propose, even before he named her, and took it in the humorous spirit that he intended. She had in fact already guessed at most of what he had said, following their conversation the previous night; and she was feeling rather pleased with herself for having been proved right, and relieved that he had not come out with anything worse. She wondered whether his passing shot about understanding the Emperor had also stemmed from their conversation, and filed it away in her mind for later thought.

'Then may we put this to the vote?' Foghlaar asked the assembly. 'Or at least, withdraw for refreshment? It seems obvious to me that the Archmage Ellen is the most level headed of the three, and, like Herusen, has the pluck to trust her own judgement when it is needed. And besides, all this talk of Ferghaal's passion and Sollonaal's corruption has given me a terrible thirst.'

'Is Sollonaal now corrupt?' said Drôshiin. 'How very droll. He shall have my vote – for all the good that will do him.'

'What is the point?' said Sollonaal crossly, standing up. 'Upon one matter, at least, the Archmage Ellen and I are in agreement: there is no purpose in waiting for this Council to debate its endless squabbles. It is clear that you have no intention of electing another *Vashta* mage as Prime Councillor, whomever else you may choose. It is also clear that this Council is now dangerously out of touch with the needs and realities of the Empire around us. You may debate your choice as long as you will, but I shall have no further part in it. Those magi who wish to serve the people of this Empire, rather than their own selfish little mystic huddle, are welcome to join me if they so choose.'

'Oh do sit down, Sollonaal,' said Ellen, with measured patience. 'Please. We do appreciate that events in Ellanguan might have gone far worse without you there.'

Sollonaal stalked to the centre of the floor, his turquoise and gold robes hissing angrily with his speed.

'That fool Hrugaar did one thing right, for a change,' he told her, 'calling for an open vote to defeat me in the assembly. Now you shall live to see all that you hold dear crumble and be swept away. I wish you joy of the sight.'

He turned on his heel and stode toward the doors. Drôshiin of Sêchral and Lirinal of Dregharis hurried after him. Morvaan sighed and gestured for the ebon doors to open, since it seemed likely that Sollonaal would batter them down did he not.

The Archmage Merrech rose like a shadow from his seat. 'It would appear that there is to be no election,' he observed. 'How shall all be in agreement, when not all are present?' He glided swiftly across the patterned floor, nodding his hood to Ellen as he passed her.

'The *Aeshta* Orders should be told, Eminence, who these servants of the demon captain are,' said Ferghaal.

The Imperial Counsellor paused just inside the doorway.

'Perhaps,' he hissed. 'But not by me. I should advise you to tread carefully. His Highness takes ill any meddling within the Imperial household; and if the danger to the Empire should increase because of your interference, your Orders Noble would be facing charges of treason.'

He turned and went out. The remaining magi sat in silence for several seconds.

'Well that was a threat, if you like,' said Foghlaar.

'I do not like,' said Ellen. 'I have grave doubts about the whole question of Rhydden harbouring the servants of the demon, especially when the *Aeshta* Orders believe that he is so close to returning. I fear that somebody may have to do something about it, even at the risk of being taken for treason.'

Somebody already is, Rhysana thought to herself, remembering Kellarn's oath – and the fact that she was still no nearer to helping him in his quest.

'We may still hold the vote,' said Trialmaster Ekraan, rearranging his snowy beard over his midnight blue robes. 'If the eight of us can agree, we carry two thirds of the total vote. The *Vashta* magi have, by Sollonaal's declaration of intent, effectively abstained. And since His Eminence did not appear to like any of our three candidates, we may safely assume his abstention also.'

'It would serve him right for leaving,' Morvaan agreed. 'But is that a lawful election?'

'Sollonaal has renounced his right to challenge, before us all,' said Ekraan. 'If two thirds of the High Council all agree, and there is no challenge made, the election is sound according to precedent. You may trust a Trialmaster to know his Council protocol.'

'But the Prime Councillor would be elected to rule over a divided Council, if Sollonaal holds to his words,' said Asharka. 'And we can not have the Ellanguan College sundered from the others.'

'Nor the Ellanguan Book Halls,' put in Rikkarn.

'May we not persuade Sollonaal to come back?' Asharka finished.

'Not this time, I think,' said Morvaan. 'Or not for a while, anyway. Or not without electing him, which I imagine that most of us would be loth to do. But no, the split between *Aeshta* and *Vashta* magi has been with us for many years. Herusen managed to smooth over the differences in his own peculiar way. Perhaps our next Prime Councillor will find another way to patch us back together again.'

'Then be so kind as to close the doors,' said Foghlaar, 'and let us make the vote.'

Kellarn awoke to the tang of wild, sweet air, and the clear call of a blackbird. He opened his eyes, blinking, and looked up at a patchwork of bright green leaves backlit by sunlight. A cool breeze brushed across his forehead, and he smiled.

'Ilunâtor,' he said.

The blackbird whistled again. A girl's face looked down at him, framed with hair of soft red gold.

'Hello, Kellarn,' she said.

Kellarn let his eyelids close, enjoying the warmth of the day, balanced by the cooling breeze. He felt rested and comfortable, though a little stiff from lying on the ground. He opened his eyes again. Dyrnalv was still there.

'The first Guardians sat at the feet of Ilunâtor, and learned wisdom of the *syldhar*,' he said.

Dyrnalv laughed. 'Where did you hear that?'

'Losithlîn told me.'

'Did she now?'

Her face moved away, so he turned his head to look at her. She was sitting on the ground beside him, clad again in her simple white shift. The lake of Alvinaah stretched out behind her.

'They did not say that to me,' she said.

'The moon fay?'

Dyrnalv made no answer.

'The *syldhar*?' he pursued.

'You should rest now,' she told him. 'We can talk later.' She began to move.

'Tell me,' he said, grasping her by the hand.

A crackle of power tore about his fingers, and the jewel of her ring burned hot against his palm. He tightened his grip, blocking the pain with a thought. The sensation of power vanished.

Dyrnalv looked down at him, her hazel eyes widening just a little in surprise. After a moment he took his hand away, and flopped back into the grass.

'What do you know of the *syldhar*, Kellarn?' she asked.

He let his eyes drift again. He had lost his train of thought. It was Ilunâtor – or the memory of him – that had saved him in the Realms of the Dead. When the moon fay had told him that only the most ancient of the great creatures might destroy the demon captain, he had thought at once of the Father of All Dragons. Ilunâtor had the power to destroy Lo-Khuma.

Why had he never done so?

'Kellarn?' Dyrnalv's voice whispered.

He struggled to remember her question. The *syldhar*. They were mentioned in the lore of Zedron, which Corollin studied, and the moon fay had spoken briefly of them. They were linked in tales with shape-shifters, and with the white horses of Dortrean legend that ushered down the mountain snows. He believed that he had seen them once in a dream, some time ago, with Ilunâtor. They had the friendship of Ilunâtor – and they had taught the first Guardians.

'You see, you need to rest now,' she told him.

'They taught you too, didn't they?' he said, suddenly understanding. 'After old Gilraen was gone.'

Dyrnalv nodded, and swept her hair back behind her ear.

'Gilraen was taken early from us,' she said. 'But be warned Kellarn: those who speak with the *syldhar* set their feet upon a different path, and fall out of step with their own kind.'

'Like making friends with the Fay?'

'Yes, very like,' she smiled.

Kellarn rolled on to his side and sat up. The effort hurt his head. His stomach felt very empty.

'Or with Ilunâtor,' he said to himself.

The dragon, the *syldhar*, the Guardians. The pieces were beginning to fit. The *syldhar* were a source for Zedron's lore – a lore which Corollin hoped might help her to use the artefact of the First Kings.

He saw a different thought behind Dyrnalv's warning.

'You think I should speak with the *syldhar*,' he said.

'I said no such thing.'

'That's why you kept asking me why it had to be Morvargh I spoke to,' he went on. '*Someone usually knows something*, that's what you said. You were trying to tell me that I was barking up the wrong tree. How could I have been so stupid?'

'You were not,' she laughed. 'You chose as you thought best, at great peril to your own life. But why do you now wish to speak with the *syldhar*?'

'Because they know Ilunâtor,' Kellarn cried.

It was not what he had expected to say, and he was surprised by the strength of his own passion. There was a commotion in the leaves overhead as the blackbird flew away. Dyrnalv looked at him gently, and smiled.

'I think that you know him as well as any of us, Son of the Living Fire,' she said.

Kellarn ducked his head away. 'What do you know of the artefact of the First Kings?' he asked her.

'Your friend Corollin has told me of it, this morning.'

'But what did you know of it before we came?' he pursued.

'I am the last true Guardian alive within the Middle Lands,' she told him. 'The *syldhar* told me that an artefact was made, for they learned that two of the pieces had been found; and now you have brought with you four more. One more remains of the seven, which they hope shall be found very soon.'

'Seven?' Kellarn demanded.

'When that artefact is made whole,' Dyrnalv went on, 'they hope that it may be used in the fight against the great demon whom of old the elevenfolk of the Fay named *Atallakûr*, the Beautiful Deceiver. And that conflict draws very near. The Enemy now stands on the threshold of the waking world; and this new moon is a Moon of Calling, when gifts that were hidden may be revealed.'

'I thought that I saw – the Enemy, in the Realms of the Dead,' Kellarn told her. 'Or his shadow, at least.'

'Yes,' she said. 'But do not think about it just yet, until you are fully rested. Let the forest do its work of healing first.'

Kellarn drew a deep breath, and tried to clear his head.

'Why did you not tell us all this before?' he asked. 'About the *syldhar* and the bars, I mean.'

'You had to find the answers for yourself,' said Dyrnalv.

'*To learn, you must take the path of unknowing*,' Kellarn grinned.

'Something like that.'

'But where are the other two bars?' he demanded. 'Or three, if there is one still to be found.'

'The two are safe enough,' she said. 'You might say that they are with the Moon. The seventh and last is the Lautun part, which Corollin tells me a friend of yours was looking for.'

'Rhysana,' Kellarn nodded. 'But do the *syldhar* know where it is?'

'No,' said Dyrnalv. 'Not yet.'

The storm had already started by the time that Rhysana and Torkhaal reached the imperial citadel, and the thunder echoed behind the chatter and bustle of the busy hallways of the river wing.

They had left Taillan safe with Ellen and Hrugaar, back at the Lautun College. Ellen was in no mood to attend Court that day, now finding herself elected to be the next Prime Councillor of All Magi. She had said that she wanted to have some time quietly to herself – though with Hrugaar and Taillan around that seemed to be a most unlikely possibility. Ellen also proposed to make a start on sorting out Iorlaas' belongings, so that someone from the Farran College could come to take them away.

'He never spoke of any kinsmen,' she said. 'I am assuming that Asharka will know whom he wished to handle his affairs.'

'What about Dhûghaúr?' Torkhaal had dared to ask.

'His mother and father are dead,' Hrugaar answered. 'He had two sisters, but I do not recall that he ever told me their names. The older one is married – to one of the lesser Dortrean nobles, I think.'

'Not to another Moraan?' Torkhaal grinned. 'How unusual.'

Hrugaar made a face. 'The other was a few years younger again. I think that she may still be a student at the College in Farran.'

'I shall ask Asharka to speak with her, Ru,' Ellen told him. 'Unless you would prefer to do so yourself?'

'No,' he said.

'Then there were his Herghin kinsmen, on his mother's side,' said Rhysana. 'Lorellin Herghin will no doubt have to come to Court, to swear her formal oaths as the new Head of House. I think that she would like to be told, especially since he played such an important part in regaining her manor house from the Easterners.'

'Is that the oath-taking that you are to attend today?' Hrugaar asked.

'No,' said Torkhaal. 'Today is the admission of the new cadets to the Imperial Household Guard. The eldest son of Mage Councillor Kharfaal of Vaulun is one of the proposed cadets.'

'Has he been tested for magical talent?' Ellen wondered.

Torkhaal shrugged. 'When his father is first cousin to the Emperor, and the Empire is on the brink of war, he has little choice but to go into the Guard. Perhaps he may come to us in a few years' time, when Rhydden has finished with him.'

'Hardly a comforting thought,' said Ellen.

The oath-taking ceremony was to be held in the great audience hall of the imperial palace, with its formal pillared arches and galleries of black stone framing walls and vaulted ceiling of white marble. The black marble floor, polished smooth as glass, was set aside for the close families of the nominated cadets; but the upper galleries on either side were open for others – such as Rhysana and Torkhaal themselves – who were either friends of those taking part or merely curious to watch.

It was rather a sombre hall at the best of times, and perhaps the more so by contrast with the chattering nobles in all their colourful attire. The dark sky of the storm beyond the high windows added to the sense of gloom, in spite of the white lamps hung along the pillars, and the air in the upper gallery seemed close and stuffy again after the cooler breeze of the hallways down in the river wing. Rhysana wished that she could have kept on the loose fitting gown that she had worn earlier, instead of her high councillor's robes of deep indigo, but it would have been unsuitable for a formal gathering in the Emperor's presence.

They found her brother Lavan near the far end of the

gallery, with his two sons, Khyrfan and Mâghan, leaning over the balustrade to look down in to the hall. All three were dressed alike in high collared tunics of deep blue bordered with silver, the colours of Telún. The Lord Aúrun of Renza was talking with Lavan, tall and fair and cheerful as ever. Nereïs and Lauraï had taken little Maïa away for a walk in one of the cooler parts of the citadel.

There were a fair number of people gathered in the hall, both above and below; though most, by their colours, appeared to be from lesser branches of the Lautun Houses, or from among the Farran and Telbray nobles. For once there were not many faces that Rhysana knew, even by sight alone. On the gallery on the far side of the hall she picked out Torkhaal's uncle, the Lord Ravaïl Eädhan, who with his dark hair and fair face looked remarkably like an older version of her husband. Ravaïl was clad as usual in a high collared tunic of midnight blue. Standing talking to him was a younger woman in a gown the colour of winter beech leaves, with dark auburn hair caught up prettily into coiled braids. Her face was flushed to rose with the heat of the hall, and she looked fully two months nearer to childbirth than Rhysana herself. A tall man of about the same age, with long curling blond hair, stood protectively behind her.

'Is that not your sister Sîlaúra?' she asked Torkhaal. 'You did not tell me that she was expecting.'

'That is because I did not know,' he replied. 'You know that I hardly ever see her.'

Rhysana looked again. She guessed that the tall man with her must be Sîlaúra's husband, the Lord Sorrachal of Aartaús. Sorrachal's younger brother, she remembered, had inherited the Dortrean House of Dhûlann and married the lovely Inghara of Rebraal, a former contender for the Empress Consort's crown. Rhysana did not think that the new Lord Dhûlann himself was at Court; and in point of fact, when she searched around the hall with her eyes she could see only one person whom she knew for certain belonged to any of the Dortrean

Houses. Down on the main floor, the Lord Torreghal Valhaes was resplendent in scarlet and gold. He was talking with one of the imperial guards, with a knight in his own livery hovering just behind him. Torreghal was the right arm of Dortrean's military strength, and would be here to represent Erkal as well as to support his Countess, the Lady Karlena. Which of the cadets he had come to see, Rhysana did not know. Of the Ladies of Valhaes, and of Karlena herself, there was as yet no sign.

'Here comes High Councillor Drôshiin,' said Torkhaal, pointing to a flash of cinnamon robes near the arched doorway at the end of the far gallery. 'I can not remember the last time that I saw him at Court.'

'Grinnaer's marriage, perhaps,' she supplied. 'I wonder if Sollonaal sent him.'

'More like he has come to cast an eye over any pretty young Ladies joining the Guard,' Torkhaal grinned. The twins laughed. Rhysana tugged at the sleeve of his dark green robes to hush him.

At that moment the noon bell sounded in the hall, and then the clamour of horns and drums that heralded the Emperor's arrival. All the nobles in the gallery crowded forward to watch.

The Emperor Rhydden came first, a dazzling figure in white and gold. At his side was the Empress Grinnaer, in a gown of cloth of gold, her right hand upraised and clenched firmly within Rhydden's gloved fist. Both wore golden circlets that flashed with glittering jewels.

Behind them came the Imperial Counsellor the Archmage Merrech, clad now in hooded robes of silver-grey silk; and behind him came the two Guard Commanders, Drômagh of Sêchral and Brodhaur Levrin, in the black and gold of their uniform. At the rear followed the Lady Karlena in a gorgeous gown of scarlet velvet, with scarlet gems flickering on the jewelled combs in her piled coppery hair. At Karlena's side, and somewhat overshadowed by her presence, was the fair haired Lady Turinda Linnaer of Solaní, dressed in gold and brown as a lady in waiting of Grinnaer's household.

The imperial party strode the full length of the hall, the Empress Consort struggling very slightly to keep abreast of her Lord and husband's pace. As they drew closer, Rhysana could see that Grinnaer's chestnut curls were hidden within a golden snood, and her face was expertly made up, with her eyes painted large and dark in deep bronze tones. It was an ancient mode of face painting, dating from a time when the horselords of Lautun had been High Kings rather than Emperors, and Rhysana had seldom seen it used among the Ladies of the Court Noble except at formal masked balls. She thought that it made Grinnaer look older, though with a remote, timeless beauty. It would also mask any signs of the beating that Rhydden was rumoured to have given her before they had left Ellanguan. This was Grinnaer's first public appearance at the Summer Court. From what Torkhaal had told Rhysana, she had not been present at the opening ball.

The Emperor sat himself down on the ebon throne prepared for him, and the Archmage Merrech and Lord Drômagh took up their positions behind. The Empress had a smaller, cushioned throne of white and gold, set upon the Emperor's left. It took Karlena and Turinda slightly longer to settle Grinnaer comfortably into place, and then Lord Brodhaur signalled for the first of the cadets to be brought in.

There were twenty-three new cadets to take their oaths that day. Lûghan of Vaulun was the first to be escorted up the hall, being the foremost among them by precedence of Blood Noble, and displaying his father's height and easy confidence. A few cadets further down the line came the fair haired Dannil of Valhaes, Torreghal's eldest son. He seemed much younger and more uncertain than Lûghan – a little too young, Rhysana thought, to be entering the Guard. She did not recall that Dannil had yet come of age to be formally recognised as Torreghal's heir designate, which prompted her to wonder at the political implications behind this apparent sacrifice.

Rhysana watched closely as Dannil knelt before the Emperor to speak his oath, placing his hands between Rhydden's own. The boy was softly spoken, and seemed almost tongue-tied by Rhydden's dazzling presence; and when she looked more intently, Rhysana realised that the unusual brightness around the Emperor himself was clearly the work of enchantment. As Rhydden returned his own oath of protection and vengeance with chilling calmness, she had the uneasy feeling that all was definitely not as it should be.

She sought and found Torkhaal's hand, and held it. Though he did not risk linking mind to mind with her here, she could sense that he was unsettled too.

Dannil of Valhaes stood up to receive his cadet's black headband from Lord Brodhaur, and Rhydden himself buckled a sword about the boy's waist. Then, with Brodhaur's prompting, the new cadet remembered to salute the Emperor and Empress in turn, and then his Commander in Chief, before being led away out of sight beneath the gallery.

The second hour of the afternoon had passed before all the cadets were done and the Emperor rose to leave. By that time Rhysana was famished, and Torkhaal's stomach was growling loudly, and the twins had grown tired of the whole affair and were anxious to be off. Nothing more had come of the strange enchantment about the Emperor, and none of the other cadets had seemed more nervous of him than might be thought usual; but Rhysana's sense of uneasiness still remained.

They walked with Lavan down through the river wing of the citadel, and then Rhysana and Torkhaal made the *leap* back to their College apartment. Hrugaar and Ellen were waiting for them there, and were glad enough to hand Taillan back to them before taking themselves off to Iorlaas' chambers to begin the work of gathering up his belongings. Torkhaal and Rhysana were soon able to sit down to a meal with their son and to enjoy a quiet afternoon to themselves.

It was not until later that evening, after Taillan had been settled to sleep in his cot and the stormclouds had rolled back to let the western sunlight stream across the slated rooftops in a glory of rosy gold, that Rhysana remembered the carved *sherunuresh* piece which she had brought back from Whitespear Head. She fetched her satchel quietly from the bedchamber, and brought out the wooden horse for Torkhaal to see.

They had been sitting together on the settle before the hearth, though the fire had not been lit. Torkhaal turned the carved piece in his hands as she sat down again beside him, and then kindled his own rich green magelight to help him to study it.

'It looks more like ash wood,' he told her; 'but very old and dried, of course.'

'I think that there is something made of metal inside,' she said. 'You can see it underneath, where the wood has cracked.'

Torkhaal turned the piece around again, to look. Then he closed his eyes, probing the wood gently with his fingertips while he searched with other, magical senses.

'Curious,' he frowned. 'There is something in there. But the wood feels as though it grew into place around it. Do you want me to take it out?'

'Can you do so without damaging the wood?' Rhysana asked. 'If it is a *sherunuresh* piece, from such an early date, perhaps we should not risk it.'

'Trust me, I am an Earth mage,' Torkhaal grinned.

'I do hate it when you say that,' she said, laughing. 'But this is serious.'

'I know,' he said. 'Watch.'

He cradled the carved horse in his hands, and breathed upon it gently. The surface of the wood grew smooth and clean again, with a soft sheen as though it had been oiled and polished. Then he held the piece between his fingers, smiled, and ran his two thumbs up the horse's back. The wood split open like a pea pod, or perhaps more like a leaf bud unfurling, and what looked like a block of metal tumbled out into his lap. Torkhaal brought his thumbs down together again, and the carved wood furled back into place with no trace of a break or scar.

'I trust you,' said Rhysana, kissing him. Torkhaal sighed, weary but content.

'Fickle woman,' he teased. He picked up the metal object from his lap and handed it to her.

Rhysana turned it over in her hand, and felt her heart skip several beats. She must have gasped aloud, for Torkhaal turned to take hold of her by the arms.

In her hands she held a bar made of a metal like white steel, about the length of her middle finger and perhaps a third of that broad. The edges at each end sloped back beneath, and the lower face curved up into an inward arch. The upper face was flat, and set in the middle with a smooth round cabochon gem of a clear tawny yellow; and flanking the gemstone on either side were engraved the stylised likenesses of two galloping horses.

'I am all right,' she heard herself saying. Her husband's *presence* was hovering about her.

This was the bar that Corollin had asked her to find, the Lautun part of Kellarn's strange artefact. Holding it in her hands now, its history became clear to her. The first Kings of Lautun – perhaps even Llaruntôr himself – had hidden the bar by their arts within living wood, and then shaped the wood into the likeness of a seated horse. Rhysana had noticed from the first how closely the piece resembled the great stone horses that marked the length of the Rolling River along Lautun's ancient boundary. When the palace of the High Kings fell, it had found its way from their treasuries into Illana's keeping. She doubted that Illana had ever even guessed at the value of what she held.

'I do not think that it was a *sherunuresh* piece,' she said aloud.

'But what is it?' Torkhaal asked. 'It does not appear to be magical.'

'Something that you should not mention to anyone yet,' Rhysana told him, 'not even to Ru.'

She offered the bar for him to look at. He took it carefully, leaving the carved horse resting in his lap.

'There is something about the stone,' he said after a moment. 'Not an enchantment, but – ow!'

A golden light flared within the gem, and then vanished.

'Torkhaal?' she asked anxiously.

He shook his head, chuckling. 'My own fault. The stone is not magical, as such. But the way the crystals are formed is something like one of your matrix patterns. When I tried to put energy into it, it bounced it straight back at me. No wonder Illana kept it hidden away.'

'I doubt that she knew it was there,' said Rhysana absently.

Her thoughts were running ahead of her. Kellarn and Corollin had not told her what manner of power the artefact had – if indeed they knew. They had said only that it was made to help in the fight against Lo-Khuma, and that they had already found four such bars. Torkhaal had wakened this one with the use of his rare mental gifts, gifts that were perhaps more like to the powers used by the Kings of old. She pictured the bars together in her mind, and suddenly she understood. They would fit together to form a circlet or crown – like the circlets worn by the carved images of Ferrughôr and Falladan in the storied frieze of Illana's throne hall; or indeed like the crown on the ancient crown monument near the East Gate in the city of Ellanguan. The ruling Heads of the Houses Noble still favoured jewelled circlets as a sign of their lordship. The clue to Lo-Khuma's defeat had been hidden so openly for so long that they had overlooked it.

But someone else had not. Kellarn had warned her that someone else, unfriendly, was hunting for the bars. Rhysana did not have to look too far to guess who that might be. The shadowfay had been in Whitespear Head before them; and when the Toad Archmage had found her in Illana's study he had asked her, *What was it that you hoped to find?* At the time she had thought it a rather obvious question, and part of his manner of playing cat-like with her when she was cornered. In hindsight, she would lay fair odds that he had been trying to discover whether she had any knowledge of this artefact of the First Kings. But, by the grace of the gods, she had deflected his question back toward Illana's lore, and found a treasure trove of Illana's writing which might keep him busy for a very long time.

'You are going to tell me what this is, I trust?' Torkhaal's growl broke into her thoughts.

'It is hope,' she smiled, taking the bar back from him and smiling. 'And perhaps the true reason why I went to Illana's fortress, though I did not know it at the time.'

'That is not a proper answer,' he said. 'Which reminds me, you have also to tell me about the *Argument of Command*.'

Rhysana sighed. Dangerous though the knowledge might prove, she supposed that she had to share it with someone. It would be more dangerous for that knowledge to be lost, or to fall into the wrong hands, should anything happen to her now. And then Kellarn might have need of Torkhaal's help anyway, to work out how to use the power of the bars. And above and beyond all this, she found that she wanted to share her secrets with him, mind to mind.

'Have it your own way,' she said. 'But not in here. Set the seals on the chamber first, so that we shall not be disturbed, and then come to bed.'

III FIRE IN THE AIR

Chapter Ten

Rhysana woke early the next morning, and washed and dressed and took herself off to the College library before her husband and son were stirring. She had agreed with Torkhaal that she would leave the Lautun bar safe in the Warden's care until such time as she could hand it to Kellarn.

Quite how she would find Kellarn, Rhysana did not yet know. From what little she had gathered from his sister Ellaïn on the evening of The Arrand's burning, it seemed that he had ridden south from Dortrean toward Telbray; but that would have been about four days ago now. She supposed that Telbray was the best place to start looking for him. But before she did so, she felt that she should at least try to speak with his mother, the Lady Karlena. For one thing, Karlena might well have more recent knowledge of Kellarn's doings. For another, Kellarn would almost certainly ask after her well being.

When she returned to her apartment, Hrugaar had arrived before her and the *chaedar* were bringing breakfast. Ellen would not be joining them that day, since she wished to prepare herself for her Rite of Ascent as Prime Councillor of All Magi, which was to take place the following morning. The two men were sitting at the table, with Taillan in his high chair between them. The carved wooden horse which had held the metal bar was sitting on the far end of the table, side by side with Taillan's own toy wooden horse, Brin.

'His name is Carbray,' Taillan told her as she kissed him.

'Is that so?' she said. 'I had thought that he was a Lautun horse.'

'He looks like a Carbray horse to me,' said Torkhaal.

'He has been playing with Brin,' Taillan added.

'Has he now?' said Rhysana. 'Well that is good, that they have made friends. But do you make sure that they play nicely together. Carbray does not belong to us, he is only visiting for a little while.'

Taillan nodded seriously. Rhysana put away her shawl and tidied herself quickly to join them for breakfast.

Torkhaal had already told Hrugaar, mind to mind, of her answer to the riddle of the *Argument of Command*. It had been Rhysana's suggestion – partly because it was only fair, in that Hrugaar had played an important role in her study of Illana's work over the years, and partly because she had hoped thereby to save herself from an endless flood of questions. Hrugaar being who he was, that hope soon faded. Though he understood the simple theory readily enough, the discussion of how it might truly be put into practice lasted for most of the meal; and Rhysana found that her confidence in her own theory, so strong at the moment of her first insight in the cave, had begun to dwindle. By the time that they left the table, none of them really felt that it was a power that they might be able to achieve for some while to come, if ever.

Nothing was said of Kellarn's artefact, or of the bar that they had found. That was a matter which Rhysana and Torkhaal had agreed to keep strictly to themselves.

After breakfast she put on her formal indigo robes again. It was not the best thing to wear for a visit to the Countess of Dortrean – let alone the Empress, if she was with her – but Rhysana had no more suitable morning gown that would still fit her comfortably. She tried to soften the effect by pinning her hair with tiny cornflowers, which Hrugaar and Taillan fetched for her from the College gardens. Then the four of them made the *leap* together to the imperial citadel and went up to the Telún apartment.

It soon became clear that Rhysana's private plans for the morning were about to be overturned. It was the first day of the formal debate of the Court Noble, which at this present Court would undoubtedly examine the recent war with the Easterners, and the current problems with the Southers and with Ellanguan, and the likely threat of another war to come. Torkhaal and Hrugaar were both to attend, as appointed delegates from the Council; and the Archmage Ellen had also asked Hrugaar to attend on her behalf. Rhysana had expected her brother Lavan to be going, while Nereïs remained behind with the children. But Nereïs, as it turned out, also wished to attend the debate – both for her own interest and because she had promised her cousin Lauraï Raudhar of Renza that she would be there.

Had they been at the Telún manor house, Rhysana would have had no qualms in leaving Taillan in the twins' care, with the household to keep an eye on them. Here in the imperial palace she had far greater concern for her son's safety and protection. And since she could not press the importance of her own errand to Karlena without drawing unwanted questions, she felt it best to offer to stay to look after the children herself. She comforted herself that Karlena would also most likely be going to the debate that morning, unless Rhydden prevented it.

That comfort did not last long. Before an hour had passed, Rhysana found herself growing restless; and the children seemed to sense her mood, and were becoming restless and fractious in their turn. The younger two were squabbling, and the twins Khyrfan and Mâghan were bored with being penned inside the apartment and wished to go riding in the park. Rhysana sympathised with them. She considered the wisdom of sending one of Nereïs' household women to enquire where Karlena was, and then decided that she might as well take the children with her and go to find that out for herself.

She made the twins put on their best deep blue tunics, and told them to bring hats if they wanted to go riding later on. When they pulled long faces at having to wear such formal gear, she assured them that she did not mind if they wore old stockings on their heads, if they so wished, as long as they had something to protect them from the heat of the day. The suggestion seemed to provoke much merriment. She pulled little Maïa into a clean dress of cornflower silk, and tied a matching bonnet with silver ribands on her golden head. Taillan had only the green velvet tunic and hat that he had brought with him, over black leggings. But fortunately – Rhysana thanked the gods – he had his father's gift for managing to appear clean and tidy no matter what he had been doing.

Some of the Telún household offered to escort them, but Rhysana thanked them and told them that they would not be needed. For one thing, armed guards would not be allowed into the Empress' presence, if that was where Karlena was; and for another, even a dozen of her brother's men unarmed would be no match for the guards of the Imperial Household. Besides, Rhysana felt quite equal to the task of protecting the children herself, should the need arise, and she did not wish to raise undue alarm by having an escort about the citadel. Instead she sent two of the younger household men down to the stables, to arrange for horses for the twins to be brought to the nobles' postern at the foot of the western wing.

Before long they set off through the tapestried hallways of the older Houses' apartments, Rhysana leading the way with Taillan and Maïa holding her hands, and the two boys trailing behind and trying well enough to behave. They made their way down to an upper courtyard garden, above and to the west of the old summer palace, and then climbed the worn stone steps up into the great square tower at the heart of the citadel where the Empress Grinnaer had her apartments.

The guards who greeted her at the top of the steps informed her rather curtly that the Empress was not there. But Maïa chose that moment to burst into tears, appearing greatly distressed; after which the guardsmen seemed to relent a little, and explained that the Empress had not gone to the debate but was taking the air with her Ladies in the garden on the far side of the tower. They allowed that it would be permitted for the children to see Her Serene Highness from the vantage of one of the upper windows, if the Lady Rhysana knew where to go.

Rhysana knew quite well where to go – though she had no intention of merely looking out through the windows – and she thanked the guards kindly. She picked Maïa up and carried her along the wide landing to leave by the carved doors at the far end. Khyrfan carried Taillan so that they could move more swifly.

Beyond the doors they came to a much wider stair in a high, shadowed lobby. Rhysana led them up and to the right, which brought them to a more homely panelled landing with the door to the Dortrean apartment. She put Maïa down and hesitated for a moment, wondering whether to knock upon the door to find out if Karlena was there. But given the Countess' present circumstances, she thought it likely that there would have been a guard outside the doorway had that been the case.

They moved on through a series of pleasant lobbies linked by short flights of steps, passing beautiful windows of coloured glass glowing brightly in the morning sunlight. None of the children had ever come to this part of the citadel before, so Rhysana pointed out to them the apartments of some of the Houses Ancient – Levrin and Ercusí, Scaulun and Vaulun – with their painted shields above the doorways, and liveried attendants standing guard. And then finally they turned down a longer stair which brought them to one of the doors of the Empress' garden.

The grey oak doors stood wide open, letting in the sunlight and fragrant air from the courtyard garden outside. A lone cadet in the golden livery of the Imperial Household Guard stood duty just inside the shadow of the doorway. He looked to be no older than fifteen, and already flushed and uncomfortable in the growing heat of the day. The sight of a High Councillor with four children in tow only served to unsettle him further.

Rhysana was not sure of the strictest Court protocol with

regard to bringing young children into the Empress' presence; though as a rule, when the Empress had her Ladies gathered about her there were seldom any children among them. She trusted to luck that the guard cadet would have no clearer idea than she did.

'I am the Lady Rhysana Telún of Carbray,' she told him. 'We have just come to pay our respects to Her Serene Highness and her Ladies, on our way to the park.'

'It's only us, Hollis,' said Mâghan, beside her. 'We won't cause any trouble.'

The cadet looked at them uncertainly.

'Are you Lord Torkhaal's wife, my Lady?' he asked.

'That I am,' she smiled; 'and this is our son Taillan.'

'That's all right then,' he said. 'I don't know if I should let you in, really. But my Lord Ravaïl Eädhan speaks very highly of you.'

'But you are in the Emperor's service now,' she reminded him.

'That's different,' he grinned, and gestured for her to go on.

Rhysana nodded her thanks, and picked Taillan up to carry him. Mâghan led Maïa by the hand. Hollis remembered to bow to them as they went out through the doorway.

The courtyard garden was one of the prettiest in the citadel, with cobbled pathways of different coloured pebbles curling in spiralled patterns around a central fountain of simple grey stone. The beds between the paths were filled with white roses in wild profusion, and everywhere there were white doves fluttering and cooing. Ahead of them now as they entered, the north face of the Empress' tower was already cast into shadow as the sun climbed higher into the open sky. The Empress Grinnaer herself appeared to be in the midst of the garden, away to their left, on the far side of the fountain pool.

'Why are the *chaedar* here?' Taillan asked Rhysana.

'The *chaedar*?' Rhysana echoed. 'They can not be. They never leave the College.'

Nevertheless she paused on the path and looked around her. If her son had sensed something, it occurred to her that there might be other, less friendly things moving around unseen within the garden. Though the use of subtle magic was frowned upon within the citadel, she decided that the use of a simple spell might be forgiven her upon this occasion. Their safety, and that of the Empress herself, might depend upon it.

Rhysana focused her magical senses and looked around the garden more carefully. She could see no sign of any hidden creatures or people, nor any particular use of magic other than her own; and yet there was indeed a faint thrill and sparkling upon the air, which she had come to associate with the *chaedar*.

'*Limminn*' me,' said Taillan loudly, pointing with his chubby fingers.

Unseen hands plucked a single rose from a bush beside them and presented it to him, with a half heard rumour of musical laughter upon the air. Taillan handed the rose to Rhysana.

'See?' he said delightedly.

'Thank you,' she said, kissing him. She moved on along the path, feeling puzzled but strangely comforted. She wondered whether the Warden had sent them to look after her.

The Empress Grinnaer had perhaps a dozen women gathered about her, mostly of Rhysana's age or younger, all lively and colourful as birds in their lovely summer gowns. Chief among them that Rhysana recognised were Grinnaer's cousins, Lisâ Sêchral of Scaulun and Irina Scaulun of Solaní – neither of whom had had much time for Grinnaer before she became Rhydden's Empress Consort. Standing out among the crowd as being a little older, and a little more modest in her attire, was the Lady Turinda. And then there was Karlena, clad again in her gorgeous scarlet gown, but with a simple straw hat to keep her fair face in the shade.

The women were making a good deal of noise with their laughter and chatter, and they had also the constant play of the fountain and the cooing of the doves, so that it seemed to Rhysana that her exchange with Taillan must have gone unnoticed by them all; for it was not until she had almost reached the near side of the fountain circle that they became aware of the intrusion. Then they all turned to face her, fanning themselves and whispering. Rhysana set Taillan down beside her and bowed toward the Empress.

'Hardly the kindest move, Rhysana,' said the golden haired Irina, 'to flaunt your own children in Her Highness' face when still she prays for her own.'

'You only say so, Sister, because you have none yourself,' said Lisâ of Scaulun. 'And Her Highness has not been married so long.'

Lisâ was a more handsome version of Grinnaer, though with slightly darker hair, and with more confidence in her own strength. Rhysana had always liked her well enough, in spite of her Sêchral lineage, but she would not have considered her as an ally at Court.

The twins had arrived by another path, and were now bowing in their turn. They had brought with them wide brimmed hats of deep blue velvet, Mâghan's with silver ribands and Khyrfan's with ribands of silver and sky blue. They bowed with several flourishes in very gallant fashion, prompting much giggling and amusement among some of the younger Ladies there.

'Doggie,' said Taillan, slipping away from Rhysana's grasp and trotting toward a honey coloured spaniel pup nearby.

'Lady Rhysana,' said Karlena, moving forward around the fountain pool, 'we had expected you to be at the debate. But I do not think that I have had the pleasure of meeting your son before.'

'This is Taillan,' Rhysana answered, circling toward her. 'Taillan, say good morning to the Lady Karlena.'

Taillan tilted his head to look up into Karlena's face. After a moment he gave a shy smile. Karlena smiled in return.

'Is he yours?' he asked her, pointing to the puppy.

'No, he is mine,' the Empress answered, arriving at Karlena's side. 'I have been trying to teach him to fetch a ball when I throw it, but I think that he is still a little too young to learn.'

Grinnaer was dressed in a full skirted gown, a shade paler than the spaniel's honeyed coat, with a high aureole collar framing the chestnut glory of her curling hair. Her face was less heavily made up that morning, allowing her a gentler beauty of her own, and Rhysana was pleasantly surprised at the easy kindness of her manner. It struck her that Karlena's influence had already done Grinnaer some good.

Taillan, however, seemed less encouraged by the Empress' arrival. He looked at her seriously for a long moment, then backed away behind the safety of Karlena's skirt.

'Please forgive us, Serenity,' Rhysana said hurriedly. 'He is not used to meeting so many new people all at once.'

'It is not easy, I know,' Grinnaer answered. 'But there is no harm in your son to forgive. We are pleased to welcome you here.'

'Thank you,' Rhysana began. But at that moment there was a disturbance among the other women. One of the Ladies had tried to pick Maïa up to kiss her, and received a slap for her trouble. Khyrfan was stammering in apology, and the Lady Turinda was elbowing her way forward through the laughing and gasping crowd.

'Me go wee,' piped Taillan.

'I think that perhaps we had better be on our way swiftly, Serenity,' said Rhysana. 'If you shall excuse us?'

'We look forward to your company another time,' Grinnaer nodded.

Rhysana bowed in answer. When she raised her head again, she discovered that Karlena was already leading Taillan away to one side, where he could relieve himself behind the bushes. Rhysana rounded up her brother's children – murmuring her apologies to the dark haired young woman who had been slapped, and coaxing little Maïa into saying sorry – and sent them back to wait at the door. Then she wound her way along the circling paths to fetch her son from Karlena.

Taillan seemed happier again, though he lifted up his arms to her to be carried. Rhysana thought that she had better do so. Karlena did not appear at all put out by looking after him.

'*Chaedar*,' Taillan whispered in her ear.

Rhysana glanced around her. Sure enough, there was the familiar thrill of their unseen presence upon the air. But now there was also a shimmering like a heat haze, and the sounds of the women and of the doves were muted and distant. She realised that the *chaedar* must have woven a spell, to allow her to speak with Karlena without being overheard.

'Have you heard from Ellaïn?' she asked, keeping her voice soft and making a show of straightening Taillan's green hat.

'But briefly,' Karlena nodded. 'I have not had much chance to speak with Jared since he returned.'

'You know that Kellarn has sworn an oath to avenge his brother?'

'Then I hope that he will stay safely away from here,' said Karlena, 'until he is fully prepared. I take it that you shall be seeing him?'

'I hope so,' Rhysana allowed.

'He should be mindful of Terrel,' said Karlena. 'Perhaps you would be kind enough to tell him that from me? Not that he will listen to his mother, I suppose. Goodbye, young Taillan. I hope that we shall meet again soon.'

'Goodbye,' he said, tilting his face up to kiss her. Karlena laughed and kissed him.

'Shall I give that to the Empress for you?' she offered, glancing at the white rose that Rhysana still held in her hand.

'Yes, thank you,' Rhysana answered. She had almost forgotten that taking flowers unbidden from the Empress' own garden would be a serious breach of courtesy.

Karlena smiled and took the rose. Then she nodded to Rhysana in farewell, and swept away along the cobbled path to return to the Empress' circle.

More than fifty leagues from the imperial palace of Lautun,

away beyond the wild reach of the Sighing Lands, Kellarn was thinking of Rhysana as he rode west toward the city of Telbray. It was a glorious morning – too glorious perhaps for the mailshirt and scarlet surcoat that he now wore, with the star shield of Heruvor slung across his back. The sun shone bright and hot in a pale blue sky, with just a few small clouds basking lazily high above, and only the easy speed of the Mairdun horse kept a gentle breeze upon his face.

The Guardian herself had led them from the holy lake of Alvinaah, through the cooler green shade of the forested hills and down to the southern eaves of the Telbray Woods; and from thence he had turned west with Corollin and Mellin, skirting the edge of the Taraas manor lands toward the Border Road that ran from Farran and the coast up to the gates of the city of Telbray. It had been Kellarn's suggestion to head for the city. That was where his sister Ellaïn had thought they were going, and thus where Rhysana might try looking for them.

'It has been less than a week since we saw her last,' Corollin had objected. 'It took us far longer to find each of the other bars, and Rhysana will be busy with the Court. She may hardly have had the chance to start.'

'I know,' Kellarn allowed. 'But she did say something about Hrugaar looking through old records.'

'And how could Rhysana leave a message there?' Corollin went on. 'Telbray is an imperial city, and holy to one of the *Vashtar*. The Sun Temple or the White Manor would be her more likely choices.'

'The Lady Idesîn of Telbray is cousin to Carstan Mairdun,' Kellarn told her, 'and Mairdun are friendly to Dortrean. Idesîn could at least tell us if Rhysana has been there.'

'The Lady Idesîn may have gone to Court,' put in Mellin.

'Perhaps,' said Kellarn. 'I still think it's worth a try, since we are so close.'

'Would there be anything in Telbray that might help us to find the Lautun bar?' asked Corollin practically.

'Probably not,' he said. 'The fortress has a library, but I doubt that they would have anything that old. Rhysana is more likely to find something in Lautun.'

'The *Aeshta* Monastery of the Tumbrachin is at the head of the Telbray valley,' said Mellin. 'Might they be able to help?'

Kellarn ran his fingers back through his hair. 'Perhaps,' he said. 'The Guardian did say that two other bars had been found. The priests might be able to find out more about that.'

Dyrnalv had said that the two bars were *with the Moon.* Ferunel of Starmere had said much the same about the Cerrodhí bar, which had later been given to them by the Guardian Losithlîn. If any of the moon fay had had the other two bars, Kellarn was sure that Ferunel would have told them. His only other guess was that they might be hidden in a place holy to the Moon Maiden Haëstren, or perhaps with one of her priests or magi – though surely Ferunel would have known of that also.

'Do you think that the servants of the Enemy have found them?' asked Corollin.

'No,' said Kellarn. 'Or at least, Dyrnalv said that they were safe. I think that the *syldhar* know where they are, if only we could ask them.'

They had tried to question Dyrnalv further upon that point; but she would say only that when the Lautun bar was found, and when the hour was ripe, they should then seek the help of the Sun Temple. The Guardian could offer them no counsel on where to search for the fifth bar. Mellin had suggested going to the *commanderie* of Mairdun, since it stood on the northern borders of Lautun, and the library there was said to house manuscripts far older than the Hyrsenite Order itself. Corollin had ventured that perhaps they should risk going to the city of Lautun, to search with Rhysana, though none of them really liked that idea. In the end – and partly for the sake of peace – the two women had agreed to ride with Kellarn to Telbray. With the Emperor's spies and the shadowfay abroad, there had been no question of the three of them splitting up once they had left the woods and Dyrnalv's protection.

The decision marked a subtle change in Kellarn's relationship with Corollin. Until now he had always regarded the quest for the bars as hers, and been content to follow her lead in most matters that concerned them. Yet since they had met with the Guardian, the focus seemed to have shifted more to Kellarn himself. So now it was his instinct that led them to the city, whither Corollin was content to follow. He wondered whether Dyrnalv had had a hand in that, or even Ilunâtor or the *syldhar*; and what that might mean, if anything, about his own relationship with the bars themselves.

Kellarn was still troubled by the memory of how he had blocked the pain from the Guardian's ring with a single thought, when he awoke in Alvinaah. He could not recall ever having done such a thing before, and had never had much success with any artefacts of power, other than swords. It had occurred to him that perhaps it was the result of being rescued from the Realms of the Dead by Ilunâtor, and that some touch of the dragon's presence had still been with him. But when he had tried privately to look within himself again, searching for the dragon, he had felt self conscious and rather guilty for doing so; and the voice of instinct had whispered within him, *not yet*.

He comforted himself that perhaps this present shift of focus, from Corollin to himself, meant only that they had to wait for the fifth bar to be found; and that whether they went to Telbray or not was of little importance to the quest. If that were the case, then Corollin would have seen no great need to continue arguing the point anyway.

The two women seemed happy enough once they were on their way, riding quietly side by side behind him. To their right were the sleepy farmland hills of the Taraas manor, which stretched from the edge of the woods to the mouth of the Telbray vale. To their left and behind them the ground grew rougher and more sparse, sprawling away beneath a tawny haze toward the borders of the Sighing Lands. Drawing ever closer ahead, the sheer cliffs and slopes of the Black Mountains rose sharp and clear in the morning sunlight, crowned by far off snowy peaks in all their dazzling beauty.

It was a journey of some seven leagues to bring them to the Border Road, and the sun had reached his noon height by the time that they rode down the last grassy slope on to the broad paved way. The mountains were now so close that they filled nearly a third of the sky, their looming faces already slipping into shadow. Kellarn judged that they were still some three leagues from the city itself, but even here the road seemed busy after the peaceful emptiness of the lands that they had crossed that morning. A merchant caravan with banners of green and gold was crawling away south in the middle distance; and there were smaller groups of travellers, mounted and on foot, moving up and down along the road ahead of them to the north.

Kellarn sighed as he patted Rúnfyr's neck. 'We shall have to be on our guard again,' he said.

'How dangerous is it likely to be?' asked Corollin.

'The ordinary people in the city are all right,' said Mellin. 'They are mostly traders and craftsmen. And the Lord Patall and Lady Idesîn are friendly to us, much more so than the Lady Eriss Telbray used to be. The ones to watch out for are the priestesses of Serbramel – and some of the merchants and nobles, of course.'

'The same as in any city,' Corollin nodded.

Kellarn frowned at the mention of the priestesses. The last time that he had been here, some years before, he had had to watch while the Guardian Gilraen was condemned, hanged and burned by the servants of Serbramel for his heathen faith. The High Priestess Kaïra had demanded the full measure of the imperial law, and even Kellarn's father had not been able to save him.

'The power of Serbramel is strong in Telbray,' he said grimly. 'You can almost feel her presence looking over your shoulder. The Emperor will no doubt have his spies there; but there are enough people who will recognise Mellin and me anyway, so there is no point in trying to keep our visit secret.'

'I could ride into the city alone,' Mellin offered. 'The two of you could go on up to the monastery, and wait for me.'

'No,' said Kellarn. 'We should stay together. Besides, Patall's guards keep a close watch on the road, so they will know that you are travelling with us. Dortrean has its own apartment up in the fortress itself, so it will seem natural enough that we should want to go there. And even if Patall and Idesîn have gone to Court, there should be someone friendly around to tell us any news.'

'Are you worried about Karlena?' Mellin asked him.

Kellarn glanced aside. He did not need the reminder.

'Rhysana is keeping an eye on her,' he said. 'I am more worried about Father, I think, and what the Southers are doing – and Rhydden.'

'Are there magi in Telbray?' asked Corollin. 'I do not recall there being a College there.'

'They have a Mage in Residence in the fortress,' Kellarn answered, glad to change the subject. 'I am not sure who that is now. And there may be one or two others.'

'Would you want to see them?' Mellin asked her.

'Probably not,' said Corollin. 'I have had little to do with the Council, except for a few close friends of my father Morvaan – Hrugaar, of course, and now Rhysana.'

'I hardly think of Corollin as a mage,' said Kellarn. 'You should see the way she fights.'

'Coming from you, I suppose that that is a compliment,' Mellin laughed.

'I hope it will not come to a fight today,' said Corollin.

The three of them turned north along the road, riding now through the outskirts of the city lands as they approached the small wayside village of Kray. The ripening fields of the Telbray vale reached deeper into the mountains, ahead and to their left, with the *Aeshta* monastery of the Tumbrachin nestled high on the cliffs beyond. The city of Telbray itself was straight ahead, raised up on a low mountain spur near the outer end of the vale on the northern side, and clearly visible even at this distance.

As Kellarn had warned, any guards out on the city walls would already have marked their approach.

The huge fortress of the Lords of Telbray stood in the midst of the city, the better part of a furlong square and towering up to half its own breadth in height. Its sheer sides were of the same black stone as the mountains, so that it seemed to have been carved from the end of the rocky spur that came down at its back. Upon either side, at about a third of the height of the fortress, were the walled terraces of the twin halves of the Upper City, set aside for nobles and some of the more prosperous merchants; and above and behind the fortress, resting on the shoulder of the mountain spur, was the walled temple precinct of the *Vashta* goddess Serbramel, Lady of Justice. The Lower City with its comparatively modest encircling wall – no more than thirty feet high – spread out in a neat square some three furlongs broad about the fortress' feet.

Had his instincts drawn him less strongly, Kellarn might have been as reluctant as Corollin to come here. Though Telbray was a fine city, renowned for its skilled craftsmen and market fairs, and though he liked Patall and Idesîn well enough, it was still an imperial city holy to Serbramel. He had made his own truce with that goddess a few months before, but he did not trust her servants; and the spiteful High Priestess Kaïra held as much sway in Telbray as did the Lord Patall himself. If Kaïra even suspected that they had had dealings with a Guardian, she could call for their deaths under the same imperial law that had condemned Gilraen. And if any of the Emperor's Black Destriers were here, that could prove dangerous enough in itself.

Neverthless, the people who passed them on the road seemed happy and friendly, and no one paid them too much attention. So though Kellarn was sweating with the heat of the sun at his back, and on edge with the knowledge of danger ahead, he had to trust that his instincts were right.

Rhysana was still in the park when Torkhaal came to find her.

She had settled herself comfortably in the shade of a stand of trees, well away to the west of the citadel buildings and with a clear view of the open ground where the twins were off riding. Taillan and Maïa had gathered handfuls of birch twigs and leaves brought down by the storm the previous day, and she was playing a counting game with them both. Maïa's temper was much improved now that they were out of doors.

The game and the peace in the park had given Rhysana time to think. The presence of the *chaedar* back in the Empress' garden still puzzled her. She had never known them to leave the Lautun College before, and she could only assume that the Warden had sent them to watch over her – which then begged the question why, since he was not in the habit of concerning himself with the private lives of the Magi. But then Rhysana enjoyed a closer relationship with the Warden than did most of her colleagues.

That Taillan had sensed their presence before she did might perhaps be explained by the fact that the *chaedar* had been around him for much of his short life, coupled with the fact that the minds and hearts of the young were more open to the magical possibilities of the world around them. It was also possible that he had inherited some of his father's extraordinary mental gifts, though that was something which Torkhaal himself would be better placed to determine. And that reminded her that the twins Khyrfan and Mâghan would also have to be tested soon, to gauge their magical ability.

And then there was Karlena. By all reports, and from what Rhysana herself had seen, the Countess appeared to be faring well enough within the Empress' household. The news of Kellarn's oath had seemed to come as no great surprise to her. Rhysana guessed that Terrel, Ellaïn's older boy, would be the next heir to Dortrean if anything should happen to Kellarn. But then Kellarn himself would surely know that, so that she wondered why Karlena had thought it necessary to mention it.

The need to find Kellarn seemed less pressing to her now,

here in the openness of the park beneath a clear summer sky; though she still meant to visit Telbray before the end of the day if she could, to see if there was word of him there. It was not until the other nobles began to come out into the park, at the end of the morning debate, that her sense of approaching danger returned.

Torkhaal and Hrugaar came out through the nobles' postern at the foot of the western wing of the citadel, which held the apartments of many of the Lesser Houses. Quite a gathering of friends and kinsmen followed behind them, and the twins rode over to escort them across the park to where Rhysana was sitting. She soon discovered that Nereïs had instructed her household to bring their noon meal outside, so that they could all enjoy the fine day for a while.

Lavan and Nereïs were there, with the flame haired Lauraï Raudhar of Renza in a wonderful floating gown of silvery silken voile. Aúrun of Renza was laughing and chattering with Hrugaar, the two looking more like brothers than ever. Torkhaal had brought Ellaïn's husband Jared along, and the Archmage Morvaan with him; and to Rhysana's surprise he had also brought Mage Councillor Drengriis and his wife the Priestess Bromaer of Kelmaar. Both Drengriis and Bromaer were dressed in the pale blue and brown of Româdhrí, so that she had to look twice to recognise them. Apart from Hrugaar and Aúrun, they all seemed strained and somewhat irritable.

The main news of the morning, which Rhysana had not yet heard, was that an army of horsemen had come down from the Highland Mountains the previous day. It was said that they had been sent by the Elders of Radbrodal, who counselled the lords of the Northern Lands. The army had met with the Northern Envoy Hakhutt in the trading village of Môstí, and was now riding south toward Lautun. Brodhaur Levrin, Commander in Chief of the Imperial Household Guard, had declared in the debate that these were friendly troops being brought by Hakhutt to help in the defence against the Easterners. Given the long history of raiding and plunder by the Northerners on

Six Kingdoms lands, not all of the assembled nobles had been persuaded of their good intent.

The question of the Souther troops had, predictably, given rise to far more heated debate. Given the recent turn of events in Ellanguan, the Emperor had proposed the withdrawal of the *Aeshta* Orders from the cities to reduce the risk of conflict, and that they should be sent ahead to guard the border lands east of Arrandin. This suggestion had received a disturbing strength of support from many of the nobles in the debate, particularly among those who came from the city ports of Ellanguan, Gorrendan and Farran. Indeed, Jared's had been the only strong voice of protest from among the cities, saying that the *Aeshta* Orders were more than welcome in Arrandin. But the War priest Môrghran of Fâghsul had pointed out that that was a matter for Jared's older brother, Lord Bradhor, to decide, once he had been formally recognised by the Emperor as the new Head of House Arrand.

'Will Kelmaar be leaving Ellanguan?' Rhysana asked.

'Most have already done so,' said Bromaer, glancing at her husband before she spoke. 'After the war, many of those who returned from Arrandin went to our *commanderie*, or elsewhere. Then yesterday the Lord Steward Rinnekh bade the rest of us be gone from the city. Some few have remained there in secret.'

'I am sorry,' said Rhysana. 'High Councillor Sollonaal was to have tried to persuade Rinnekh against that.'

Drengriis and Bromaer looked at one another. 'We have not heard a word of his doing so,' he said. 'But Sollonaal has been much occupied with gathering the *Vashta* magi to himself. It seems as though he intends to break away from the Council.'

'We had feared as much,' said Morvaan. He studied his half eaten pastry with an unusual lack of enthusiasm. 'He could take nearly a third of the Council with him, you know. Poor Ellen.'

'But Rinnekh is a fool to think that he can be rid of us so easily,' said Bromaer. 'Kelmaar could take Ellanguan whenever they choose. The sea would be our ally.'

'But could they hold it against the Emperor?' wondered Lauraï.

The priestess shrugged in answer. 'Some of our Order are coming hither, to the Temple of Maësta in Lautun,' she told them quietly. 'We have heard the words of the Easterner prophecy. We fear that there may be more trouble within the Imperial Household.'

'The Môshári have had the same thought,' said Torkhaal. 'And Gravhan has gone to see if he can find out more about Hakhutt's army, and why the Elders sent it.'

'Is that not spreading your forces rather thin?' Aúrun asked.

'Perhaps,' said Bromaer. 'But remember, like the Magi we may move from place to place very swiftly in time of need.'

'Is the Emperor in danger?' asked Lauraï.

'Perhaps,' said Rhysana.

'Though perhaps you could try to look a little less cheerful at the thought, Lauraï,' Hrugaar grinned.

'There may be others, outside the Household, at greater risk,' Rhysana explained, ignoring him.

'The Emperor has that foul Archmage of his to protect him,' said Aúrun.

'It is a pity that Rhydden has not provided himself with an heir,' said Drengriis. 'If anything should happen to him, the struggle for power at Court would severely weaken our defence against invasion.'

'*Your strength will crumble, from the centre to the rim*,' said Bromaer. 'Perhaps that is what the Easterner wizard meant?'

'Would the throne not pass to his kinsmen of Vaulun?' asked Hrugaar.

'Knight Captain Jochaîl of Vaulun is his nearest heir,' Drengriis nodded. 'He is the oldest of three sons of the late Lady Loghrana Lautun of Vaulun, who was Rhydden's closest surviving kin of Lautun blood by birth. But Jochaîl has not been formally recognised as heir designate. He is only Rhydden's fourth cousin, and comes from a secondary branch of House Vaulun. His father is only third cousin to the present Earl.'

'You may trust a Scholar of Blood Law to give you a long and difficult answer,' said Bromaer fondly.

'There will be other Houses,' Drengriis added, 'especially Sêchral and Scaulun, and probably Levrin, seeking to use their ties with Vaulun to further their own power. And none of Loghrana's children are yet married.'

'My brother Kierran was proposed as husband to the sister a few years back,' said Jared, 'though nothing came of it.'

'But who would be the next nearest to challenge his succession?' Rhysana wondered. 'Apart from Jochaîl's brothers.'

Drengriis gave a wry smile. 'That is one of the first jokes that every Scholar of Blood Law learns,' he said. 'Rhydden and Loghrana shared a common forefather in Korgan Lautun, Rhydden's fifth ancestor, the son of the Emperor Urzael. Had Urzael not amended the Blood Law so that succession passed to the oldest surviving male heir, then his daughter Mirren – Korgan's older sister – would have inherited the imperial throne. As it was, Mirren of Lautun married Terrel, then Earl of Dortrean, who is Erkal Dortrean's fifth ancestor in direct line.'

'So what is the joke?' asked Hrugaar.

'Were it not for the amendment of Urzael, it would be Dortrean, not Lautun, who now sat upon the imperial throne,' Drengriis explained. 'And by Dortrean Blood Law, Mirren would still have held the prior claim. Perhaps you have to be a Scholar of Blood Law to see the humour in it.'

Rhysana was only partly listening. As soon as Drengriis had spoken the name, she had guessed what Karlena's message truly meant. Karlena was not simply telling Kellarn to think of his nephew Terrel, and of the succession to Dortrean, but of Dortrean's claim by blood to the throne of Lautun itself.

'How strong is Dortrean's challenge to Jochaîl's claim?' she demanded.

Drengriis frowned. 'Strong enough to cause problems,' he

allowed. 'Jochaîl has Lautun blood from his mother, though from a secondary line, and his kinsmen have powerful allies in the imperial Court. Erkal's Lautun blood comes only from Mirren; but that was the senior bloodline in her generation, and Erkal himself has far greater personal precedence than Jochaîl. Dortrean also has far more popular support than Vaulun throughout the Empire as a whole.'

'And he would make a much stronger leader in time of war,' said Jared.

'But both Dortrean and Lautun must surely know about this,' said Lauraï.

'The Emperor certainly would,' Drengriis agreed. 'Dortrean, possibly. After so many generations, only the Scholars of Blood Law keep track of such things as a rule.'

'It casts a new light on Solban's death,' said Morvaan, 'since Erkal now has one less heir with which he might try to fill the imperial throne. I do not like where that thought is leading me. But perhaps we should be thankful that your boys are safe at home, Jared.'

'I like the mood of this Court less and less,' said Lavan. 'The Lady Ellaïn has shown more wisdom than most of us. I think that Nereïs and the children should return to Telún.'

The twins cried aloud in protest.

'Especially after Maïa's behaviour in the Empress' garden this morning,' Lavan went on firmly. 'Half the Court must have heard of that by now.'

'Oh for goodness sake,' said Rhysana, 'she is only a little girl. And no great harm was done.'

'Only that she slapped Arienn of Tersal,' her brother returned; 'who just happens to be Môrghran of Fâghsul's favourite niece, and sister to the new Lord Cardhási – both of whom have enough influence in imperial circles to cause us a great deal of trouble. I will not have them bending the Emperor's ear about my badly behaved children.'

'We behaved with all courtesy, Father,' said Mâghan.

Rhysana nodded her support. The twins had been most well

behaved. Once they had left the Empress, however, she had discovered that the blue riband tied around Khyrfan's hat had in fact been a blue woollen stocking. The stocking was now hidden safely away in a pocket of her robes, and she did not think that Lavan needed to hear about it.

'But we wanted to see the Summer Fair,' said Khyrfan.

'That is a good ten days away yet,' said Nereïs. 'Your father is right. We shall be better off at home.'

'Could you perhaps take Taillan with you?' Rhysana ventured. 'We have Ellen's Rite of Ascent as Prime Councillor tomorrow morning, and then Torkhaal and Hrugaar are to be admitted to the High Council; and I have much to do in the next couple of days.

'Would you like to go to Telún with your Aunt Nereïs?' she asked her son. 'It would help me very much.'

He looked up at her, and then nodded seriously. Rhysana leaned over and kissed him.

'I should be happier if you went with them,' Lavan told her. 'You should not be overdoing things with another child on the way.'

'My place is here,' she demurred.

'Torkhaal and I can make the *leap* to take you to the manor house,' offered Hrugaar.

'I should be grateful,' Lavan thanked him. 'I have actually managed a *leap* or two of my own you know, in the last few weeks, but I should hesitate to take anyone with me.'

'That is wonderful news,' said Rhysana, greatly pleased for him. 'It will not be long before you are ready to join the Council.'

'A while yet,' he returned modestly. 'Though it does seem to me that you could do with at least one person with some sense among you.'

'But that would never do,' laughed Hrugaar.

Torkhaal made the *leap* to Telbray, since he had better

knowledge of the fortress and its people than did Rhysana. They had first to return to the College in Lautun to gather Taillan's things, and to see him safely on his way with Hrugaar and Nereïs, and then Rhysana had to visit the Warden; so the second hour of the afternoon had passed by the time that the two of them reached the Magi's landing in the upper part of the Telbray fortress. They hurried along a passage of black stone, past the door to the chambers of the Mage in Residence – at present Councillor Stellaas – and then down a stair and along a broader winding passage to reach the main entrance hall.

Upon their left as they came in to the hall were tall windows looking out on to the upper courtyard of the fortress, with the square gate tower beyond that led to the temple precinct of Serbramel. To their right a double stair swept down in a stately crescent, with open doorways above and below. The far wall held a high gallery, half hidden in shadow; and below it were hung the green and orange banners of some of the Houses Lesser of Telbray and Farran, their colours glowing brightly in the gentle northern light from the windows. There were several settles and sideboards of dark wood around the borders of the hall, lending it a welcoming air, but there were very few people – just one or two folk of the household going quietly about their errands.

'Well this is a day for visitors,' said a voice from behind them.

'Sir Kyeruk,' said Torkhaal, sounding pleased and a little relieved.

Rhysana turned around to greet him. Sir Kyeruk of Telbray was a pleasant man in his early forties, clad in green and black as a senior officer of the city guard and with a sword at his side. His dark blond hair was turning to grey at the edges, but he was as fit and trim as a man of half his years. Rhysana thought that she remembered him.

'I do not recall if you have met my wife,' Torkhaal was saying.

'Our Lady of Justice forbid that I should ever forget such a pretty face,' returned Kyeruk gallantly; 'though I think she was her own mistress then.'

'And still am, I trust,' she smiled. Kyeruk raised one eyebrow in amusement.

'My Lord Patall is away at Court,' he went on, 'as no doubt you are aware. But the Lady Idesîn is here, and perhaps she is expecting you?'

'I was not,' said Idesîn from the stair. 'But they are ever welcome nonetheless.'

Coming as they had done from the splendour of the imperial Court, it struck Rhysana that the Lady Idesîn did not appear to have dressed for visitors. She was clad in a slender gown of simple grey, tied with a girdle of black and green, and her dark hair was divided into two long braids plaited with ribands of silver and gold. Yet her gentle beauty needed no more. Her simple attire brought to mind that she was also a priestess of the Hyrsenite Order, and like many of her kinsmen of Mairdun she was possessed of powerful mental gifts. Rhysana remembered that Idesîn had been a Truthsayer here in Telbray before she married the Lord Patall.

'We shall not keep you long,' Rhysana told her, once they had made their formal greetings. 'We were just hoping for a quiet word.'

The Lady Idesîn looked at her strangely, and then nodded and led the way through the open doors beneath the crescent stair.

'You did not bring your son,' she said as they went. 'But then my own young ones are asleep at the moment. They are much better for a rest in the afternoon, particularly with the long summer days.'

'Another time,' Torkhaal promised.

They went along another wide passage, lit with flickering lamps, with more doors and stairs on either side. At the far end Idesîn turned right and took them through into a huge chamber, which Rhysana later learned was aptly named the

Green Hall. Sir Kyeruk followed them in, shutting the doors behind him.

The hall must have been nearly fifty paces square and fully four fathoms high, with six wide round pillars in a ring about the centre part of the floor, and it was lined throughout with polished malachite. A row of high windows along the south and west walls let in the early afternoon sunlight, so that the chamber had the feeling of a forest grove or of a cave beneath the sea. Two high backed ebony chairs had been set to face one another in the midst of the pillar ring, with a number of smaller chairs on either side; but they did not seem to belong here, and there were no other furnishings to be seen, so that Rhysana wondered whether they might have been brought in for visitors other than themselves.

'I have been hearing of your great deeds in Arrandin and the east,' said Idesîn, leading them toward the chairs. 'I am sorry for the loss of your Prime Councillor Herusen. We can but pray that the peace which you have brought us may last.'

'The peace with the Easterners has brought other quarrels to the fore again,' Torkhaal sighed. 'But that was only to be expected, I suppose.'

'That is perhaps in part why we are here,' said Rhysana. 'Has anyone from Dortrean passed through the city within the last few days?'

The Lady Idesîn smiled. 'Why yes,' she said. 'I might have guessed that that would have something to do with the timing of your visit.'

At that moment there came the sound of voices from the passage outside, and then the panelled doors were flung open. The Reverend Mother Kaïra, High Priestess of Serbramel in Telbray, sailed in. Behind her came Mage Councillor Stellaas in his robes of laurel green. One of the temple handmaidens was kept back by a guard at the door.

Kaïra was short of stature, with a pale, pinched face that matched her spiteful nature, and the dark hair piled upon her head was now streaked with steel grey. Despite the summer heat she wore a full skirted green gown beneath a heavy black over-robe with a high aureole collar. The ebon staff of her office struck a loud and regular beat against the floor as she bore down upon them.

'Reverend Mother,' said Idesîn patiently in her deep, gentle voice, 'is there something the matter? We have noble guests.'

'If they bring news from the Court, I have heard it from Councillor Stellaas,' Kaïra returned. 'I am in haste, Idesîn. I dare say your noble guests will excuse us for a short while.' She favoured Rhysana and Torkhaal with an acid smile. 'I told the Dortrean boy to wait outside.'

Idesîn's grey eyes widened visibly. 'Sir Kyeruk, fetch him in at once,' she said.

'We can wait outside,' said Rhysana, glad of the opportunity. She had no doubt that the Dortrean boy to whom they were referring was Kellarn.

'I shall not hear of it,' Idesîn demurred. She signalled for Kyeruk to be gone.

'At least there is some courtesy left among the Houses Noble,' said Kaïra, nodding to Rhysana. 'I remember that you stood against my Lady Eriss Telbray in the hope of becoming the new Empress Consort. Clearly you were not Rhydden's second choice.'

'Actually I was his first choice,' Rhysana returned smoothly. 'I turned him down.'

Kaïra snorted. 'His Highness knew better than to take a heathen Consort. You should learn from his wisdom, Idesîn. To bring the heathen in the way of the goddess' work is to set your face against her. I am the voice of the goddess in this city; and I need hardly remind you that your own Order is now being questioned by the High Servants of War, on suspicion of heresy. Even welcoming the heathen into your home, no matter how noble, places you in grave danger.

'See now the proof,' she went on, pointing a black gloved hand toward the doorway, 'where the guest comes bearing a sword into your presence.'

'It is a holy blade of the *Aeshtar*,' said Idesîn calmly. 'None shall take it from him.'

Kaïra made a spitting noise, like an angry snake.

Kellarn came striding across the hall, with Corollin and Mellin Carfinn a few paces behind him. He wore a red surcoat over his mailshirt, worked with a leaping gold lion, and the holy blade of Fire was at his side. But though his sandy fair hair had been neatly brushed back, his grubby boots and breeches suggested to Rhysana that he was but newly arrived in the fortress. Mellin's dark green riding habit and Corollin's leathers told a similar tale. He went down on one knee to honour the Lady Idesîn as their host, and then stood to nod to the magi.

'Had I wanted to kill you, Reverend Mother,' he said, 'I would have done so already. Though I am more minded to let my Lady cousin here teach you some courtesy with the flat of my blade.'

'You would dare strike a priestess?' Kaïra challenged.

'Only with just cause,' said Kellarn. 'And here only with my Lady of Telbray's permission.'

'I had rather that you did not, my Lord,' said Idesîn, motioning for him to be seated. Kellarn offered a high backed chair to Rhysana, and then sat down to her right. Idesîn took the high backed chair facing them. Mellin and Corollin found places for themselves. The three men and Kaïra remained standing.

'You said that you were in haste, Reverend Mother,' Idesîn prompted. 'What is the matter?'

'The Emperor has called for the heathen Orders to withdraw from the cities,' Kaïra told her. 'The motion has received much support in the debate of the Court Noble this morning. I must go to Lautun at once.'

'My Lord Patall is there to speak for Telbray' Idesîn pointed out. 'And besides, the *Aeshta* Orders have no school here, and little enough presence.'

'Of course not,' Kaïra smiled. 'This is a holy city. But the other cities need our support – Farran in particular. We have already seen the proof in Ellanguan of how the heathen Orders stir up trouble against the Southers and the Emperor's servants, and make a mockery of peace. We can not stand idly by while the same happens in Farran, and perhaps even Gorrendan and Lautun itself. The Emperor knows this. But your husband has grown soft in his service of the goddess since he married you, and may be too slow to speak out where it is needed.'

'The situation is not so simple in Ellanguan,' said Torkhaal, his deep voice echoing between the pillars around them. 'It is said that some of the *Vashta* priests may have played a part in the burning of the Kelmaar School. It might be wise to learn the truth behind that rumour, Reverend Mother, before raising Ellanguan as an example.'

'I note that you wear no token of mourning for the loss of Prime Councillor Iorlaas,' said Kaïra coldly. 'No doubt your heathen magi were only too glad to be rid of him so soon. I have heard it said that he was beguiled by your own Order into going there, for that very purpose.'

'Iorlaas went there of his own choosing,' Rhysana told her, 'in the hope of bringing better peace to Ellanguan. He was a worthy man, and much respected among the Council. And one of our heathen magi, as you call them, lost his own life trying to defend him.'

'Nevertheless the attempt was ill advised,' said Stellaas. 'All servants of the old gods in Ellanguan are now viewed with fear and suspicion. Prime Councillor Sollonaal is moving to restrict the Ellanguan College to those of the *Vashta* faith alone – at least until the present crisis has passed.'

'Is Sollonaal your new Prime Councillor?' Kellarn asked Rhysana.

'Only of the Ellanguan Magi,' she said, 'as he was before. But no mention of this has yet been made to the High Council.'

'But it is a wise move,' said Kaïra. 'If the heathen Orders are to be removed from the cities, then so too should be the heathen magi. It is certainly high time that they were gone from Farran, Ellanguan and Lautun, though perhaps the border city of Arrandin would still welcome them.'

Rhysana did not point out, as well she might, that the Arrandin College had neither the buildings nor the resources to provide for the students of all four Colleges. Nor was she minded to waste time debating the matter with one so notoriously outspoken against them.

'The Council remains neutral, Reverend Mother,' she said calmly. 'Sollonaal has yet to present the matter to us, or to the Court Noble. But if you wish to attend the debates of the Court Noble, it is of course a proposal that you may make for yourself.'

'The afternoon debate will already have started,' Torkhaal added. 'Though I am not sure whether the priests from the new Sun Temple will be there to speak today.'

Kaïra's pinched little face shifted colour, taking on a rather sickly pallor from the reflected green light of the hall.

'My women are making ready for the journey,' she said. 'Councillor Stellaas will take us there.'

The Telbray mage fidgeted uncomfortably. 'There are quite a few in the High Priestess' train,' he said. 'Councillor Torkhaal, I hesitate to ask, but if you are returning to the Court—'

Torkhaal smiled and bowed. 'We should be honoured to help carry the servants of Justice to Lautun,' he purred. 'We shall not be here long.'

Kaïra looked sickened at the very thought, but she gave a curt nod of acceptance.

'I wish to leave within the hour,' she said. 'My Lords.'

She bowed her head more graciously in farewell. Everyone stood to watch her leave. She stalked away across the hall, her ebon staff sounding its steady drumbeat again against the polished stone floor. Stellaas glided silently beside her. Sir Kyeruk followed them to see them out, shutting the doors firmly behind them.

'I am sorry about that,' said Idesîn, gesturing for them all to be seated.

'The gall of the man,' said Mellin Carfinn, tugging the netted snood from her head to let her yellow gold hair run free. 'Asking you to take them to the Court.'

'I think that it was his way of apologising,' Torkhaal explained. 'It does show some measure of trust in our good will.'

'Even though they are planning to throw you out of your Colleges,' she returned. 'I call it adding insult to injury.'

'I had not heard of this latest move of Sollonaal,' said Rhysana. 'But that is a matter for the High Council. Lady Idesîn, what did Kaïra mean about Mairdun being questioned?'

'The Emperor suspects us of heresy because of the role we played in the war,' Idesîn sighed. 'No doubt it stems from the jealousy of the other *Vashta* Orders.'

'More likely it's because of us,' said Kellarn. 'Abbot Commander Carstan lent us horses, and helped us to escape the imperial guards.'

'In a conflict between Dortrean and Lautun, Mairdun would side with Dortrean,' said Idesîn; 'and we have a great respect for the long wisdom of the *Aeshta* Orders. You might say that we have a tradition of being accused of heretical thought. Yet still we are here. It is no great matter, I think.'

'Dortrean may need to call upon your support again one day soon,' said Kellarn.

'You shall have it, my Lord,' Idesîn promised. 'But for now you will excuse me. I must speak with my household before Kaïra spreads this news abroad.'

She signalled to Sir Kyeruk and the two of them went away, leaving by another set of doors on the northern side of the hall.

'I knew that you would come here, looking for me,' Kellarn told Rhysana.

'Did you now?' she smiled.

'He is insufferable when he is proved right,' Mellin sighed.

'And Kaïra is just plain insufferable,' said Torkhaal. 'It

worries me what else she might say at Court. Rhydden will soon learn that we were all here, meeting together.'

'She is a spiteful creature,' Rhysana told Kellarn. 'Your attack upon her was perhaps a little too pointed, under the circumstances.'

'She deserved it,' said Kellarn. 'You were not here when she forced Patall to condemn the Guardian Gilraen to death. It may be imperial law, but Father could have helped Patall to avoid it had it not been for her. She took such a savage delight in it. Actually I do want to kill her. I just need to find a lawful reason to do it.'

'You are probably not alone there,' said Torkhaal.

'So why are you here, Rhysana?' asked Mellin. 'Did you really come looking for us?'

'I had hoped to hear news of you,' Rhysana allowed.

'Have you brought good news or bad?' Kellarn demanded.

'A little of both, as usual,' she answered. 'May we speak freely?'

The question was addressed as much to her husband as to Kellarn himself. Though she trusted the Lady Idesîn, and though she had not sensed any sign of magical eavesdropping at work in the chamber, with Kaïra and Stellaas around she would hardly have considered the fortress the safest place for them to talk. And the Emperor had spies in many places.

Torkhaal frowned, sweeping the hall with his dark gaze.

'Probably,' he said softly. 'But better safe than sorry.' He placed his hands together and breathed out slowly. A veil of deeper green light shimmered into life around them, arcing up to form a dome above their heads.

'Now no one outside can hear us,' he explained, for Mellin and Kellarn's benefit.

'First there is this,' said Rhysana. She reached into her pocket and brought out the Lautun bar, wrapped in a square of milk white silk. 'I think that this is what you asked me to find.'

Kellarn seemed to forget whatever qualms he may have had

about Torkhaal's warding spell, and grinned broadly. He took the small parcel from her and weighed it in his hands for several seconds, as though savouring the moment before opening it. Corollin and Mellin stood up from their chairs to come and look. The yellow gemstone winked up at them from between the silken folds.

'Where did you find it?' he asked.

'That is too long a tale to tell you now,' Rhysana replied. 'But I may say that it was in the Council's care, though we did not know it. And I now believe that the Emperor's Archmage was also searching for it, and perhaps the shadowfay with him.'

'We should have guessed,' said Kellarn grimly.

'The bar was hidden within a wooden carving,' Rhysana told them. 'Torkhaal helped me to retrieve it, and he may have discovered something about the nature of its power.'

Corollin and Kellarn looked up at once.

'Not much,' Torkhaal confessed. 'The stone may be a form of matrix for mental energy. But when I tried to focus energy into it, it bounced straight back at me.'

'I imagine that all the bars would link together to form a circlet,' added Rhysana, 'such as the one on the old crown monument in Ellanguan.'

'Yes, that would make sense,' Corollin nodded.

'May I ask how you are faring with your own search?' Rhysana ventured.

'Let's just say that this is the last piece that needed to be found,' said Kellarn. 'Now we have to go to the Sun Temple, to find out what to do with them.'

'We can take you there, if it would help,' said Rhysana. 'Or to the Carfinn manor house, at least.'

'Better not, thank you all the same,' said Kellarn. 'We shall need to take the horses with us. Besides, you have risked more than enough to help us already.'

'The need of the Six Kingdoms is great,' she returned. 'You are our best hope, as well as our friends.'

Kellarn smiled, and put the bar away in his pocket.

'I have a message for you from your Lady mother,' Rhysana told him, remembering that they might have little time left before Idesîn returned. 'She said that she hopes you shall stay safely away from the imperial palace, until you are fully prepared. She also said that you should be mindful of Terrel.'

'Terrel?' he echoed.

'That is what she said.' Rhysana debated briefly in her mind, and decided that it would be better to let Kellarn interpret Karlena's words as he would. 'I spoke to her this morning, and she appeared very well. I may also tell you that his Grace your father has now arrived safely at the Braedun *commanderie*. It seems that the Souther move there has gone more peacefully than anyone expected. How long he will remain there before coming to Court, I do not know.'

'But what happened to the Kelmaar School?' asked Mellin. 'And to Prime Councillor Iorlaas?'

'And who will succeed Iorlaas?' Kellarn added. 'Sollonaal?'

Rhysana sat back in her chair, and nodded for Torkhaal to end his warding spell.

'That is a longer tale,' she said. 'Yet if the gods are kind, then tomorrow morning the Archmage the Lady Ellen of Raudhar will be our new Prime Councillor.'

'Good,' said Kellarn. 'Someone whom we can trust.'

Chapter Eleven

The following morning, being the tenth day of Röstren in the year 1524, on that day of the week held holy to Temrbrin, *Aeshta* Lady of Earth, the Archmage the Lady Ellen of Raudhar faced the challenge of her Rite of Ascent. By tradition she should have spent the previous night alone in the great assembly chamber, preparing herself in private vigil. But since Torkhaal and Hrugaar were both to join the High Council that day, it had been agreed that they should keep their own silent vigil there with her.

Admission to the High Council, as Rhysana knew, required no further test of magical skill; for it was an honour granted only by the existing High Council to those who had already proved their worth through outstanding insight or achievement. As such, Torkhaal and Hrugaar would face a simple ritual challenge from one of the Trialmasters or Archmagi, and then be led through a maze of passages beneath the College. There they would meet the Warden of the College Libraries, who would reveal something of his secret nature to them, as he saw fit, and then they would be brought to the assembly chamber to swear their oaths to their fellow High Councillors. Nevertheless, it occurred to Rhysana that the challenge of spending an entire night without speech might prove a more rigorous test for Hrugaar than any of the ordeals which he had undergone to earn his seat as a Mage Councillor.

The rites were set to take place at the latter end of the morning, when the crescent moon and the sun were in the sky together. But though Rhysana was not permitted to see any of the three before then, she was not left entirely to her own devices. The Archmage Morvaan arrived early on, and they broke their fast together. It was rather a frugal meal, by either of their standards, for they needed to keep their wits about them for the work at hand.

Morvaan brought only small news from the Court, and seemed less inclined to talk about it. The debate of the previous afternoon had come to an early close, with those in favour of removing the *Aeshta* Orders from the cities ahead by only a slight margin when Lord Brodhaur put it to a testing vote. Since Rhysana and Torkhaal had taken the priestesses of Justice to the city harbours of Lautun, to make their own way by ferry to the imperial citadel, the Reverend Mother Kaïra had arrived too late to join in the debate. She had now taken over the Telbray apartment – her Order having no chambers of its own within the citadel – obliging the Lord Patall Telbray to remove himself to his kinsmen's chambers of Logray. Kaïra would no doubt be sounding forth to the Court Noble that morning. The Emperor had made it known that he wished for a decision to be made before the end of the second day.

'I cannot see the sense of it,' said Rhysana. 'If the Southers turn nasty, the city guards will need the strength of the Orders for defence.'

'That point was made,' Morvaan nodded. 'The burden will otherwise fall on the knights of the *Vashta* Orders and armies raised by the other Houses – which is why, I think, the margin of the vote fell so slight as it did. But it seems that the Emperor trusts the Southers more than the Easterners, for now. I spoke with Bradhor last night. As Acting Head of House Arrand, he has enough sense to welcome all the strength that the *Aeshta* Orders can spare for the protection of Arrandin. Whether he would say the same if the Emperor commanded him otherwise, I am not certain. He has his father's stubbornness, but not his father's wisdom.'

'Kaïra would have the *Aeshta* magi turfed out of the Colleges as well,' Rhysana told him.

Morvaan snorted. 'That woman! No doubt she would. But that is hardly likely. After the show that we put on in Arrandin, there is not a city or manor in the Kingdoms that would turn down our help in time of war, whatever they may think of us. We have you to thank for that, my dear.'

'And Ellen,' she said. 'Which brings us back to this morning. Is she still worried about the rite?'

'She is worried about the role thereafter,' Morvaan corrected her. 'I must say that I can not blame her, especially with this business of Sollonaal. But I hope that the rite which we have chosen will help to encourage her in her own sense of worth.'

Iorlaas' Rite of Ascent had been a solemn but rather modest affair, tailored to the traditions of his *Vashta* faith. For the Archmage Ellen, Morvaan intended to go back to a more ancient and powerful working which had been used for the late Prime Councillor Herusen several years before.

The rest of the High Council met with them in the great assembly chamber in the middle morning, by which time Ellen, Hrugaar and Torkhaal had been led away to wash and dress themselves elsewhere in the College with the help of the unseen *chaedar*. Of the three *Vashta* magi who might have been present, only the reluctant Lirinal of Dregharis was there. Morvaan went through the rite with them all, explaining to each their various roles; and then they had time for a short break before the ceremony itself began.

Rhysana hurried back to her chambers to freshen herself, and to put on her formal robes of deep indigo with the double sash of the High Council. The *chaedar* fluttered around her, setting her silver fair hair to rights and fetching out fresh silken slippers, and bringing her a tumbler of chilled cordial to sip; and then, as the last hour of the morning drew nigh, she made the *leap* back to the great assembly chamber. The ebon doors swung shut behind her as she went in.

The other magi were already drifting toward their places. Rhysana murmured her apologies, gliding forward to the middle of the chamber, but no one seemed to mind. The central stone of the patterned floor had by now been raised up into a circular pillar, waist high, in the manner of an altar; and upon it were set three crystal bowls of water, salt and incense about a single tall candle. The white steel rod of the Prime Councillor stood upright against it on the eastern side. She bowed to the altar as she circled it, and moved on to take up her appointed position four paces in from the northern edge of the floor. The North was more truly Ellen's place, being the Quarter of the Lords of Earth. But since Ellen could not do it, and they had magi of Air to spare, Morvaan had asked Rhysana to stand there. He said that Ellen herself had requested it.

Ferghaal, Asharka and Trialmaster Ekraan made up the three remaining Quarter points. Trialmaster Foghlaar stood nearer the centre of the chamber with the two other Archmagi, Morvaan and Merrech. High Councillors Rikkarn and Lirinal stood at the very edge of the chamber before their misericord seats, to the south and northeast respectively. When all were ready, Morvaan thanked them for coming and invited Ferghaal to begin.

Ferghaal unsheathed a long sword from his side, and held it up to the crystal dome high overhead. Then he drew a deep breath and began to sing in his roughened tenor voice. It was a hymn from the dawn rites of the Braedun Order, in praise of the Sun, Moon and stars that filled the air with light, bringing joy to the life of the world. He brought down the tip of the blade, and hooked up a riband of blue-white light from the floor at his feet; and then he held the blade level across his chest and walked sun-wise around the chamber, singing as he went. The riband of light spun out behind him, floating steadily in the air. He passed outside Asharka and Ekraan, and then on behind Rhysana herself, until he returned again to the East whence he had begun and the riband formed a circle around them. Then he touched the sword point to the floor, and swept it up high in an arc above his head, and down and round before his feet. The riband of light sprang wide, running up to form a dome above them and down into an unseen dome below, sealing them off from the world outside.

'The outer circle is cast,' said Ferghaal, bringing his sword upright before him. He strode forward across the floor to Morvaan, who received the sword from him in an exchange of bows.

'We stand at the meeting of many paths,' declared Morvaan, 'at the meeting place of many Realms. We stand at the still point that is the very heart of the dance of the gods, where all hopes and fears are past.'

'The wisdom of the gods is endless,' came the Archmage Merrech's silken voice.

'And also their joy,' said Foghlaar.

Morvaan returned the sword to Ferghaal. 'Let the Witnesses come forth,' he said.

Ferghaal sheathed his sword and bowed, and turned back to face the East. He raised his arms in prayer and began to sing softly, calling upon the Lord of Air. A cool wind sprang up around them, buffeting Rhysana's robes and ruffling through her hair; and then the ghostly image of a huge eagle, twice Ferghaal's height, blurred into life just inside the shimmering wall of the dome. His wings seemed to span more than half the width of the chamber as he shook them out before settling down, and his eyes were the bright blue of the summer sky. Rhysana loved him at once, passionately. But she bowed in awe, as did all the other magi.

Asharka then stepped out across the floor, and turned to summon the Witness of Fire. The wind burned suddenly dry with a desert heat, and a winged serpent reared up before them. It was nearly as large as the eagle, and its body was all of crimson and violet flame; and its serpent eyes shone bright as twin suns as they glared down upon the bowing magi.

The desert wind turned to summer rain as Ekraan summoned the Witness of Water, and steaming clouds gathered to flicker with lightning in the upper part of the dome. The liquid shape of a tall man stood forth in the West, with a face like a great cat and a bright rippling mane. And then it was Rhysana's turn to step out across the floor, and to turn and call forth the Witness of Earth.

Had she been married to anyone other than Torkhaal, she might have been daunted by the task appointed to her – especially in her wet, windblown and bedraggled state. But because of his love for the Lords of Earth, and her own love for him, Rhysana found herself at once humbled and proud to do so.

'Holy Maachel, great Lord of All Earth,' she breathed, standing still as she could beneath the storm; 'look now with favour upon us, and send your great messenger to strengthen us with order and peace.'

The pale light of the dome deepened to tawny gold before her, and then a lion of the Môshári filled her sight. The storm fled away as he spread his feathered wings, and a gentler sunlight filled the chamber. His breath upon her face was warm and sweet. Her first thought was to run to him and embrace him, and to bury her face in his soft mane. But he raised one velvet eyebrow at her, and Rhysana recovered herself and remembered to bow instead.

The four magi who had summoned the Witnesses then shifted round to the halfway points between the Quarters, moving closer to the edge of the warding dome. The three who had stood near to the centre spread out, taking up their places halfway between the centre and the edge. Morvaan stood to the south, Foghlaar nearest to Rhysana in the northeast, and the Archmage Merrech to the northwest.

The next part of the rite was something that Rhysana had never seen; for the three senior magi then called upon an inner circle of Witnesses who faced outward from the altar pillar. Morvaan began with a sun dog of Torollen to the southeast, the great hound as tall as the Archmage himself even when sitting upon its haunches, and its smooth coat as bright as copper flame. The Archmage Merrech called upon the twin sea serpents of Sherunar to the southwest, and the black panthress of the Moon Maiden Haëstren close before him. And then Trialmaster Foghlaar invited in a golden mare of Temrbrin to the north, and a gryphon for the Tumbrachin. And when the gryphon reared and beat its wings, a second dome of power sprang up at the creatures' backs, swirling with muted rainbow hues as fine and delicate as a soap bubble.

'The Witnesses have come forth,' said Morvaan, when all was done. 'We are honoured by your presence.'

'We render honour in return,' said Foghlaar, and all the magi bowed again.

'Let she who wishes to be our next Prime Councillor be brought in,' Merrech purred.

Ferghaal, Asharka and Ekraan circled round between the inner and outer domes to join Rhysana in the northeast. Though the great messengers of the *Aeshtar* filled her with wonder and joy, she found herself relieved that she did not have to make that journey beneath their watchful eyes. When Ferghaal reached her he gestured with his right hand toward the wall of light, and then drew aside a small part like a curtain to allow them to pass through.

'Hoods up,' came Morvaan's voice from behind them.

They all drew forward the hoods of their robes, so that their faces were hidden in shadow. Ekraan led the way off along the line of misericord seats, with Asharka and Ferghaal following, and the three of them went to take up their positions outside the circle of power. Lirinal came across to stand a short distance from Rhysana, on the far side of where Ferghaal had opened a way for them to come out.

They could see through the wall of light as through a shimmering veil, so Rhysana still had a fair view of the magical creatures and the senior magi within. But she could only dimly make out the blue and red shapes of Ekraan and Asharka as they circled the far side; and from here the inner dome of power seemed as dense as a slow waterfall, so that the altar pillar and the central part of the floor were no more than a half guessed blur.

They waited for some time until the elderly Ekraan was in place; and then at last the ebon doors were opened, and Rhysana caught a flash of scarlet robes in the East as High Councillor Rikkarn fetched Ellen inside.

Ellen, like the other magi, had to make the traditional circuit of the chamber to the left; so it was not until she had passed by her accustomed High Council seat in the North that Rhysana had her first proper sight of her that morning. She was clad in a simple gown of russet silk, which would later sit comfortably beneath her formal robes. Rhysana tilted back her head so that she could peek beneath the brim of her hood, and saw that Ellen's heavy bronze hair had been scooped up more softly than was her wont into a plaited crown. For a woman who had spent the previous night awake, and the two days before that worrying, she appeared remarkably rested and confident. Only the slightest frown upon her brow, and the tighter set of her strong jaw, warned of the strength of her focus and determination.

Rhysana smiled and bowed, clasping her hands before her chest in formal Council greeting. She could not see whether Ellen acknowledged her; but as the Archmage came to a halt beside her, she reached out to hold Rhysana's hands briefly.

'Here you may carve a way to pass within,' said Lirinal, his rich voice catching a little in his throat. Given that he was a *Vashta* mage in the presence of so many powerful *Aeshta* creatures, Rhysana could hardly fault him for that. He drew out a silver bladed dagger, and presented the hilt of polished blue steel toward Ellen for her to take.

'I come not to carve a way, but to ask it,' Ellen replied. 'She who would lead must first serve.'

Lirinal bowed in answer. Ellen bowed and then turned to the wall of light, resting her palms against it as she sought to find a way in.

How she saw the danger in time, from within the confines of her hood, Rhysana never fully knew. Perhaps some instinct warned her. She knew only that she saw Lirinal raise the dagger up in both hands, poised to bring it down upon Ellen's back. And then he shuddered, switched the angle of the blade, and plunged it down toward his own heart.

'No!' she cried, lunging blindly toward him.

Lirinal punched himself on the chest, staggered and fell back.

Rhysana held the dagger in her own hand.

Ellen whirled round and grabbed her arm. Rhysana breathed deeply, trying to calm her racing heart and steady her tumbling thoughts. Lirinal groaned, and began to drag himself to his feet.

'What is it?' came Morvaan's voice, as though from a great distance.

'No matter,' said Ellen firmly.

She released Rhysana's arm and took hold of Lirinal instead. Rhysana pulled her hood back halfway to see what was happening. The *Vashta* mage was white faced and trembling.

'You had better come with me,' Ellen told him sternly.

Lirinal shrank back, but had not the strength of will to resist. Ellen reached one hand into the wall of power, opened a way and hauled him through. The three senior magi had all turned to face her in concern.

'Stay there please, Councillor,' said Ellen to Lirinal. 'Sit down, or kneel if you would find that more comfortable. But do not try to leave.'

She left him three paces in, bowed to the senior magi, and then moved toward the eagle in the East.

Lirinal glanced at the huge creatures all around him, the divine messengers of gods whom he did not serve. He hugged himself deeper into his blue and white robes, and went down on one knee with his hooded head bowed.

Rhysana checked that the wall of light before her was made whole again after Ellen's passing. Then she pulled forward her own hood a little way, so that she could still see to watch what followed. She had nowhere safe to put the dagger, so she set it down on the floor and covered it with the hem of her robes.

Ellen bowed deeply to the great eagle, and then spread her arms wide in formal welcome.

'Hail, Son of the Skies,' she said, her deep voice now muffled and remote to Rhysana's ears because of the wall of light between them. 'Hail, messenger of the most high Lord of Air, who brings knowledge and learning, the gifts of the skilful mind. Without your gifts we fail and fall.'

She bowed and moved on to the South, to honour the winged serpent of Fire, and then on to the West and the North; and then circled to greet each of the five Witnesses around the inner dome in their turn, in the order that the magi had called them. When all were done, the three senior magi came to join her. And then Morvaan opened a way into the inner dome, between the sun dog and the gryphon, and all four of them passed inside.

What followed next was veiled from Rhysana's eyes, no more than shifting shadows glimpsed within a pool of water. But she knew that Ellen would receive the four symbols of the elements which were waiting upon the altar pillar, and the white steel rod of the Prime Councillor; and that thereafter she would come forth to release each of the Witnesses in their proper order or *ascendancy*, whence the Rite of Ascent took its name.

While the hidden part of the rite went on, Rhysana fell to wondering about the dagger. Her hand had been nowhere near Lirinal's; and yet the dagger had come to her, quite possibly sparing the poor man his life. Had they been anywhere else, such a feat could have been achieved with a relatively simple spell – and perhaps a few more seconds' warning. Yet here in the assembly chamber such spells did not usually work. But then again, the presence of so many messengers of the *Aeshta* in the council chamber, and of such powerful warding spells, was highly unusual. She wondered whether one of the great creatures themselves had commanded it.

The other possibility now hovering at the edge of her mind was that she had done it herself, using that power which Illana had never mastered but only grasped at in the *Argument of Command*. Rhysana labelled that as an *unlikely possibility*, and filed it away firmly at the back of her mind for later thought.

Why Lirinal had done what he had at all was no doubt a question that would very soon be asked of him.

Before long the inner dome rippled again and Trialmaster Foghlaar came out, with Merrech and Morvaan behind him. Last of all came Ellen, now arrayed in her high councillor's robes of russet and green, but with her hood thrown back. She held the white steel rod in her hands.

'The Prime Councillor of All Magi has been chosen,' Morvaan declared. 'We honour her before the Witnesses of the gods.'

'We honour her,' Rhysana repeated. The other magi outside of the dome of power echoed the words. Morvaan, Foghlaar and even Merrech went down on one knee in homage.

'May the gods grant that I serve all the Magi in wisdom, humility and truth,' Ellen returned.

The three senior magi rose and trod the path together around the inner dome, pausing to honour each of the nine Witnesses in turn. Then they came on through the wall of light just to Rhysana's left, leaving Ellen to finish her Rite of Ascent alone, and circled the edge of the chamber to return to their proper places. Lirinal looked up at them as they passed, but Morvaan shook his head and signalled for him to stay put.

Ellen turned first to the gryphon of the Tumbrachin, holding her rod of office level before her between her two hands, and spoke words to him that Rhysana could not catch. The gryphon opened its great beak and seemed to be answering her. Ellen nodded, and then bowed deeply. The gryphon turned and flew back into the watery dome behind it, vanishing from sight.

As far as Rhysana could tell, Ellen did the same with each of the other Witnesses around the inner circle; honouring them as she gave them leave to depart, and receiving some form of answer from them in return. When all five were done, she raised her hands above her head – the rod held lightly in the right – and brought them down slowly upon either side. The swirling bubble of the inner dome flowed down into the floor and was gone.

Rhysana had expected Ellen to repeat the same pattern with the four outer creatures, beginning in the North and working her way back round to the East as the rite unwound. But instead she went first to the great eagle of Telúmachel, leaving the lion of Earth until last. As an Archmage of Earth, the choice was understandable.

Ellen spent longer in conversation with the eagle, and at one point she looked in Rhysana's direction and smiled before making answer. Rhysana had no idea what they were saying, and doubted that Ellen would ever tell her. But at last Ellen bowed very deeply, and the great eagle brushed one wing lightly across the back of her head as it turned and vanished. When Ellen stood up again, she seemed somehow taller and more imposing than before.

Her exchange with the winged serpent of Fire was much briefer, as was that with the Witness of Maësta. And then at last she came round to the North, and the golden lion went down on to his belly so that she stood between his huge forepaws. They seemed to study one another for some time without speaking, unless they were talking mind to mind. And then the lion breathed upon her, so that Ellen was wrapped in a mist of glittering light; and then to Rhysana's eyes he seemed to fly out through the dome and out through the wall of the assembly chamber itself with a roar like thunder.

Ellen moved back toward the centre of the floor, the last wisps of the lion's breath still glimmering about her, and turned to face the East.

'The Rite of Ascent is ended,' she said aloud. 'Blessed are the Lords of the *Aeshtar*.'

'Blessed are those who serve them,' the other magi answered.

Ellen lifted her hands above her head again. But now she grew swiftly taller, and her robes shimmered and shifted hue. Her arms spread into wings, and her handsome face lengthened into a dragon's snout of burnished bronze; and a great tail unfurled around the altar pillar, setting the candle flame dancing wildly.

Lirinal's courage failed him at last, and he scrabbled back against the encircling dome.

'Know this of me,' the dragon told him, her voice so deep that the floor trembled beneath Rhysana's feet. 'I am Prime Councillor of All Magi.'

Then the dragon curled in upon herself in a rush of gold and bronze, and she was Ellen again. She swung the white steel rod about her head and brought it down to touch the floor, and the outer dome rolled down like a scroll and vanished.

'The paths unfurl,' she said, 'the world turns, the stars take up their dance.'

She turned and bowed to the altar pillar, and then moved round to stand on its western side facing the ebon doors.

'Please be seated, all of you,' she said easily. 'I think that it is time now for our two new members to be admitted. High Councillor Rhysana, would you be so kind as to join me?'

Trialmaster Foghlaar helped Lirinal to stand and led him back to his High Council seat. Rhysana picked up the dagger and took it with her, trying to keep it hidden behind the folds of her sleeve. Ellen took it from her and laid it calmly upon the altar between the crystal dishes, as though there was nothing untoward about its presence there.

Torkhaal and Hrugaar were led in by Morvaan, since he had been their chief proposer. The two were clad alike in belted shirts over breeches and soft boots – Torkhaal all in black and Hrugaar in creamy beige – which to Rhysana's mind suited them rather handsomely. Morvaan presented them by name, and made the last formal request for any challenge to their admission. But fortunately there was none, and so Ellen welcomed them on behalf of all. Hrugaar, Rhysana noticed, was grinning broadly through most of the brief ceremony, as though he could hardly contain his joy at being here. Her husband was more subdued and thoughtful, as was his wont, but he managed a smile of relief when the ritual exchanges were done.

Their councillors' robes were brought for them, and Ellen and Rhysana helped them to put them on; and then the Prime Councillor herself presented each of them with the double sash of the High Council. And then Hrugaar went to sit in the southwest, and Torkhaal in the north, and Rhysana returned to her accustomed place in the east. Ellen bowed to the altar pillar, snuffed out the candle flame, and went to take up her Prime Councillor's seat in the west.

'I shall not keep you much longer,' she told them. 'I know that there is work to be done, and I expect that we shall hold another assembly a few days hence. I am pleased to have begun on a high note, welcoming our two new High Councillors. But before we leave, I feel that there is one matter of which we should speak.

'High Councillor Lirinal, I note that Sollonaal, Prime Councillor of the Ellanguan Magi, is not here. While I understand that a rite rooted in the *Aeshta* faith might be at odds with his personal beliefs, are you aware of some pressing need that has kept him in Ellanguan at this time with no word to us to explain his absence?'

Lirinal had to clear his throat twice before he could answer her. 'Sollonaal has no interest in this election, Prime Councillor,' he told her. 'As he has said in previous assemblies, he believes this Council to be mired by outworn traditions and its own self interest, and of no further use or support to magi of the imperial faith or to the needs of the Empire.'

'So does he intend to set up his own Council?' asked Ekraan.

'Not that I have heard, as yet,' Lirinal replied. 'He says that he wishes to offer another choice to those magi who have lost faith in the leadership of this present High Council.'

'I have heard that he wishes to keep the Ellanguan College for the use of the *Vashta* magi alone,' came Torkhaal's deep voice from the north.

'That is out of the question,' Asharka objected.

'But not entirely so, perhaps,' said Ellen. 'We know that even now the Court Noble are debating whether the *Aeshta* Orders should be asked to withdraw from the cities. From what High Councillor Torkhaal has told me, it seems likely that the Reverend Mother Kaïra will be proposing that the *Aeshta* magi of our own Order should withdraw as well. I doubt that that is a battle which she could win. But given that the *Vashta* magi number a third of our Order, and given that the staffing of all of the Colleges has now to be considered following our losses in the war, it seems to me that the proposal of one College specialised in the training of *Vashta* magi is worthy of our attention. Whether Ellanguan would be the College most suited to that purpose is another matter.

'If Sollonaal has this in mind, High Councillor Lirinal, then he is welcome to present his case to the Council. Whatever he may think of us, we are pledged as a body to remain neutral in all matters of faith and politics; and he may achieve more by working with us than by labouring in our despite.'

'I fear that he has lost faith in the Council and what it stands for,' said Lirinal. 'He would not accept your help, since it would be given on your own terms. He would rather see you fail, and himself build something new; and there are many among the *Vashta* magi who agree with him.'

'But you do not,' said Rhysana.

Lirinal shifted awkwardly in his seat. 'I come from a House Merchant,' he said. 'I believe that the Council should remain neutral.'

Rhysana felt that there was more to it than that. She had seen Lirinal turn the blade from Ellen to strike toward his own heart. She wondered how great a hold Sollonaal had over him, and whether he had urged Lirinal to make the attempt on Ellen's life; and if so, then whether Lirinal had been driven to turn the dagger upon himself for fear of the High Council or for fear of the wrath of Sollonaal. But that was not a question which she felt that she could put to him with some of the other magi present.

'You are not on trial here, High Councillor Lirinal,' said Ellen. 'But I need to understand what is happening in Ellanguan, so that I may attempt to heal this rift between us.'

'Iorlaas tried that, and failed,' said the voice of the Archmage Merrech.

'I would not lose even one mage from this Council, if I can prevent it,' she countered.

'I fear that you may be too late, Prime Councillor,' said Lirinal.

Linaelin, daughter of Hirulin, daughter of Heruvor of the moon fay of Starmere, watched from the parapet arches of the high orchard garden as her kinsman Tinûkenil arrived. In spite of the noonday sun upon her back, she shivered as though a cloud shadow had passed over her. The long years of waiting were over. Her hour of judgement was at hand.

She tugged her dark blue cloak around her and settled herself more comfortably on the wide parapet ledge. She had grown fond of sitting here of late, looking north toward the shimmering splendour of the golden birches of Hellenur, spread out like a mantle over the rolling hills. On the nearer slopes the gold was bordered with the coppers and greens of beeches and chestnuts and oaks, and alders and willows in the narrow stream valley that came down into the half moon bay. At the foot of the steep wall below her the cobbled streets and steps of the Monastery Isle of Telúmachel wound their way down between clustered buildings of many colours to the outer gate tower, through which Tinûkenil and his friends had come. The great Temple of Telúmachel, where many of the isle's inhabitants were now gathered for the noon rite, stood behind and above her on the far side of the orchard garden, with the tall cloistered buildings and towers set aside for the priests and holy knights of the Braedun Order.

The tide had not long turned from the full when Tinûkenil had arrived on the mainland shore. Three came with him – a tawny haired man, and a dark haired woman all in deep blue, and a warrior of the *noghru* in a scarlet cloak. A rowing boat had been sent over to fetch them, since it would be some time before the causeway was clear, and Linaelin had come here to say her private farewells. Only Tinûkenil himself, as a priest of the Moon, would be permitted to come so high within the cloistered terraces of the isle to find her. The rest would be invited to wait for him in one of the guest halls for pilgrims, down close by the outer gate.

The Lady Aramen – sister of the Earl of Vansa and now wife to the High Priest the Lord Tirrel of Braedun, and a priestess of Temrbrin in her own right – had gone to welcome them. She said that Tinûkenil and his friends were well known to her, and that the tawny haired man was one of her own people, held in high honour at her brother's seat of Caer Vansa. Linaelin could see her now, her golden hair and light green robes fluttering in the sea breeze as she greeted their guests. In the short time that they had known one another she had come to love Aramen, with her gentle manner, and the deep wisdom and sense born of running her brother's household for several years before marrying somewhat later in life. She would miss her as much as any of the folk here whom she had known for far longer.

Aramen led the three guests away and Tinûkenil came on up the winding streets, his long silver hair and white tunic shining in the shadows as he followed one of the younger novices. Of course Linaelin could remember a time, long before he was born, when there had been no streets or buildings there at all; when the lower part of the isle had been covered in grass and evergreen oaks, and this pleasant walled orchard had been no more than a rocky bluff used as a nesting place by gannets and gulls and terns. She had been here then, as now, as an Honoured Priestess of Telúmachel; and in other places under other names in the long years between, serving the Lord of Air in the hidden life of the cloister while the lives of mortal men flew by and her true name and lineage were all but forgotten. But when the moon fay Tinûkenil had found her, in the Monastery of the Tumbrachin above the Telbray vale, it had not taken him long to discover her secret. And now Heruvor knew that she lived, and the great Enemy was about to return, and the long twilight of her life was ending.

The sea birds wheeled and called above the rooftops as Tinûkenil climbed higher. One of the grey gulls of the isle flew up to perch beside her on the parapet wall, chattering in excitement.

'I have seen,' she told the bird. 'And you might have seen him the sooner, had your belly not been so full of mackerel. He comes to fetch me. We have work to do, far away from here.'

Gone, gone, the gull cried pitifully.

'For a little while,' she said. 'You shall soon have forgotten me.'

The bird cocked his head to fix her with one yellow-rimmed eye, then flew down again to spread the word in wailing calls and to summon his brethren.

By the time that Tinûkenil reached the orchard garden, more than six score sea birds were gathered atop the walls and parapet arches or strutting and bickering upon the grass before Linaelin's feet. He had to clear a way through them to reach her.

'Welcome kinsman,' she said, standing slowly. He hurried forward to help her, but she laughed as she took his hand.

'I am stronger than I look,' she told him. 'Yet this frailty is no guise. Though I have lived centuries more easily than those around me have counted decades, the mortal blood of my father takes its toll.'

The moon fay looked at her kindly. He was less tall than she had been in her youth, though he stood head and shoulders above her now; and his priestly tunic was of silver-white silk, bright as the midwinter moon and bordered with silver threads, over simpler garb of grey. A silver torc in the likeness of a panthress was curled about his arm, and a circlet set with white jade and deep blue jasper adorned his silver head. A staff of mother-of-pearl was cradled in his right arm, and about his throat was the sash of violet silk that Linaelin herself had given to him.

'Our last meeting was unexpected,' she said. 'Today I have been waiting for you.'

Tinûkenil turned his head aside, almost diffident. 'I have come to ask your help, my Lady,' he said.

Linaelin sat down again. 'You would take me to ask forgiveness of one whom I have not seen since the earliest days of my youth,' she said, 'and abide his judgement.'

He wrinkled his nose, as if puzzled. 'I have not come to take you to Starmere,' he told her.

'No indeed.' She sighed softly to herself. 'We must go to the new Sun Temple that that young friend of yours has built.'

Tinûkenil's fair face broke into a smile. 'How much do you know, my Lady?' he asked.

Linaelin chuckled, shooing a grey-backed shearwater further along the ledge so that he could sit down beside her.

'Too much,' she said, 'and too little. Yet if you mean, *how much do I know of your errand*, then the answer is little more than that. I had a visit from a priestess of Aranara.'

'Ilumarin?' Tinûkenil ventured.

Linaelin nodded. 'A pretty girl – but as riddling as any Moon priestess I have ever met.'

There had been something else about the girl, some sense of *otherness* which even Linaelin with all her years of wisdom had not been able to make out, and of which the messengers of the Lord of Air would not speak. But the Lady Aramen had said that Ilumarin was known to her as a friend and companion of Tinûkenil; and Linaelin trusted that the gods or Tinûkenil would make the rest clear to her when the time was ripe.

'We have found something which may help to drive the ancient Enemy back,' he told her. 'Yet we may need your help to understand it.'

'This much I understand,' she said, 'and I shall help you as I may. But do not place too much hope in my power to help, Tinûkenil. The wisdom of Starmere might serve you to better purpose.'

'Not in this, my Lady,' he answered.

The second day of the Court debate turned more strongly against the Emperor's proposal. The efforts of the High Priestess Kaïra, rather than fanning the flames of righteous hatred against the heathen as had been her intention, had only served to remind the gathered nobles that the *Aeshta* Orders and Magi had been far more effective in the war against the Easterners than had their *Vashta* counterparts. It was also mooted from several quarters that the attitudes of some of the *Vashta* Orders served only to compound the present problems with the Southers in Ellanguan and Farran.

In the afternoon debate the focus of blame shifted, perhaps inevitably, to the Southers themselves. The young Lord Tarrek Cardhási – himself a follower of the imperial gods, and nephew to the War priest Môrghran of Fâghsul – suggested that the continued military presence of the Southers in Ellanguan could only serve to provoke further conflict and was the main cause of many of the recent troubles. The Lady Melissa of Vanbruch, on behalf of the city merchants, was minded to voice her agreement with him. She observed that trade with the Souther merchants, in particular the T'gaim, would be the sweeter without the presence of the troops and was a surer way to promote peace; and that although she was reluctant to question the wisdom of the Earl of Dortrean or the Lord Steward Rinnekh in their dealings with the Souther Ambassador T'Loi, she felt that they had erred in allowing T'Loi to retain so great a number of his warriors in Ellanguan. Melissa's speech won much support; and there was a general demand, led by the Earl of Ercusí, as to why Rinnekh and T'Loi were not there to make answer in the debate.

All this Rhysana watched from the lower of the two balconies that circled the round hall, with Ellen sitting beside her. Though weary from her overnight vigil and the demands of the morning, Ellen had been determined to see at least one session of this debate before the vote was taken. Torkhaal and Hrugaar stood protectively behind them. Gravhan Dârghûn of Môshári had joined them part way through the afternoon, and now stood with his back to the brown marble pillar just to Ellen's right.

'Whom would Rinnekh trust to govern Ellanguan while he was away?' Ellen snorted.

'They could hardly make a worse job of it than he has,' said Torkhaal.

'Whom would Rhydden trust, more like,' said Hrugaar. 'The Emperor may have told him to stay there.'

'Someone who did not like Sollonaal might be of more use to us,' said Ellen. 'His stand against the Council might have gained less support without Rinnekh's favour. I wonder whether the alliance between them was Rhydden's idea.'

'No,' said Hrugaar. 'Or at least it began with Sollonaal, I think. The Emperor may have encouraged it.'

'But I doubt that the Toad would have done so,' said Rhysana. 'Not unless he misjudged Sollonaal's strength to draw so many magi after him.'

The hooded shadow of the Archmage Merrech was down on the raised dais, below and to their right, on the near side of the Emperor's great black-winged throne. The eight lesser thrones of the Imperial Council were arranged in an arc to either side, of which five were filled that afternoon. The Earls of Vaulun, Ercusí and Scaulun were there, as were the War priest Môrghran of Fâghsul and Knight Commander Drômagh of Sêchral, each with their own advisers at their side. Rhysana had noticed that Mage Councillor Kharfaal sat next to his elder brother of Vaulun. The kindly Brodhaur Levrin, the sixth member of the Council present, stood at the front of the dais with his staff of office, attempting to keep some kind of order among the crowded nobles on the main floor of the hall as the debate progressed. Erkal Dortrean and the Lord Steward Rinnekh were notable by their absence – though Torreghal Valhaes sat on a low stool beside one of the empty thrones, clad in the formal scarlet and gold of his House, to speak on Dortrean's behalf.

The Emperor himself sat back in his winged throne, partly hidden from Rhysana's view. By custom he did not speak in the debate, unless formally requested to do so. He was clad that afternoon in the simplest of gold tunics over black, with only a plain fillet of gold on his dark head; but about his throat in all its glittering splendour hung the Easterner necklace of many green gemstones which had been sent to him from Herghin. Hrugaar had noticed that at once, with his keen sight; and he had noticed also that there was now some new glamour or enchantment upon the jewel, which had not been there before.

'Perhaps the imperial priests have put some blessing upon it,' Rhysana had said to him. 'Or the Toad may have done something.' But Court protocol prevented them from using magic to discover anything more just then; and besides, with Rhydden wearing the jewel and the Archmage Merrech standing right next him, it would have been a most dangerous undertaking.

Lord Brodhaur did invite the Emperor to make answer on behalf of the Lord Steward of Ellanguan; but Rhydden declined in favour of Lord Drômagh, as Knight Commander of his Imperial Household Guard. Drômagh simply told the assembled nobles what they could have guessed for themselves: that Rinnekh felt obliged to stay in Ellanguan to ensure the city's continuing safety and peace, and that T'Loi was better able than any to command the Southers there. His answer did nothing to stem the growing tide of the debate.

At last Lord Brodhaur called upon all the Court to rise for the final vote; and, as had by now become clear, the Court upheld that the Orders Noble should not be required to leave the cities. A second proposal, put forth by Edhrin Ercusí, that the Souther Ambassador T'Loi should instead be required to remove his military strength from the city of Ellanguan, was also comfortably carried.

The Emperor Rhydden sat forward on his throne to hear the vote, displaying his most dangerously radiant smile.

'We hear the voice of our Court Noble,' he said, when Lord Brodhaur invited him to speak. 'Since our proposal does not meet with your wise approval at this time, it behoves us to withdraw it.

'Nevertheless, in light of the continuing threat to our Empire from the Eastern Domains, we shall be calling upon the Orders Noble to provide more active defence in the near future upon our borders east of the city of Arrandin. And since in its wisdom this Court requires us to remove the threat of the Souther forces from within Ellanguan, we shall command that they be sent to the shores of the Galloppi River at this time – together with other armies now promised to us by the God-King. We are confident that our subjects of Linnaer and Galsin, Braedun and Levrin, will make every effort to welcome the armies of our K'tarim allies within their lands.'

There was an uproar of protest at this latest command, subsiding swiftly into an uneasy silence as the Emperor stood up. The Easterner necklace shimmered like green fire upon his breast.

'We would remind you that our Empire is upon the brink of another war,' he said firmly. 'If this Court Noble wishes to empty its own coffers to match the resources that the God-King is providing for us, and to raise, train and maintain armies of equal strength for our immediate defence, then should we be only too pleased to let the Souther armies return home. But until, or unless, that should come to pass, the need of our Empire demands that we accept the help of the God-King. No doubt that is a matter which this present Court will wish to consider in the next debate.'

He strode forward and down from the dais, the Archmage Merrech following swift as a shadow at his heels. The crowded nobles parted and bowed before him like grass in the wind. The remaining members of the Imperial Council gathered themselves and hurried after him.

'We should have seen that coming,' said Ellen wearily.

'We did,' said Gravhan, 'for the most part. We all know that another strike from the East is possible, unless the High Clan Chieftain can prevent it; and the *Aeshta* Orders and the Magi are our best defence. And Braedun have foreseen that the Southers might try to spread out along the Galloppi, given half the chance, and have sent some of their own knights in secret to keep watch for that.'

'At least Erkal is still down there,' said Ellen.

'What interests me more,' said Gravhan, 'is that Rhydden was so ready to move the Southers out of Ellanguan. It may be a sign that Rinnekh and he are at odds over what is happening there.'

'Perhaps Lirinal can tell us more of that,' said Rhysana.

After the High Council assembly that morning, Lirinal had been led away by the Archmage Morvaan and Trialmaster Foghlaar – partly at Rhysana's own quiet suggestion, though she gathered that Ellen herself had also requested it. Foghlaar was wise in the ways of all manner of enchantments and the beguiling of the mind, and how to deal with those who had fallen prey to them; and Morvaan was a Truthsayer and skilled in the inner magic of the mind, and also more aware of the political situation in Ellanguan than was the reclusive Foghlaar. Between them they hoped to uncover what had driven poor Lirinal to make an attempt on Ellen's life, and then upon his own, and what measure of danger he might be in should he return to Ellanguan; and in what manner, if any, they might help him. It was among the most ancient traditions of the Council to care for any mage who was oppressed or constrained against his will, and to offer safe refuge. But such a thing had rarely happened in Rhysana's time; and to her mind it was yet another sign that Sollonaal had chosen a most perilous path for other magi to follow.

'What worries me,' said Hrugaar, 'is that the new Souther troops are of the K'tarim. It was they who brought war to our coasts to aid the Easterners' cause.'

'Could the sea fay help against them?' Torkhaal asked him.

'They may, or they may not,' Hrugaar answered. 'If they come to our shores beneath a banner of peace, then it is not the sea fay's part to hinder them.'

'It is the part of the Court Noble,' said Ellen; 'which Rhydden has clearly overruled. Even the Imperial Council seemed surprised by the news.'

'I wonder if Erkal knows of it,' said Rhysana.

'No doubt he soon will,' said Gravhan.

The Emperor Rhydden returned straight to his private apartment after the debate, telling the guards upon the door that not even their senior commanders nor members of the Imperial Council should be allowed to disturb him. He went through into the cooler shade of the murrey chamber, and suffered the attendants there to pull off his boots and bring him wine before sending them all away. The hooded Archmage helped himself to wine from the crystal jug.

'His Highness seems pleased with his afternoon's work,' Merrech observed softly.

'In part,' said Rhydden. 'That damned woman Kaïra may have done us a service by reminding the Court Noble of the dangers of intolerance.'

'She herself is an example,' said the Archmage.

'Or perhaps we should make one of her,' Rhydden offered. 'What if the Reverend Mother were staked out in the temple square of Serbramel in Lautun, for the temple cats to come and feed upon?'

'The idea is tempting, Sire.'

The Emperor stretched back on the velvet couch. The Easterner necklace weighed heavy as a *noghr* sitting upon his chest, making it hard to breathe. He found the sensation both frightening and strangely exciting.

'Of course the end result is the same,' he said, smirking. 'Whether the *Aeshta* Orders be welcome in the cities or not, they will be sent east to provide for our defence. We trust that your new Prime Councillor will see the wisdom in that?'

'The Archmage Ellen laboured hard in the defence of Arrandin,' Merrech nodded, 'and she works well with the Môshári. Her sense of duty lends her great personal commitment to the defence of the Empire. She also labours to heal the rift within the Council precipitated by Sollonaal. Her good intentions in both directions will serve His Highness' purpose for now.'

'And our clever Rhysana will support her,' Rhydden mused. 'You are certain, Counsellor, that Rhysana had no knowledge of the Crown of Ferrughôr when you found her at Whitespear Head?'

'She spoke only of the work of Illana, Sire. I saw no sign in her that she sought for anything else.'

'And the shadowfay have found no part of it there?'

'None yet, Sire,' Merrech nodded again. 'It may be that the Lautun part was taken by the *noghru* of the Black Mountains, after Illana fell. The shadowfay have sent word to their kinsmen in the west to hunt for it.'

'If Illana had it at all,' Rhydden scowled. He had to move round on the couch, to shift the weight of the necklace on his chest.

'These Northerners from Radbrodal come sooner than expected,' he said. 'We like not the thought of their coming too close to our city of Lautun. Have them sent east toward Ellanguan, but let the Envoy Hakhutt come on to appear before us.'

'And what of the Southers, Sire?' Merrech prompted.

Rhydden scowled again. 'Send word to Baelar in Ellanguan. Have the Souther troops stand down from the guard at once, and out of the city before sunset tomorrow. Let them march south along the road, if there are not ships enough to bear them. Rinnekh should not have defied us by keeping them there so long.'

'Your Rinnekh was no match for the subtlety of T'Loi,' said Merrech. 'Nor, it would appear, did His Highness' Destrier foresee how T'Loi would turn the burning of the Kelmaar School to his own advantage.'

'Either that,' said Rhydden, 'or like your High Councillor Sollonaal they are making their own bid for power. Let Rinnekh and T'Loi come hither, to make answer before us and before the Court. Sollonaal can bring them. We trust that Baelar may still be relied upon to see the removal of the Southers from Ellanguan.'

'He will do so or die, Highness.'

'Good.' Rhydden knocked back the rest of his wine, and brightened again. The hooded Archmage fetched the crystal jug.

'There remains the question of the Souther armies along the Galloppi River, Sire,' Merrech's voice purred as he poured the wine. 'To garrison them at the Braedun *commanderie* was one matter; to give them free rein to settle elsewhere is to risk letting His Highness' own lands fall into the God-King's hands. The Court Noble shows wisdom in voicing its concern.'

'And you question our wisdom in commanding it?' Rhydden countered.

'For once I would add my voice to theirs. That alone should give His Highness cause for thought.'

'We have thought on it,' the Emperor snapped. 'But our time is running short. The K'tarim are our allies, and we need them in a position of strength. We have less than a twelvenight before the moon is full. Everything must be ready for when the Master returns.'

'Of course, Sire,' Merrech bowed. 'Erkal Dortrean is still down there. Should he stay, or be summoned to Court?'

Rhydden twirled his goblet slowly, studying the shadowed patterns of the cut crystal through the pale golden wine.

'We can no longer trust Dortrean to serve us,' he said. 'Erkal let the Vengru off too lightly at Khôrland, and left T'Loi too strong a force of men in Ellanguan. He has allowed certain priests of Braedun to remain at their *commanderie* when all should now be gone. He worked closely with the Magi in Arrandin, and now we hear that High Councillor Rhysana has been to Telbray to speak with his son Kellarn.'

'Then should he be brought hither, Sire?'

'No,' said Rhydden. 'Have him killed. But tell the K'tarim to do it discreetly – we would not have the *Aeshta* Orders spreading word of his death just yet. Those of Braedun who remain at their *commanderie* should be required to leave or be taken captive. And then let Kellarn be summoned to Court.'

'And Karlena, Sire?' Merrech ventured.

'Not yet,' the Emperor smiled. 'Her children, and her children's children, should die before her. We want her to be the last.'

In the early evening the Earl of Dortrean sat down to a simple supper in his borrowed chambers. Father Enghlar and Sir Rowan – two of the older members of the Braedun Order who had stayed behind in the *commanderie* – had come up to join him. Kierran of Arrand and Father Dharagh, the *noghr* priest of Fire, also sat at the table with them.

Kierran fiddled restlessly with a soft skinned peach, glancing out through the open window. They had been given chambers high up in one of the eight white towers of the old *commanderie* keep, looking east toward the falls of the Galloppi River and the upper end of the valley. The green hills beyond were still in bright sunlight beneath a pale, hazy sky, and the sultry heat of the afternoon lingered even in their shadowed chambers. The weight and heat of the mailshirt beneath his Arrand surcoat only added to his discomfort.

They had gone armed since their arrival here two days before – Kierran with his sword and the *noghr* with his axe – and he had badgered Erkal until he had agreed to carry a knife for his own defence. In truth, the Earl had not needed much persuading. In happier times, none of them would have thought to bear weapons while guests within the hallowed walls of an *Aeshta* monastery. But with unknown Southers around every corner, and with the memory of their unwanted visitor on the eve of their departure from the Steward's palace in Ellanguan, they could ill afford to take any chances.

The welcome presence of Boldrin of Levrin had not lasted for long. Before the end of the first day the holy knight had said his farewells and ridden away east toward Arrandin, taking a score or more of the *commanderie* folk with him. The handful that now remained, like Father Enghlar and Sir Rowan, kept quietly to themselves, as reserved in their dealings with Erkal as with the Souther leaders. Sir Rowan was one of the older knights of Braedun, grey haired and dark eyed, and seemed to be responsible for answering any of the problems brought by the nearby villagers – usually with Erkal's advice. Father Enghlar had been introduced to them as the Master of the Temple, and seemed mostly intent on the welfare of the holy places within the *commanderie* itself. He was more or less of an age with the Earl, though his rounded build and wandering manner put Kierran more in mind of a bumble bee. Neither of them, Kierran thought, would stand much chance in the face of a direct challenge from the Souther leader Talarkan. And though Boldrin had told them that there were others of the Braedun Order nearby, none had so far made themselves known to the Earl during his tours of inspection around the valley.

Erkal had discovered little more of the Souther chain of command, which – as he had admitted privately to Kierran – gave him some cause for concern. The lesser folk of the *ilionin* served themselves, as was their wont, under the guise of running errands for the more powerful Souther nations who were paying them. T'Loi's people of the Su'lorim were under the command of a likeable captain named Nadan, who was settled in the outer buildings of the *commanderie* with a sizeable number of his own men. Nadan was courteous and competent, and worked well with Sir Rowan of Braedun to maintain a general measure of peace and harmony between the Southers and the village folk; but he ranked below Talarkan of the K'tarim. The Su'lorim had also at least three priests of the God-King with them, who were housed in a golden pavilion down on the meadowlands well to the south of the *commanderie* hill. Kierran had met the three briefly on the second morning of his stay here when they were presented to the Earl's party, clad all in white with sashes of deep cinnamon silk and veils across their faces. They were treated with honour by all the Souther people who came near them; yet whether they had any real say in the command of the gathered armies was as yet impossible to fathom.

Thus, so far as they knew, it was the K'tarim who had the greatest strength here, and the Most Worthy Talarkan who spoke on their behalf. Father Dharagh had found out by asking that Talarkan's brother stood very high in the favour of the present God-King, which seemed to be the main reason for his role as commander; and thus it might be hazarded that his orders came from the court of the God-King beyond the sea, rather than from Ambassador T'Loi in Ellanguan. The Most Worthy and a score or more of his captains had taken over the greater part of the *commanderie* keep, each with their own train of guards and attendants and slaves; and it was they who provided the food for Erkal's table now that the Braedun people were gone, so the fare was sparse and to Souther taste. Kierran had carefully avoided the spiced meats and suspicious looking kettle broths, but his stomach was beginning to tire of the sweet southern fruits and the coarse, heavy bread.

He set down his peach half eaten on the table. Dharagh was trying to lift the mood by regaling their Braedun hosts with tales of the feasts of his childhood home, where succulent meats and berries were wrapped in golden pastries by the cunning fingers of pretty dwarven maidens. Father Enghlar, who had eaten scarcely more than Kierran, had tears in his eyes as he listened.

Dharagh's tale was interrupted by a knock at the outer door, and the Most Worthy Talarkan strode in. He was followed by four of his bodyguards, clad in their black trimmed with murrey and gold, and the two mastiff hounds on tight leashes. There was also another man with them whom Kierran had not seen before, clad in ochre robes.

The five at the table rose to their feet. The chamber seemed suddenly very crowded.

'Your pardon, your Grace,' said Talarkan bowing briefly. 'There is news from your Emperor. If the priests would leave us?'

Erkal exchanged glances with Enghlar and Rowan, and nodded. The two men bowed and made their way out past the Souther guards.

'Your work here is ended,' Talarkan went on, as Rowan reached the doorway. 'Your Emperor commands your return to his palace.'

'I must go where my Emperor commands,' Erkal replied evenly.

From what Kierran could see and hear, there seemed to be other guards waiting on the landing outside to lead Rowan and Enghlar away. The sultry air of the chamber grew thick with danger. He stepped back around the long table on the window side, keeping himself between the Southers and the Earl. Father Dharagh did the same upon the other side, to his right. One of the Southers closed the door.

'Your pardon, Most Worthy,' said Erkal, 'but it seems to me that a message from the Emperor of Lautun should be brought by one of his own envoys. If there be one come hither from Lautun, I wish to speak with him.'

Talarkan smiled. 'I speak here for Rhydden Lautun.'

'You seem to speak for a lot of people,' Dharagh muttered; 'whether they wish it or not.'

The tall Souther laughed, and the pale blue gem danced and glittered upon his brow. 'Three days you have been here,' he mocked, 'and still you are deaf and blind. I have served your Emperor in my own lands since the days of S'Taran, who came before T'Loi, in the days of the God-King Ascended. Who else would he choose to command here? Not that trained ape Nadan, or the veiled priests of the God-King Among Us.'

'That's a lie,' Kierran burst out. But he had a sickening fear that it was true.

'His Highness did not see fit to tell us of this,' Erkal amended. 'I shall need to speak with Master Enghlar, Most Worthy. The Braedun ship that carried us here is long gone.'

'One of our own ships will bear you,' said Talarkan easily. 'Rather, he who we name Sikhatis here will place your faces on three of our own people, who will take ship this night.' He nodded to the Souther in ochre robes, who stood just behind to his left.

Sikhatis, Kierran now saw, was nearly as tall as Talarkan himself; but he was gaunt and haggard, and looked a good deal older. His robes were covered with swirled symbols of black and gold, and he wore a long-panelled leather cap like a scribe's, sewn with tiny jewels. The hair and beard beneath were snow white, dyed with streaks of fiery red, and his eyes glittered black and spiteful as a weasel's. There was a tattoo on his left cheek like a horse's skull, with a long mane curling up and around on to his brow, which stirred an uneasy memory at the back of Kierran's mind. He had heard childhood tales of wicked sorcerers of the South, but he had never met one before face to face. He did not like the feel of the man at all.

'Alas, that ship will founder when she leaves the river for the open sea,' Talarkan went on, 'and all on board her shall be lost. Your bodies will not be found.'

'Indeed?' said Dharagh, readying his axe. Kierran drew his own sword.

'This is madness,' said Erkal calmly. 'His Highness would not cast aside so powerful a playing piece as the Earl of a House Ancient – not without a gain to match the loss. Are we to be held hostage in secret? Or is Ambassador T'Loi to be forfeit also?'

'You are no more of worth to your Emperor,' said Talarkan;

'so you have no value to us. His Grace must prepare to meet his gods.'

'At least spare the boy,' said Erkal. 'The Emperor has no quarrel with him, and he is a proven warrior and will serve well in battle. And do not bring a curse upon your house by slaying an anointed priest.'

'They'll get more than a curse if they try,' said the *noghr*.

'Enough,' said Talarkan, signalling to his men.

The four guards rushed them, letting the hounds run free. Kierran kicked a chair beneath the legs of one man. He went down, taking the nearest dog with him, his weapon skittering across the stone floor past Kierran's feet. Then he brought down his sword upon another, robbing him of his curved blade and the use of his hand as he clove through the man's wrist. The Souther screamed as he fell against the wall.

There was another scream as Dharagh plied his axe. The *noghr* was shouting something in his own tongue.

The shadows in the chamber had grown sharp, and there was a brightness of magic around where the sorcerer Sikhatis stood. But he was too far away for Kierran to reach. The young Lord barged past the guard still trying to free himself from the chair, and launched himself at Talarkan. The hound came bounding beside him.

Talarkan was waiting with a barbed blade of white steel. He turned Kierran's blow with disdainful ease, stepping aside to let the boy's own speed carry him headlong to the floor. Kierran lost sight of him as he fell. He rolled and stood up again to get his bearings.

One of the Southers was groping sideways along the wall toward the door, his face bloodied and ruined by Dharagh's axe. The *noghr* hewed at the legs of another, shattering the knee as he took him down. Talarkan was heading toward Erkal.

Sikhatis pointed at the Earl and spoke three words in a deep, grating voice. Erkal gasped and staggered, as though struck a blow to the stomach, and then uttered a breathless cry. Talarkan was nearly upon him.

'No!' Kierran shouted, running forward and up on to the table, trying to get there first. The *noghr* sprang the other way, calling the hounds to him as he bore down upon the sorcerer.

Pewter and glass smashed and clattered around Kierran's feet. The last guard left standing swung at him with a chair. Kierran swerved aside to dodge the blow, and came down off the table to land on the man with the shattered knee. There was a burst of red fire behind him, and a dizzying shriek seared the air. The hounds yipped and howled.

Talarkan punched down with the barbed blade, plunging it deep into Erkal's chest. There was far too little blood. And then Kierran reached them.

The Souther ripped the blade from the Earl's sagging body with near inhuman strength. He moved too slowly. Kierran swung round his sword to strike him in the lower back. The grey steel clove sheer through the black silk of the panelled tunic, and cut deep through the Souther's spine. Talarkan arched backward with a cry, crumpled and fell, cracking his dark head against another chair as he went down. His smeared blade steamed and hissed as it tumbled to the floor.

The Southers who could still move were fleeing. The one with the ruined face had already gone, leaving the door open behind him. A black reek of smoke billowed up from Sikhatis' lifeless body.

Kierran knelt down beside the fallen Earl, knowing that he was too late. There was a wide and ragged wound in his chest, but too little blood flowed out; and the flesh inside had a pale greyness to it. His handsome face was a stretched, distorted mask, like that of a man hanged.

'Help me to block the door,' said the *noghr*. 'Quick! Before there are more of them.'

'We cannot get shut in,' Kierran said mechanically.

The heat and smoke caught in his throat, and made his eyes water. He was not yet ready for grief. He could not imagine how he would tell Kellarn.

'We shall not,' said the dwarf. 'But nor can we fight our way out. I have another plan.' He tugged gently at Kierran's shoulder.

They carried the long table between them and overturned it against the outer door, heedless of where the food and dishes fell. The man with the shattered knee had stopped trying to drag himself across the floor and simply lay where he was, moaning and cursing. Kierran saw that Sikhatis' jewelled cap and skull had been cloven in two like a cracked walnut.

'The bastard son of a stoat had some sort of rebuking spell on him when he died,' Dharagh muttered. 'Damned near took my beard off.'

'Erkal—' Kierran faltered.

'I know,' said the *noghr*. 'We shall take him with us. Now run and grab our things, while I make ready.'

Kierran forced his legs to obey, dragging himself through the other doorway into their shared bedchamber. They had brought little enough with them, and most of it was still stowed in their one pair of saddlebags. Father Dharagh had only his simple pack. Erkal had said from the first that they should be prepared to leave swiftly.

He tarried briefly, gathering a few more of their belongings that were scattered around the room, until the *noghr* called to him to make haste. Then he picked up the saddlebags and pack and went out. The sight that greeted him in the outer chamber made him drop what he was holding.

A huge serpent of Fire reared up before the blockaded door, its spreading wings spanning a third of the vault overhead. Before it, dwarfed indeed by the size and splendour of the creature, Father Dharagh stood wreathed in crimson and violet flame. The Souther man lay whimpering in terror, the smell of his emptied bowels now adding to the reek upon the air.

'This is a messenger of holy Hýriel,' the *noghr* explained calmly. 'She will grant us passage through the Realm of Fire.'

The boy will not endure the flame, the serpent's thought echoed around them, rich and deep.

'That can be mended,' said Dharagh, coming over toward Kierran. The young Lord shrank back a little, in spite of himself.

The *noghr* smiled and made a sign of *Aeshta* blessing between them. Then he took Kierran by the hands, and the flames ran up over his arms and furled around him from head to toe. There was a coolness to the flames' touch, and a thrill of freshness, which was not at all what he had expected. Kierran found that he could breathe more easily.

'I can manage the bags,' Dharagh told him. 'But you shall have to carry the Earl.'

'Is it far?' Kierran asked. He did not know how far he could carry a full grown man unaided.

There was a loud bang against the outer door, and an answering flash of red fire around its frame.

'The way begins here,' Dharagh answered, picking up the bags. 'And in the Realm of Fire it is strength of will, not strength of arm, that will sustain you.'

'But will the Fire not harm him?'

'My power protects the living,' said the *noghr*. 'He has gone now beyond all help or harm. But we shall not leave him here.'

Kierran went over to gather up Erkal's ruined body. He was less heavy than he had feared. He glanced once in hatred at the fallen Talarkan, and then at the whimpering guard. There was another bang at the door, and the sound of angry voices.

'What about them?' he asked, picking his way toward the *noghr*.

They are mine, said the serpent's voice. *Come now*.

She curled up her tail and caught it between her jaws. A great disc of scarlet flame sprang to life within the ring of her body. Whether through the serpent's power or the protection of the *noghr*, Kierran could feel no heat from it; but it was like gazing into a furnace, or the hottest part of a smithy forge, so that his eyes were dazzled by the fierce brightness.

There was a louder crash from beyond the door, and the great wings beat upon the air.

'Let us leave this place,' said Dharagh, stepping over the scaled threshold of the serpent's body and vanishing into the flames.

Kierran hefted Erkal's weight in his arms, ducked his head against the brightness, and followed after him.

Chapter Twelve

The summer evening was fading toward twilight when Kellarn crossed the fords below the Tungit Isle. The heads of the Black Mountains were veiled in clouded mists, smouldering here and there in memory of the vanished sun, and the lands between the mountains and the river lay under a pall of shadow. The double peak of the Twin Watchers stood pale against a deepening sky. Kellarn shivered in the cooler river breeze.

They had left Telbray the day before, riding east around the borders of the woods, taking the route most favoured by the merchants and travellers of the Six Kingdoms. The way was a little longer, and their pace had been slower with the heat of the day. Kellarn had taken off his mailshirt when they reached the safety of Dortrean lands, preferring the cooler comfort of a simple shirt. Mellin Carfinn had borrowed his spare shirt and breeches; and even Corollin had shed her leather tunic, for once favouring comfort over self discipline. The horses had suffered patiently, grateful of shaded rest whenever it was offered to them. There had been no urgent need to press the pace. There had been no trouble along the way.

They had not seen the Guardian again, yet it had seemed to Kellarn that he could sense the quiet strength of her presence at rest everywhere along the eaves of the Telbray Woods. It was within the slow pulse of the life of the trees themselves, and nestling hidden among the undergrowth; and in the flight of the birds among the branches, and rumoured in the hazy brightness of the air. It also seemed to Kellarn that his own senses had grown keener since his meeting with the Guardian, that he should be able to see such things at all. But when he had said so to Corollin, early that morning, she had replied only that if he would go eating silver moon apples and journeying to the Realms of the Dead, he could hardly expect to remain unchanged.

'Besides,' she added, 'the pulse of the life of Earth flows strong within Telbray Woods. You can almost feel it throbbing.'

Kellarn grinned broadly.

'Don't start,' she warned, forestalling his cheeky comment. His attempt to look innocent failed to fool her.

Nevertheless, as they left the woods behind and made for the old causeway, Kellarn's heightened awareness of the world around him remained. He felt like a small boy again, on a holiday outing, gazing at each new thing with wonder and delight. Their quest for the artefact of the old Kings was nearly done, with all the promise of new hope that came with it, and the troubles of the imperial Court and the shadow of war seemed far away. As they rode further north he began to look ahead for the Flaming Woods, hoping even to catch a glimpse of Firinaakr, the red-golden dragon who dwelt there. But by the time that they drew level with the trees on its southern borders the sun was already well down in the western sky, and the brightness dazzled him.

They forded the grey waters below the rocky cliffs of the Tungit Isle, Kellarn's bay horse Rúnfyr staying calm and biddable as he had been throughout the day. A shout went up from the island, and a man in a red tunic waved from the clifftop and disappeared among the pine trees.

'No chance of sneaking in quietly now,' said Mellin, as she came up on to the western shore beside him. 'And look! Someone has already crossed over to meet us.' She grinned at Kellarn, teasing.

'Some two,' Corollin corrected. 'A man and a *noghr*. Not your steward Markhûl, I think. I do not remember seeing any *noghru* at the Sun Temple before.'

'They come down to visit from the mountains,' said Mellin easily. 'Father Torriearn earned their friendship.'

Kellarn was only half listening, intent on the two figures ahead as they rode toward them. They were standing at the near end of the shallow ford which linked the island to the mainland shore. The man was tall and slim with long dark hair, clad in a pale grey shirt and breeches, and barefoot upon the grass. The *noghr* stood two paces behind him, taller than most of his kind, in a surcoat of fiery red and with an axe beneath his belt. The cool breeze from the river seemed suddenly chill.

'That's Kierran of Arrand,' said Kellarn.

'Kierran?' Mellin echoed. 'What in the world is he doing here?'

'Perhaps he brings word from your father,' said Corollin.

'No,' said Kellarn quietly. He slowed Rúnfyr to a halt, and dismounted. The women drew rein just ahead of him.

'You two go on,' he told them. 'Mîsha – take Rúnfyr, would you? I need to speak with Kierran alone.'

Corollin looked doubtful. Mellin came back to take the reins from him.

'We could wait here,' Corollin offered.

Kellarn looked around. Kierran and the *noghr* – Father Dharagh, he remembered – were barely a stone's throw distant. Already there were more people coming down from the temple hill at the farther end of the isle, and gathering to meet them on the grassy shore before the stables.

'We'll deal with them, Collie-dog,' Mellin told him, following his gaze. 'Come and find us, when you want us.'

She nudged Wynborn forward, nodding with her yellow gold head for Corollin to go first. The horses moved on at a walk. Kellarn followed more slowly on foot.

Kierran came along the shore to meet him halfway, and they stood facing one another at arm's length. Kierran's face was pale, and his eyes reddened from recent tears. No further words were needed. Kellarn knew his friend. Kierran would not have left Kellarn's father in danger. If his tidings were good, he would have ridden out to greet them. For him to tarry here weeping could mean only one thing.

'Col,' Kierran faltered, his voice roughened in his throat.

'How?' Kellarn asked simply.

Kierran's face went even paler. 'You know?' he managed.

'Of course I know, now, you idiot,' Kellarn returned. 'Just look at you! But how did it happen?'

'The Southers, at Braedun,' said Kierran. 'I tried to stop them. They had a sorcerer – and some bastard of the K'tarim for a leader.'

'A sorcerer,' said Kellarn quickly, remembering his brother's death. 'Did they summon a demon?'

'No.' Kierran shoook his head. 'He burned from within, I think. Some devilry of Fire. Father Dharagh could tell you. I should have stopped them, I was too slow. Too bloody stupid.'

'Why?' Kellarn demanded. 'Why now? What had he done? What could they gain?'

'Rhydden commanded it. He said he had no more use for him. Talarkan served him – the Souther leader – served the Emperor, I mean. I killed him. I should have stopped him. I should have seen it coming.'

'We all saw it coming,' said Kellarn, through gritted teeth. 'First Solban, now my da. I should never have left him.'

'You had to,' said Kierran. 'I didn't. I didn't leave him. It's my fault.'

'No it's not,' Kellarn snapped.

It was Rhydden's fault. Rhydden who had had his brother killed. Rhydden who had commanded the Souther leader – though what that might mean about the Emperor's relationship with the Southers, Kellarn could only begin to guess. And those guesses were deeply disturbing.

His own emptiness numbed him – whether through shock, or because the shock had already been half expected. What worried him more at that moment was to see his friend so wretched. To have Kierran standing there, head bowed, heaping blame after blame upon himself, was just what Rhydden would have wanted.

'How is it your fault?' he demanded, shoving him.

'I should have saved him,' said Kierran, in a small voice. 'I failed you.'

'How is it your fault?' Kellarn repeated, shoving him harder toward the river bank.

'I tried.' Kierran's voice gathered strength. 'I am not the swordsman you are.'

'You fight well enough,' Kellarn countered, pushing him again. 'Or you used to. Was your head so far up your Souther lover-boy's arse that you didn't see what he was doing?'

Kierran gave a choking cry and pushed him back, the colour returning rapidly to his face. They glared at one another for a long moment, and then sprang forward. The two of them went down tumbling and wrestling upon the grass.

'Should we not do something?' Corollin ventured.

The two women had drawn rein on the near side of the ford, and were waiting with Father Dharagh. The *noghr* had confirmed their guess about the news.

'No,' said Mellin. 'Let them slug it out. It may do little to heal the grief, but even a little helps. At heart, they are friends.'

'Both now are fatherless,' said Dharagh.

'And Kellarn is now Earl,' said Mellin. 'Or shall be, when he is presented to the Scholars of Blood Law in Lautun and swears his oath of fealty to the Emperor.'

'That will not be easy for him,' said Corollin.

'It never is, for any of us,' said Mellin. 'And I doubt that he has given it much thought at all. Like me he was raised as a younger child, expecting only to serve below the Head of his House. To become Head himself, and with no overlord to stand between him and the very Emperor whom he blames for his plight, is no easy change to suffer. He will need all our help – though whether he will accept it is another matter. We shall have to give him time.'

'That may be something that we have not left to give,' said Corollin.

The tussle did not last long. Kierran had the slight advantage of height and weight, but Kellarn was the stronger and more slippery to grasp; and neither of their hearts was really in it. In the end Kellarn let himself be rolled on to his back, with Kierran kneeling astride him and leaning forward to pin his arms to the ground. They looked at one another, breathing heavily.

'I tried, Col,' Kierran told him. 'I really did.'

'I know,' said Kellarn. 'I'm glad that you were with him. I'm glad that you are here now, with me.'

He shifted his hips a little beneath Kierran's weight. Kierran stroked his wrist with one finger. They looked at one another, and smiled. And then they remembered where they were.

'The priests will be waiting,' said Kierran, sliding back and off him. Kellarn rolled to his feet.

'Did you bring him here?' he asked.

'No,' said Kierran. 'Dharagh brought us here through the Realm of Fire. I carried his body into the flames, and he had his Rite of Burning there. We did not leave him for the Southers. Talarkan and the sorcerer are dead.'

Kellarn nodded in silence. They walked along the shore together, to where Dharagh and the women were waiting for them.

'My heart grieves for your loss, my Lord,' said the *noghr*. 'Your father was a most worthy man.'

'He was honoured by your friendship,' said Kellarn. 'Thank you.'

He did not know what else to say. He could now see more than a score of people gathered on the island shore, most of them clad in white or red, all waiting to greet him in the fading light.

'The moon fay Tinûkenil is here,' Mellin told him; 'and some of his friends, I think.'

She led the way across the ford, now riding the spirited Rúnfyr. Corollin went behind on Mistwise, with Father Dharagh on Wynborn's broad chestnut back. Kellarn and Kierran brought up the rear on foot.

Mellin Carfinn seemed to contrive to make the crowd scatter even as she reached the island shore. She had the horses led away to the stables, and knights bowing and withdrawing, and herself engaged the silver white figure of the moon fay and led him off toward the temple with more than half a dozen people accompanying them. By the time that Kellarn waded ashore, barefoot with his boots in his hand, only Holy Father Ûrsîn and two of the lesser priests were still waiting to intercept him. He braced himself to greet them, bowing in reply to their kindly words of welcome and sorrow.

'We have sent word to the Lady Ellaïn at the White Manor,' Ûrsîn told him in his quiet, homely voice. 'We have also sent two of our brethren to the imperial Court, to speak with the Lord Valhaes. We thought that Valhaes himself should break the news to your Lady mother, in your absence. I trust that we have not presumed too far, Your Grace?'

Kellarn shook his head. He had not yet thought about his mother or his sister, or how safe either of them might now be. His mother, at least, knew better than he how to protect herself at Court; and Rhysana would no doubt be keeping an eye on her. But Ûrsîn's words had struck home another fact of his father's death, which he had avoided until now.

'I am not yet truly *Your Grace*,' he told the priest. 'Not until the Scholars of Blood Law acknowledge my formal claim before the Court Noble. But tomorrow I shall play the Earl, and we shall speak further. For tonight I am weary and wish to rest.'

'Of course, my Lord,' Ûrsîn bowed. 'We have prepared such simple rooms and fare as we have, for your welcome.'

Kellarn shook his head again. 'You honour me, Holy Father. But I am not ready to pass through your temple doors. Not yet

– not in my present mood, I mean. For tonight I shall sleep on the Dragonrest, beneath the trees.'

'My Lord?' said Ûrsîn doubtfully.

'You can bring food and blankets to the edge of the trees, if you would,' said Kierran. 'I can fetch them in.'

Ûrsîn looked hardly comforted.

'If I may stay with you?' Kierran added, turning to Kellarn.

Kellarn gave in, and smiled as he nodded. Then he bowed to the priests and turned away, with Kierran following behind him.

Kellarn ate little and spoke less while Kierran told him the full tale of his father's death; and then he slept deeply for several hours, lulled by the gentle roar of the river waters below. When he awoke the rosy light of dawn was already stealing between the pine trees, and the blackbirds were tuning their whistles in the branches overhead. Kierran was sleeping at his back, with one arm wrapped around him beneath their shared blankets.

Kellarn snuggled back against him, grateful for the warmth in the chill dew of the morning air. He laced his fingers between Kierran's, listening to the birds and the water and the rumour of the breeze, and enjoying the quiet stillness of the moment. And then presently the light grew stronger beyond the pine trees, and the faint sound of singing drifted down from the temple as the priests began their day.

He crept out carefully from beneath the blankets, and climbed down the rocks to the water's edge to relieve himself. The eastern sky was now fiery gold, with ranks of clouds gathering away beyond the grassy hills, promising rain to come.

When he climbed back up, Kierran was awake. Kellarn padded over and sat down beside him, wriggling his legs beneath the blanket again. Kierran propped himself up on one elbow.

'Are you ready to face the priests yet?' he asked.

Kellarn made a face. He was not sure that he would ever be ready. He would just have to brace himself to do it.

'We've a while yet,' he said.

Kierran chuckled softly.

'I need you to understand,' said Kellarn. 'When I pass through the temple doors, many things may change. Or at least, my life *has* changed; and when I go in there I must face up to it.'

'I know,' said Kierran.

Kellarn looked up at the rough bark of the trees. When he had been here before there had been things about Lo-Khuma and the Emperor that he had avoided telling the priests, for fear that they might act in haste, and for fear of what they might expect from him. But now his father was dead, and all the bars had been found; and the Guardian had said that he should seek help from the Sun Temple, when the hour was ripe. It seemed that that hour was at hand. He must take up the burden of care for all Dortrean. And when the Sun priests were told – as they must surely be told – of the bars and the Enemy, and of the role of the Emperor, it might push them to the brink of civil war. And then there was his own oath of vengeance, to which Rhydden must make answer.

'There are other things I must do,' he said, 'about the demon captain and the Emperor. We may be at war with Lautun very soon.'

'After last night, I already am,' Kierran told him. 'Where you go, I shall follow.'

'I cannot ask you to follow,' said Kellarn.

'You don't have to,' said Kierran. 'Sun and Moon, Col, don't send me away.' He rested one hand on Kellarn's shoulder, pleading.

Kellarn looked at him and smiled. 'I don't suppose I could if I tried,' he said. 'What kind of leader does that make me?'

'The best loved, I think,' Kierran grinned.

It was Mellin Carfinn who came to find them some time later, clad again in her dark green riding habit, and with the golden glory of her newly washed hair still damp and tied back into a single fat braid. She took a long look at the pair of them, as if to reassure herself that they were indeed ready to face the demands of a busy day; and then she led them up to the temple building and through empty passages and halls to the guest chambers prepared for them, where they could bathe and dress and make themselves presentable. Perhaps because of Mellin's familiar ease, or the absence of anyone to meet them, it was not at all the formal ordeal that Kellarn had expected. Everyone else, Mellin told them, was already at breakfast in the main dining hall downstairs; and they could come and find them when they were ready.

By the time that they emerged from their bath – freshly scrubbed and shaved, and scattering water liberally as they chased each other around the room – the formal breakfast must have ended; for a tray had been brought up for them piled with milk rolls and fruit and cheese, and a tall jug of tea, and a covered dish filled with piping hot sausages. There were also fresh shirts and breeches of soft white linen laid out for them to wear, and black sashes of mourning.

It was thus well over an hour later before they made their way down the stone stair and out into a cloistered yard to the west of the main temple. The yard was paved in black stone, with several bench seats of golden oak set back along the pillared walkways, so that Kellarn guessed that it must be used for sparring practice rather than more bookish lessons or quiet contemplation. But at this hour of the day there were only a few of the younger members of the Order there, cleaning the flagstones with large wooden scrubbing brushes. He discovered by asking that Holy Father Ûrsîn was now in the teaching halls. The Lady Mellin and the other guests had gone down to the stables, or to the old watchtower on the eastern shore.

Between them they found their way back to the south lobby with its steps and floors of precious stones, and then out on to the grassy hillside. The storm clouds had marched closer, filling the eastern sky, and the air was growing sluggish and thick. Mellin was down by the stables, with Wynborn already saddled to ride. A broad-faced man clad in green and black was talking with her, running tanned fingers through his curling mane of auburn hair as he spoke. Kellarn recognised him as Gwydion, the borderlander from Vansa, who had no doubt come here with the moon fay Tinûkenil.

'There you are,' Mellin called, catching sight of them. 'I did not want to leave without seeing you again.'

Kellarn felt suddenly lost. He hurried down the slope.

'You're leaving?' he said.

'There is little more that I can do here,' she told him sensibly. 'I shall go to the White Manor.'

'I thought you were coming to Court,' said Kierran.

Mellin shook her yellow gold head. 'Not while Rhydden lives,' she said. 'He robbed me of a father and brother too, remember. And Kellarn would only worry about me if I were there. But Ellaïn may have need of me, with Jared away. And with Erkal gone, Dortrean's debts and duties shall have to be reckoned.'

'Markhûl can see to that,' Kellarn objected.

'I dare say that he can,' she returned. 'But Ellaïn will fret. You have not the time to go to her now, but I have. And then Carfinn needs me, and I must play my part in Dortrean's defence. I feel the need to work, just now,' she added.

'But you will not ride there alone?' asked Kierran.

'This is my home ground,' Mellin smiled. 'But no, two of the temple knights will come with me. Ûrsîn insisted upon it.'

'Good,' said Kellarn.

Mellin looked up at Kierran. 'I needn't tell you to look after Collie for me,' she said. 'But take care of yourself as well. If the gods are kind, we shall all meet again.'

She patted Kellarn's stomach with the back of her hand. 'Corollin was looking for you,' she told him. 'Don't stay to watch me leave – that would be too much like saying goodbye.' She handed Wynborn's reins to Gwydion, and went away into the timbered stable block. Gwydion looked at Kellarn, and shrugged.

Apart from the stable workers and themselves, there seemed to be few other people outside the temple building. At the far end of the small western bay, close to the rocky rise of Dragonrest, two more of Tinûkenil's companions were sparring with wooden practice swords. Odhragh, the *noghr* from the Black Mountains, looked as though he would have been more comfortable wielding his black-bladed axe. The woman Skaramak, clad in close fitting tunic and breeches of dark charcoal grey, was putting him through his paces with the grit of a stern taskmaster.

Kierran tugged at Kellarn's elbow and pointed away to their left, where the low spur of the temple hill stretched down the eastern shore of the isle. Corollin had come out from the ruined walls of the old watchtower and was jogging down the slope toward them. They ran to meet her halfway.

'Tinûkenil is here,' she told them quietly, leading them back toward the tower. 'He has brought the Farodhí bar. He said that they found it in the Wood at the World's End, west beyond West.'

'We should never have thought to look for it there,' said Kellarn. 'Besides, the tale runs that no one comes back from there alive.'

'It seems that they did,' she said. Her face was as serious as ever.

'What bar is this?' Kierran demanded.

'I'll tell you later,' said Kellarn. 'But that makes only six. Where is the seventh bar?'

'That will be made clear to us when the hour comes,' said Tinûkenil, appearing in the open doorway ahead of them.

'I should have guessed it would be you,' said Kellarn.

The moon fay wrinkled his nose in question.

'You who found the bar, I mean,' Kellarn explained.

'Gwydion found it,' said Tinûkenil. 'I played a part. But come! There is one here whom you should meet.'

They followed him into the little paved court of the tower's base, still deep in shade at this early hour. The air was heady with the sweet scent of honeysuckle, and the softer musk of the holm oaks outside.

The Moon mage Dakhmaal was standing near the far wall, clad in black robes bordered with silver and holding a staff of white wood capped with silvery steel. He was somewhat short of stature, as were most of the folk of Farran, and his long brown hair was tied back. Though he was of an age with Rhysana and Torkhaal, and had now earned his own seat on the Council of Magi, Kellarn did not think that Rhysana knew him well. Dakhmaal was another of Tinûkenil's travelling companions, and had – or had had – the good will of Erkal Dortrean; but on the few occasions that they had met, Kellarn had always been slightly wary of him. That was in part because Dakhmaal was a mage, and particularly careful of his privacy. And also, though he was pleasant enough, there was an air of self interest about him that put Kellarn on his guard.

Sitting on the wooden bench, and standing as they came in, was a much older woman in a cloak and gown of dark blue. Her white hair was plaited into a crown about her head, soft and billowing as high cloud, and her skin seemed soft and delicate as wild white rose petals. The eyes that met Kellarn's were a bright cornflower blue, with the shadow of deep memory as unfathomable as the vault of the summer sky overhead. In spite of the frailty of age she carried herself as a great Lady; and Kellarn accepted her as such, and bowed.

'This is Linaelin, Honoured Priestess of Air from the monastery isle of Telúmachel,' the moon fay told him.

'Linaelin?' Kellarn nodded and then frowned, half remembering the name.

'Memory grasps toward the truth,' said the Lady, sitting herself down again. 'Ferrughôr's daughter of Hauchan am I, and my mother was Hirulin, daughter of Heruvor of Starmere. Well met, son of Dortrean.'

Kellarn's world staggered. He sank down on one knee before her.

'Honoured Lady,' he stammered. 'High Queen of Hauchan's

line. How is it that you are here? I had thought that you were lost long ago, when Hauchan fell.'

'So I was,' she said. She reached forth pale fingers beneath his chin, and tilted his face up toward her. 'I was safely hidden for many years, until Tinûkenil found me and came to disturb my peace.'

There was gentle laughter in her face and voice, as though she had not really minded.

'Then the bars should come to you,' said Kellarn. 'They were not meant for us at all.' He fumbled for his pack, forgetting it was not with him.

'Perhaps, or perhaps not,' Linaelin said. 'In truth, son of Dortrean, heir of Khêltan, I never heard my father speak of them; and only in the last few days have I learned a little of their story. But now the Enemy returns, and these bars have been found, and Tinûkenil has brought me hither to offer such help as I may. It is only fitting that Ferrughôr's daughter should make amends where her father failed.'

She gestured for Kellarn to sit beside her. As he stood up he realised that Kierran had knelt with him, and was still staring at Linaelin as if in a dream. He tugged at his shoulder for him to rise. But instead Kierran shuffled round on the flagstones to sit at Kellarn's feet.

'But Ferrughôr did not fail,' said Corollin.

'Nor did he wholly succed,' Linaelin replied. 'And so the Enemy returns. My father was brave and generous of heart, and the gift of foresight was his, but he had not the wisdom of his years. Nor was he always willing to heed the counsel of others. When the great demon was overthrown, he and his brother Falladan made an end as they saw fit; and then they built their two cities of Hauchan and Ellanguan, while others were left with the work of driving back the evil that remained in the land.

'It was my father who called the first Court of Kings, where the rulers of the Six Kingdoms sat down together to forge the bonds of peace. Yet before I was born Falladan went away, leaving no heir to follow him, and the Kingdom of Ellanguan passed under stewardship. Then when my father's kinsman Llaruntôr, First King of the horselords of Lautun, grew envious of the growing wealth and power of Khêltan, my father was beguiled by his lies of danger and betrayal, and Hauchan did nothing to prevent Khêltan's fall. And when my father died, and Ellanguan rose against me because of my fay blood, the horselords of Lautun would not come to my help. So now Hauchan is long gone, and Cerrodhí and Farodh have fallen; and Ellanguan founders, and the line of Llaruntôr of Lautun is coming to an end. And now these bars of the First Kings are revealed and gathered together, and Ferrughôr's daughter must play her part to see them joined.'

'But when shall they be joined?' Kellarn asked. 'And how, if only six are here?'

'Tomorrow is Ochsha,' said Linaelin, 'the day of the week holy to Osîr and all the Lords of the *Aeshtar*. There is one other who must come, when all is made ready. But as the gods are kind, tomorrow we shall see all seven joined as one.'

'You said that Llaruntôr lied,' said Corollin. 'We have seen the buried ruins of Khêltan; and there the sword of Ferrughôr, which Kellarn had, perished in a demon's heart. Is it not true that Halgan, First King of Khêltan, fell into evil ways, and that his kingdom was destroyed by avenging fire?'

'He did not turn to evil,' Tinûkenil answered her. 'It was the envy of Lautun that brought about his kingdom's fall.'

'The feud between Dortrean and Lautun stretches back even to the days of the Bright Alliance,' Linaelin told Kellarn. 'But now this Sun Temple is rebuilt, and it is you as the heir of Halgan who have gathered the bars together. It is meet that I, as Ferrughôr's daughter, should serve you in this. I shall listen to your wisdom.'

'But I have no great wisdom,' Kellarn protested. 'It was more Corollin's quest than mine.'

'There will be many who wish to speak,' said Corollin. 'But

perhaps we should wait until all seven bars are here. You said that there was someone else still to come.'

'At least one,' said Tinûkenil; 'and perhaps others with him. All shall soon be made clear.'

Rhysana was with her kinsmen at the Telún manor house when the summons to the High Council reached her. The call came not from Prime Councillor Ellen herself, but in the person of Hrugaar. His fair face was unusually pale.

'Erkal Dortrean is missing,' he told her. 'We fear that he may be dead.'

The household had cleared away the noon meal, and Rhysana was sitting with Taillan on her lap. She hugged him close, until he squirmed and whined in protest.

'If we do not know that he is dead,' said Torkhaal, 'how do we know that he is missing?'

'Braedun,' said Rhysana.

Hrugaar nodded, saying no more.

They took their leave of Nereïs, and Torkhaal promised the twins that he would go riding with them another day. Taillan was tearful as they kissed him goodbye. They made the *leap* straight back to the Lautun College.

'I heard the news from Jared of Arrand,' Hrugaar told them, as they hurried into their apartment. Grey rain streaked the windows and filled the cloister garden outside. 'The story at Court is that Erkal took ship from the Braedun *commanderie* at dawn, and is coming to Lautun. But the Sun priests from Dortrean have brought word to Torreghal Valhaes that Erkal was betrayed, and that the *noghr* priest Dharagh fled to the Tungit Isle taking Kierran of Arrand with him. Valhaes told Karlena and Jared, as they are Erkal's close kin.'

'Kierran would not leave Erkal willingly,' said Rhysana. 'I fear that there is little hope.'

'Might he be held captive on board ship, or at the *commanderie*?' Torkhaal asked.

'The Sun priests say that Erkal's body was burned in the

Realm of Fire,' said Hrugaar sadly. 'Or so Jared was told by Valhaes. The priests of Torollen may leap to swift answers, yet my heart tells me that in this they speak the truth.'

Rhysana sat down on the edge of the bed. Torkhaal knelt behind her to hold her. She pushed him gently away. There would be time later for grief.

'We must get dressed for the Council,' she said.

Ellen was there before them when they reached the assembly chamber, enthroned on her Prime Councillor's seat. Ferghaal and Asharka of Braedun sat silent in the grey light. The Archmage Morvaan came in just behind them, and then the hooded shadow of the Archmage Merrech; and then the elderly Trialmaster Ekraan, his blue and silver robes billowing around him in his own personal storm. No others of the High Council attended.

The tidings told in the assembly were no better. Ellen spoke to them mind to mind, by virtue of their High Council seats, as though perhaps she did not trust her own voice to hold.

They heard from Ferghaal that those of the Braedun Order who remained at the *commanderie* were now confined to their cells, but that they had been told that Erkal Dortrean was taking ship for Lautun. Ferghaal had no word from outside to confirm whether the Earl had left. There was rumour, however, that the Southers there were now in conflict among themselves, and that their leadership had changed. The Archmage Merrech allowed that the Emperor had heard as much, and that it seemed that the captain of the K'tarim had been slain. The K'tarim blamed the *Aeshta* priests, or else the commanders of the Su'lorim. The Emperor had found no ground to doubt the word of the Southers that Erkal had taken ship.

The priests of Hýriel say that Dortrean was slain by the Southers, and that his body was returned to the flames, said Ellen.

'I have no word of that,' Merrech replied. 'If Dortrean is gone, his loss shall be felt by all. But the priests of Hýriel have no love for the Southers, and may speak too swiftly in judgement. Perhaps the priests of Braedun are better placed to learn what truth there may be in this tale.'

'I shall send word to the *commanderie*,' Ferghaal promised.

No one mentioned Kierran's flight to the Sun Temple, or questioned what might have happened to him or to Father Dharagh if Erkal had been slain. Their distrust of the Archmage Merrech held them to silence.

'Does not Ambassador T'Loi have command over the Southers down there?' demanded Ekraan. 'Should he not be required to make answer?'

T'Loi has been summoned to Court, said Ellen. *Even now he makes ready his ship to sail from Ellanguan. The Steward Rinnekh will escort him to Lautun.*

'I thought that T'Loi's ship had been seized by the Emperor,' said Ferghaal.

He has another, Ellen returned. *It is said that he will bring all his people with him from the city. I do not like the feel of it at all. But at least Ellanguan may rest easier with him gone.*

T'Loi or Rinnekh? said Hrugaar.

Ellen turned her head to frown at him.

'What of Sollonaal and the Ellanguan Magi?' asked Asharka.

Mage Councillor Drengriis tells me that they continue the work of the College, said Ellen. *How far Rinnekh will trust Sollonaal in his absence I do not know. We must hope that they still have the best interests of Ellanguan at heart. Archmage Morvaan?*

'There is news from Arrandin, Prime Councillor,' he nodded. 'The Easterner loremaster Aghaira returned to the city this morning.'

'Kata Aghaira is here?' cried Hrugaar. 'Then must the return of the Enemy be very nigh.'

Rhysana felt her own heartbeat pounding in sudden fear.

'Not quite yet, High Councillor Hrugaar,' Morvaan assured him calmly. 'Aghaira came to the Arrand palace, but she has gone away again – for now.

'Less welcome did she receive from Bradhor than she enjoyed in the days of The Arrand, his father. Well, the war has soured

Bradhor toward the East, I suppose. But I managed to speak with her before she left. The High Clan Chieftain is beset with troubles of his own, in far off Kara Ko-Daighru, as more of the clans fall under the sway of the servants of the demon Lo-Khuma. He is sending an envoy to Lautun, with assurance of his own good will, and Aghaira herself will return in the envoy's train. But there is also rumour that a new muster of armies is being prepared at Ko-Vengru, in defiance of the High Clan Chieftain; and those armies may march on our borders before the waning of the year. So Kata Aghaira has gone away again, to learn what else she may.'

'That is no more than we had already feared,' said Torkhaal.

'Aghaira sends this Council her most honoured greetings,' Morvaan added. He looked as if he were about to say something else, but then thought the better of it.

'Lord Bradhor will have to come to Court soon,' said Ferghaal, 'to make his claim before the Scholars of Blood Law and to swear his oath of fealty as the new Arrand.'

'He will come,' said Morvaan. 'He has very kindly allowed that I should bring him, nearer the time. His brother Lord Jared has spoken with the Scholars.'

'The Dortrean boy should come too, if what we hear is true,' said Ekraan wearily.

I shall speak with the Countess of Dortrean, said Ellen. *Karlena will not thank the Council for bearing her such tidings. But Erkal honoured us with his trust in the defence of Arrandin, and we shall not betray that trust now.*

'Karlena must choose her own path,' said Asharka. 'She is more skilled than any of us in the ways of the Court Noble, to know how Dortrean should respond.'

Of course, Ellen nodded. *But in the matter of her husband she has a right to know what we know; and better that she hear it from us than from the whispered rumours among the Empress' household.*

The assembly came to an end, and the shimmer of Ellen's warding spell faded from the encircling wall. The ebon doors swung open.

'Rhysana?' the voice of the Archmage Merrech whispered around her. Rhysana looked up. The other magi had begun to rise, but the shadow of the Toad Archmage still lingered in the alcove of his seat on the far side of the chamber. Since no one else seemed aware that he had spoken, she guessed that he had addressed her mind to mind. Her first instinct was to leave her High Council seat, to move beyond his reach. But he would simply follow her, or corner her later when she was alone. She would be safer here, with her husband and the other magi around.

In light of this debate, Merrech sent to her, *His Highness may consider commanding Kellarn of Dortrean to come to Court. It is known to us that you have met with him in Telbray of late.*

I spoke with him while I was there, she allowed. *I have no certain knowledge where he now might be.*

I trust that you will oblige His Highness by finding him, Merrech sneered.

What part did you play in Erkal's death? she countered.

I was but the messenger, he returned smoothly. *I regret the loss of the Earl, and my own counsel was against it. But it was a point that I had to yield, in the hope of gaining greater influence with the Emperor in matters of far more dire consequence.*

Such as the return of Lo-Khuma?

His Highness believes that he can control the Enemy when he comes, Merrech told her, *and bind him to his own will, to prevent him from destroying all.*

Rhysana felt herself trembling in her seat. The enormity of Rhydden's folly, and of his arrogance, appalled her. And how far had Merrech followed him – or led him – down this road?

'And hence the *Argument of Command*,' she murmured.

That is what His Highness wants, he sent.

There was an irony to the thought, begging the question of what the Toad Archmage himself might intend. Rhysana did not waste her failing energy in trying to ask him. For one thing, that would have been a direct attack upon his personal privacy and he would only have answered her in riddles. For another, she could guess that he would serve his beloved Emperor as best he could, but seek to save his own hide in the end.

'You look far too pale,' said Torkhaal, taking hold of her hand.

She looked past him, but Merrech's High Council seat was now empty.

'It is the dim light,' she said, bracing herself to stand. 'Or perhaps the shock is catching up with me. I am well enough.'

Kellarn was sitting among the pine trees of Dragonrest again when Rhysana reached the Tungit Isle. The sun had run down to the peaks of the Black Mountains, racing ahead of the stormclouds, and the western sky was kindling to red-golden flame. The wind had died away, and a stillness spread over the isle as the temple made ready for the sunset rite at the end of a busy day.

'Magi,' said Kierran, touching Kellarn's shoulder and pointing across the river.

A little way up the mainland shore, dwarfed beneath the high double peaks of the Twin Watchers, three robed figures were making their way down across the grass toward the ford. Two of them had pale fair hair, shining softly in the evening light. The third carried a large rucksack.

'Not just magi – Rhysana,' said Kellarn, scrambling to his feet; 'and Hrugaar and Torkhaal with her. Come on!'

'Are they the ones we are waiting for?' asked Kierran hopefully, springing after him.

'No,' Kellarn answered. 'Tinûkenil knows that we know them. He would have said. They are probably here about my father.'

They jogged and skidded their way down the rocky rise, and splashed across the ford to reach the mainland shore. The three magi were approaching at a gentler pace, so the two of them had time to catch their breath again before they arrived. Hrugaar waved to them in greeting.

Kellarn had had a day of visitors and meetings, beginning with the wonder of Linaelin, High Queen of fallen Hauchan, and then the more familiar company of Tinûkenil and his friends. There had been more formal talks with Ûrsîn and the priests and knights of the Sun Temple, and the rather solemn splendour of the noon rite in which Father Dharagh had been invited to play a part; and as the afternoon wore on he had met once again with the tall Lord Rinnakhal Dhûlann, and with commanders of the household guards of Valhaes and Tarágin, who had been summoned to the Tungit Isle by riders from the Temple to pay homage to Kellarn and to speak of the defence of his Earldom of Dortrean.

Though he supposed that the Sun priests meant well enough, and were mindful of the perils of the days to come, Kellarn felt that he would have liked a little more time before all this was thrust upon him – time at least to see the seven bars joined, so that their chief hope against Lo-Khuma would be prepared and his mind left free to turn to other things. Thus when the magi appeared, part of his purpose in crossing the ford to meet them was to stand on his own ground of Dortrean, outside of the Sun priests' domain. There was also the fact that if they brought news from the Court, he wanted to hear it alone. And above either of these, he suddenly realised that he was both pleased and relieved to see them.

He bowed as they came down to join him, and then hugged Hrugaar hard and kissed Rhysana more gently. Torkhaal grasped his arm warmly in friendship.

'I am glad that Kierran is with you,' said Rhysana, studying the pair of them. 'You look better than I might have hoped.'

'But you look a little pale,' Kellarn told her. 'Is there other news from Court.'

'No worse than you have heard,' she said; 'and nothing that can not wait a while longer. I am just a little tired and sad. The Archmage Ellen has spoken with your mother, and we have come now from the White Manor. Mellin is there with Ellaïn – but then of course you would know that.'

'Can you stay until tomorrow?' he asked, leading the way to the ford. 'I should like you to be here. And we may need Torkhaal's help.'

'What will happen tomorrow?' asked Hrugaar.

Rhysana glanced at her husband, and then smiled in understanding. 'If the Sun priests will have us,' she said.

'You can have our room,' Kierran offered. 'Collie and I don't mind.'

Rhysana paused to fix him with her gaze, and raised one delicate eyebrow. 'I should not dream of it, my Lord,' she told him.

She turned her attention back to the ford, taking a slow, deep breath. A silvery mist gathered over the surface of the water, arching up into a slender bridge spanning from shore to isle. To Kellarn's eyes it looked delicate as gossamer brushed with morning dew; but Rhysana gave a faint smile of satisfaction, and walked out across the bridge as calmly as though it were carved of solid rock. Hrugaar sprang lightly after her.

Kierran and Kellarn exchanged glances. Torkhaal gave a deep chuckle, and waded through the water with his dark green robes hitched up above his knees. Kellarn followed behind him gratefully. Kierran hesitated, then climbed up on to Rhysana's misty bridge.

'Serve you right if you fall in,' Kellarn told him.

'Is the Sun Temple so short of space for guests?' asked Hrugaar when they reached the other side. By now a handful of people were coming down the hill to greet them.

'You don't know the half of it, Ru,' Kellarn sighed. 'But yes. Tinûkenil and all his friends are here.'

'And Corollin, and Father Dharagh,' added Kierran.

'You may want to invoke the Magi's right to privacy,' said Kellarn. 'The gods know, I wish that I could myself.'

They all went to the sunset rite in the Temple of Torollen, with its golden dome and white walls and twelve pillars of deep red jasper, and then to supper in the panelled dining hall to the east of the temple cloister. During the meal, Kellarn discovered that the rooms prepared for him were in what Father Torriearn had originally intended to be a tower for the use of magi; after which he renewed Kierran's offer to Rhysana that she should stay there, and insisted until she gave in. He and Kierran then fetched their own clothes and gear, and took themselves off to Dragonrest armed with lantern and blankets. Father Ûrsîn saw the wisdom in letting them go without making further protest.

The clouds had all fled to the mountain heights, now silvered beneath the waxing moon, and the sky above the pine trees was clear and filled with stars. The two of them stretched out beneath their shared blankets, glad of the peace after the chatter of the dining hall. Kierran was soon fast asleep; but Kellarn lay awake for a while, listening to the gurgle of the river and the whisper of the pines, and the soft sound of his friend's breathing beside him.

When he awoke the sky had grown pale, and the land around them was stirring into life. Kierran was awake and leaning over him, stroking the hair back from his face with gentle fingers. Kellarn rolled on to his back and grinned up at him, and reached up to stroke Kierran's cheek. Then the memory of the day's work returned to him.

'I am glad you are here,' he said seriously.

'I know,' said Kierran, stroking his stomach beneath the blankets. Then he gave Kellarn a wry smile and sat up. 'This is a holy place,' he said.

'I know,' said Kellarn, stretching the night stiffness from his joints and sitting up beside him. 'I know. But we shall not stay here forever.'

He sought and found Kierran's hand, and took it between his own; and together they sat and looked west toward the mountains, watching as the first light of dawn kindled the snowy peaks of the Twin Watchers to flame.

'What is that?' Kellarn asked presently.

A white mist was flowing down from the north, hugging

close around the feet of the Twin Watchers. It drew swiftly nearer, growing brighter and clearer, travelling at impossible speed; and then it wheeled to the east, heading straight toward them, and Kellarn laughed aloud in delight.

'Look! Oh look!' he cried, scrambling to his feet and dragging Kierran up with him.

A herd of white horses, more than a hundred strong, came galloping joyfully toward them – the white horses of Dortrean tales, who ushered down the snows from the mountains. They had the beauty of snow under sunlight, and the fluid movement of light upon water; and at their head was a great stallion, all rose-gold and bright as the sun, with a single golden horn upon his brow.

The unicorn cleared the ford in a single leap, and galloped on toward the rising sun. The white horses ran behind him, their bright hooves skimming across the water. And then they were gone, leaving the two men alone in the stillness.

'What have we seen?' breathed Kierran at last. He was still holding Kellarn's hand.

'It is a sign,' said a warm voice from behind them. 'The Son of the Sun returns.'

Kellarn knew before he turned that it was a dragon's voice. There could be no mistaking. He kept a firm hold of Kierran's hand, for his friend's sake rather than his own.

'Firinaakr,' he said.

A huge head rested on the ground between the pine trees, with scales of deep red-gold and eyes like living rubies. Behind the head a long neck swept up into a gold ridged back, with great wings folded close. He was nowhere as large as Ilunâtor, and far more solid, and his breath was like a warm bath around them.

'So it would seem,' said the dragon. 'I am sorry to be such a disappointment.'

Kellarn was about to stammer in protest. But then he caught the gleam of mischief in Firinaakr's eye, and instead he laughed.

'Who is the Son of the Sun?' he asked.

'Now there is a question,' said the dragon. 'The unicorn goes by that name, as does Torriearn who rebuilt the Sun Temple; and Halgan was so called, who was priest and King in Khêltan. All three you shall see here today.'

'Halgan?' Kellarn gasped. 'But I thought he was dead – or worse.'

'That is his own tale to tell,' said Firinaakr. He blinked once, and then vanished from their sight. A moment later there was a rush of warm air, and then the buffeting of great wings taking flight.

Kierran was shaking hard, and his eyes were wide and bright. He sat down upon the ground. Kellarn fetched the blankets and wrapped them around him.

'I'm all right,' Kierran managed. 'Just—'

Kellarn nodded, rubbing his back and holding him until the trembling passed. The dawn light grew brighter around them.

'I suppose we should get dressed,' he said presently.

Kierran hummed his agreement. 'What did you mean about Halgan being dead, *or worse*?' he asked.

'That is the tale in Dortrean,' said Kellarn. 'It is told that he turned to evil ways, and brought about the fall of Khêltan; and that his spirit still waits deep beneath the mountains, until evil men call upon him to return. So he is called *Halgan the Chill* in children's tales, as a figure of fear and terror.'

'But Tinûkenil said that was a lie of Lautun,' said Kierran; 'and Holy Mother Linaelin agreed with him.'

'I know,' said Kellarn. 'Perhaps—'

He broke off, listening. Somewhere in the distance a horn call was sounding. Faint at first but clear, it grew and took life upon the air until the very stones of Dragonrest were singing. It was a call of triumph, and a call to battle.

'That's not coming from the temple,' said Kierran.

Kellarn tugged on his boots and shirt, and caught up his sword and shield. Kierran was right behind him. They ran through the trees and leaped down the rocky slope toward the shadowed bay.

Tinûkenil was there ahead of them, shining silver-white as he strode easily toward the shore. Corollin was at his side, half running to keep up with him, in her robes of strawberry gold that were the gift of Starmere. The High Queen Linaelin came down the winding path at a gentler pace behind, resting on the arm of a dark haired woman all in blue; and behind her came Holy Father Ursîn and other folk from the Sun Temple.

Kellarn and Kierran ran on, slowing to a halt as they joined the moon fay at the water's edge. Corollin glanced pointedly at Kellarn's untucked shirt, and then turned to look out across the river.

Three people came down to the mainland shore at the far end of the ford. In the lead was a young woman robed in midnight blue, with long golden curls that shimmered and danced in the dawn light. Behind her came two men, walking side by side. The taller of the two Kellarn guessed to be Father Torriearn, with his long white tunic bordered in gold, and breeches and cloak of bright scarlet. A long sword hung from his belt, and also a curved ox-horn bound with rings of gold upon a scarlet cord.

The second man was in full panelled robes that were more like the magi's, all of the soft rose-gold hue of sunstone, and in his hands he carried a great sword in a crimson sheath. He was half a head shorter than either Torriearn or the girl, and of stockier build, and looked to be comfortably into his middle years; yet there was something in the air about him which told Kellarn that this must be Halgan.

The young woman stood barefoot on the bank and raised her arms in greeting to Tinûkenil. The moon fay spread his arms wide in answer. They stood in silence like that for several heartbeats; and then Kellarn realised that the girl was singing, her voice as soft and liquid as the waters between them.

Tinûkenil was singing too, in the elven tongue, his fair voice blending with hers like moonlight rippling upon the waves.

Kellarn stepped back, sensing that magic was stirring. The waters of the Grey River slowed in their course, and then drew back, shaping themselves into a low crested wall like a wave curl poised to fall. The rocky river bed of the ford ran dry.

Then Torriearn and Halgan walked forward together, passing dry-shod across to the isle. The woman came three steps behind them; and the wave curl broke and flowed on again at her heels.

Tinûkenil bowed to the two men as they mounted the shore.

'I am glad to see that Ilumarin has nursed you back to health,' he said to Torriearn.

The Sun priest made a low squawking sound, like a disgruntled falcon. The moon fay shook his silver head, and laughed.

He led them first to meet Corollin. Torriearn gave a slight bow as she was presented, and favoured her with a sign of *Aeshta* blessing. But Halgan bowed very low, pressing his sword sheath to his forehead.

'And so we meet again,' he said in a warm, mellow voice.

He had his back to Kellarn at this point, but the look of startled wonder was clear on Corollin's face. Halgan chuckled softly as he stood up.

'Forgive me,' he said. 'Our meeting was in my past, but for you it is yet to come. Time is such a curious thing, is it not?'

If he had startled Corollin before, he had now lost her. She nodded and smiled faintly, but Kellarn recognised the look. She had turned in upon herself, weighing what she had heard in her mind until she could find a way to understand it.

'And this is Ilumarin, Chosen Priestess of Haëstren,' said Tinûkenil, beckoning forward the golden haired woman who had brought them.

Someone tickled Kellarn's back. He turned his head, and saw Hrugaar's fair face grinning down at him. Rhysana and Torkhaal were not there, but he saw that Linaelin was standing close by. Her white hair was mostly hidden by her hood, but her pale face was clear and serene in the morning light. The dark haired woman with her was one of Tinûkenil's companions, the Lady Skaramak.

Halgan had handed his sword to Torriearn, and now came striding toward them. Kellarn began to bow, suddenly aware of how scruffy he must appear. But Halgan came to a halt before Linaelin, and the two of them stood and studied one another. The Lady Skaramak stepped back.

Seen from close to, Halgan had the look of a kindly and rather homely man. His soft grey-blue eyes were a blend of laughter and common sense, set in a rounded face as much wrinkled with merriment as with care. Though the sense of veiled power within him was almost staggering, it was nothing terrible. He was a man that others would find easy to like.

There was a silence for some time while Halgan stood before Linaelin, as though much passed between them without words. But then at last she parted her cloak and began to kneel before him. He moved swiftly to stop her, going down on one knee himself and taking her hand between his own. There were tears in his eyes as he kissed her pale fingers.

'My Honoured Queen,' he said. 'You have borne the burden of the long years, while I have slept in peace. Now my heart sings to see you again, for we were ever friends.'

'The tongues of men are changed,' said Linaelin in her clear voice, 'yet your words are still as sweet.'

'The Kingdoms of men are changed,' said Halgan, 'and much is now strange to me. I shall have need of your wisdom to guide me.'

Linaelin laughed, and gestured for him to rise. Then she sent a private smile to Kellarn, and led Halgan away toward the waiting line of priests and knights on the temple hill.

IV FIRE EXALTED

Chapter Thirteen

Firinaakr had been right that Kellarn would see the Sons of the Sun, but it proved to be little more than that that morning. Compared to a legendary priest of Fire and the Sun from the dawn of the Six Kingdoms – and to the return of Father Torriearn – the heir apparent of Dortrean was small wonder and old news. Thus while Halgan toured the Sun Temple discussing the war with the Easterners and the problems with the Southers, the preparations against the return of Lo-Khuma and the doings of the other *Aeshta* Orders, Kellarn had the somewhat mixed relief of being left in peace to watch and listen. Torriearn divided his time between the priests and Tinûkenil and his friends. The priestess Ilumarin kept quietly to the background, when she was to be seen at all. The three magi also watched quietly from the lists, though Torkhaal seemed to be keeping the inquisitive Hrugaar on a tight leash. Corollin and Kierran stayed quietly with Kellarn, waiting with measured patience.

It was not until the afternoon that Torriearn led them aside to the great round tower of the chapter house, where they gathered to join the white metal bars. The circular chamber was lined with the same white stone as the temple, with a single central pillar supporting the great vault; but the floor was covered with glazed tiles of red and gold, each showing the ancient symbol of Fire and the Sun. A long bench seat of white stone ran the full circuit of the outer wall, with a line of round archways let in to the wall to make individual seats. Higher up to the north and west was a row of arched windows, bright with jewelled glass of many colours, and filled with the likenesses of all manner of birds and beasts.

There were far more people gathered there than Kellarn might have hoped, so that what he had come to regard as their private quest seemed now to be a matter for many others. He felt less than comfortable with the change. Apart from Corollin and himself – now washed and much more presentable – the three magi were there at his invitation. He had thought it only fair, since Rhysana had found the Lautun bar. Halgan and Linaelin were there, since they knew better than any about the magic of the First Kings. Torriearn was with Halgan, and the priestess Ilumarin was with Linaelin. Tinûkenil was there with all the rest of his companions; and then Kierran was there, because he had begged Kellarn to let him come, and he had brought the *noghr* priest Dharagh with him.

He was more aware of the crowd because they were all standing together in the northern part of the room. A table had been set there, spread with a plain white cloth, and a chair had been brought in for Linaelin. At Halgan's request Kellarn brought out the five bars, and laid them slowly side by side along the table; and then Tinûkenil brought out the sixth and set it beside them – the bar of Farodh, with a deep green stone and the likeness of flying swans carved upon either side.

'There are still only six,' said Corollin. 'Who holds the seventh?' She looked at Tinûkenil, and then Halgan.

'Six were commanded by Ferrughôr,' Halgan told her. 'One from each of the Kings. But we foresaw that one more would be needed – one not of the Kings, shall we say – which would bind all together in unity, and wield the power that they gave.

'It was I who had the seventh part made; and for long it was held by the wizards of the *noghru* in their hidden tower, high among the snows of the Black Mountains. It had no gem of its own like the six, but only an empty space; for the one who would wield it must bring their own key to the power.'

'But who has it now?' Kellarn demanded.

Tinûkenil and his friends were exchanging glances and whispering to one another. Corollin wove her way past them to stand before the Moon mage Dakhmaal.

'I think that you know where it is,' she told him.

'I have been to the mage tower of the dwarves,' he allowed; 'and so have others with me.'

Corollin gazed at him steadily. Dakhmaal gazed straight back.

'I believe that you have it,' she said. 'Now, for the love of the Moon Maiden and for all that we hold dear, I beg you to fetch it for us, so that the circle of seven may be complete.'

The Moon mage reached into the shadow of his robes and brought out the final bar.

'I'm sorry,' he said, with a wry grin of apology. 'The old dwarf who gave it to me was most particular that I should be asked for it directly.'

Corollin bowed in thanks as she took it from him, and then hurried back to the table. Kellarn leaned forward to see. The seventh bar was just as Halgan had described it – like to the other six, but with a round hollow where the stone should have been and no markings of any kind.

'Then who has the gem for this bar?' he asked.

He looked to Linaelin, but she smiled and shook her white head. Kellarn turned back to Halgan.

'I was the King of Khêltan,' Halgan told him. 'This bar, as you call it, was for one not of the Kings. It is your friend Corollin who holds the key.'

'I have no gemstone such as this,' said Corollin. 'Nor have I the powers of the First Kings.'

'A stone might be found,' offered Tinûkenil.

'You have a focus for your power, do you not?' said Halgan, staying the moon fay with one raised hand.

'My staff,' said Corollin doubtfully.

'And what else?' Halgan pursued. 'Something small and round – a *talisman*, perhaps, about your neck?'

Corollin and Kellarn exchanged glances. 'The pendant of Zedron,' she said softly. 'Of course.'

The finding of that pendant had brought about her first meeting with Kellarn, and it had been the cause of their first run in with the priests of Lo-Khuma in the Holleth Woods north of Arrandin. It had been the key to finding the forgotten lore of Zedron; and Corollin believed that it had been made for her by Zedron himself.

She reached beneath her strawberry gold robes, and brought out the pendant on its silver chain. It was made of a soft grey metal like pewter, a filigree of spirals and whorls within an encircling ring. The size of it looked more or less right to fit the seventh bar.

The three magi pressed forward behind Kellarn to see. Tinûkenil and his friends were alert and watchful. Kellarn had the uneasy feeling that something else was happening.

'Hold on,' he said, taking Corollin by the wrist. 'How did you know about that?'

The servants of Lo-Khuma had shown an interest in the pendant from the first; and the name of the Enemy among the Fay was *Atallakûr*, the Beautiful Deceiver. Though Halgan seemed wise and kind, and Linaelin and the moon fay held him innocent of great wrong, fifteen hundred years of dreadful legend cast a shadow in Kellarn's mind.

'We have met once before, in my past,' Halgan told him. 'On the eve of the fall of Khêltan, it was Corollin who came to save me.'

'She is the Hope of the *Syldhar*,' said Tinûkenil.

Corollin let go of the pendant and stared at him, her eyes wide and deep jasper blue. Kellarn felt his own heart leap at the sound of the name.

'It is time to take off the rings,' said Halgan. 'For their purpose is fulfilled, and the Crown and the Hope are here.'

He slipped a band of pale ivory from his finger, and placed

it in the centre of the table. Tinûkenil and Torriearn did the same; and other hands moved forward, until six rings all lay in a circle beside the white-metal bars.

And now other people stood around them in the white chapter chamber. They looked to be of Kellarn's height and age, young and fair of face, some male and some female. They were more like to humans than fay; yet there was a brightness of life about them, an *otherness*, which reminded Kellarn of something else. Five were in simple tunics of different colours, with bare arms and legs and feet. The sixth had a hooded robe of black, and her face was veiled.

'*Syldhalië*,' Corollin breathed.

'Even so,' said Halgan. 'When I came to Khêltan I met the *syldhar*, and set my feet upon a different path; and when my city fell they took me in. They offered me the gift to change my life – as Zedron did, and Ilumarin – to dwell in joy with them. But instead I asked them to lay me to sleep for all these long years, to wake again when the Enemy returned – to fight him, not to join him, Kellarn of Dortrean.'

'But why?' said Corollin. 'At one with the *syldhar*, could you not still have fought him?'

'Oh yes,' Halgan nodded. 'But the *syldhar* make their home in another Realm that borders the waking world. If the Enemy returns here, within the waking world, he could draw the veil between the Realms and drive them back. While I remain a mortal man, he can not so drive me away. And you are the heir of Zedron, with the lore that he learned from the *syldhar*; and you are also a mortal woman, and bound to the waking world while you live.'

'And what are the rings?' asked Corollin.

'We made them with Halgan,' answered one of the *syldhar*. He was clad in a tunic of sky blue, with short brown hair, and was standing closest to Torriearn. 'Six of us pledged ourselves to the rings, one for each of the Kingdoms of men; and we worked with those who wore them, to bring about this day.'

'I saw you,' said Kellarn, suddenly understanding. 'In a

dream, at Khôrland I think. You were with Tinû and Corollin, and the dragon was behind you.'

'We can not hide from one who has seen the dragon,' the *syldha* smiled at him. 'Your friend Corollin is the Hope of the *Syldhar*, but you are the Joy of Ilunâtor.'

Kellarn felt the blood rush to his cheeks. He wanted to laugh and to weep and to shout for joy at the very name. And yet he was deeply embarrassed, and wished that he could have been somewhere else alone.

'You knew of the *syldhar*, and you never told me?' cried Corollin. But she had rounded on Tinûkenil, not Kellarn.

'You never asked,' said the moon fay.

'Which is just as well, knowing Tinû,' Gwydion laughed.

'The Fay have no fear of the truth,' said Tinûkenil calmly.

The *syldhar* had all vanished – almost, Kellarn thought, as though they were granting his wish to be left alone. The chapter chamber seemed dimmer by their absence, but scarcely less crowded.

'Perhaps now we should join the bars,' said Linaelin.

Halgan bowed to her. 'May I?' he asked Corollin.

Corollin looked at Kellarn. He nodded. Since Halgan had been alive at the time of their making, he clearly knew better than any of them what had to be done.

Halgan took the ivory rings from the table and handed them to Torriearn, then laid out the white metal bars in a circle – Ellanguan, Farodh, Lautun and Cerrodhí, Hauchan and Khêltan. The seventh bar completed the circle, on the side nearest to Corollin.

'When the Crown was first made,' he told them, 'it was thought that each of the Kings would bring their own part. Then they would join together their strength of will, and the Crown would be made whole. Alas, that can no longer be. Yet there are some here, I think, who may help us in this, in whom the gifts of the First Kings live on. I shall stand for Khêltan.'

'And I for Hauchan,' said Linaelin.

'The Moon mage Dakhmaal would be the best choice for Farodh,' said Halgan, 'if he is willing.'

Dakhmaal nodded, and came round the table to stand beside the Farodhí bar.

'Torkhaal managed something with the Lautun bar,' said Kellarn, 'and Rhysana found it.'

'I have not such gifts of the mind,' Rhysana demurred

'Let Torkhaal stand for Cerrodhí,' said Linaelin. 'The love of Earth is strong within him.'

'And Hrugaar for Ellanguan, if he will,' said Corollin. 'He has been my teacher and friend, and the ways of his mind are known to me.'

The two magi came forward, needing no second bidding. Hrugaar's face shone with delight as he took up his place between Dakhmaal and Corollin.

'There remains one other,' said Linaelin. 'Who shall stand for Lautun?'

There was silence in the chamber.

'Gwydion, perhaps?' Dakhmaal offered.

The borderlander exchanged glances with Tinûkenil, and shook his tawny head. 'Better not,' he said.

'Let Kellarn stand,' said Rhysana in her clear, sweet voice. 'It is his right.'

Kellarn looked at her in surprise. Everyone else seemed to be looking at him.

'This quest has been yours, as much as Corollin's,' Rhysana explained.

He had the feeling that there was something else, some other thought that she had not spoken. He wondered whether she was thinking of his oath of vengeance against Rhydden.

'I have not the gifts of the mind,' he said in his turn.

'That remains to be seen,' said Linaelin. 'Yet that is of little matter. There are others who can work the joining of minds, and we shall guide you. Your strength has helped to achieve this quest. I hold that the choice is good.'

Kellarn looked down at the bars, avoiding Linaelin's bright

eyes. He supposed that she was right. The bars – the Crown – had become so much a part of his life in the past year. Yet this was not how he had imagined their joining.

'Does it have to be Lautun?' he muttered, to no one in particular. He went to take up his place beside the table.

Corollin had used her gifts with him a few times before, and he had seen things as though looking through her eyes, so he had some small notion of what to expect. It was not the most comfortable prospect. Halgan made the seven of them hold hands in a circle, to begin with a physical bond. Everyone else went and sat down on the bench around the wall, to give them room to work.

Kellarn stood there for what seemed to be some time, holding himself ready for something to happen. He let his gaze drift down to the Lautun bar, all too aware of the powerful people standing around him, and feeling rather young and foolish by comparison. He would have liked to have had Corollin or Hrugaar beside him; but at least he had the comfort of Torkhaal's presence upon his left, warm and supportive. The Moon mage to his right held his hand firmly, imparting confidence, yet with a cooler and more elusive brightness.

What did not help was the soft strength of Torkhaal's fingers as they gently stroked his left hand. Kellarn's skin seemed to blossom beneath their touch, and the sensation was deeply arousing. He was finding it hard to focus; and increasingly aware of Torkhaal's *presence* beside him, and of Torkhaal's awareness of him. He tried to turn his attention elsewhere, to other people in the circle. And then Torkhaal was with him in his mind, and guiding him; and shielding his embarrassed thoughts from those around them with the impression of feathered wings.

His awareness of the circle had now changed. Beyond the warm shadow of Torkhaal's comfort, as secret and alive as the deep forest, the beauty and power of the High Queen Linaelin was bright and vast as the clear sky above the high mountains. Halgan shone as glorious and triumphant as the dawn. The wild salt freshness of the sea was with Hrugaar, the wideness of the ocean beneath a summer sky, and the laughter of the waves as they tumbled upon the shore. Dakhmaal had the pale glory of the waxing moon, at once present and remote, shadowed with violet and deep green; and there was a fathomless silence about him, overlaid with the rumour of hidden streams.

Amidst all these, Corollin seemed simply herself. But her blue jasper eyes looked right through him, almost painfully bright and sharp, and every part of her was radiant with life. It was as though he had only seen her sleeping, in all the time that he had known her, and now she was awake.

What everyone else might make of him, Kellarn did not know, and Torkhaal did not show him. Nor could he glimpse himself through other eyes. Each focused on a vision proper to the Kingdom of their bar; and Corollin nudged him gently back, reflecting an image of himself as in a mirror. He tried to think of the wide plains of Lautun, and the joy of the horses that galloped there. But it was not much good. And then Torkhaal prompted him to look down again at the Lautun bar, with its two carved horses circling the tawny yellow gemstone.

The stone, like Corollin, seemed closed to him, so that at first he saw only his own ghostly likeness masking the shadowed depths within. He tried to look past it into the heart of the jewel, and failed. But when he focused upon his own face, a burst of glittering light filled all his vision, dazzling him with flashes of silver and red and gold. He seemed to drift or fall for several moments in a world of whirling light. And then other hues and colours flowed around him, shrinking and steadying into a tall rainbowed column before his eyes; and at the base of the rainbow the seven bars were joined as one upon the snow white cloth, while all around held hands.

Kellarn was now more keenly aware of the gathered minds around him – the merriment of Hrugaar, and the wonder in Torkhaal's heart, and Linaelin's sense of achievement. But already the bonds were fading, and the rainbow pillar dimmed and blended into the coloured light from the western windows. Dakhmaal let go of his hand.

'Feel your feet upon the floor,' Torkhaal told Kellarn quietly. 'Walk up and down a little. You must return fully to the waking world.'

Kellarn squeezed his hand shyly in thanks, and then walked around the table. Linaelin's chair was being brought for her, and the other people in the chapter chamber rose and gathered round.

The Crown of the First Kings stood upon the table, a circlet of white metal with seven jewelled facets. Corollin's silver chain still lay on the cloth beside it, from when she had taken off her pendant. She was standing gazing at the crown, smiling at its simple beauty. Kellarn rested his hand on her shoulder, sharing the moment.

'Well, now that we have it,' said Torriearn, 'what do we do with it?'

'Destroy the demon,' said Skaramak.

'Corollin will use it against the demon,' Linaelin amended. 'We shall help her as we may.'

Torriearn shifted his tunic irritably.

'But how will she do so, Honoured Mother?' asked Rhysana, stepping forward at Kellarn's side. 'Has she yet the knowledge to master this power? Or is this something that you may teach her?'

Kellarn glanced at her. Fond as he had become of Rhysana, he wished that she could forget that she was on the Council for once. He supposed that she was only doing her duty, as she understood it, to ensure the proper control of power. And he had to admit that she was raising an important question.

'Corollin is master of the Crown,' Linaelin answered. 'That much now is clear. It will take what power she gives, and return it sevenfold and more, and focus it to her will. As with any tool, it may take a little time to tame it to the hand. Yet that is but a matter of self control, which she already has in good measure.'

'Then how can the Enemy be destroyed?' asked Corollin. 'Or can he only be defeated and banished once more? That is what the moon fay of Starmere seemed to think.'

'The Crown may help you there,' said Halgan. 'That was our hope. When the Enemy was overthrown at the cliffs you call The Steeps, the Kings Ferrughôr and Falladan joined hearts and minds and chased after his fleeing spirit. They were Air and Water, and he was Earth and Fire; and together they hounded him through the Realms, striving with him through strength of will until he was left empty and powerless. And when at last they could do no more, they returned to the waking world.

'In the years that followed, after Ferrughôr became King, he foresaw a time when the demon would also return. And it came to his mind then that had others been with him and his brother, drawing power from all of the Lords of the *Aeshtar* and not just Air and Water, then an end might have been made of the Enemy forever. So for that purpose he called together the Court of Kings and commanded the Crown to be made; so that when the Enemy came again he could be challenged with the strengths of all the great Lords of Life.'

'So I am to strive with him through strength of will,' said Corollin, 'guided by the lore of Zedron.'

'The lore of Zedron comes from the *syldhar*,' Halgan reminded her. 'And you are the Hope of the *Syldhar*.'

'I shall be there with my sword,' said Torriearn, 'and all the strength that Torollen grants me.'

'And so shall I, and many others,' said Halgan.

Corollin bowed in thanks, and picked up the Crown to study it more closely. Then she offered it to Kellarn. He took it from her slowly, half reverent and half fearful. It weighed strangely heavy in his hands, as the bars had done, but there seemed to be no feel of magic about it at all.

'The Crown is here,' said Hrugaar, 'but where and when will the Enemy return? Did Ferrughôr or the First Kings have foreknowledge of this? For no lore has been passed down to us.'

'He will come where a way is opened for him,' Linaelin answered. 'The Enemy has servants in many places.'

Halgan and Torriearn exchanged glances.

'The Lord of the Sun guards the thresholds between the Realms,' said Torriearn after a moment, 'and grants us great power over evil creatures from outside the waking world. The Sun Temple was raised to challenge the Enemy and draw his attention, in the hope that he would try to strike here before other places. We shall gather our strength here, watching for the moment of his return. Wherever he appears, we shall be ready to meet him. Remember we can travel very swiftly through the Realms when speed is needed.'

'All here are free to stay with us, if they so choose,' said Halgan.

Corollin looked at Kellarn. She suddenly looked as tired as he felt.

'We need to rest first, I think,' she said, 'before we do any choosing.'

'Not that I seem to have much choice at all,' said Kellarn, some time later.

The two of them had excused themselves from the gathering and gone down to sit in the shade of the holm oaks, near the old watchtower. Kierran was sprawled full length on the grass at Kellarn's side. The three magi had come to join them, bringing a tray piled with buttered tea cakes and tall jugs of crushed raspberry ice. Rhysana had just broken the news that the Emperor was summoning Kellarn to Court.

'There is always a choice,' she said, helping herself to another tea cake; 'even if all courses run ill. Besides, your mother counselled you to stay away from the imperial palace until you were fully prepared.'

'I don't know that I ever shall be, really,' said Kellarn. 'But things could only get worse if I stay away, and my mother is there. The quest for the Crown is over. I must deal with Rhydden now.'

'And how shall you deal with Rhydden, Col?' Corollin asked him.

'Challenge him before the Court Noble, I suppose,' he said. 'Him and his foul Archmage – and Rinnekh and the Southers, if they are there.'

'Rinnekh is sailing from Ellanguan,' said Hrugaar, 'and Ambassador T'Loi with him. They should reach the imperial palace soon.'

'Good,' said Kellarn. 'The Court Noble shall hear the full tale of the evils that they have done, and decide what to do with them.'

'I shall come with you,' said Kierran; 'and Father Dharagh will, too. We were with your father. We can tell the truth of what happened at Braedun.'

'You shall forgive my saying so,' said Torkhaal in his deep voice, 'but the Court Noble might not be persuaded.'

'Father Dharagh is a Chosen Priest of Hýriel,' Kierran protested.

'Which means that many of the imperial nobles would doubt his word,' Torkhaal returned. 'And too few of the Houses Noble these days favour the *noghru* so well as do Dortrean and the Arrands.'

'The Emperor will try to turn your tale against you,' said Rhysana. 'And remember, he has the argument of treason to fall back upon. Even were the Court Noble persuaded in their hearts of his guilt – as I do believe would be the case – they may be loth to act against him. And they will fear the turmoil of another interregnum, should Rhydden be removed without an heir apparent to follow him.'

'Are you telling me to leave Rhydden alone?' asked Kellarn.

The three magi looked at one another.

'No,' Rhysana answered. 'We are warning you not to rely on the strength of the Court Noble to support you.'

'What about the Council?' Kellarn countered.

'Some of us will support you,' she said, 'some will support the Emperor.'

'Prime Councillor Ellen says that Rhydden must be stopped,' Hrugaar added.

'How much have you told the Sun priests?' Rhysana asked in turn.

Kellarn ducked his head. 'They know that there are servants of the Enemy within the Emperor's household. But they will need all their strength for the Enemy's return, even with Corollin and the Crown. He may bring a whole army of demons with him, as he did before. I can not ask them to come with me now. This is my own oath of vengeance, which I must fulfil or die in the trying.'

'And what shall become of Dortrean if you fall?' asked Hrugaar.

Kellarn scowled. 'The Dortrean Houses are prepared to stand against Lautun,' he said. 'The Sun Temple and Mairdun will fight beside them. I have to see the Scholars of Blood Law anyway at the imperial palace, so I can confirm my heirs with them. The line will pass to Ellaïn's children.'

'Terrel and Korren,' Rhysana nodded.

'Then again,' he said, 'if the Enemy returns with his armies, there may be no Dortrean left to speak of.'

'Korren is an Arrand name, I think,' said Rhysana, taking the last tea cake, 'but whom was Terrel named after?'

Kellarn ruffled his hair, confused by her change of direction. But eccentricity was part of Rhysana's charm.

'One of the previous Earls of Dortrean,' he said, 'four of five generations back, I think. He married—'

Kellarn stopped short, remembering. Rhysana was nodding for him to go on.

'He married Mirren of Lautun,' he said slowly, 'oldest daughter of the Emperor Urzael. She would have been Empress, had Urzael not changed the Lautun Blood Laws.'

That was what his mother had tried to tell him, when she had told him to be mindful of Terrel – not just the safe succession of the Dortrean line, but a Dortrean claim to the imperial throne. He realised that Rhysana had known all along.

'Dortrean has Lautun blood?' demanded Kierran, sitting up beside him.

'I have spoken with one of our Scholars of Blood Law,' said Rhysana. 'The blood is less strong than in Rhydden's nearest living kinsmen of Lautun blood, in Vaulun; but they are only his distant cousins, and come from a lesser branch of the imperial line. Should Rhydden die without an heir, the Scholars would consider Dortrean to have a strong enough claim to make challenge.'

'Do you mean that Kellarn could be Emperor?' gasped Corollin.

'Or his nephews,' Rhysana nodded.

'They're my nephews too,' said Kierran excitedly. 'Dortrean and Arrand on the imperial throne. That would be revenge against Rhydden indeed!'

'Stop it! All of you!' Kellarn roared. 'In case you have forgotten, there may be no Six Kingdoms left at all very soon. I never wanted to be Earl, and I don't want to be Emperor. And I don't need my mother and the Magi and half the damned Court Noble interfering in my life.'

'Would you have Rhysana do nothing?' Corollin threw back at him. 'Or do you intend to deal with the Emperor, and his Archmage, and all the servants of the Enemy, single handed – not forgetting the shadowfay of course, and perhaps the Enemy himself?'

'Why not?' said Kellarn. 'Or is that your job, now that you have the Crown?'

There was an awkward silence. Kellarn suddenly felt too tired to argue, and even more than usually foolish.

'I'm sorry,' he said quietly. 'You know how much I hate the thought of being at Court.'

'You shall have us with you,' said Corollin.

Kierran handed him a bowl of raspberry ice.

'What about the Crown?' said Kellarn. 'The Emperor's Archmage has been searching for it.'

'There is a new danger there,' said Rhysana. 'His Eminence

has told me that Rhydden now thinks to control the demon Lo-Khuma when he comes.'

'What?' cried Kierran.

'He *told* you?' Corollin demanded.

Kellarn found that his mouth was hanging open.

'Has Rhydden gone mad?' he gasped. 'Or has the Archmage led him to this?'

'The Emperor is what Merrech made of him,' said Rhysana, 'for the most part. Yet when a wedge was driven between them for a while, a few years ago, we discovered that Rhydden grew worse left to his own devices. For better or worse, the Archmage Merrech still tries to control him. But I fear that his hold over Rhydden may be slipping.'

'But he could not use the Crown, could he?' said Corollin.

Rhysana hesitated for a moment. 'He would not have to,' she answered. 'He needs only to prevent you from using it. We can not let him take it from you.'

'Could you leave it here, with the priests?' asked Kierran.

'Not really,' said Corollin. 'I have yet to master the use of it, and that will take some time.'

'Perhaps you should stay here,' said Kellarn glumly.

'It would seem wise,' she agreed. 'Yet my heart tells against it. Will my father Morvaan be at Court?'

'Most likely, if you are there,' said Rhysana. 'Lord Bradhor makes less call upon his time than did The Arrand.'

'Bradhor is a bull-headed oaf,' Kierran snorted. 'Jared would have made a much better Head of House.'

'Tempt not the gods by saying so,' Torkhaal warned him.

Kellarn sipped from his bowl of melting ice. 'Where do you think the Enemy will return, Ru?' he asked.

Hrugaar gave a wry smile. 'Wherever his servants call him,' he replied.

Kellarn stared at him, waiting, until Hrugaar sighed and gave in.

'The Easterners are mustering again,' he said, 'but I do not think that they will bring him with them. We know that he has servants among the K'tarim. The *noghr* Dharagh told us that their sorcerer bore the mark of a horse's skull, like to the skull-headed demons that were seen at the siege of Arrandin, that of old were among the Enemy's most deadly servants.'

'Damn!' said Kierran. 'I knew that I should have recognised that tattoo. But the sorcerer is dead now. Dharagh killed him.'

'One is dead,' said Hrugaar, 'there may be others. They may try to bring the demon back at The Steeps, where Ferrughôr defeated him. That is one place that the *Aeshta* priests will be watching.'

'But you don't think it will be there,' said Kellarn. Hrugaar shook his head.

'The K'tarim leader was in Rhydden's service, until I killed him,' said Kierran. 'Who commands them now?'

The three magi looked at one another.

'One of T'Loi's captains, we believe,' Rhysana answered. 'But if that were the case, it seems likely that Rhydden will be seeking to regain control of them through another of his agents.'

'And if the Emperor wants to control the demon, The Steeps are a long way from Lautun,' said Corollin.

'The Sun priests believe that the Enemy is more likely to return beneath the Black Mountains,' Hrugaar went on. 'That is where Torriearn drove him back last year, and there are shadowfay waiting for him there; and from thence he can strike swiftly at this Sun Temple.

'There is also Illana's fortress of Whitespear Head, where we know that both the Toad Archmage and the shadowfay have been. That is a stronghold not easily taken, and in the heart of the Six Kingdoms.'

'*He rises in the heart; strength crumbles from the centre to the rim,*' Rhysana quoted. 'It does seem a more likely place than most.'

'That would be an embarrassment for the Council,' said Kierran.

'Torriearn is mindful of this,' said Hrugaar. 'That is but one more reason why he wishes to keep the strength of the Sun Temple within Dortrean, with Whitespear Head so near to the east.'

Kellarn twirled his bowl slowly between his hands, grateful of its coolness. He felt that they were all missing something. The Emperor wanted to control the Enemy when he came. The Sun priests wanted to draw him here. The Archmage Merrech had been to Whitespear Head. Perhaps the place was less important than who – who among the Enemy's servants would summon him? In the Realms of the Dead, it had been Tighaún who called upon him; and only the memory of Ilunâtor had saved Kellarn.

And then he remembered. In the Realms of the Dead, the Empress' brother Goshaún had told him. The Emperor himself would summon Lo-Khuma.

'Where would Rhydden choose?' he said aloud.

Someone else had been speaking, but he startled them all to silence. Rhysana seemed to grasp his thought quicker than the rest.

'Rhydden wants to control him,' she nodded. 'He will try to control when and where he comes. Whitespear Head could well be his best choice. It is warded by the strength of the High Council.'

'I need to get to Court,' said Kellarn. 'How soon is he likely to try?'

'The dark of the moon is when the servants of the Enemy are strongest,' said Torkhaal. 'That is still some weeks away.'

'And at the end of the Summer Court,' said Rhysana. 'That gives him time to prepare.'

'It gives us time to stop him,' said Kellarn.

'When do we leave?' asked Kierran.

'We must be going soon,' said Rhysana. 'You may come with us if you will. Or the priests can bring you when you are rested, if you prefer.'

'We shall come with you,' said Kellarn.

*   *   *

They gathered themselves together and went back to the temple building to fetch their belongings. Tinûkenil and his friends were in the south lobby, taking another look at the precious stones of the floor and steps. The High Queen Linaelin was sitting quietly beside the fountain pool.

'It's a bit colourful to my way of thinking,' Gwydion was saying as Kellarn came in.

'That's your problem,' said Father Torriearn.

'Gwydion thinks?' mused the *noghr* Odhragh, his eyebrows raised in surprise.

Tinûkenil turned and bowed to Kellarn's party. 'We were just coming to take our leave of you,' he told them.

'But I thought that you were to stay here, with Father Torriearn,' said Kellarn.

'The temple is fair,' said Tinûkenil, 'but I have another calling. The shadowfay are abroad in Fystenur, the great forest, and already the realm of Starmere has been assailed. I must go to my kinsmen.'

'But Starmere will be safe, will it not?' asked Corollin anxiously.

'Safe enough – for now,' he nodded. 'The power of the moon fay is still strong in Starmere, and the Nets are well woven to ward them.'

'Then why do you need to go there?' asked Kellarn.

Tinûkenil smiled. 'As in *sherunuresh*, there are many kinds of victory in this world. It is Heruvor's hope that some of the shadowfay may yet be saved; that there remains some spark of the life of the Fay – no matter how small and mean – within the empty shells of their being, which may be woken again. That is one reason why he has tarried so long in Starmere, on the borders of your mortal lands, because the shadowfay are close at hand beneath the Blue Mountains. It may be a small hope, yet I shall help him as I may. And since the shadowfay have long served the Enemy, it is another part of the battle against him.'

'Everything is part of everything else in the great dance of life,' Corollin nodded.

'And shall you be going to Starmere, my Honoured Queen?' asked Kellarn, kneeling before Linaelin.

'Not yet,' she smiled sadly. 'I must bear the burden of my mortal father for just a little while longer, until the great challenge comes. I shall stay here with Halgan.'

'And the rest?' asked Corollin.

There was an awkward silence.

'The Lady Skaramak and the *noghr* Odhragh will not be coming to Starmere,' said Tinûkenil.

'We have another errand,' said Skaramak firmly, interrupting him.

'Kellarn has a right to know,' the moon fay told her. 'They go to join the son of the King of the Elves of the North, wherever he may be. I believe that your friend Kôril is with him. The Moon mage Dakhmaal will take them.'

'Will you be staying here, now that you have the Crown?' Father Torriearn asked Corollin.

She looked around her, as though uncertain how to answer.

'Kellarn is going to Court,' she said at last. 'I think that I should go with him.'

'Lo-Khuma has servants in the Emperor's household,' Torriearn frowned. 'Perhaps I should come with you.'

'No, thank you,' said Kellarn quickly. 'I must challenge the Emperor over the death of my father, and my brother, and I must do so alone. You can not risk your neck for Dortrean. Your strength is needed here, for the greater battle.'

'Then Corollin should stay here, by the same argument,' said Torriearn.

'I know,' said Kellarn, looking at her.

'I need to run my sword through that black Archmage anyway,' Torriearn added, 'for what he did to Carfinn.'

Hrugaar cleared his throat.

'No,' said Kellarn. 'That is Dortrean's battle. Nor can you simply strike down a member of the Court Noble – and of the Imperial Council – no matter how much he deserves death.'

'I want to go to Court,' said the borderlander Gwydion, 'if the magi will take me there. My Lord Saerl Vansa will be there, and Patall Telbray, and of course the Lady Karlena. I should be of more use there. And one of us needs to keep an eye on Kellarn.'

'I have not seen the Earl of Vansa at Court,' said Hrugaar.

'My Lady Aramen said he was going,' Gwydion countered.

'You would not be allowed to enter the imperial citadel,' Kellarn told him, 'unless you were part of a household serving those of noble blood. And again, I am loth to risk taking you as part of Dortrean.'

'The Môshári would gladly have him among their number, if Vansa is not there,' offered Torkhaal.

'But would you not be better here, keeping an eye out for the Enemy?' said Kellarn.

Gwydion shifted on his feet uncomfortably. 'I might be better keeping away from him,' he said.

Kellarn looked at him in question. From what he had heard, in every other battle Gwydion had been brave to the point of recklessness.

The borderlander ran one hand back through his mane of hair. 'When we fought the demon last year,' he said, 'in the mines beneath the Black Mountains, I was possessed by him.'

'He was not wholly himself at the time,' Tinûkenil explained quickly. 'A deadly venom had taken him. But the elvenfolk of the Summer Lands healed him, and brought him back to life.'

'The Enemy tried to use me to summon him into the waking world,' Gwydion went on. 'I may be healed, but I'd rather not risk being too close when he tries to come back again.'

'But could not the *syldhar* protect you from him?' Corollin demanded. 'Or were they not with you then?'

'The poison got into my blood,' said Gwydion. 'I had to take off the ring.'

'How did you come by the rings, anyway?' she asked.

'Torriearn found them, a few years ago,' said Tinûkenil; 'around the time that he woke Halgan, I think. They have been with us for many of our adventures. It seems strange not to have them with us now.'

'But they will come back to fight the Enemy, won't they?' asked Kellarn.

'Perhaps,' the moon fay said. 'The *syldhar* try not to interfere with the doings of other folk in this world. Yet in such a great matter, they might.'

'And Ilunâtor?' Kellarn wondered.

Tinûkenil shrugged in answer. A bell sounded in the silence that followed.

'This is for you,' said the moon fay. He brought out a large pearl with a pale lilac sheen. 'If you are beset with great danger, then hold this and call to me, and I shall come. Or if I can not come, then I shall send what help I may.'

Hrugaar took Kellarn by magic as far as the river wing of the imperial citadel. Kellarn thought that it might have been better for him to take the ferry ship across the estuary from the city of Lautun, as was usual for the sons and daughters of Blood Noble; but Rhysana told him that since she had been more or less commanded to fetch him there anyway there was little point in disguising the fact that the magi had brought him. He found that he was too tired to argue.

Corollin went to stay in the College of Magi in Lautun, where she would be close at hand if he had need of her. They felt that the Crown would be far safer there than within the walls of the imperial citadel. Torkhaal took Gwydion to the Môshári, until they could find out whether the Earl of Vansa was now at Court. After some debate, Father Dharagh had stayed behind in the Sun Temple with Linaelin.

The river wing was cool and peaceful in the late afternoon, and there were few people around to mark Kellarn's arrival as he trudged up the long stairs and hallways with Kierran at his side. They cut through the old summer palace, where the white stone walls were carved with a huge frieze of life-sized horses frolicking among the clouds, and so on up to the Dortrean apartment in the central part of the citadel.

When at last they reached the panelled landing they found two guards in the red and gold of Valhaes outside the door. Though Valhaes was a retainer of Dortrean, it was not quite what Kellarn had expected. Yet the guards had a familiar look about them, and as he came closer he recognised the bright blue eyes of Boldrin of Levrin twinkling at him. His companion was the Lady Haësella, another holy knight of the Braedun Order.

'What are you doing here?' Kellarn whispered, both surprised and pleased.

'Your Lady mother asked the Emperor to take his guards away,' Boldrin told him quietly. 'Since there are few of her own household here, and since for some reason Valhaes sent most of his people straight home from Farran, Haësella and I are taking our turn on the door.'

'That is not what I meant,' said Kellarn. 'I thought that you were supposed to be in Arrandin.'

'So I was,' the knight agreed. 'I was to have come here with Lord Bradhor, a few days hence. But when we heard the news—' He looked at the two of them kindly. 'Let us say that the request came from the highest ranks of my Order.'

Kellarn thought of Linaelin, and nodded.

'Is Bradhor here?' Kierran asked gloomily.

'Not yet,' Boldrin smiled. 'You have a few days of freedom left. But your brother Jared is at Court, and may be glad of your company for a while; and the Lady Karlena is waiting for you now.'

Karlena was sitting in what had been Erkal's favourite chamber in the apartment – a square room panelled with dark oak, with coloured windows showing the magical creatures of the *Aeshtar*. The windows were open to let in the sweet air from the orchard garden below, and she was sorting through a box full of papers and scrolls. Meghîsen, the young priestess of Fire from the Dortrean house in the city of Lautun, was sitting on a low stool beside her.

Kellarn thought that his mother looked pale and tired in her scarlet gown, and perhaps a little smaller and thinner than he remembered. But her hands had lost none of their gentle strength as she held him close, and kissed his face and hair. She embraced Kierran in the same way, and then stepped back to study them both; and then she bade Meghîsen put away the papers for another time.

They spent most of that evening with her, going over all that had happened at the Braedun *commanderie* and then turning to lighter things. Karlena spoke little about her own doings at the Court, except to say that she was bored half to distraction by the silliness of the Empress' Ladies. They did not tell her about the Crown, or whom they had met at the Sun Temple; but with Kellarn's mother it was always difficult to gauge how much she guessed or already knew.

The following morning Lord Brodhaur, Earl of Levrin, came early to the Dortrean apartment. As Commander in Chief of the Imperial Household Guard, and for long a friend of the family, he had taken it upon himself to bring the official tidings that the Souther ship carrying Erkal to Lautun had been lost at sea soon after she had sailed out of the Galloppi River estuary.

Kellarn and Kierran were still at breakfast when Lord Brodhaur arrived. Karlena was sitting further down the long table from them with her own jug of steaming tea, and looking a healthier colour in her dressing gown of creamy white silk. She invited the Earl to join her.

'You are deceived, my Lord,' Kellarn told him. Kierran's presence alone should have been enough to give the lie to Brodhaur's words. 'My father never sailed from Braedun. The Southers murdered him there.'

The Earl looked at him steadily. 'I have heard the same tale rumoured around the Court,' he said. 'I should think twice before repeating it if I were you, young Collie-dog. Feeling against the Southers already runs high. We can ill afford a war with them at this time.'

'The tale that he was lost on one of their ships will hardly endear them to the Court Noble,' Kellarn countered.

'I know,' Brodhaur sighed. 'But you know what has happened in Ellanguan. The same may be happening now in the south. Already they are taking over along the coast of Linnaer, and spreading across the borders of my own lands of Levrin. They are demanding horses of Galsin. There was conflict among them after one of their leaders died.' He glanced pointedly at Kierran. 'We believe that a man named Nadan leads them now, who is one of Ambassador T'Loi's people.'

'Nadan is of the Su'lorim,' Kierran nodded.

'This morning the Court Noble will begin the debate on whether we should send the Southers home,' Brodhaur went on; 'or more to the point, whether the Empire can raise the strength and resources to fight its own war against the East. Would that your father were here. He could keep reason in the debate more readily than could I. When Ambassador T'Loi arrives tomorrow, he may find that he has much to answer for. We must pray that he does not answer with steel.'

'Do the Southers serve T'Loi or the God-King?' asked Kellarn. 'Or will they serve the Emperor?'

Brodhaur shook his head. 'That was never certain. We shall miss your father greatly in the days to come, I fear. But I must warn you that there is an evil rumour abroad in the Court that he betrayed us to the Southers, and reaped his just reward. It is clear that Dortrean now has many enemies.

'If you feel that you can not hold your peace in the debate, then you were best to stay away. If you want my advice, go and do some sparring practice out in the park. His Highness has commanded a grand tourney in just over a week's time, and it will be expected that one of your reputation will wish to take part.'

'Isn't that too easy a way for someone to arrange my untimely death?' objected Kellarn.

'Perhaps,' Brodhaur allowed. 'But I meant that the two of you should spar together. Take no other partners.'

The Earl climbed wearily to his feet. 'I grieve for the loss of your father,' he said. 'I do not intend to lose any more of Dortrean while you are here under my guard.' He bowed to the three of them and went away.

'Why am I worried by his advice?' said Kellarn, when he had gone.

'He has a point,' said Karlena. 'The sparring yard and the stables are among the most likely places for news, and where many deals are made. Besides, nothing will be decided in the debate before T'Loi and Rinnekh arrive to have their say.'

'I am not like Father,' he reminded her.

'I know,' she said, smiling sadly. 'But we can honour his memory by being who we are, and who we were born to be. That is what pleased him the best.'

In the end Kellarn decided to ignore Lord Brodhaur's advice and went to the debate, though he kept quietly to the background behind one of the pillars in the upper gallery. Kierran went with him. They did not much like what they heard.

The debate began with the imperial treasurers' proposal that a levy of at least two tenths would have to be raised from every person in the Empire to pay for a war without the Southers. This prompted the call from many sides that the God-King should send gear and supplies rather than warriors. One of the more foolish Ercusí suggested that the dwarves of the *nohgru* should be made to supply weapons and smithcraft in tribute, since they had the benefit of the Emperor's protection. The idea was greeted with hoots of derision by some, and stony silence by others. The more seasoned members of the Court Noble then pointed out that the harvest was coming, and that there was too little time to train raw farmhands and traders if the Easterners were expected again before winter came. It was felt by many of the Lautun and Farran Houses that the

Souther troops should remain for now, allowing time to train an imperial army while the winter snows kept the Easterners at bay. The Houses from Ellanguan and the eastern part of the Empire, who already bore the burden of the Southers' presence, were loth to accept the delay. They began to list their grievances against the Southers, and the price of the uneasy peace that kept them here; and there were not a few who openly doubted that the Easterners could muster any great strength for a second assault that year.

What hurt Kellarn the most, amid all the bickering and backbiting, were the slurs against his father's name. When his uncle the Lord Forval Sentai lamented Erkal's loss, a whole volley of comments ensued to the effect that Dortrean had made matters worse with both the Southers and the Easterners in the way that he had dealt with them, and that he should carry the blame for much of the Empire's present plight. Though some spoke in Erkal's defence – and among them Prime Councillor Ellen and Lauraï Raudhar of Renza, and Kierran's brother Jared of Arrand – the lack of gratitude or respect for his father's work left a bitter taste in Kellarn's mouth. Had Kierran not been there to calm him, he doubted that he could have held his tongue.

They left the debate before the noon bell rang and fled back to the stillness of the Dortrean apartment; and then in the afternoon they went out into the park as Lord Brodhaur had advised, and found a shady place to practise their sword-play alone.

The sparring helped to block the debate from Kellarn's mind, but not all of his fears for the future. Though Kierran was a good swordsman, and could have held his own against all but the most seasoned warriors even among the Imperial Household Guard, Kellarn was worried that he might not be good enough. He was quick and nimble, but too used to gauging his moves to an opponent with a weapon in one hand; so that Kellarn wielding his longer blade two-handed put him a little out of reckoning. That was a habit that could cost Kierran his life.

Nor would he have Kellarn's experience in fighting non-human foes. Kellarn had no knowledge of what the morrow might bring, nor much hope that he might live very long after he had challenged the Emperor, but he wanted his friend to survive. He needed Kierran to live, whatever the Emperor or the Southers might throw against them; and then there would be the greater challenge of Lo-Khuma thereafter.

Whether from this need for Kierran to survive, or from his own frustration with the morning debate, Kellarn pressed him hard, putting him through his paces as best he could, until the heat of the afternoon and the salt air of the sea left them exhausted; and then they walked back to the Dortrean apartment once more. Whatever befell, they were as ready as they could be in the time that was now left to them.

For Rhysana the day was strangely normal. Torkhaal and Hrugaar went with Ellen to the Court, to hear the familiar squabbles of the debate. Rhysana went to the library, to try to catch up on some of her own neglected work. The journeyman Corollin spent much of the day working quietly in the Lower Library like any other student, or in her guest chambers on the south side of the cloister garden. The unseen *chaedar* were under strict instructions to warn Rhysana at once if anyone tried to disturb Corollin's peace, or if the Archmage Merrech should arrive in the College. But the day passed without incident.

Nevertheless Rhysana did not feel like her everyday self. For one thing her son Taillan was still away at the Telún manor house, and though she was glad of the chance to concentrate on her work she missed his company greatly. She had reluctantly agreed with Torkhaal that it was best to leave the boy with her kinsmen until Kellarn had had out his quarrel with the Emperor; for if there was trouble in the imperial citadel they might need to be free to act swiftly.

Then there was the lingering wonder of their visit to the Sun Temple. When she had gone to Whitespear Head, Rhysana had glimpsed the fallen splendour and terror of a fortress out of legend, and discovered treasures kept hidden for a thousand years. At the Sun Temple, heroes from older legends still had simply walked into her life beneath the light of day, bringing with them the knowledge and hope to defeat the ancient Enemy. She felt strangely out of step with time, or as though she stood poised on the threshold between a vision and the waking world. Everything around her seemed brighter, more real and alive; and yet she herself felt somehow apart from it, waiting for something else.

The sense of waiting made it difficult to settle to her work; nor did it help that the hooded figure of the Warden kept drifting in and out of the *aumery* library, as if keeping his own watchful eye upon her.

At length, in the middle afternoon, the Warden came to stand beside her.

'Mistress,' he said. 'You do not study the lore of she who was named Illana.'

'Yes and no, Warden,' she replied, setting down her pen and sitting back from the faldstool desk. 'You will recall that there is a squared floor pattern in Illana's study chamber. I am trying to gather my memories of the spell, and to consider how such a matrix of energy might be constructed.'

Rhysana was suprised that he had mentioned the subject of Illana at all. Though the Warden had been grateful for the few treasures that she had brought him from Whitespear Head, he had been less than comforted that Illana's hidden books and papers were now in the hands of the Archmage Merrech. Rhysana had not yet told him of her own guesses concerning the *Argument of Command.* And then with the forging of the Crown of the First Kings, and Corollin's arrival in the College, there had been other things to think about.

'You believe that the Journeyman Corollin will suffice to defeat the demon captain, Mistress?'

'She will have others to stand with her,' Rhysana returned,

'and the help of powers older than our own Council. It appears to be our best hope.'

The Warden nodded slowly. 'The lore of the *syldhar* is a thing apart,' he recited. 'The great mage Zedron did not share his lore with the First Council.'

The comment seemed to beg a question that Rhysana was not sure how to ask. Halgan, she remembered, had said that Zedron's lore came from the *syldhar*; and that Corollin could use it to wield the Crown of the First Kings.

'What do you know of the *syldhar*, Warden?' she asked carefully.

'The lore of the *syldhar* is a thing apart,' he repeated. 'I must trust your wisdom in this, Mistress.'

'The power of the First Kings will be with Corollin,' she reminded him; 'and the strength of the *Aeshta* Orders, and many of the Council, and the sword of Kellarn of Dortrean. My own wisdom has little enough to do with it.'

The Warden leaned closer to her. 'And what of His Eminence, Mistress?'

Rhysana found herself unsettled by the reminder. She knew that Merrech would stay loyal to the Emperor, even though his hold over Rhydden's reason was failing. Unless—

'Does he know about the *Argument of Command*?' she gasped.

The Warden straightened himself and stood back, impassive as ever. Of course he could not answer such a question, in breach of a mage's right to personal privacy.

'The Archmage Ellen, Prime Councillor of All Magi, knows well the wisdom of discipline,' he said. 'She will rebuild the Council and the Colleges, for the good of all the Magi. Yet it is not she who can save the Magi from themselves.'

Rhysana looked at him in confusion. 'What do you mean, Warden?' she demanded.

The Warden made no answer. He turned and moved silently to the door, and let himself out on to the landing. But as the door closed behind him, his dull voice drifted back to her in a murmur. 'Not His Eminence, Mistress.'

* * *

In the early evening Prime Councillor Ellen gathered together the Council delegates to the Summer Court, and Rhysana was invited to join them. They met in the privacy of the *daurzha* – a small chamber set aside for Council use within the College of Lautun, and almost impossible to find if one did not know where to look for it. The *daurzha* had a crystal dome, similar to that of the great assembly chamber but on a much smaller scale, to let in the light of the sun and moon, and crystal lamps around the wall that could be kindled to shed a warm golden light.

There were eight high backed chairs around the ebony table, all cushioned with moon white silk, but only seven were filled that evening. The Archmage Morvaan sat facing Ellen, with Torkhaal and Hrugaar on either side. To Ellen's left was Drengriis of Româdhrí, being still the bursar of the Ellanguan College; and between Drengriis and Hrugaar, still looking a little uncomfortable, was the unfortunate High Councillor Lirinal. There had been no new delegate found for the Farran College, and Mage Councillor Ghîlsaan had not been seen in the imperial citadel that day.

Ellen touched only briefly on what had passed in the debate of the Court Noble, since most of those present had been there to hear it. She seemed more concerned with tidings from the world outside. The Steward of Ellanguan was sailing to Lautun in Ambassador T'Loi's ship, with two larger Souther warships now providing escort – and far more than the number of Souther warriors who had been in Ellanguan.

'T'Loi does not need so large an escort,' said Torkhaal. 'It looks as though they are preparing to make trouble.'

'Or preparing for T'Loi's defence,' Lirinal offered. 'They will have heard of Dortrean's death. They will not suffer T'Loi to be taken and killed.'

The other magi were silent.

'I don't suppose Rhydden has done anything about it?' ventured Morvaan, glancing around the table.

'Not that I have heard,' said Ellen. 'But then he has ships of his own here, and guards enough at the palace. He may not consider a thousand Southers too much of a threat.'

'The God-King has fleets enough to follow,' said Morvaan. 'Can the sea fay help us here, Ru?'

'Perhaps,' said Hrugaar, 'yet not willingly. While Lautun has peace with the Southers, T'Loi is a guest on these shores. And even were the God-King to send a hundred ships against us, the sea fay may wish to have no part in a war between humans. There are worse things than Southers stirring in the deeps.'

'The Môshári are making ready,' put in Torkhaal.

'And Kelmaar,' said Drengriis.

'But what of Ellanguan, now that the Southers are gone?' Rhysana asked.

'Not all of T'Loi's people have left,' said Lirinal. 'A few of his advisers and womenfolk remain in the Steward's palace. The city guard and the guildmasters keep the peace for now, but Ellanguan is too quiet. The Southers who had lived in the city before are keeping to themselves, and there are too few visiting merchants to bring trade.'

'It is early days yet,' Ellen pointed out, 'and there are the summer fairs in Arrandin and Lautun to draw trade away.'

'It is more than that,' said Liniral gloomily. 'It seems likely that T'Loi intends to return.'

'The Northern Envoy has arrived at Court,' said Torkhaal, trying to sound a brighter note. 'Or he should have reached the citadel by now. His army is making camp up in the hills, and the knights of Mairdun are with them.'

'The Northerners have little love for the Southers, at least,' said Drengriis.

'And little love for the Six Kingdoms, as a rule,' Ellen reminded him. 'The Môshári tell me that they were sent by the Elders of Radbrodal to help in the fight against the servants of Lo-Khuma. How far they will serve at Rhydden's command remains to be seen. Why Mairdun rode with them is still far from clear – though I hear that it was to keep the Northerners out of mischief along the way.'

'Carstan Mairdun is wise in the ways of *sherunuresh*,' said Hrugaar. 'He moves his knights where they may both defend and challenge.'

It occurred to Rhysana that Carstan was also cousin to the Lady Idesîn of Telbray, and that Idesîn had pledged Mairdun's support to Dortrean. It seemed to her more than timely that the knights should have arrived here now, with Kellarn come to Court to challenge the Emperor; but she did not feel that she could say so with Lirinal at the table.

'Did Carstan come to Court with the Northern Envoy?' she asked aloud.

'Not that we have heard,' said Torkhaal. 'But we can look for him tomorrow.'

The next morning marked the beginning of the second quarter of the Summer Court. It was also the second day of the week, being the fourteenth day of the month of Röstren, and thus held holy to Hýriel and Torollen. No formal rites of the *Aeshtar* were permitted within the imperial palace; but Kellarn rose early and went out on to the pillared balcony of his bedchamber, which looked down into the smaller shadowed courtyard in the centre of the wing, and brought his own hopes and fears before the gods in the stillness of the dawn. Kierran came out and stood beside him.

There was to be no debate that day, for the Souther Ambassador was expected to arrive in the afternoon and a great feast was being prepared for his welcome. There had of course been a mixed reaction among the nobles to this news; but since the Emperor was paying for it and he was their host, they did not complain too loudly.

Kellarn went down to see the Scholars of Blood Law, to have his succession to the Earldom of Dortrean confirmed. It needed but a simple formal exchange, since the blood lines had been established some years before, when Kellarn's brother Solban had been made heir designate. Karlena came with him, as Erkal's widow; and his brother-in-law Jared bore witness, both on Ellaïn's behalf and as father of Kellarn's own heir apparent, young Terrel of Arrand.

It was Mage Councillor Drengriis of Româdhrí who spoke on behalf of the assembled Scholars, with the fair haired Eonnaï of Gadhrai from Ellanguan standing beside him. But if Rhysana had asked Drengriis to prepare another claim on Kellarn's behalf, for the blood line of Imperial Lautun, there was no sign of it in his voice or face as he droned through the familiar words.

Lord Bradhor of Arrand was also there that morning, though his exchange with Drengriis was even briefer than Kellarn's since he had been the lawful heir designate of The Arrand for many years. Jared and Kierran stood as witnesses for their older brother, and for once the three of them reached agreement without dispute.

What Kellarn had not expected was to see the Empress Grinnaer and her Ladies gathered farther down the hall. It appeared that they had come because Karlena was there – though his mother would not have invited them – and because they wished to see for themselves the next Earl of Dortrean. Most of the women were little older than himself, and they were giggling and whispering behind their gloved hands, and studying him from head to toe as though he were a yearling brought up for auction.

There was nothing for it but to speak to Grinnaer before they left the hall, and indeed the Empress herself seemed most eager to meet with him. Kellarn remembered her from childhood visits, though the two of them had not really been friends. She had been tormented by her older brothers growing up, and she seemed put upon now by the gaggle of women that flapped and pecked around her. He had expected to feel more sorry for Grinnaer than he did. But to Kellarn's eyes her queenly bearing – so carefully nurtured and groomed by his mother in recent months – was but another layer of the gowns and make-up that she had put on. Beneath was the flawed and fawning creature that he remembered. She was a water spaniel watching the birds, and likely to spring without warning; and the Emperor's shadow lay upon her.

'You shall have to get used to it,' Kierran teased him, as they beat a hasty retreat from the hall. 'Every unmarried daughter of Blood Noble will soon be dragged out of the closet and paraded before you, until you choose your new Countess.'

'Dortrean is hardly in favour just now,' said Kellarn; 'and I have no intention of getting married. Besides, the prettier ones will all be making eyes at you.'

'They'll be wasting their time then,' Kierran laughed.

They took Jared and Bradhor with them, and went riding out into the sunlit glory of the Shining Hills, away west beyond the encircling wall of the park. Kellarn was half minded just to keep riding westward, to lose himself in the golden forest of Hellenur and not to come back; but he knew that that choice was no longer his to make. They returned for a noon meal in the Arrand apartment, though Kellarn had no appetite for it; and then he and Kierran took themselves off to the Dortrean apartment to make ready for T'Loi's arrival.

Kellarn sat down on the edge of the bed, studying his booted feet without interest. Kierran sat down beside him.

'Can't you leave dealing with Rhydden,' he asked gently, 'until after this business with Lo-Khuma is over? After all, if we manage to defeat the demon, then his servants won't have any power to back Rhydden up.'

'I know,' Kellarn sighed. 'But if we take away his servants, we take away some of the Enemy's strength within the waking world. That might give us a better chance to defeat him. Besides, I have sworn an oath before all the gods to avenge my father and my brother, and now that oath has found me. The gods are waiting.'

'Can't they wait a little longer?' said Kierran. 'I don't want to lose you, Col.'

Kellarn smiled in spite of himself. 'You aren't going to

lose me,' he said stoutly. But he could not meet Kierran's gaze.

Kierran took him by the hand and said nothing.

'Here,' said Kellarn presently. 'Take this.' He pulled out the pearl that the moon fay Tinûkenil had given to him, and pressed it into Kierran's palm. 'You have a better chance of remembering to use it than do I.'

They looked at one another then, and Kierran nodded. And then they got washed and dressed to do battle.

Kellarn put on his mailshirt beneath his scarlet surcoat with the leaping gold lion, and slung the holy blade at his side. He looked at the star shield of Heruvor, but decided reluctantly that he would be better off without it. Kierran also wore a mailshirt of grey steel, beneath a scarlet surcoat borrowed from the Dortrean household, and carried his own grey sword with him.

They went down to the river wing to watch the Souther Ambassador's arrival, choosing the vantage of one of the higher windows above the quay. Several score of the warriors of the Imperial Household Guard were outside below them, all in the tawny gold and brown of Lautun; and a larger number of nobles lined the inner edge of the quay, colourful as a garden border in all their finery.

The three Souther ships lay at anchor well out in the deeper waters in the middle of the estuary. T'Loi's own vessel had been taken from him in Ellanguan, and he seemed to have come in one of the smaller trading ships of the Souther Islanders which was rather dull and ordinary by comparison. But this was flanked by two of the huge K'tarim warships, glittering with gold and jewels in the early afternoon light. Their tall masts with furled mulberry sails were as high as the line of hills behind, even from Kellarn's vantage; and their long decks of polished oars stirred dark memories of his own captivity in Souther hands.

Five smaller boats were lowered to the water and filled rapidly with the folk of T'Loi's train, all clad in dazzling white.

They were rowed to shore with the music of strings and pipes and deep voices carrying faintly on the breeze ahead of them. A fanfare of horns and drums greeted them as they reached the quay.

Kellarn and Kierran left the window and made their way slowly to the great audience hall at the heart of the imperial citadel. There Rhydden would receive T'Loi, and lead him to the feast thereafter.

The sombre hall was a scene of quiet activity when they arrived. Imperial guards were posted before each of the twelve black pillars beneath the pale crystal lamps, and stood in pairs beside each of the open doorways. A couple of dozen nobles drifted across the polished black stone floor, murmuring to one another or to their liveried attendants, and more were gathering in the upper galleries that stretched the length of the hall on either side. Many more were starting to arrive behind them.

It was not usual for members of the Court Noble to go armed about the citadel, and Kellarn had fully expected to be challenged by the guards on the doors. But on this occasion they appeared willing to turn a blind eye; and looking around him at the gathering crowds, he realised that many others also bore weapons that afternoon. Given the presence of two Souther warships at anchor just outside, Kellarn guessed that the imperial guards would secretly welcome any help that they could get if it came to a fight.

They found Rhysana and Torkhaal halfway up the hall to the right, both in their formal high councillors' robes. Prime Councillor Ellen was with them, clad in splendid robes of russet and apple green embroidered with all kinds of birds and beasts in golden thread. The magi greeted them kindly, though with the traditional reserve of the Council when dealing openly with the Court Noble. Corollin, they told them, had stayed behind in the College, but could be fetched if Kellarn had need of her.

If the magi were worried as to what Kellarn might plan, they still managed to convey an air of cool confidence that was as balm to him in the crowded heat of the hall. They pointed out where Hrugaar was standing with the handsome Lord Aúrun of Renza, up on the western gallery across the hall from them. The Archmage Morvaan was farther along the gallery to the right, with Boldrin of Levrin in his blue and white as a holy knight of the Temple Guard of Telúmachel in Arrandin; and Gravhan and Imarra of Môshári were there with them. The borderlander Gwydion had now found the Earl of Vansa, and they were with the Lord Patall Telbray somewhere up on the eastern gallery above. The Lord Torreghal Valhaes, who captained most of Kellarn's military strength of Dortrean, was down on the main floor directly across from them, talking with the Earls of Ercusí and Vaulun.

The bells had sounded the passing of the third hour of the afternoon by the time that everyone was gathered, and the outer hall beyond the southern doors was filled with the white mass of T'Loi's train. The imperial guards herded the nobles back behind the line of the pillars on either side, in beneath the high galleries. And then there was a loud braying of trumpets, and the echo of drums all around, and the imperial party came in through the far side door at the northern end of the hall.

The Lords Brodhaur Levrin and Drômagh of Sêchral came first to clear the way, clad in gold and black as the senior commanders of the Imperial Household Guard. The Emperor himself strode behind, in tunic and cloak of cloth of gold, and with a glittering circlet crowning his dark head. About his throat and spreading down across his chest hung a necklace of many green gems, bright as rainwashed leaves in the sunlight, which drew Kellarn's gaze at once; for he had seen that necklace before, and slain the Easterner woman who had worn it. The brightness of the jewel half dazzled him, so that a glow of greenish gold seemed to linger about the Emperor as he came up on to the dais. He found that he hated Rhydden more than ever, now that the moment of challenge was upon him.

The black shadow of the Archmage Merrech came in behind

the Emperor, and then the Empress Grinnaer with the Lady Turinda and Kellarn's mother carrying her long train. Grinnaer had changed out of the russet gown that she had worn earlier, and was now clad all in cloth of gold like her Lord and husband. Her chestnut hair was piled up beneath a simple circlet, but she wore no other jewels; and her eyes were painted large and dark, which lent her an otherwordly beauty that Kellarn found faintly disturbing.

So intent was Kellarn on watching that Kierran had to tug at his arm to remind him to bow. When Lord Brodhaur gave them permission to rise again, the Emperor was seated in his carved ebon throne. Grinnaer sat behind and to his left in a smaller white throne, with Karlena and Turinda standing behind her. Lord Drômagh and Brodhaur stood to attention at either side of the dais. The hooded Archmage lurked close in behind Rhydden's throne, so that from where Kellarn was standing he looked almost to be a part of it.

A second fanfare sounded, and the imperial guards at the southern doorway stepped aside. Ambassador T'Loi came in, unhurried and graceful in his billowing robes of pale primrose silk. The five jewels of his high office danced and glittered on his olive-skinned brow, and his long raven hair fluttered gently at his back. At his right hand, moving with near equal grace, walked Rinnekh Solaní of Ellanguan. He was clad in a high collared tunic of blue-green over white leggings, with the white steel circlet of the Lords Steward of Ellanguan upon his dusty brown head, and a long sword hung in a scabbard at his side.

Behind these two came a shorter man in his middle years, with greying dark hair, clad in gorgeous robes of turquoise bordered with gold. He lacked the easy confidence of Rinnekh and T'Loi before the Court, and did not smile. After a few moments Kellarn guessed that he must be Sollonaal, Prime Councillor of the Ellanguan Magi, and he glanced sideways to see Rhysana's reaction. But the three magi had now moved beyond the pillar to his right, and he could not see their faces.

A half circle of six Souther guards escorted T'Loi up the hall, but no more were permitted beyond the doors. They were clad in long white tunics over black mail, with white silk hoods covering their dark heads and curved swords sheathed at their sides. Their tanned faces were handsome and proud, with a serene dignity that seemed wholly impassive to their surroundings. Kellarn had no doubt that they were hand picked from among T'Loi's finest swordsmen.

It felt like an age for T'Loi to walk the length of the hall, and the more so because he would pause and bow deeply to the Emperor after every couple of steps. But at last he came to a halt some six paces from the edge of the dais, with his guards in a half moon behind him and Sollonaal at his side; and Rinnekh took three paces forward and went down on one knee, drawing his sword and presenting it hilt first toward his Lord and Emperor.

Rhydden stood up and came down from the dais. He smiled at his beloved favourite – a smile more loving than any father ever bestowed upon his child, so gentle and beautiful that it caught at the heart, so that even Kellarn found his own throat tightening with a sense of grief and loss.

'There are those,' said Rhydden, his voice low but clear, 'who would tell us that Ellanguan has betrayed us and now serves another master. Yet when her Lord Steward kneels thus before us, how may we doubt his loyalty and love?'

'Ellanguan has ever served His Highness,' said Rinnekh, his head still bowed. 'It is our duty and our joy, and our greatest honour.'

Rhydden took the sword from his hands and tested its weight, and then tapped the point lightly beneath Rinnekh's chin in signal that he might look up. Rinnekh tilted back his head to gaze up into his Emperor's face, his own face now radiant with reflected light and love.

Then Rhydden turned the sword in his hand, and swept off Rinnekh's head with a single stroke.

Chapter Fourteen

There were one or two screams in the shocked silence. Blood fountained from Rinnekh's neck and spattered down across the dais and throne. The Emperor had stepped clear.

'We accept your loyal service,' said Rhydden calmly. 'Seize them.'

The six Souther guards sprang into a circle about T'loi, unsheathing their curved swords. The imperial guards were moving, some to the Southers and some to the outer doors. Kellarn's legs were numb beneath him.

High Councillor Sollonaal drew himself up, clasping his staff in both hands. The nearest of the Souther warriors grabbed him by the hair and jerked back his head. There was a quick flash of steel as the curved sword slit his throat; and then the Souther let him fall, and he sank into a heap of turquoise and red-stained gold.

The white hood of the warrior had slipped back, revealing a woman's face of rather severe beauty, with silky raven hair strained back into a fish-plait braid. Her lip curled into a sneer as she stepped back into the ring, sweeping up her sword in readiness before her.

A horn call sounded from the outer hall. Kellarn found his feet and began to move.

The golden figures of the guards were ahead of him, closing in a second ring around T'Loi. Kellarn kept well clear of them to the right as he made for the dais. The Emperor had already moved back to stand before the throne, with Lord Brodhaur and Lord Drômagh flanking him to either side.

There was a flurry of movement around the Southers, and their blades leaped and writhed like living serpents in their hands. They cried out in fear, and cast their weapons down. Lord Brodhaur barked a command and the imperial guards rushed in.

'Hold!' cried Kellarn, skidding to a halt before the dais steps.

Lord Drômagh moved forward, barring his way to the throne. The imperial guards ignored him, intent on taking the Southers away. The six white garbed warriors now submitted without demur, presumably at some signal from T'Loi. The clatter of steel and battle echoed from the outer hallway.

Rinnekh's head was staring up at him from the bloodied floor.

'Do not be deceived!' Kellarn cried, appealing to the dumbstruck nobles. 'This show of judgement and strength is but a mummers' play. Your Emperor has been in league with the Southers from the first. It was he who commanded my father's murder, at the hands of his own men among the K'tarim; and he it was who murdered my brother Solban in Ellanguan. For this Emperor before you serves the same great demon as the Easterner clans who brought war upon Arrandin, the great Enemy of our forefathers. And so also do the K'tarim worship that demon, and so did Rinnekh and Sollonaal, and so does His Excellency the Souther Ambassador T'Loi.'

The crowds were moving now, stirring and whispering like reeds in the dawn wind. There were catcalls and cries from the gallery and the floor, and a commotion at the far end of the hall as the Southers pressed their attack against the defending guards. Ellen and Rhysana were standing ready by their pillar, and Kierran was at Kellarn's side. He could not see where Torkhaal had gone. A tall man in blue and black was coming forward up the hall.

Ambassador T'Loi had not moved, though he now had two imperial guards watching over him. His white garbed warriors were being led away to Kellarn's right, toward the northern door where the Emperor had come in. T'Loi was studying Kellarn in wry amusement, as though watching a sideshow at a fair.

'Rhydden Lautun must be brought to account!' Kellarn had to shout to make himself heard above the gathering noise. 'He must stand trial before the Court Noble, for he has betrayed us all!'

A volley of shouts flew back at his words, in support or denial he could not tell. Then the Emperor raised his hands and flashed his most brilliant smile, and the shouting died away.

'The boy is clearly overwrought at the sad loss of his father,' said Rhydden indulgently.

'I have heard the same tale,' called the tall man, drawing level with Rhysana and Ellen. He was not much older than Kellarn, with curling dark hair cropped short; and from his height and powerful build, and his deep rolling voice, it was easy to guess that this was the Northern Envoy, Hakhutt. 'Our wisest elders of Radbrodal have seen this evil in the stones, though till now I had but half believed it.'

'Listen to him!' cried the Empress, stumbling forward at Rhydden's side. 'The Emperor worships the great demon. He murdered my brother. He will betray and murder us all!'

Rhydden turned and ran her through with his sword. Grinnaer gave a voiceless cry. He jerked the blade free in a spray of blood, and let her crumple to the floor. Lord Drômagh scrabbled back to kneel at her side.

'They are all raving,' said Rhydden. 'They still do not understand.' He signalled to the guards.

Kellarn and Kierran drew their swords. Lord Brodhaur stepped forward from the dais, warning them with his hand to back off. The two guards left T'Loi and hurried toward them.

'Get Mother out of here!' Kellarn told Kierran. 'Go!'

Kierran turned and was gone. Kellarn moved to block the guards. He had the blurred impression of a blue and white figure leaping down from the gallery beyond, and then the first guard was upon him.

Kellarn brought his blade round and ripped open the man's side, sending him staggering across the floor. He went down and did not get up again. Kellarn whirled and followed through, dealing the second guard a pommel strike to the head. She did not remain standing.

Torreghal Valhaes had moved out on to the floor, a curved Souther sword in his hand. Boldrin of Levrin was sprinting toward T'Loi. Kellarn turned to look for his mother on the dais, and found the great bulk of Lord Drômagh bearing down upon him.

He moved too slowly to parry the blow well, and Drômagh's sword sliced down across his thigh. Kellarn cursed him for the bastard that he was. But then the blue and black mass of Hakhutt shouldered him aside, driving Drômagh back and dealing him a mighty cross-stroke with his broad Northerner blade. The Knight Commander bellowed like an angry bull and sank down upon the dais steps, letting his sword fall. A wide wound gaped across his belly, spilling blood and innards across his tunic of imperial gold. Drômagh laboured to staunch the flow with his heavy hands.

Kellarn looked up on to the dais. His mother and Turinda had gone. He glanced to the right, and gasped in relief as he caught the familiar flare of Dortrean red. Karlena and Kierran were both there, and Torkhaal was with them.

The hall had gone quieter again, though there was still the ring of steel upon steel. Kellarn turned back to the fight. Valhaes was now just to his left. The doors at the far end were shut, and perhaps half a dozen guards in the gold of Lautun were coming up the hall toward them. Only Boldrin and T'Loi were fighting, circling one another in their own private duel. The hooded Archmage had moved to the far end of the dais. Lord Brodhaur and the Emperor did not appear to have moved at all.

Then Kellarn looked at the Emperor again, and understood why the hall was so quiet.

Rhydden stood with his dark head bowed, so that his

hair fell forward across his face. He seemed to be breathing deeply. One bloodied hand was clasped to his chest; and there was blood smeared all over his golden tunic, and over the glittering necklace about his throat. He held his sword level across his thighs.

Yet with each breath he seemed to grow a little taller and broader, and the blood upon him was fading. And then he lifted his head to look down the hall, and his face was no longer his own. The same features were there, the proud nose and strong jaw and the wide, all generous smile. But now they were sharpened to a feral beauty, and a more terrible radiance shone forth; and his eyes burned with a dark opalescent fire.

He flicked his gaze around the hall, and the smile curled to a sneer. The Radiant. The Beautiful. The Deceiver. Lo-Khuma had come among them.

The silence of the hall was shattered. Men and women screamed and wailed, surging this way and that along the galleries and stumbling across the lower floor to the outer doors, trampling whoever fell. Even the mighty Hakhutt gave a cry of dismay, and dropped his weapon and fled. Lord Drômagh rolled on to his face and grovelled.

Kellarn looked back over his shoulder. Rhysana was not far behind him.

'Get Corollin!' he shouted to her above the din. She nodded, already signalling to Torkhaal. Prime Councillor Ellen was a few steps behind her, with arms upraised and eyes closed as she called upon the power of Earth.

Kellarn turned and charged at his double foe, now both Emperor and demon.

The Enemy glared at him. The force of his look hurled Kellarn back through the air, smashing him in to a pillar. He fell to the floor, gasping.

Kierran and Valhaes were there to help him up. 'Torkhaal has gone,' Kierran told him. 'Karlena went with him.'

Kellarn could hardly hear him above the noise, but he nodded.

'You must leave here, my Lord,' urged Torreghal Valhaes. 'This is a foe beyond your strength. Dortrean will have need of you.'

'There will be no Dortrean,' said Kellarn, 'if I don't fight now.' He hauled himself to his feet.

Lord Brodhaur was fighting the Enemy. Boldrin was running to join him. Kellarn hefted his sword and charged forward again, with Kierran at his side.

Rhysana had watched in horror at Rhydden's growing madness and the slaughter before the throne. The magi had held themselves ready to support Kellarn, though in a straight fight against the imperial guards he seemed to have little need of them; and someone else – perhaps Merrech, she thought – had transformed the Souther swords into serpents. She had seen Hrugaar and Aúrun leaving the gallery early on, and guessed that they had gone down to join the battle in the outer hall.

But when Rhydden lifted his head to show an altered face, she knew that far greater peril was upon them all, and that Corollin and the Crown were needed. It had been a gift from the gods that Karlena had been brought to Torkhaal's side, so that he could carry her to safety in his *leap* to the College. How to hinder the Enemy until he brought Corollin here was quite another matter.

She had hoped that Kellarn would hold him back; for though Rhydden was possessed he was still a mortal man and Kellarn was the better warrior, and Kellarn had the holy blade of Fire. But when she saw him flung aside with a glance – and had to dodge as he crashed into the pillar just behind her – she knew that more would be needed.

Her thoughts flew, searching for a way that she might help. Rhydden was possessed, which was more a matter for the priests than the Magi. Gwydion of Vansa, she remembered, had been possessed; and the elvenfolk of the Fay had been needed to heal him.

And then she remembered what the Toad Archmage had told her: that Rhydden had hoped to control the Enemy, and to bind him to his will. To do that, Rhydden would need the help of his Archmage, and probably the lore of the Southers or Easterners.

He had the Easterner necklace about his throat.

At last Rhysana understood what they had done. They had woven spells about the necklace and made it a thing of power, so that Rhydden could call upon the Enemy and bind him to himself while he wore the jewel. The necklace was the link. And if she could break the spell, she could break the link between the Enemy and the waking world, driving him out again.

Boldrin of Levrin had passed T'Loi and was moving toward the dais. The Souther Ambassador had fallen, his gorgeous robes turning swiftly from primrose to red. His curved sword lay on the floor, a severed hand still grasping the hilt.

Lord Brodhaur stood fighting the Emperor on the dais steps, wielding his staff of office with all the skill of the seasoned warrior that he was. Yet now he seemed no match for Rhydden; and the staff shivered as it struck the Emperor in the chest, leaving Brodhaur staggered.

'It is you who should withdraw, my Lord,' she told Valhaes as Kellarn left them. 'Your Souther sword can not touch the Enemy.'

She did not wait for his reply, but turned inward to focus upon her spell. It would have helped had she had the jewel close by her, and without someone wearing it and moving around; but she sought only to break the enchantment, not to lay each strand of power to rest. Such reckless loosing of unknown power without rendering it wholly harmless was against the strictest Council precepts. Yet given the urgent need, she had no better choice. And if Rhydden suffered the backlash, she considered that to be no more than he deserved.

Rhysana fixed her gaze upon the jewel, squinting against

the brightness, focusing all her trained mage's senses upon the woven strands of power. It helped that Kellarn was shorter than Rhydden, and lower down on the dais steps, so that he did not wholly block her view. She was aware of Ellen's power surging into life behind her, and the noise of the crowds grew fainter. And then she glimpsed the twisted spells that she sought, bent all her will toward them, and strove to tear them asunder.

The strength of will resisting her was terrible. It had the slippery feel of the Archmage Merrech, and the baleful glare of the Enemy, and the arrogance of Rhydden Lautun. But her own strength prevailed, and the binding spell broke in a flare of emerald power. Rhysana gasped with the effort.

Yet she did not achieve her purpose. The figure of Rhydden grew swiftly brighter and taller, rearing up to half again Kellarn's height. The ebon hair and cloth of gold faded and were gone, and face and form grew handsome beyond words. He was of human shape, with cat-like eyes and grace, and a long mane of flowing hair, and a simple tunic open from neck to waist; and he was pale and translucent as alabaster lit from within, with a sheen of pale blue like a topaz.

The spells that had bound demon to man were gone, but it was the demon who had remained. Rhysana wept.

'Bugger,' said Ellen, hurrying past her toward him. 'I should have brought the Prime Councillor's rod.'

Kellarn hated Rhydden. There was no other word for it. He hated him even more because the demon within him gave him far better strength and skill at arms than Rhydden had ever bothered to master for himself. Lord Brodhaur had been driven back, to hunt for another weapon; and Rhydden could hold off the three of them – Boldrin, Kierran and himself – so well that as yet they had not touched him.

It did not help that he was above them on the dais, with his back to the heavy throne, and that the steps were slick with blood beneath them; and that, to Kellarn's right, Kierran's feet were hampered by the body of the fallen Empress.

And the brightness of the Easterner necklace half dazzled them.

Then the clustered jewels shattered in a burst of green flame – though Kellarn did not see who had hit it – and the broken fragments tore at his cheeks and hands as they flew past. Rhydden gave a cry, but it was too much to hope for that he was defeated. And then the Enemy himself came forth, transforming Rhydden's body completely.

It struck Kellarn at once that he did not find Lo-Khuma particularly beautiful, except in an irritating sort of way. He supposed that that was partly because he knew what the Enemy really was, though he hardly had the time to think about it just then. With his added height it was now more like fighting a giant – of which Kellarn himself, at least, had had some experience. But the Enemy was far swifter and more canny, and a superb swordsman, parrying strokes from all three of them with negligent ease, without even bothering to move his feet.

Kierran and Boldrin moved up on either side, trying to get behind him. Kellarn doubled his effort from the front, enabling Boldrin's blade to strike home. Lo-Khuma dealt the knight a lazy backhand swipe that sent him reeling, and fought on.

Kierran gave a cry and pointed beyond Kellarn's back, but he dared not turn round to see. There was a loud crack, like a lightning strike, and a shrill scream. The Enemy glared past him. Kellarn seized the moment and drove his own blade home.

Lo-Khuma parried too late. The holy blade of Fire bit into his leg above the knee, and a glow of red light flared from within the pale blue. A growl of fury rumbled around him. Kellarn sprang back, beyond his sword's reach, trying to draw him down. But the demon did not follow.

Kellarn realised with a start that Ellen was just beside him, chanting in her deep voice. The hooded shadow of the imperial Archmage was just beyond Boldrin, with arms raised high, and a flicker of dark opal fire played around him. There were dark lines creeping across the demon's pale tunic, like black gossamer or shadowfay bonds.

Kierran was struggling. Kellarn leaped back into the fray. Boldrin barged into the Enemy's flank, and Kellarn's sword bit deep once more. With a second growl the demon flung them all aside, thirty feet across the floor. Kellarn and Ellen landed in a heap together, close to Rhysana again. They pulled themselves to their feet.

A dome of light now filled the northern end of the hall, like a huge bronze bubble, which Kellarn guessed must be the work of the magi. The galleries and what remained of the crowds were dim and hushed beyond. Near at hand, Lord Brodhaur fought with another demon, a curved Souther sword in his hand. The demon was of man shape, with the head and tail of a horse, and shone a pale golden green like ripening corn under a summer sun.

Then blue-white power crackled from Rhysana's hand, and the creature withered and fell into dust.

Lo-Khuma was moving, taking two strides across the dais to strike at the hooded Archmage. The bubble of power burst, and another horse-headed demon appeared across the hall. And then there were more people coming up the hall from Kellarn's left – Gravhan and Imarra in their deep Môshári green, and the fair-haired Aúrun of Renza, and the tawny haired borderlander Gwydion. But Corollin was still not there.

Kellarn left them to deal with the horse-headed demon, and bounded toward the dais. Lo-Khuma turned back toward him with a sneer. As he ran he could see that Lord Drômagh was on his feet again, barring Kierran's way with his sword. Kierran would have to manage Drômagh without him.

Boldrin was running in from Kellarn's left. Lo-Khuma stepped back into place before the throne. Kellarn and Boldrin both roared, and leaped at him together. Boldrin snared the demon's sword hand, drawing steaming white blood with his blade. Kellarn's sword sang as it came down, sinking deep into the demon's left shoulder. Holy fire flared to life through Lo-Khuma's massive chest, and his dark eyes flashed briefly to gold. He snarled and staggered, forced to fend them off with his feet. Kellarn scrabbled on the slippery steps. Kierran came running along the edge of the dais to join them.

The red fire in Lo-Khuma died, and the contempt in his bright face turned to hatred. Two more of the horse-headed demons came into view on either side behind him. A wall of dark opalescent flame sprang up beyond, dimming the light in the hall so that the demons shone all the brighter. A second wall of light flew up in front of it, shimmering with deep bronze; and there was a stirring on the air that thrilled the heart like the freshness of a garden after rain, or the joy of the first spring flowers that challenge the winter snows.

And then a creamy white light broke over them, wild as the mountain air and as breathtaking as a wave in the long bay of Ellanguan; and it filled the heart with a shout of triumph, and hung like a clear bell note upon the air that did not fade; and there was a voice singing, with words that Kellarn could not quite catch. But he knew the voice and he knew what had just begun. Corollin was using the Crown.

Lo-Khuma gave a great shout in answer. The force of his voice and thought ripped past and through Kellarn like a hurricane, leaving him breathless. A horse-headed demon sprang down from the dais, passing out of sight to their right. Two more blurred into view where it had stood. Lo-Khuma swept down with his sword, slicing across Kellarn's forearm. The demons were moving forward, leaping to either side. Aúrun sang as he leaped up to challenge them.

Corollin's light was still bright all around them, but a second wave of power pulsed through it. A second shout from Lo-Khuma tore through them. A darkness gathered behind the Enemy's head, and split into two circling shapes in the air above the dais. Kellarn could guess that they were more demons, coming to fight for their master; and he knew that he would send them all against Corollin.

Kellarn redoubled his efforts, driving the Enemy back. The

ebon throne toppled and fell. Kellarn hewed at the demon's thigh, and his blade blossomed with red-golden fire. Boldrin and Kierran struck in from either side. The dais shook with the Enemy's roar.

The hall around them changed. The walls of light and flame vanished and the black stone shifted to shimmering silver grey. Corollin's light and strength were still around them; but now also there was a half heard music, or voices singing, behind the din of the battle. And Kellarn knew, with a great rush of hope, that the *syldhar* had come to help them.

But the Enemy himself had changed. Where he had been pale and bright before, he had now the deep lustre of black opal. He drove them back with a great sweep of his sword, and dark flames kindled on the air all around him, searing their hands and faces with sudden cold.

Four more dark shapes appeared in the air behind him, and flew out across the hall; and then more behind them. Lo-Khuma lunged forward, dodging past Kellarn's blade, and thrust his sword deep into his belly. Kellarn howled, and then stumbled and gasped as the demon ripped the blade away.

A burst of scarlet fire flew over Kellarn's head and smote the Enemy full in the chest. The dark flames devoured it greedily, and Lo-Khuma laughed.

Boldrin had turned aside, battling a winged demon to his left. Kierran gave a yell of fury and launched himself at the Enemy. Lo-Khuma batted his blade aside, and then hewed down with his sword to cleave deep into Kierran's shoulder. Kierran buckled beneath the blow, lost his footing on the steps, and sprawled beside the fallen Grinnaer.

Rhysana tugged the scorched and tattered glory of her high councillor's robes about her, and braced herself against the pillar where she had stood for most of the fight. Corollin and Torkhaal, just beside her, looked as ragged as she felt. The High Queen Linaelin and the *noghr* priest Dharagh were hurrying up the hall to join them.

Corollin still stood upright, surrounded in the creamy aureole of her own power. Her eyes were wide and unseeing, and wholly deep jasper blue, and the jewelled Crown of white metal bars flashed and glittered upon her head as she strove with the Enemy in thought. She grasped her white wood staff before her in both hands, but had not used it once to defend herself. It had fallen to Rhysana and Torkhaal – and others whenever they could – to protect her from physical attack.

How Lo-Khuma could battle Corollin in thought and still wield a sword against Kellarn, Rhysana did not know. She dreaded to think what else he might have been capable of, had Corollin and the Crown not been here. She supposed that things might have been easier, had she herself not been so foolish as to break the spells that kept him bound to Rhydden.

That Lo-Khuma was driving all his creatures against Corollin was clear; and it was due to the valour of Gravhan and Aúrun, Gwydion and the rest, that the lesser demons had been mostly kept away. Rhysana and Torkhaal had used their own power against the horse-headed demons – which were far more comely than they had any right to be, she thought – and battled against the hail of fire that the creatures had called down. Ellen had laboured for the most part to keep a dome of warding power about the whole area, mainly to shield the foolish or fascinated crowds who still lingered at the farther end of the hall. She had also summoned the rest of the Council; though if and when they would appear was impossible to guess.

What the Archmage Merrech had been attempting earlier, Rhysana also did not know; but he had raised his own dome of power to shield the hall, just before Corollin had begun to challenge the Enemy. Both shields had been brought down when Halgan and Torriearn arrived, bringing Linaelin and Father Dharagh and two of the Sun Temple folk with them. Rhysana could see from the way that he was standing that Merrech had now begun to raise another dome.

'*Gorghaim*,' said Linaelin as she reached Torkhaal's side, pointing up to the winged creatures.

'Demons of earth and stone,' said Ellen grimly.

Rhysana was distracted. The Sun priests had paused in their progress up the hall. Halgan pointed his sword at the dais, and a burst of scarlet fire seared through the air to strike the Enemy. Father Torriearn had turned aside, and was bearing down upon the Archmage Merrech. Before Rhysana could move or cry out, his sun-bright sword had run the Archmage through. The hooded shadow fell back and did not stir again.

Father Dharagh had run on to join Gravhan, swinging his fiery axe. The winged demons – the *gorghaim* – flew screeching overhead around the galleries, and two stooped down upon Halgan and Torriearn. Two more came down upon the dais. To Rhysana's eyes they seemed to be part dragon and part ape, with heavy jaws and huge gnarled fists. Their bodies had the look of ruddy stone, like cooling lava, and their long tails curled through the air with the strength of battering rams.

The floor lurched beneath Rhysana's feet, and shards of polished stone flew up around them. Imarra's voice cried out in pain, and Torkhaal swore and held his head. Blood trickled from his brow beneath his fingers.

'Beware the *gorghaim*,' said Linaelin. She lifted up her frail hands, and lightning streaked up from her fingers toward the high vault. Two of the winged demons burst asunder at her stroke, and their shattered bodies fell like dark hail in the hall.

Dharagh hewed down a horse-headed demon. One of the *gorghaim* smashed Halgan to the ground, breaking his arm beneath him. Gwydion was leaping to Torriearn's side.

Corollin stamped her staff upon the floor, and her power flared brighter about her. Another wave of challenge and hope rolled through the hall. And an answering note, or many notes, came from somewhere else, like many voices joined in song. The last horse-headed demon, and all but four of the *gorghaim*, turned and faded, and were gone.

But then a harsher sound, like grinding stone, echoed back from the dais end of the hall. The northern wall grew dark, and two huge figures stepped through. They were like to the horse-headed demons, but far greater and more terrible; and their bodies seemed wasted, and their heads were more like to horses' skulls, with manes of yellow fire that smeared to black. More than twice as tall as their master they were, so that their flaming eyes were level with the gallery parapet; and in the oldest tales of the *Aeshta* Orders they had been among Lo-Khuma's mostly deadly servants.

'Oh, for the defences of Arrandin,' said Ellen.

The high music was cut off, and the hall around them grew dark. But the light of Corollin's power still stood like a beacon, and the swords of Kellarn and Gwydion and the Sun Priest Torriearn shone doubly bright. Rhysana gathered her strength to do battle.

Kellarn knew that he was dying. His insides grew colder with every passing moment, and his own blood now trickled down inside his boots. He fought with Lo-Khuma alone. Boldrin still battled with the winged demon to his left, and a golden figure was with him, probably Lord Brodhaur. Aúrun and Valhaes fought another to his right. There was the clash of battle and power behind. Kellarn parried and struck beyond weariness, a match for the demon even at his last strength. Or perhaps Lo-Khuma was also weakening. But then the Enemy had only to wait, and soon Kellarn would fail and fall.

It was not that he minded dying. There were times when he had longed for it; and in truth he had held little hope of outlasting this day alive. But he was failing too soon. He could not leave yet, not with the Enemy still standing. The gods would not cheat them thus – it was not in their nature – after all their hard effort to come here. He must spend his last strength holding back the Enemy, so that Corollin could finish what they had begun.

Kierran was not dead. He had crawled up the steps, keeping

close to Grinnaer's body, giving Kellarn more room to move. Kellarn prayed that Lo-Khuma had forgotten him.

When the darkness came, and the great demons came forth, his heart quailed within him. He had heard of the skull-headed demons, though he had not been there to see them when they appeared at the siege of Arrandin. But the great demons ignored him, leaping high to either side and passing behind him down the hall. A deeper darkness and the reek of burning trailed in their wake.

There came a rush of wind overhead, and the clouded air burned golden bright for a moment, so that the darkness seemed thicker still when it had gone; and then there was the crack of splintering stone. And then the creamy light of Corollin's challenge rolled over them once more, and Lo-Khuma stepped back against the ebon throne.

Kellarn pressed forward, striking beneath The Enemy's guard. The demon seemed hardly to notice him. The darkness grew paler, and the creamy light was now tinged with the rosy gold of dawn.

Then Lo-Khuma drew himself up to his full height, and sneered. The strength of Corollin's challenge broke with a snap, and the hope of her light was gone. The Enemy stretched out his left hand and grasped the air – and held the Crown of white metal bars.

Corollin staggered when the Crown was torn from her head, and let fall her white wood staff. Rhysana moved swiftest to catch her.

The skull-headed demons stood between them and the dais, with humans and *gorghaim* milling all around. The Crown was beyond their reach.

The farther of the two great demons stamped his foot upon the floor. The stone shook beneath them. A crack ran across the width of the hall, shuddered, and sprang suddenly wide. Gwydion pitched down, and Torriearn fell with him, and the skull-headed demon leaped down into the crack behind them.

The *noghr* Dharagh made a mighty leap, crossing the gap to the dais side where the second great demon still stood.

Torkhaal threw himself down on the floor, singing loud and strong in his deep bass voice as he poured his power into calming the stone. Ellen clung to the pillar at Rhysana's right hand, sending her own strength up to hold the gallery and the vault. There were screams and shouts from the southern half of the hall, heard even through the warding wall of the Archmage Morvaan's rosy gold power.

Lo-Khuma held up the glittering crown, and laughed. Kellarn was fighting him for it.

Imarra of Môshári stood farthest from the dais, with her back to Morvaan's wall of light. Morvaan himself was beside her. She raised her hands in prayer, heedless of the shaking floor, and began a song of *Aeshta* blessing and the faithful strength of Earth. Linaelin was also singing; and her hood was thrown back, and she seemed to have shed her long years, and the glory of her moon fay heritage shone silver-white amid the reek.

Halgan whirled his sword about him, and his robes flared bright as the sun. He leaped through the air across the gaping floor, and sped straight toward his ancient Enemy.

The *gorghaim* that was waiting there caught him by the throat and crushed him. The second skull-headed demon sprang over the *noghr* and landed before Linaelin, punching straight through her ribs to the heart.

Rhysana cried out in dismay. Corollin pulled free of her grasp and strode toward the great demon, whirling her staff about her as she went. Her aureole of power flared in challenge. Gravhan of Môshári was running to join her.

Morvaan sent a flare of golden power arcing straight up the hall to the dais. It shimmered and failed around the Enemy's head.

Lo-Khuma still held the Crown high with his left hand, while fighting off Kellarn with his right. Boldrin was joining the fray. Kellarn seemed almost to be trying to climb up the demon, struggling to get to the Crown.

It struck Rhysana suddenly that Lo-Khuma was just like Rhydden Lautun. Rhydden had always behaved like an overgrown child, teasing or tormenting those younger or less powerful than himself. Had they come to no more than this, that the demon would play with them and tease them like a spoiled brat, while worthy people laid down their lives striving against him? That had been the story of Rhydden's life, all along. She felt suddenly weary – and furious with him. It was time to make an end of it.

'Give Kellarn the Crown!' she commanded.

Somehow the wind must have got into her words, or perhaps some grace from the gods was given to her. For above the shaking of the hall and the screams of the *gorghaim*, the Enemy heard her. He turned his face toward her, both in hatred and surprise, and her heart laboured within her in sudden dread.

Then Lo-Khuma lowered his arm and gave the Crown into Kellarn's hand.

There was no time for doubt. Though his arm shook with the effort, Kellarn put the Crown on his own head.

Rainbowed light exploded behind his eyes, spiralling into white. His vision of the world around him changed.

The wrack of the hall was still the same. But behind and somehow *through* that he saw the Enemy as he had seen him once before – a cloud of shadow looming over him, with the impression of vast spreading wings. Two cat-like eyes glared down at him from the heart of the cloud, seething with malice.

In the First Realm of the Dead, Kellarn had fled from the shadow. Now he had another purpose.

The cloud that was Lo-Khuma swept down around him, driving to overwhelm him. Kellarn knocked it back with a thought, encircling the shadow within the ring of his will. He let fall his sword, and grabbed the Enemy by the tunic with both hands.

You're coming to meet Ilunâtor, he told him.

He turned in thought, dragging the Enemy with him. The Crown bound them together. Perhaps that had been part of its purpose, to keep the Enemy in rather than to drive him out.

The dragon was waiting for them – two enormous eyes twinkling with starlight, with just the hint of a ridged brow edged with rainbowed hues, and great starlit wings enfolding them. It was the dragon's wings that pinned the cloud of Lo-Khuma in. Was the Crown a part of Ilûnator?

Not as such, the dragon told him.

It was hardly a battle at all after that, to Kellarn's way of thinking. He had all of his determination and stubbornness, but freed from the weariness that weighed on mortal strength; and Ilunâtor was bright and terrible and fearlessly joyful.

And yet it was still a battle. Lo-Khuma was strong, evasive and slippery. Nor could Kellarn simply resist him, letting the dragon do all the work. He had to move and block and watch ahead for his tricks, as though they were still crossing blades. The Enemy mocked and belittled him, or flattered his strength, or offered friendship and love, and service to bring great power for the good of all. He shifted in form from cloud to man, or became a thing of scales and wings, or slithering coils, or fluid and formless as molten rock. But Kellarn fought on, forcing him back or chasing after him; and Ilunâtor was always with him, and full of his dragon's wiles, and around every corner waiting.

They hounded the Enemy through a world of blue ice, like the home of the northern fay; and over mountaintop realms of wind and snow, and through sun-filled cloud, and deserts of rock and ash. And then he fled before them through tunnels and chasms down into the deep places of the earth. They passed through mazes of darkness, through halls of chains and wheels and grilles, and sudden pits, and doors of iron and brass; and rough caverns filled with living jewels, and jagged rocks sharp as knives. The shadowfay were there, and the winged horrors of the *gorghaim*, and nameless creatures of claw and slime and bitter cold. And then they went deeper still, to where the rock of the world's heart burned with fire unquenchable; and then up through vents and passages of smoke and steam, and out into the endless vault of the heavens.

They came at last to an empty realm of bare mountain peaks, where no snow had ever fallen nor living thing grown. The sky overhead was utterly dark, save for the flicker of rainbowed starlight on the wings of the Father of All Dragons himself. The Enemy had abandoned all other shapes and forms, and stood before them like a pillar of stone and fire. But the stone was fluid and clouded; and the fire burned around it and through it, so that it roiled and seethed without rest.

I am of the stuff of which the world is made, said the stone, *and the life of the gods is within me. You can no more destroy my undying spirit than you can destroy your own.*

'That does not matter,' said Kellarn. 'Ilunâtor can destroy us both. And though he slay me, yet still shall I love him.'

There was a stirring on the air around them, and the first light of dawn bled up into the sky. The stone surged more strongly within itself, and the flames flared and spat.

Ilunâtor was waiting for him. Kellarn thought that he understood.

'The Sun is Fire and Air,' he said. 'That you can never be, nor were you meant to be. Nor would you be happy, being that. You can love the Sun for what he is – or who he is – and love him because he is different. But you are Fire and Earth. It's a difficult mix. I know.'

The Enemy mocked him, and his laughter was the roar of a landslide. *You know*, he sneered. *You know nothing. You are a spark, a pebble on the mountains of the world. Your wisdom is shorter than a day. I do not want your pity. I am the pain and terror of the gods, the force that destroys form and turns the wheels of the world. I am what the gods made me to be.*

Kellarn ran his hand through his hair. The mockery did not touch him. He could see beyond the words. The pain and terror were the Enemy's own; he suffered them within, and so he flung them at all the worlds around. He was Fire and Earth out of balance. On a far lesser scale – a pebble to a mountain – he knew the problem. It was the balance that he had had to find within himself. He did not claim to have all the answers, or even a particularly good answer, but he had to offer something.

He felt Ilunâtor's breath upon his back. He knew that he was right.

'Let me show you,' he said. He braced himself, sent a last thought of love back to Ilunâtor, and stepped into the roiling stone.

Fire ripped all around and through him. Earth and gravel smothered and filled him, chill and slick as mud. There was terror and pain beyond enduring, and the horror of endless dying and devouring. But Kellarn did not shrink back. He let the Fire and the Earth take him, ravaging every part, until they – or he – should be thoroughly spent. And there was still Ilunâtor with him.

He passed through darkness and fire until all thought and memory fled, and all that was left to him was the oblivion of peace.

When Kellarn came to himself he was lying on a grassy bank in the sunlight. There were mountain slopes on either side and a steep ridge ahead of him, all mantled in clean snow, and a clear blue sky overhead, so that the place had the feel of a high valley. There was the sound of falling water nearby.

Kellarn sat up and stretched, more from habit than any stiffness of limb. A little way off, near the base of the ridge, stood a single slender tower. It was square, without windows or doors, nor decoration of any kind. It looked to be made of the same rare stone as the White Manor of his Dortrean home.

At the foot of the black stone cliff, immediately below the tower, reared two large statues of winged dragons, one black and one white. They stood back to back, with tails entwined, and there was an archway in the rock between them; and a small waterfall came down on either side, pouring from their raised forepaws. A wide pool spread out about their feet, and spilled over into a little stream not far from where Kellarn sat.

There was a whispering on the breeze, and Ilunâtor's great head appeared on the ground before him. The dragon was stretched out across the grass, trailing the tip of his long tail in the waters of the pool. He shone like newly washed crystal in the mountain sunlight. The two of them looked at one another for some time, quite comfortable in the silence.

'What became of – him?' Kellarn asked at last.

'What he *will* become,' Ilunâtor corrected him, in a voice wild and deep and full of great joy, 'is in the hands of the Lords of the *Aeshtar*. But his evil is ended, and the Fire and Earth within him are at peace. Now he flies, like the rest of us, to find his own place in the great harmony of the dance.'

Kellarn looked at the statues. 'Were you and he – opposites, then?' he asked.

The dragon snorted. 'You know better than that.'

Kellarn wiggled his bare toes in the grass contentedly. He had thought at first that he was in the Realms of the Dead, but the feel of this place was different from how he remembered them. It seemed somehow familiar, and homely.

'Is this where you live?' he asked

'I come here at times,' answered the dragon, sounding amused. 'The *syldhar* made it. But you can not stay here, Joy of my Joy. You must return.'

'To the Realms of Dead?' said Kellarn. He did not want to leave Ilunâtor.

'No, to the waking world. You must take up the rule of Lautun. The Guardians have ordained it. See, where they come!'

Kellarn stood up and turned around. He could see the rest of the valley now, filled with grass and trees, with a tall mountain peak to either side. Three women were walking toward him from different parts of the valley.

From his left came the tallest and fairest, clad in a gown of simple white. Her hair shone yellow gold, rippling down in unbraided tresses to well below the long sash of her hanging girdle, and a splendour of power shimmered on the air all around her. Kellarn knew without being told that she was Aranur of the golden fay, far older and more powerful than even Heruvor of Starmere himself; and she was the Guardian of the golden forest of Hellenur, west of the Shining Hills of Lautun.

From his right came the moon fay Losithlîn, Guardian of the great forest of Cerrodhí, in her gown of silver green and with a garland of purple flowers in her flowing silver hair. And coming up the valley from the far end was Dyrnalv, Guardian of the Telbray Woods, now clad all in bright scarlet, with her hair shining like burnished copper in the sunlight.

The three women arrived together just a few paces from where he stood. They bowed deeply to Ilunâtor, and then to Kellarn himself. He bowed awkwardly in return.

'But I thought that I was dying,' he said to the dragon.

'You were,' Ilunâtor told him. 'Even now you stand on the very brink, between the Living and the Dead. There are friends who call you back, and friends who call you on.'

'He must go back,' said Aranur in her deep, glorious voice. 'He must heal the land, and bring the Kingdoms to harmony and peace. For this Halgan and Linaelin gave their lives, and many others with them through the long years. This he can do well, and the people of the Kingdoms will listen to him.'

'Yet others might do this also,' said Losithlîn. 'He should go on, in measure with the great dance of life and death. He has earned his rest. We may ask no more of him.'

'We may ask,' said Dyrnalv, 'but the choice should be his. We can only open the way. Kellarn must choose whether he wishes to walk through.'

Kellarn's first instinct was to say no. He had achieved what he set out to do, and fought well enough. He had not loved his life in the world so much that he wanted to go back to it; and the burdens of the Court and everyday human things were not what he wanted at all. Losithlîn was right, he had earned his rest.

Yet he could not stay here, high in the mountains with Ilunâtor, where he was at peace. And there were other things in the world, apart from humankind, that he loved. The mountains were there also, and the forests and the Fay, and the Guardians themselves, and all manner of wonderful creatures. And then of course there was Kierran, and friends like Corollin and Mellin; and the Court would be in turmoil, and the Kingdoms would soon be at war, and Rhysana and the Magi seemed to be relying upon him. And besides, he could not sit around and do nothing forever. He had to be doing something. That was part of who he was.

'Shall I ever see you again?' he asked Ilunâtor.

'I am always with you,' the dragon said. 'Besides, you have much to learn. It would be most unsafe to leave you alone.'

Kellarn laughed for simple joy. And then the dragon breathed on him, and the world melted into a cloud of rainbowed brightness all around.

The brightness faded into darkness, but warm and comfortable. There was a chirruping of small birds nearby, and the high calls of sea birds in the distance. Kellarn caught the scent of polished wood and soap. He opened his eyes slowly, and found himself in his own bed in the Dortrean apartment. The shuttered windows were open on to the balcony, and the soft light of late afternoon came in from the shadowed courtyard outside.

A young woman was sitting on the edge of the bed looking down at him, her red gold hair swept back behind her ears. Dyrnalv, the Guardian of Telbray Woods.

'I love you,' said Kellarn.

'That was part of the problem,' she said.

'What problem?' He went to sit up, but his stomach was still too tender. She pushed him back gently, and smiled.

'You must rest a while yet,' she told him. 'Imarra has healed you, and her gifts are great even by the measure of the Môshári.

But you should not go running around for a day or two.' She patted his shoulder and stood up.

'I saw you,' he said. 'In the valley, with Ilunâtor.'

'I know,' Dyrnalv nodded. 'You have given us a gift beyond price. You are well named the Joy of Ilunâtor.'

Kellarn closed his eyes, remembering. There were too many questions in his head for him to catch.

'Are the other Guardians here?' he asked, turning his head on the pillow to look at her.

'They are,' she said. 'The *syldhar* called to us when the Enemy came; and you already know that it was we who urged that you should be healed. But we have other work that calls us away just now. If you ask, we shall come back to see your crowning – or your wedding.'

'I do not want to be crowned,' said Kellarn. 'And I have no intention of marrying anyone.'

Dyrnalv smiled sadly. 'That is what Corollin said that you would say,' she said.

'Is she all right?' he asked.

'She has been waiting to see you,' said Dyrnalv. 'I shall send her in. But I should be gone – I promised your mother that I would not stay too long.'

She picked up her heavy stole of red and gold from the foot of the bed. Kellarn now realised that she was robed all in black. He struggled within himself. There was something else that he must ask her.

'Linaelin?' he managed.

Dyrnalv came back and sat down beside him, taking him by the hand.

'She has gone to the long home of the Fay,' she told him; 'and Halgan and Torriearn are no longer with us, in this life. Gwydion was lost too, alas! Father Dharagh has taken their bodies back to the Sun Temple, and Father Ûrsîn with him. What remains of the Emperor's body, and the Empress and the others, will have the Rite of Burning at sunset. Your friend Carstan Mairdun is seeing to that, since their kinsmen have chosen the rites of the *Vashta* faith.'

'I ought to go,' said Kellarn.

'You ought to rest,' she said firmly. She leaned forward and kissed him on the forehead. 'Never stop loving us,' she whispered, 'even when we do not deserve it.' Then she stood up and went away.

Kellarn lay quietly, feeling the tears trickle down the sides of his face. He grieved for Linaelin, though he had known her for such a short time, and for all the other friends and kinsmen that he had lost. He wondered who else might have fallen.

There was the murmur of low voices outside the door. Kellarn lifted his hand to wipe his eyes. It was the arm that had been slashed by the Enemy's sword. There was still a faint red line running nearly from wrist to elbow, and the whole arm ached with stiffness; but it was no worse than that.

The voices continued, but the door opened a little and Kierran of Arrand slipped inside. He had changed into a loose grey shirt, and his left arm was in a sling. He padded over quickly to the nearest side of the bed and took Kellarn by the hand.

'Your mother sends her love,' Kierran told him. 'Lord Brodhaur needed her for something.'

'That sounds like Mother,' Kellarn sighed. 'Is she running the palace already?'

'She was here until ten minutes ago,' said Kierran. 'But that is typical of your timing.'

Kellarn lifted Kierran's hand to his lips and kissed it, and the two of them grinned at one another. And then the door opened wider and Corollin came in, with Mellin Carfinn behind her. Kierran fetched over a chair for Mellin with his good arm, while Corollin found one nearby.

'I am sorry that you had to come back to all of this,' she said; 'but glad to see you.'

Kellarn smiled in answer. 'And Mîsha,' he said, looking at Mellin. She was dressed in a formal gown of bright Carfinn green, with her yellow gold hair hidden beneath a black snood. 'Why are you here?'

'To see my Lord and Emperor,' said Mellin.

'Don't,' said Kellarn.

'And future husband, some say,' Kierran teased, sitting down on the bed beside him.

'Don't,' said Kellarn again. 'Mellin deserves better. I've said all along that she should marry Boldrin.'

'I have hardly met the man,' Mellin protested.

'You'll like him,' said Kellarn. Then a shadow fluttered at the back of his mind, and he glanced at Kierran. 'Is Boldrin all right?' he asked. 'And Rhysana and the magi?'

'A little bloodied and battered, but they'll live,' Kierran assured him. 'They're at a Council meeting just now.'

'Are *you* all right?' asked Corollin. 'What happened, exactly?'

Kellarn closed his eyes briefly. 'The Enemy is gone,' he told them. 'His evil is ended.'

Corollin's face shone with relief. Kierran thumped his leg through the bedclothes, and Kellarn winced.

'It was Ilunâtor who did it, really,' he told Corollin. 'But we could never have managed it without all of you. I'll tell you the rest later.'

'I shall hold you to that,' she said.

'But what happened in the hall, once I had the Crown?' he asked.

Corollin frowned, and then sighed. 'No more demons came, I think,' she said. 'The Enemy had been drawing on their strength to resist me, when I challenged him with the Crown. After he fell, and you fell on top of him, no more of them came.

'The great demons opened a chasm across the hall. One of them leaped into it with Father Torriearn and Gwydion, and one of the knights from the Sun Temple. Prime Councillor Ellen rescued their bodies, and we believe that the demon itself was destroyed. Imarra of Môshári banished the other great demon, with Gravhan and Dharagh to help her. Between the rest of us we destroyed the *gorghaim*.'

'We thought that we had lost you,' said Kierran, his voice catching in his throat.

'We were very worried for a while,' said Corollin, interrupting him. 'But now you are safely healed, and the Enemy is destroyed, and this palace is as peaceful as I guess it ever can be. And you need to get some rest. We can talk about everything later.'

Kellarn opened his mouth to speak, then thought the better of it and simply nodded and smiled.

The two women kissed him and went out. Kierran shut the door quietly behind them, and came back to the bedside.

'What happened to the Crown?' Kellarn asked him.

Kierran went over to the press and lifted out a tray covered with a white cloth. He carried it a little awkwardly, balancing it in one hand, and set it down on the bed where Kellarn could see it. The seven white metal bars were laid out side by side, their coloured gems winking softly in the dim light. Corollin's pendant had gone from the seventh bar.

'It fell apart when you fell on top of him,' Kierran explained. 'That was partly why everyone was so worried. You were so cold.'

'When did I fall?' asked Kellarn.

'Very soon after you put it on,' said Kierran. 'But the Enemy was shrinking by then. By the time I could get to you, you were lying on top of the Emperor. Or what was left of him.'

'Ugh,' said Kellarn. 'I don't want to think about that.'

He looked again at the bars, and then up at his friend's face. There were tears in Kierran's grey eyes.

'I am here,' Kellarn told him gently. 'Just sit with me for a little while.'

Kierran put the tray down on the floor, sat down on the side of the bed and took him by the hand. Kellarn rested his head back on the bolster, smiled, and let his eyelids drift shut.

* * *

When he opened his eyes again the light in the courtyard had grown dimmer, and there was the coolness of approaching rain. A yellow lamp had been lit in the bedchamber. Kierran had left his side, and was talking quietly to two more people in the doorway. Both of them had silver fair hair that seemed to shimmer in the lamplight.

'Ru,' Kellarn smiled. 'Rhysana.'

Kierran let the magi come in.

'We shall not keep you long,' Rhysana promised. 'But we heard that you were awake.'

She had put on robes of dark grey and her face was unusually pale. She looked as tired as though she had not slept for a week; but her face was all smiles, and her sweet voice was as clear and steady as ever.

'Torkhaal is well?' Kellarn asked her. He thought it a safe enough question.

'He is well, thank you,' she said, sitting herself down in the chair that Corollin had used earlier. She glanced down at the floor by her feet. 'He is with Ellen just now. They are trying to make the stonework of the audience hall a little safer. I am afraid that it may have to be rebuilt.'

Kellarn smiled. 'And is this to be my problem?' he asked. 'Do you still want me to make the claim for the throne of Lautun?'

Rhysana smoothed the folds of her robes into place. 'The whole citadel must have heard the tale of your triumph by now,' she said, 'and those who were not there, or who left the hall early, have embroidered it in the telling. But yes, the Guardians have advised it, and the Scholars of Blood Law have agreed that you have a strong claim to challenge Vaulun for the throne. And the vote of the Court Noble would probably support it.'

'You should have seen Mage Councillor Drengriis' face when he spoke with the Guardians,' grinned Hrugaar. 'Yet he would have supported you anyway.'

'As shall we all,' said Rhysana. 'The Emperor's crown is yours for the asking, Kellarn – if you wish to make challenge, that is. I know that the thought will hardly fill you with joy.'

'You shall have to be Emperor,' said Hrugaar, 'if I am to be Lord Steward of Ellanguan. For I shall serve none other.'

'You shall serve all your people as Steward,' said Kellarn.

'You sound like an Emperor already,' said the mage.

'Not really,' said Kellarn. 'That is the whole point of Blood Noble, Ru. We are born and raised to serve the people of the Kingdoms – not just to use them, as the imperial nobles seem to think. Perhaps that was where Lautun went wrong.'

'One of the many places,' said Kierran.

'Besides,' said Kellarn, 'I do not want to be called Emperor. Could I not be called Earl of Lautun, or Lord Steward, or something?'

'High Earl?' Hrugaar offered.

'The name matters less,' said Rhysana. 'If you will take the throne, Kellarn, then take it; and I for one shall be very glad. But I think that you may have to suffer being called Emperor to begin with.'

'Just don't mention marriage or children to him,' said Kierran.

'I should not dream of it,' Rhysana smiled.

Kellarn twisted his fingers in the quilt, trying to think. He was still tired and rather hungry, though he was not sure how well his stomach would cope with food.

'You mentioned Ellanguan, Ru,' he said. 'What is happening there now?'

'We have talked about that in the Council,' Hrugaar told him. 'With Rinnekh and T'Loi gone, and High Councillor Sollonaal, the city should soon be a happier place. The *Aeshta* Orders are planning how to defend it, in case the Southers should come soon.'

'There is still the problem with the Braedun *commanderie*,' Rhysana added. 'But with a new Emperor, and with Lo-Khuma now gone, the Southers there may be persuaded to leave without a fight.'

'And the Easterners may not come at all,' put in Hrugaar.

'The *Aeshta* Orders will keep watch there for now,' said Rhysana, 'until you are strong enough to think about it.'

'The Southers,' said Kellarn, sitting up. The sudden pain made him gasp. He drew his knees up beneath the quilt and hugged them. 'What about the warships outside?'

'They are taken,' said Rhysana, looking at him anxiously. Kellarn looked back at her, and nodded.

'Tell me, please,' he said.

The two magi exchanged glances. 'In brief, then,' Rhysana allowed.

'When the horn call sounded,' said Hrugaar, 'we knew that the warships would attack. The Southers would be trying to reach T'Loi, and the palace guards might be hard put to turn back many hundred K'tarim warriors unaided.

'I went down to the river wing, with Haësella of Braedun and others. There were imperial guards there before us, but not many. Yet Kelmaar and the Môshári were prepared, and their ships were not far away. And Tinûkenil came, bringing the sea fay.'

'Tinûkenil?' Kellarn echoed.

'You should have seen it,' Hrugaar said, his fair face shining in the lamplight. 'Tinûkenil brought the Northerner host, and the knights of Mairdun; and the sea fay brought them all under the river waters, and up to board the Souther ships in mid-stream. And then the sea fay themselves came up on to the quay, in the shape of tall warriors made all of water, with glittering spears and shields.'

'I should have been there,' said Kellarn.

'You cannot be everywhere,' Hrugaar pointed out.

'There were many who died, on both sides,' said Rhysana. 'And there was some fighting within the citadel, with those loyal to the Emperor and the Enemy.'

'We had other help there,' said Hrugaar. 'Korîl came, and the son of the King of the Elves of the North, and Tinûkenil's other friends with them. The citadel is at peace again now.'

'Is Tinûkenil here?' asked Kierran.

'No,' said Hrugaar. 'He was shy of coming into the citadel. They have gone back with the knights of Mairdun to the Northerner camp beyond the city.'

Kellarn lay down again carefully. He was finding it too much to take in. But at least the Enemy was gone, and the Emperor and Rinnekh.

'What happened to the Emperor's Archmage?' he asked aloud.

'He is dying,' Rhysana told him. 'Father Torriearn struck him down, even as he said he would. The Guardians have taken him prisoner. They asked Mellin Carfinn to pass judgement on him – they felt that it was her right to do so.'

Kellarn nodded to himself. He guessed that Dyrnalv would have suggested that.

'What did Mellin say?' he asked.

'She went to visit him,' said Rhysana. 'Mellin may perhaps tell you the tale herself, when she is ready. But she did tell me that she left the Guardians to deal with him, according to their own wisdom.'

'And how do the Council feel about that?' asked Kellarn.

'He is a mage under our protection,' she allowed. 'Yet for his part in what happened today he would have to make answer to the Council, and might well be stripped of all his power. And since he will probably not live long enough to stand trial anyway, the question is a moot point. It might be kinder to let him just pass quietly away. Prime Councillor Ellen will speak to the Guardians.'

Kellarn nodded in answer. The room fell quiet. He could hear the spattering of the first raindrops on the balcony parapet outside. There was one last question that he had wanted to ask, but he could not remember it. And then Kierran asked it for him.

'High Councillor Rhysana,' he said, 'how did you manage to make the Enemy give Kellarn the Crown?'

Rhysana smoothed the folds of her robes again, and looked

around the panelled walls. Hrugaar leaned forward in his chair, as if he too wished to hear her answer.

'I think,' she said, 'that it was simply the grace of the gods, to help us in our hour of need.

'And besides,' she went on, standing up, 'being the mother of a two year old boy is good practice for making oneself heard.'

She touched Kellarn's hand lightly in farewell. Hrugaar grinned and gave a bobbing bow, and the two of them went away.

'Do you think that there is something she isn't telling us?' asked Kierran, when they were left alone.

'Oh, probably,' said Kellarn. 'But Rhysana has a good heart. Perhaps that was the best answer that she felt able to give.'

He let his eyes drift closed again. Kierran got up and began to move around quietly, putting away the tray and the chairs and setting the bedchamber to rights; and then he pulled off his boots and lay down on the other side of the bed.

Kellarn stilled his mind from all the turmoil of the day – the horror, the victory and the loss – and thought simply of the peace of the moment. The bustle of the citadel still went on all around them, though hushed and distant here, heard only faintly through the open windows. The cries of the sea birds had gone silent. There was just the gentle sound of their own breathing, and the cool evening breeze drifting in from the courtyard; and the steady beat of the falling rain, lulling them to sleep as it washed all things clean and new.

Index of Names

A'lil – a captain of the K'tarim fleet.

Aartaús, House – Median House Noble; horsebreeders with land northeast of the Lautun plains.

Aeshtar, The – ancient elemental gods revered by the Six Kingdoms; still worshipped by many within the empire, and by most of the magi. [*gen. pl.* **Aeshta**].

Aghaira, Kata – gifted loremaster and storyteller from the Eastern Domains.

Aidhan of Dârghûn, Lord – one of Herusen's grandchildren; son of Serinta.

Aramen Vansa of Braedun, Lady – sister of the Earl of Vansa and wife to Tirrel of Braedun; priestess of Maachel.

Aranara – lesser contemplative Order of the *Aeshtar*, devoted to Haëstren.

Aranel – *Vashta* Lord of Faithfulness; one of the Twin Gods.

Aranur – a woman of the golden fay, serving as the Guardian of Hellenur.

Arienn Farási of Tersal, Lady – favourite niece of Môrghran of Fâghsul and sister to Tarrek Cardhási.

Arrand, The – Head of House Arrand and ruler of the city of Arrandin; father of Bradhor, Jared, and Kierran; former member of the Imperial Council.

Asharka of Braedun, High Councillor – Principal of the College of Magi in Farran; sister-in-law to Ferghaal.

Atallakûr – name used among the Fay for the demon captain Lo-Khuma.

Aúghan Vaulun, Lord – Earl of Vaulun and Head of House

Vaulun; elder brother of Kharfaal, and first cousin to the Emperor Rhydden; Imperial Counsellor.

Aúrun of Renza, Lord – husband and lesser kinsman of Broneïs.

Baelar, Father – Black Destrier; Truthsayer and priest of Fraërigr from the Temple of War in Ellanguan.

Bars, The – Kellarn's name for the jewelled white metal bars thought to be parts of an artefact made by the First Kings.

Black Destriers – elite and most secret body of imperial spies and inquisitors, fanatically loyal to the person of the Emperor himself.

Blackbeards, The – ancient dwarven clan of the Black Mountains, legendary for their smithwork and rich mines.

Blood Laws – ancient and complex laws governing marriage, inheritance and title within the Six Kingdoms.

Boldrin of Levrin, Lord – holy knight and senior guard officer in the Temple of Telúmachel in Arrandin.

Borderlander – name given to the people of the Six Kingdoms living east of Arrandin or in the hills west of Farran.

Bradhor of Arrand, Lord – eldest son and heir designate to The Arrand.

Braedun, House – Greater House Noble; principals of the most senior religious Order of the *Aeshtar*, devoted to Telúmachel and the Tumbrachin.

Bright Alliance, The – legendary alliance of humans, *noghru* and Fay in the wars before the founding of the Six Kingdoms.

Brin – Taillan's toy wooden horse.

Brodhaur Levrin, Lord – Earl of Levrin; Commander in Chief of the Imperial Household Guard; Imperial Counsellor.

Bromaer Kelmaar of Româdhrí, Lady – priestess of Maësta; sister to Miranda and Camarra and wife to Drengriis.

Broneïs of Renza, Lady – Regent of Renza; wife to Aúrun and sister-in-law to Lauraï Raudhar of Renza.

Brörigr – *Vashta* Lord of Knowledge and Poetic Rhetoric; Head of the House of Arts; rival brother of Fraërigr.

Camarra Kelmaar of Dârghûn, Lady – journeyman mage; sister to Bromaer and Miranda and wife to Haldrin Dârghûn.

Caraan – legendary mage of the early sixth century; founder of the first Council of Magi.

Carstan Mairdun, Lord – Head of House Mairdun; Abbot Commander, Lord Priest and supreme head of the Hyrsenite Order of Mairdun; gifted scholar with formidable psychic skills.

Cavalry, Imperial Household – mounted division of the Imperial Household Guard.

Chaedar, The – collective name for the invisible, non-human attendants in the College of Magi in Lautun.

Col – childhood name for Kellarn; also **Collie** or **Collie-dog.**

Corollin – journeyman mage; adopted daughter of Morvaan.

Corrimaer, Mage Councillor – Junior Lecturer at the College of Magi in Farran.

Council of Magi, The – ancient assembly comprising all ranking magi, established to govern the ethical practice and welfare of their art.

Court of Kings – assembly of the rulers of the Six Kingdoms; forerunner of the Court Noble.

Court Noble – collective name for all those with noble precedence, either by right of birth or conferred through achievement of rank within the religious Orders or the Council of Magi.

Dakhmaal, Mage Councillor – itinerant mage from Farran; friend of Tinûkenil.

Dalzhaúr, Mage Councillor – lecturer at the College of Magi in Arrandin; temporarily relocated to Ellanguan.

Dannil of Valhaes, Lord – eldest son and heir apparent to Torreghal Valhaes.

Demon Captain, The – *see* ***Lo-Khuma***.

Dernam Rebraal, Lord – Head of House Rebraal and ruler of the lesser port of Rebraal; father of Inghara.

Destriers – *see* ***Black Destriers***.

Dharagh, Holy Father – a *noghr* from the Highland Mountains; Chosen Priest of Hýriel.

Dhûghaúr of Moraan, Sir – Mage Councillor; lesser kinsman of the borderlords of Herghin.

Dhûlann, House – Lesser House Noble of Dortrean.

Drengriis of Româdhrí, Lord – Mage Councillor; bursar of the College of Magi in Ellanguan; husband to Bromaer.

Drômagh of Sêchral, Lord – Knight Commander of the Imperial Household Cavalry; Imperial Counsellor; uncle to Grinnaer.

Drôshiin of Sêchral, Lord – High Councillor; lesser kinsman of Drômagh and Grinnaer.

Dukhoi – a mage of the sixth century.

Durlan – a borderlander from the city port of Farran; drowned in the wreck of the Souther fleet off the coast of Sentai.

Dwarves, The – *see* ***Noghru, The.***

Dyrnalv – Guardian of Telbray Woods.

Eädhan, House – Median House Noble with lands north of Ellanguan and on the coast south of Sentai; kinsmen to Torkhaal on his mother's side.

Easterners – name given to the peoples of the ancient domains lying east and north of the Blue Mountains.

Edhrin Ercusí, Lord – Earl of Ercusí and Head of House Ercusí; Imperial Counsellor.

Ekraan of Eädhan, Lord – High Councillor; Trialmaster for the Council of Magi.

Elders of Radbrodal, The – mystic loremasters and seers of the Northern Lands, dwelling in permanent retreat in the forests north of the Highland Mountains.

Ellaïn Dortrean of Arrand, Lady – daughter of Erkal and Karlena; wife to Jared of Arrand and mother of Terrel and Korren.

Ellen of Raudhar, Lady – Archmage; most senior female member of the Council of Magi in terms of magical rank.

Elvenfolk, The – *see* ***Fay, The.***

Eminence, His – honorific title for an Imperial Counsellor; also used as a derogatory epithet for the Archmage Merrech.

Enemy, The – *see* ***Lo-Khuma.***

Enghlar of Braedun, Father – priest of Telúmachel; Master of the Temple at the Braedun *commanderie*.

Eonnaï of Gadhrai, Lady – priestess of Brörigr and bursar of the *Vashta* School in Ellanguan.

Eörendin – *Vashta* Lady of Creativity and Earthly Love; consort of Brörigr.

Eralaan, Mage Councillor – Senior Lecturer at the College of Magi in Ellanguan.

Ercusí, House – Ancient House Noble, most senior of all the Houses of Ellanguan; renowned for being eccentric and outspoken, and habitually divided among themselves upon all matters.

Eriss Telbray, Lady – former Head of House Telbray, and late cousin of Patall; murdered by the shadowfay.

Erkal Dortrean, Lord – Earl of Dortrean; husband to Karlena and father of Solban, Kellarn and Ellaïn; Imperial Counsellor.

Falladan – founder and first King of the ancient kingdom of Ellanguan; younger brother of Ferrughôr.

Farási, House – Median House Noble of Lautun; horsebreeders specialising in swift running coursers.

Farran, Lord Steward of – *see* ***Rhodhar Farran, Lord.***

Father of All Dragons – *see* ***Ilunâtor.***

Fauns, The – magical forest creatures, half human and half beast. *See also* ***Forest Folk, The.***

Fay, The – immortal elemental beings, in mystic harmony with one or more aspects or qualities of the elemental nature of the created world (hence sea fay, moon fay etc.); also known collectively as the Elvenfolk.

Ferghaal of Braedun, Lord – High Councillor; Principal of the Braedun Order in Farran.

Ferrughôr – founder and first King of the ancient kingdom of Hauchan; elder brother of Falladan.

Ferunel – one of the moon fay; sister of Losithlîn and kinswoman to Heruvor.

Firinaakr – a red-golden dragon.

First Council – the original Council of Magi founded by Caraan in the year 512; refers more generally to the Council of Magi during the period from its first founding until the end of Caraan's rule as Prime Councillor of All Magi.

First Kings – name given to the early rulers of the Six Kingdoms in the first century following the triumph of the Bright Alliance; more properly the first King and founder of each of the Six Kingdoms, namely Ferrughôr and Falladan, Llaruntôr, Halgan, Cyresodha (first King of Cerrodhí) and Morvargh.

Flower of the Staff – magical name of Herusen Dârghûn.

Foghlaar, High Councillor – Trialmaster for the Council of Magi; expert in the magical arts of glamour and beguilement.

Forest Folk, The – collective name for the magical creatures inhabiting the forests of the Middle Lands, in particular the fauns, centaurs, and wilder spirits of trees, water and stone; rarely used to refer to the Fay.

Forval Sentai, Lord – Head of House Sentai; widowed brother-in-law of Erkal Dortrean.

Fraërigr – *Vashta* Lord of War; Head of the House of War; rival brother of Brörigr.

Galsin, House – Ancient House Noble from the borders of the Endless Plains.

Ghîlsaan of Telbray, Sir – Mage Councillor; lecturer at the College of Magi in Farran.

Ghomughr – a legendary monster from the ancient tales of the Eastern Domains, part artefact and part creature.

Gilraen – former Guardian of Telbray Woods.

God-King, The – supreme ruler of the Souther empire beyond the sea.

Golden Age of the Magi – historical period associated with the greatest flourishing of the Magi's art, reckoned from the founding of the First Council until about the year 1000.

Gorghaim, The – winged demons of earth and stone.

Goshaún of Sêchral, Lord – youngest brother and personal guard of Grinnaer; murdered by Rhydden.

Gradhellan Ellanguan, Lord Steward – former ruler of Ellanguan.

Gravhan Dârghûn of Môshári, Lord – holy knight and commander of the Môshári Order; Herusen's oldest surviving son; husband to Imarra.

Grinnaer Sêchral of Lautun, Lady – Empress Consort to Rhydden; niece to Drômagh.

Guard, Household – personal liveried military force retained by a House Noble. *See also* ***Guard, Imperial Household.***

Guard, Imperial Household – personal household guard of the Lautun Emperors, comprising mounted and foot soldiers; only those of Blood Noble admitted to its ranks. *See also* ***Cavalry, Imperial Household and Household, Imperial.***

Guardians, The – ancient wardens of *Aeshta* lore and power; hunted down and eradicated by the rulers of the Lautun Empire in the second half of the fifteenth century, in an attempt to break the tenacious hold of the elder faith of the Six Kingdoms.

Gwydion – warrior from the borderland earldom of Vansa; friend of Tinûkenil.

Haësella of Braedun, Lady – holy knight of the Braedun Order.

Haëstren – *Aeshta* Lady of the Moon; daughter of Maësta, and bride of Torollen; depicted variously as maiden, queen, withered crone or guardian panthress.

Hakhutt – Envoy to the Emperor Rhydden from the Northern Lands.

Haldrin Dârghûn, Lord – eldest grandson and heir designate to Herusen Dârghûn; son of Rogheïn Aartaús of Dârghûn.

Halgan – founder and first King of the ancient kingdom of Khêltan; Chosen Priest of Hýriel and Torollen.

Hannaï of Braedun, Lady – priestess of Telúmachel; Weather-master for the Braedun ship during Erkal's voyage south to the Braedun *commanderie*.

Hendraal of Tarágin, Sir – Mage Councillor; lecturer at the College of Magi in Ellanguan.

Herghin, House – Lesser House Noble of the eastern borderlands, under the overlordship of The Arrand.

Herusen Dârghûn, Lord – former Head of House Dârghûn and Prime Councillor of All Magi; late father of Gravhan.

Heruvor – one of the moon fay; lord of Starmere.

High Clan Chieftain, The – greatest of the Easterner chieftains; ruler of the city of Kara Ko-Daighru.

High Council, The – elite inner circle of the Council of Magi, comprising all High Councillors and Archmagi.

High Servant of War – name given to senior priests of the *Vashta* House of War.

Hirulin – one of the moon fay; daughter of Heruvor, and mother of Linaelin; estranged from her father after her marriage to Ferrughôr.

Hollis of Eädhan, Sir – cadet of the Imperial Household Guard.

Household – collective term for the body of servants belonging to a House Noble. *See also* ***Household, Imperial***.

Household, Imperial – all non-military servants and attendants of the Imperial House Lautun.

Hrugaar, Mage Councillor – newly appointed Secretary to the Council of Magi; unrecognised son of the late Sîraelin of Ellanguan and one of the sea fay; close friend of Rhysana and Torkhaal.

Hýriel – *Aeshta* Lady of Fire; divine mother of Torollen, Lord of the Sun; patron goddess of Dortrean.

Hýriel, Order of – military religious Order of the *Aeshtar*, devoted to Hýriel and Torollen.

Hyrsenites – priests, knights and lay brothers of the military religious Order of Mairdun, devoted to the goddess Hýrsien; principal *commanderie* at Mairdun.

Hýrsien – *Vashta* Lady of Peace and Motherhood; consort of Fraërigr and divine mother of Serbramel.

Idesîn Mairdun of Telbray, Lady – Hyrsenite priestess; wife to Patall Telbray and cousin to Carstan.

Ierodh of Valhaes, Lord – lesser commander of the Valhaes troops sent to Farran.

Ilionin – islander peoples dwelling off the coast of the Souther mainland; generally looked down upon and abused by other Souther nations.

Illana – legendary mage of the early sixth century; author of the *Mazes and Psychic Constructs* and disputed author of the *Argument of Command*; renowned for technical brilliance and an irredeemably evil disposition.

Ilumarin of Aranara, Lady – Chosen Priestess of Haëstren, released from the contemplative vows of her Order.

Ilunâtor – Father of All Dragons; held to be the first and greatest of all dragonkind.

Imarra of Môshári, Lady – Chosen Priestess of Temrbrin; wife to Gravhan.

Imperial Council, The – formal advisory council to the Emperor, by custom having representatives from at least four Houses Ancient among its eight principal seats.

Imperial Counsellor, The – frequently used epithet for the Archmage Merrech; formal title for any member of the Imperial Council.

Inghara Rebraal of Dhûlann, Lady – wife to Rinnakhal Dhûlann, and daughter of Dernam Rebraal; formerly held eligible as a candidate for Rhydden's second Empress Consort.

Interregnum, The – name given to the period of political and civil chaos during the regency and early years of Rhydden Lautun's reign.

Iorlaas, Prime Councillor – newly appointed Prime Councillor of All Magi; most senior mage of Serbramel within the Empire.

Irina Scaulun of Solaní, Lady – niece of Khadrôgh Scaulun;

sister-in-law to Rinnekh Ellanguan and to Lisâ Sêchral of Scaulun.

Irzael of Farran, Lord – elderly Mage Councillor; former Principal of the College of Magi in Farran.

Islanders – *see* ***Ilionin.***

Jared of Arrand, Lord – second son of The Arrand; husband to Ellaïn.

Jochaîl of Vaulun, Lord – Knight Captain of the Imperial Household Guard; eldest son of the late Lady Loghrana Lautun of Vaulun, and thus Rhydden's closest surviving kinsman of Lautun blood.

K'tarim – rich and powerful nation of warriors and sorcerers from the coastal lands of the Souther empire, related to the God-King's people of the Su'lorim; known among themselves as the *Kentorim.*

Kaïra, Reverend Mother – High Priestess of Serbramel in the city of Telbray.

Karlena Serra of Dortrean, Lady – Countess of Dortrean and wife to Erkal; mother of Solban, Kellarn and Ellaïn; foster mother to Mellin Carfinn.

Kellarn of Dortrean, Lord – younger son of Erkal and Karlena; now heir apparent to Dortrean.

Kelmaar, House – Greater House Noble; principals of the military religious Order of Kelmaar, devoted to the *Aeshta* Lords of Water.

Kentorim – *see* ***K'tarim.***

Khadhrôgh Scaulun, Lord – Earl of Scaulun; Imperial Counsellor.

Kharfaal of Vaulun, Lord – Mage Councillor; younger brother of the Earl of Vaulun and first cousin to the Emperor Rhydden; held to be the mage of highest noble precedence by right of blood.

Khyrfan of Telún, Lord – elder son of Lavan Telún and Nereïs; twin brother of Mâghan.

Kierran of Arrand, Lord – youngest son of The Arrand.

King of the Elves of the North – ruler of the moon fay in the far north, beyond the Blue Mountains; brother of Heruvor.

Korgan Lautun, Emperor – second Lautun Emperor of the Second Dynasty; reigned 1375-99; later named *the Weak* for his inability to control the dominant factions of the Court Noble; son of Urzael and younger brother of Mirren.

Kôril – one of the fay; friend of Corollin and Kellarn.

Korren of Arrand, Lord – younger son of Jared and Ellaïn; nephew to Kellarn.

Kyeruk of Telbray, Sir – Guard Commander in the city of Telbray.

Lauraï Raudhar of Renza, Lady – Regent of Renza; sister-in-law to Broneïs of Renza and niece to Ellen of Raudhar.

Lavan Telún, Lord – Head of House Telún; elder brother of Rhysana.

Lïall of Solaní, Lord – lesser cousin of Rinnekh; estranged from his Solaní kinsmen, and friend of the Kelmaar Order.

Liertiis, Mage Councillor – Junior Lecturer at the College of Magi in Lautun.

Linaelin – daughter of Ferrughôr and Hirulin; Queen of Hauchan after her father's death, and High Queen of the Six Kingdoms; lost when the city of Hauchan was overthrown in the year 89.

Linnaer, House – Greater House Noble, with lands on the coast beside the Galloppi River estuary.

Lirinal of Dregharis, Lord – High Councillor; lecturer at the College of Magi in Ellanguan.

Lisâ Sêchral of Scaulun, Lady – first cousin to Grinnaer; sister-in-law to Irina Scaulun of Solaní.

Llaruntôr – founder and first King of the ancient kingdom of Lautun; kinsman to Ferrughôr and Falladan.

Lo-Khuma – Easterner name for the great demon captain overthrown by the armies of the Bright Alliance; known as *Atallakûr* among the elvenfolk of the Fay.

Loghrana Lautun of Vaulun, Lady – formerly Rhydden's closest surviving cousin of Lautun name and blood by birth; late mother of Jochaîl.

Logray, House – Lesser House Noble, under the overlordship of Telbray.

Lorellin Herghin of Arrand, Lady – daughter and heir apparent to the late Lord Herghin.

Lorghan of Kelmaar – young guardsman in training at the Kelmaar School in Ellanguan.

Losithlîn – one of the moon fay, serving as the Guardian of Cerrodhí; kinswoman to Heruvor.

Lûghan of Vaulun, Lord – elder son of Kharfaal.

Maachel – *Aeshta* Lord of Earth.

Maëghlar of Kelmaar, Lord – elderly High Councillor, now living in permanent retreat.

Maësta – *Aeshta* Lord of Waters; divine father of Sherunar and Haëstren.

Mâghan of Telún, Lord – younger son of Lavan Telún and Nereïs; twin brother of Khyrfan.

Maïa of Telún, Lady – young daughter of Lavan Telún and Nereïs.

Mairdun, House – Lesser House Noble; principals of the Hyrsenite Order of Mairdun, the only *Vashta* Order to hold a bloodline of noble precedence. *See also* ***Hyrsenites***.

Markhûl – a *noghr*; Steward of the White Manor of Dortrean.

Master, The – *see* ***Lo-Khuma***.

Mataún of Fâghsul, Lord – knight of the Imperial Household Cavalry; nephew to Môrghran.

Meghîsen of the Order of Hýriel, Lady – priestess of Hýriel from the Temple of Fire in the Dortrean Valley, appointed to the Dortrean city house in Lautun.

Melissa of Vanbruch, Lady – pretty daughter of Lord Farad Vanbruch and heir to the Greater House Merchant Noble of Vanbruch.

Mellin Carfinn, Lady – Head of House Carfinn; lesser kinsman and favoured retainer of Erkal Dortrean; fostered by Karlena after her mother's death.

Merrech, Archmage – Imperial Counsellor; boyhood tutor and principal adviser to the Emperor Rhydden.

Mijal – a woman of the Su'lorim.

Miranda of Kelmaar, Lady – holy knight of the Kelmaar Order; sister to Bromaer and Camarra.

Mirren Lautun of Dortrean, Lady – eldest daughter of the Emperor Urzael; wife to Terrel Dortrean.

Mîsha – childhood name of Mellin Carfinn.

Mistwise – gray mare from the Hyrsenite stables.

Moraan, House – Lesser House Noble of the Farran region; notorious for marrying their own kinsmen, though seldom beyond the accepted bounds laid down by Blood Law.

Môrghran of Fâghsul, Lord Priest – Imperial Counsellor; zealous priest of Fraërigr and one of Rhydden's personal favourites.

Morvaan of Braedun, Lord – Archmage of the Sun; adoptive father and tutor of Corollin; renowned for his prodigious appetite.

Morvargh – founder and first King of the ancient kingdom of Farodh.

Môshári, House – Greater House Noble; principals of the religious Order of Môshári, devoted to the *Aeshta* Lords of Earth.

Nadan – captain of the Su'lorim armies.

Nereïs Raudhar of Telún, Lady – wife to Lavan Telún and sister-in-law to Rhysana; mother of Khyrfan, Mâghan and Maïa.

Nets, The – a vast web of enchantment spread through the northern part of the Whispering Forest, devised by the moon fay to guard the hidden vale of Starmere.

Neutral Theatre, The – a theoretical condition free from all influence of place or circumstance, used as the basis for the determination of the primary gradations of noble precedence according to Blood Law.

Noghru, The – fabled dwarvensmiths of the Black Mountains; also used as a collective term for all the dwarvenfolk. [*s*. **noghr**].

Northern Envoy – *see* ***Hakhutt.***

Northerners – name given to the folk inhabiting the coastal regions north of the Highland Mountains; believed to have shared a common ancestry with the founders of the Six Kingdoms.

Ochsha – the sixth and last day of the week according to Six Kingdoms reckoning.

Odhragh – a *noghr* from the Black Mountains; friend of Tinûkenil.

Ogh – *Aeshta* Lord of Mountains, chiefly revered by the *noghru.*

Oghraan, Mage Councillor – bursar of the College of Magi in Lautun; former Secretary to the Council of Magi.

Opening Ball – festive gathering of the Court Noble which marks the formal opening of an imperial Court; usually held on the first night of the new moon.

Orders Noble, The – religious Orders conferring noble precedence to their members by virtue of hierarchical rank and achievement, even where those members had no prior claim to precedence by right of birth; Braedun, Kelmaar, Môshári and Mairdun hold family bloodlines of noble birth in addition to this conferred precedence, while Aranara and the Order of Hýriel do not.

Osîr – *Aeshta* Lord of the Stars; First Father, from whom all other Lords of the *Aeshtar* are held to have sprung.

Panthress of the Heavens – animal guise of Haëstren.

Patall Telbray, Lord – Head of House Telbray and ruler of the city of Telbray; holy knight of Serbramel; husband to Idesîn.

Radhraan, Mage Councillor – lecturer at the College of Magi in Arrandin; temporarily relocated to Ellanguan.

Ranzhaar of Stanva, Lord – Mage Councillor; lecturer at the College of Magi in Arrandin.

Ravaïl Eädhan, Lord – Head of House Eädhan; uncle to Torkhaal.

Rhodhar Farran, Lord Steward – Head of House Farran and ruler of the city port of Farran.

Rhydden Lautun, Emperor – supreme ruler of the Lautun

Empire; earned the epithet of *Peacemaker* for ending the factious rivalry of the Houses Noble that had ravaged the Empire during the Interregnum under the regency of his mother, the late dowager Empress; rumoured to have divine or inhuman blood.

Rhysana Telún of Carbray, Lady – High Councillor; Honorary Lecturer at the College of Magi in Lautun; wife to Torkhaal.

Rikkarn, High Councillor – itinerant mage, working mostly with the craftsmen of the city of Telbray.

Rinnakhal Aartaús Dhûlann, Lord – Head of House Dhûlann; lesser retainer of Erkal Dortrean; younger brother of Sorrachal of Aartaús, and husband to Inghara.

Rinnekh Solaní Ellanguan, Lord Steward – upstart ruler of the city and lands of Ellanguan; nephew to Drômagh of Sêchral and first cousin to the Empress Consort Grinnaer; one of the Emperor's personal favourites; Imperial Counsellor.

Rinnir – a musician and storyteller from the city port of Farran; badly burned during the Easterner attack on the village of Fersí.

Rogheïn Aartaús of Dârghûn, Lady – widow of Herusen's firstborn son and chatelaine of the Dârghûn manor; mother of Haldrin.

Röstren – the fifth month of the year according to Six Kingdoms reckoning.

Rowan of Braedun, Sir – knight of the Braedun Order.

Ru – shortened name for Hrugaar.

Rúnfyr – bay gelding from the Hyrsenite stables.

S'Taran – former Souther Ambassador, replaced by T'Loi.

Saelwan – a mage of the sixth century.

Saerl Vansa, Lord – Earl of Vansa and Head of House Vansa; brother to Aramen.

Salbaar – former Mage Councillor; slain during the Easterner attack on the village of Fersí.

Saraï, Mistress – blind harper, affiliated to the Harperschool in Ellanguan; unrecognised niece of Gradhellan Ellanguan.

Sarnîl – one of the stone fay.

Scaulun, Earl of – *see* ***Khadhrôgh Scaulun, Lord.***

Selîn of the Order of Hýriel, Lady – lesser priestess of Torollen, serving in the Sun Temple on the Tungit Isle.

Serbramel – *Vashta* Lady of Justice; divine daughter of Hýrsien and Fraërigr; patron goddess of the holy city of Telbray.

Serinta of Dârghûn, Lady – priestess of the Order of Aranara, released from her contemplative vows; daughter-in-law to Herusen, and mother of Aidhan.

Serra, House – Lesser House Noble of the border hills north-west of Farran; paternal kinsmen to Karlena of Dortrean.

Shadowfay, The – evil corruption of the elvenfolk of the Fay. *See also* ***Fay, The.***

Shaünar, Abbot – priest of Sherunar; principal of the monastery school of Sherunar in Ellanguan.

Sherunar – *Aeshta* Lord of Oceans; divine son of Maësta; patron god of Ellanguan city; name means *the Dancer*.

Sherunuresh – ancient board game with sophisticated protocols; used widely in the Six Kingdoms as a vehicle for teaching both mystic and political principles, and as a tool for diplomatic negotiation and philosophical debate; name means *the dances of the gods*.

Sikhatis – a sorcerer of the K'tarim.

Sîlaúra Carbray of Aartaús, Lady – older sister of Torkhaal; wife to Sorrachal of Aartaús and sister-in-law to Rinnakhal Dhûlann.

Skaramak – mercenary warrior from Farran; friend of Tinûkenil.

Solaní, House – Greater House Noble of Ellanguan.

Solban of Dortrean, Lord – late elder son of Erkal Dortrean and brother to Kellarn; found murdered in the city of Ellanguan.

Sollonaal, High Councillor – Prime Councillor of the Ellanguan Magi; Principal of the College of Magi in Ellanguan.

Son of the Living Fire – mystic name for Kellarn, used by the moon fay Losithlîn.

Son of the Sun – mystic name for the Chosen Priest Torriearn.

Sorrachal of Aartaús, Lord – elder son and heir designate to Lord Mönal Aartaús; brother of Rinnakhal and husband to Sîlaúra.

Sóryontel – *Vashta* Lord of Trickery and Material Wealth; divine son of Eörendin and Brörigr.

Southers – name given to the peoples of the southern lands beyond the sea, under the rule of the God-King.

Stellaas, Mage Councillor – appointed Mage in Residence in the city of Telbray.

Sturannan of Kelmaar, Lord – senior knight and armsmaster at the Kelmaar School in Ellanguan.

Su'lorim – kinsmen and people of the God-King; most powerful nation of the Souther empire.

Syldhar, The – secretive magical race, little known even among the Fay; linked in folklore with dragonkind and shape-shifters; believed capable of assuming human form. [*s.* **syldha**].

T'gaim – a nation from the vast plains of the Souther lands; renowned for their swift horses and deadly mounted archers.

T'Loi – Souther Ambassador; first cousin to the God-King.

Taillan of Carbray, Lord – young son of Rhysana and Torkhaal.

Takshar of Dregharis, Lord – late son of Soltran Dregharis; former member of the Arrandin City Guard.

Talarkan, Most Worthy – a warrior of the K'tarim; leader of the Souther forces garrisoned at the Braedun *commanderie*.

Taraas, House – Lesser House Noble of Telbray.

Tarrek Farasí Cardhási, Lord – young Head of House Cardhási; nephew to Môrghran of Fâghsul and brother to Arienn Farási of Tersal.

Telghraan, Mage Councillor – Honorary Lecturer at the College of Magi in Ellanguan.

Telúmachel – *Aeshta* Lord of Air.

Temrbrin – *Aeshta* Lady of Earth and Fruitfulness.

Terrel of Arrand, Lord – elder son of Jared and Ellaïn; nephew to Kellarn.

Terrel Dortrean, Lord – former Earl of Dortrean; husband to Mirren of Lautun.

Tighaún of Vaulun, Lord – Black Destrier; former knight of the Imperial Household Cavalry, and friend of the shadowfay; slain by Sarnîl.

Tinû – shortened name for Tinûkenil.

Tinûkenil – one of the moon fay; Chosen Priest of Haëstren; son of Neriel, and kinsman to Heruvor.

Tirrel of Braedun, Lord – Chosen Priest of Telúmachel; senior priest of the Braedun Order on the monastery isle of Telúmachel; husband to Aramen.

Toad, The – Hrugaar's epithet for the Archmage Merrech.

Torkhaal of Carbray, Lord – Mage Councillor; lecturer at the College of Magi in Lautun; husband to Rhysana.

Torollen – *Aeshta* Lord of the Sun; divine son of Hýriel and husband to Haëstren.

Torreghal Valhaes, Lord – Head of House Valhaes; principal retainer of Dortrean.

Torriearn of the Order of Hýriel, Lord – Chosen Priest of Torollen; instigator and co-ordinator of the rebuilding of the Sun Temple on the Tungit Isle; lost during the siege of Arrandin.

Tree-spirits – spirits of living trees, assuming the form of comely humans or elvenfolk. *See also* ***Forest Folk, The.***

Trigharran of Kelmaar, Master – former priest of the Kelmaar Order and Principal of the Kelmaar School in Ellanguan; found murdered in the streets of Ellanguan.

Tumbrachin, The – *Aeshta* Ladies of Lightning; the daughters of Telúmachel.

Turinda Linnaer of Solaní, Lady – handmaiden and companion of Grinnaer.

Twin Gods, The – divine twins Aranel and Arredin; numbered among the *Vashtar*, but not specifically aligned either to the House of Arts or to the House of War.

Ulhennar, The – demonic creatures spawned during the Wars of the Gods.

Ûrsîn of the Order of Hýriel, Lord – Chosen Priest of Torollen; senior priest in charge of the Sun Temple on the Tungit Isle.

Urzael Lautun, Emperor – first Lautun Emperor of the Second Dynasty; reigned 1348-75; secured his succession by changing the Blood Laws to favour the first male heir above a female with precedence; father of Mirren and Korgan.

Valhaes, House – Greater House Noble of the earldom of Dortrean; renowned for military prowess.

Valroc Dhûlann, Lord – former Head of House Dhûlann; late uncle to Rinnakhal.

Vashtar, The – the imperial gods, first introduced to the Six Kingdoms around the middle of the thirteenth century; divided into two rival factions of War and Arts, with Fraërigr and the related *Vashtar* of War in the ascendancy during Rhydden's reign. [*gen. pl.* **Vashta**].

Vaulun, Earl of – *see* ***Aúghan Vaulun, Lord.***

Vengru, The – a greater clan chief of the Eastern Domains.

Virlaas – former Archmage and Prime Councillor of the Ellanguan Magi, succeeded by Sollonaal.

Warden, The – enigmatic custodian of the libraries in the College of Magi in Lautun.

Wars of Power, The – name given to the chaotic wars between the Six Kingdoms during the fourth and fifth centuries, before the Council of Magi was established to curb the excesses of uncontrolled and abused magical power.

Wars of the Gods, The – name given to the initial age of strife between the Lords of the *Aeshtar*, in which the created world was forged; also used to include the extended period of warfare thereafter, until the ways between the waking world of humankind and other mystical Realms were effectively closed.

Wynborn – chestnut gelding from the Carfinn stables.

Zedron – legendary mage of the sixth century.

[illegible] the Order of Hawk. [illegible]
[illegible]
[illegible]
[illegible]
[illegible] Dynasty [illegible]
[illegible] Blood [illegible]
[illegible]
[illegible]
[illegible]
[illegible]
[illegible]
[illegible]
[illegible]
[illegible]
[illegible]
[illegible]
[illegible]
[illegible]
[illegible]
[illegible]
[illegible]
[illegible]
[illegible]
[illegible]
Wars of the Gods. [illegible]
[illegible]
[illegible]
[illegible]
[illegible]
[illegible]
[illegible]
[illegible]

Index of Places

Alvinaah – sacred lake in the heart of Telbray Woods.

Arrand Palace – principal residence and hereditary seat of The Arrand, dominating the southwest part of the Old City of Arrandin.

Arrandin – border city at the southern end of the Blue Mountains, built on a spur of the Footstool Hills looking out across the Endless Plains; governed by the hereditary rulers of House Arrand; famous for its glassware and market fairs.

Assembly Chamber – circular meeting hall in the College of Magi in Lautun; principal venue for formal debates of the Council of Magi, and accessible only by Council members; also referred to as the Great Assembly Chamber.

Aumery Library – restricted collection within the libraries of the College of Magi in Lautun, normally only accessible to mage councillors accompanied by the Warden.

Black Mountains – mountain range forming the northwest borders of the Lautun Empire, beyond the earldom of Dortrean; legendary domain of the *noghru*.

Black River – river flowing from the lake of Sîrnae down to the Grey River, forming the southern border of the Carfinn manor lands; waters poisonous to man and beast.

Blue Mountains – highest mountain range adjoining the Lautun Empire, forming its eastern border; also called the *Diadem of Ogh* by the *noghru*.

Book Halls of Ellanguan – arguably the most extensive libraries of the Six Kingdoms, and among the most ancient; established in Ellanguan city in the year 106.

Border Road – old paved road running north from Farran to the city of Telbray.

Braedun, Commanderie of – principal monastery and fortress of the Braedun Order; located on the northern bank of the Galloppi River.

Caer Vansa – hereditary ancestral seat and fortress of House Vansa and principal residence of the Earl of Vansa; stands at the head of a narrow valley at the southwest end of the Black Mountains.

Cardhási – greater manor on the northwest border of the Lautun plains, beside the Rolling River; hereditary seat and principal residence of House Cardhási.

Carfinn – lesser manor occupying the western part of the earldom of Dortrean; hereditary seat and principal residence of House Carfinn.

Carfinn Hills – spur of foothills running along the north and eastern borders of the Carfinn manor lands.

Cerrodhí – the great forest in the northeast reaches of the Lautun Empire; formerly the Fifth Kingdom.

College of Magi in Arrandin – smallest of the colleges, following an eclectic tradition and with no formal building complex of its own; founded in 784 after the raising of the Easterner siege upon the city.

College of Magi in Ellanguan – greater of the two ancient schools restored by the First Council; originally founded in 106 with the Book Halls of Ellanguan; claims a more ancient tradition than that followed in Lautun, and reserves the right to elect its own Prime Councillor in addition to the Prime Councillor of All Magi.

College of Magi in Farran – youngest of the four colleges; founded in 1064, after the end of the Golden Age of the Magi; essentially a junior branch of the Lautun college.

College of Magi in Lautun – oldest of all colleges in the Six Kingdoms, and the most orthodox and prestigious; originally founded in the year 56; governing centre of the Council of Magi.

Daurzha, The – small domed chamber hidden within the College of Magi in Lautun; set aside for the use of the Council of Magi.

Dârghûn – rich farmland manor lying northwest of the Lautun plains, on the east bank of the Rolling River; principal residence and hereditary seat of House Dârghûn.

Dhûlann – lesser manor in the southwest part of the earldom of Dortrean; hereditary seat and principal residence of House Dhûlann.

Domains – *see* ***Eastern Domains***.

Dortrean – earldom in the northwest region of the Lautun Empire, between the arms of the Black Mountains; formerly the Fourth Kingdom.

Dortrean Forest – old forest occupying a sizeable part of the earldom of Dortrean.

Dortrean Manor – hereditary ancestral seat and fortress of the earls of Dortrean, built on the cliffs of the Black Mountains near the upper reaches of the Grey River; principal residence of Erkal; also called the **White Manor** because of the peculiar semi-translucent white stone from which it is built, which defies the arts of the Magi.

Dortrean Valley – deep mountain valley in the northwest corner of the earldom of Dortrean, where the Grey River flows down from the Black Mountains; location of the Dortrean Manor and the Temple of Fire.

Dragonrest – rocky hill at the southern end of the Tungit Isle.

Eastern Domains – name given to the lands inhabited by the Easterner clans, lying east and north beyond the Blue Mountains.

Ellanguan – southeastern coastal region of the Lautun Empire; formerly the Second Kingdom.

Ellanguan, City of – traditionally independent city port at the mouth of the Great River; former ruling centre of the Second Kingdom; seat of the Lords Steward of Ellanguan.

Empress' Garden – courtyard garden lying to the north of the summer palace and the Empress' tower in the imperial citadel of Lautun; set aside for the Empress' personal use.

Empress' Tower – square tower near the centre of the imperial citadel of Lautun, to the east of the old summer palace; principal residence of the Empress Grinnaer and her household.

Farodh – formerly the Sixth Kingdom, west of Farran and south of the Black Mountains; now uninhabited marshland.

Farran, City of – imperial city port on the southwest coast of the Lautun Empire; effective successor to the lost Sixth Kingdom of Farodh; seat of the Lords Steward of Farran.

Fersí – borderland village on the road east of Arrandin, under the care of the Lords of Tollund.

Flaming Woods – small woodland area on the western shore of the Grey River, to the south of the Tungit Isle; named for the fiery colours of its leaves in autumn.

Fystenur – name given by the Fay to the great forest of Cerrodhí.

Galloppi River – long river which flows southwest from the Blue Mountains to the sea; name more usually applied only to the lower stretch of the river, after it resurfaces from the hills southwest of the Glymn Pool.

Gorrendan – small imperial city port built at the point where the old West Road crosses the White River; once notorious for slave trading.

Great Forest – *see* ***Cerrodhí.***

Green Hall – large meeting chamber in the upper part of the Telbray fortress, faced entirely with polished malachite.

Grey River – central river of the earldom of Dortrean; joins the Black River and flows into the Rolling River, to become the White River of Lautun.

Harperschool – oldest and most prestigious music school in the Lautun Empire; located next to the College of Magi in Ellanguan.

Hauchan – the lost First Kingdom, founded by Ferrughôr; name also used for the ruined remains of Ferrughôr's city, on the banks of the Great River in the upper part of the Hauchan Valley.

Hellenur – the golden forest, stretching along the coast to the west of the White River estuary; principal location of golden birch trees within the Six Kingdoms, and traditionally a hiding place for many strange and magical creatures.

Herghin – lesser borderland manor in the far eastern reaches of the Footstool Hills; hereditary seat and principal residence of House Herghin.

Highland Mountains – lower mountain range forming the northern border of the Lautun Empire beyond the great forest of Cerrodhí.

Holleth – lesser manor centred in a village clearing in the Holleth Woods, where the Old North Road crosses the Galloppi Stream; principal residence of House Holleth.

Holleth Woods – remnants of an ancient forest stretching to the north and west of Arrandin; notionally under the care of the Lords of House Holleth.

Igaerwa – ocean lying to the south and west of the Six Kingdoms; name means *the Wide*.

Imperial Citadel – principal citadel and hereditary ruling seat of the Emperors of Lautun; built up around the original summer palace of the horselords of Lautun, on the western shore of the White River estuary; access restricted to those of Blood Noble and their immediate households; also referred to as the Imperial Palace.

Imperial Palace – palace buildings and apartments of the Emperors of Lautun within the imperial citadel on the White River estuary; name also used more generally to refer to the whole of the imperial citadel.

Imperial Plains – *see* ***Lautun Plains***.

Kara Ko-Daighru – ancient citadel of the High Clan Chiefs of the Eastern Domains; located some two hundred leagues to the east of the Blue Mountains.

Kelmaar School – oldest and most important academic school of the Kelmaar Order, located in the western part of the city of Ellanguan.

Khêltan – the original Fourth Kingdom, founded by Halgan; destroyed in the first century, but later reclaimed and renamed as Dortrean; name also used for the lost ruins of Halgan's city, by tradition buried somewhere in the region of the Dortrean Valley.

Khôrland – easternmost borderland manor, in a broad vale beneath the cliffs of the Blue Mountains; hereditary seat and principal residence of House Khôrland.

Ko-Vengru – ancestral fortress and ruling seat of the clan chiefs of the Vengru; located in the western part of the Eastern Domains, on the eastern slopes of the Blue Mountains.

Lautun, City of – imperial capital; largest city and port within the Lautun Empire, built on the eastern shore of the White River estuary.

Lautun Empire – name now given to the combined lands and peoples more traditionally referred to as the Six Kingdoms; under the supreme rule of the Emperors of Lautun.

Lautun Plains – central grassland plains of the Empire, still used primarily for the Emperor's horse herds; formerly the main part of the Third Kingdom, and the ancestral domain of the horselords of Lautun.

Levrin – earldom lying to the west of Arrandin; ancestral domain of House Levrin.

Linnaer – greater manor on the southeast coast, beside the mouth of the Galloppi River; hereditary seat and principal residence of House Linnaer.

Lower Library – largest collection within the libraries of the College of Magi in Lautun, accessible to all College students and magi.

Mairdun, Commanderie of – principal monastery and school of the Hyrsenite Order of Mairdun; located near the upper reaches of the Rolling River, at the eastern end of the Black Mountains.

Middle Lands – name given to the continental area stretching west from the Blue Mountains and south to the far edge of the Endless Plains, of which the Six Kingdoms form but a part; sometimes used in error as a synonym for the lands of the Six Kingdoms or the Lautun Empire.

Monastery Isle of Telúmachel – *see* ***Monastery of Telúmachel.***

Monastery of Maësta – monastery temple of the *Aeshta* Lords of Water, built high on the cliffs of the northern side of the Hauchan Valley; under the care of the Kelmaar Order.

Monastery of Sherunar – oldest monastery and school of the *Aeshtar* in Ellanguan, occupying the northern part of the city beyond the Temple of Sherunar.

Monastery of Telúmachel – ancient holy citadel on an island off the coast west of the imperial city of Lautun; principal temple of Telúmachel within the Empire, under the care of the Braedun Order; also called the Monastery Isle of Telúmachel, or the Telúmachel Isle.

Monastery of the Tumbrachin – old monastery retreat of the Braedun Order, located on the mountain slopes at the upper end of the Telbray Valley.

Môstí – trading village on the northern border of the Lautun Empire, guarding the mountain pass to the Northern Lands.

Murrey Chamber – small living chamber within the Emperor's private apartment in the imperial palace of Lautun; so named for its furnishings of mulberry velvet.

Neridh – fishing village and harbour at the head of the Galloppi River estuary, under the care of the Lords of Linnaer.

Nobles' Postern – name given to the small gate in the west wing of the imperial citadel of Lautun, giving access to the enclosed park.

Nobles' Quarter – restricted and guarded area within a city, reserved primarily for the city houses of the Lords of the Court Noble.

Northern Lands – name given to the coastal regions north of the Highland Mountains.

Old Kingdoms – another name for the Six Kingdoms.

Radbrodal – sacred meeting place and retreat of the wisest Elders of the Northern Lands; located in the forested hills to the north of the Highland Mountains.

Raudhar – farmland manor lying between the forest of Cerrodhí and the coast; ancestral seat and principal residence of House Raudhar; renowned for its rich pasture land and fine yellow cheese.

Rebraal – fortified ferry town and lesser port on the Strong River; principal residence of House Rebraal.

Reddit – small trading and fishing village on the north bank of the Galloppi River, close to the Braedun *commanderie*.

Renza – *see* ***Watchful Isle.***

Ringstream – tributary stream of the Grey River in the Dortrean Valley.

River Wing – largest wing of the imperial citadel of Lautun, built upon the eastern side on the shore of the White River estuary.

Rolling River – eastern border river of the earldom of Dortrean; joins the Grey River to become the White River of Lautun.

Seaward Tower – square tower forming the northwest corner of the Kelmaar School in the city of Ellanguan.

Sêchral – greater manor to the west of the Lautun Plains, bordering the Rolling River; ancestral seat and principal residence of House Sêchral.

Sentai – greater manor on the southeast coast, governed by House Sentai from the castle of Arveil; fertile hill region, renowned for its vineyards and fine wines.

Shining Hills – low hill range running down to the coast between the White River and the forest of Hellenur; set aside for the Emperors of Lautun and visitors to the imperial citadel.

Sighing Lands – largely uninhabitable moorland region to the west of the White River and south of the Grey River.

Sîrnae – small lake at the head of the Black River, to the west of the Carfinn manor; name means *ebony waters*.

Six Kingdoms – traditional name for that part of the Middle Lands claimed by the victorious human leaders of the Bright Alliance and their descendants; now also referred to as the **Lautun Empire**; in practice, the original political division of six distinct kingdoms under one High King did not survive beyond the end of the first century.

Souther Empire – vast conglomeration of kingdoms lying to the south, beyond the ocean of Igaerwa; under the suzerainty of the God-King of the South.

Starmere – name given to the hidden dwelling place of Heruvor and the moon fay, in a mountain valley east of the Whispering Forest; more properly the name of the lake within that valley.

Steeps, The – sheer cliffs stretching west from the southern end of the Blue Mountains; traditionally the site of the final battle and victory of the Bright Alliance, and still holding a sinister reputation in folklore.

Steward's Palace – principal residence of the Lords Steward of Ellanguan, in the eastern part of Ellanguan city.

Summer Lands – hill region beyond the western borders of the marshlands of Farodh, thought to be the dwelling place of some of the elvenfolk of the Fay.

Summer Palace – oldest part of the imperial citadel, originally built as a summer residence for the High Kings of Lautun.

Sun Temple – ancient monastery temple on the Tungit Isle in the midst of the Grey River of Dortrean; in ruins for centuries, but recently rebuilt at the instigation of the Sun priest Torriearn with the help of the elvenfolk of the Fay. *See also* ***Temple of Torollen***.

Taraas – lesser farmland manor lying between Telbray Woods and the city of Telbray; hereditary seat and principal residence of House Taraas.

Tarágin – farmland manor of Dortrean, lying between the Grey River and the Twin Watchers; hereditary seat and principal residence of House Tarágin.

Telbray, City of – fortress citadel near the southern end of the

Black Mountains; holy city of the *Vashta* goddess Serbramel; ancestral seat of House Telbray, under the overlordship of Farran; renowned for its artesans.

Telbray Woods – wild and ancient forest to the east of the city of Telbray.

Telúmachel Isle – *see* ***Monastery of Telúmachel.***

Telún – greater manor lying east of Ellanguan and south of the Great River, among the steep foothills of the Blue Mountains; ancestral seat and principal residence of House Telún.

Temple of Maësta in Lautun – largest surviving temple and monastery of the *Aeshtar* within the imperial city of Lautun, dedicated to the Lords of Water; located on the estuary shore at the northern end of the harbour district.

Temple of Serbramel in Lautun – principal temple to Serbramel within the Empire; located near the harbour district of the imperial city of Lautun.

Temple of Sherunar – largest temple to the *Aeshtar* in Ellanguan city, and principal temple of Sherunar within the Empire; renowned for its huge silver-blue dome and ancient peal of bells.

Temple of Telúmachel in Arrandin – oldest and largest monastery temple of the *Aeshtar* in Arrandin, dedicated to Telúmachel and the Tumbrachin; located in the western part of the Old City.

Temple of Torolien – principal temple building at the heart of the Sun Temple monastery on the Tungit Isle. *See also* ***Sun Temple.***

Tollund – lesser borderland manor in the hills northeast of Arrandin; hereditary seat and principal residence of House Tollund.

Tungit Isle – holy island in the midst of the Grey River, east of Carfinn; location of the newly rebuilt Sun Temple.

Twin Watchers – great double-peaked mountain, extending from the main body of the Black Mountains between Carfinn and the Dortrean Valley.